Praise for Robert Dunn's earlier music novels:

Pink Cadillac:

Real rock 'n' roll literature—a book with all the wily literacy of a Chuck Berry song.
　　—David Hajdu, author of *Positively Fourth Street*

The characters are larger than life and yet believable in the way that it takes giants sometimes to effect cultural change. The author knows blues and early rock in the intimate way of a guitarist caressing people's lives out of his guitar strings. This is one super book.　　　　　　　　—Book Sense citation

Pink Cadillac brings both of its milieus, the present world of record collecting and its 1950s Memphis setting, to brilliantly vivid life. Dunn has a remarkable ear for the nuances of dialogue, and he never misses a note. His astonishing portrayal of Thomas (Bearcat) Jackson as a brilliant, flawed, larger-than-life tragic hero is achingly real.
　　　　　　—Karen McCullough, *Scribes World*

The pervasive passion for music provides the novel with a steady heat.　　　—*Kirkus Reviews*

Cutting Time:

A heady mix of blues myth and blues nitty-gritty by a writer who knows the passions and pleasures of music from the inside.
—Michael Lydon, author of *Ray Charles: Man and Music*

Dunn's novel is a great look into the Chicago blues scene of the 1960s. . . . It is very hard to describe music with mere words. That task is even tougher when trying to describe music as passionate as the blues, but Dunn does a very fine job.　　　—Greg Shaw, *Bomp Bookshelf*

The Fleur-de-Lys Records
Soul Cavalcade Spring 1964
No. 1 with a Bullet Tour

Friday, April 17, Pittsburgh
Saturday, April 18, Richmond, Va.
Sunday, April 19, Raleigh, N.C.
Monday April 20, Columbia, S.C.
Tuesday, April 21, Charleston, S.C.
Wednesday, April 22, Macon, Ga.
Thursday, April 23, Atlanta
Friday April 24—Mobile, Ala.
Saturday, April 25—New Orleans
Sunday, April 26, 1964—Shreveport, La.
Monday, April 27—Jackson, Miss. (Day free)
Tuesday, April 28, Jackson, Miss.
Wednesday, April 29, Memphis
Thursday, April 30—Nashville
Friday, May 1, Pensacola, Fla.
Saturday, May 2, 1964—Jacksonville, Fla.
Sunday, May 2, Spartanburg, S.C.
Monday, May 4, Columbia, S.C.
Tuesday, May 5—Washington, D.C.
Wednesday, May 6, Washington, D.C.
Thursday, May 7 1964—Philadelphia
Friday, May 8, New York City
Saturday, May 9, New York City
Sunday, May 10—New York City

Featuring: The Daisies, the Cravattes,
Orlando Calabrese, Mary Hardy, and the Shags

Tickets available at all local outlets.

Soul

Cavalcade

A novel by
Robert Dunn

oral press

ISBN: 0-9708293-4-5
Library of Congress Control Number: 2005902853
Manufactured in Canada
1 3 5 7 9 10 8 6 4 2
First Edition

Cover Design: Monica Fedrick
Cover Photograph: Jon Hobein
Author Photo: Nancy Ramsey

www.coralpress.com

For Sky, always helping make 'em better

To the girls she said, "Hey, have a seat," then went back to her puzzling over the puzzling sheets of paper.

There was a big potted rubber plant, and Esmé took the seat beneath it. She had her gaze trained down the hall, waiting for Mr. Chapman, whom she was sure she'd recognize from his recent picture in the *Detroit Free Press*, when she felt a sharp nudge in her side. "Esmé, look!" Annette whispered. The front door had just opened, and three strikingly handsome men strode in.

These were the Cravattes, one of FDL's hottest groups, and they were glamorous, drop-dead dressers who sang with the harmonies of angels, though so far none of their records had clicked. Here in Detroit and in the ears of Young America, Fleur-de-Lys was playing second fiddle to Motown, but it was no fly-by-night, imitative company. FDL had come into existence in the late '40s, a decade before Motown, as a jazz label, had dipped into blues in the '50s—they'd put out sides on John Lee Hooker and Detroit Shorty—and now was moving into this soul music that in 1964 was busting out all over.

Of all the FDL acts, the Daisies had so far charted the highest, breaking the national Top 10 with *Love Is a Changing Game*. The Shags and Orlando Calabrese, a single act, had cracked the Top 30. A couple other girl groups, the Kittens and Penny and the Thoughts, were doing all right. But the Cravattes' first two records never made the national charts; the third had spent a week at Number 43, a fourth at 38 before falling back.

"Which is your favorite, Esmé?" Annette whispered, eyes wide.

"Don't know if I have a favorite."

"Man, I love that Otis." Otis Handler was the tallest of the group and moved with storklike finesse. He wore a Zantrel/cotton sport coat and a purple viscose shirt. A wide-brimmed black hat with a well-worn silk band topped his head. "Grace, what about you?"

"I like that Mitch Williams," Grace said. "Even if he does have a beard."

"What about Robert Warwick?" Esmé said, referring to the Cravattes' bespectacled singer, bringing up the rear and stopping to talk to the receptionist. He had wide, inquiring eyes behind thick black frames, a firm chin, and an all-business way about him.

"Ew, a boy with glasses," Annette cried, almost loud enough for the men to hear. "How gross!"

"But they're cool glasses," Esmé started to say, half to herself. "Big, neat-looking black—"

"Yeah, and he's . . . short," Grace interrupted. "I don't think I could go with a man I couldn't look up to." She was trying to keep her voice soft but in her excitement not succeeding. "Essie, what about you?"

Esmé winced. Sometimes these girls. "Ladies, please," she whispered, then when the Cravattes had bustled down a hallway, she added, "Decorum."

"Deeee—what?"

"Behave!"

At this sharp word the three Cravattes turned and looked at the girls. Otis Handler winked and tipped his hat. Mitch clearly mouthed to his friend the words, *Nice-looking ladies*. Annette and Grace preened. Esmé kept her gaze on the shorter Robert Warwick. He didn't even bother to look their way.

"Yes, Mom," Grace said as the male group disappeared through a wooden door.

The foyer empty, the three girls sat back in their straight-back chairs to wait some more. A few minutes later the front door opened again, and Annette let out a short yelp. "Jesus," she cried, "it's Orlando!" She clapped her knees together. "Oh, my!"

Orlando Calabrese was a famously tall, fine-cheeked—it was said he had Indian blood in him—and gloriously handsome black man, and at least half of Detroit had a crush on him. Back home in her bedroom even Esmé had photos of Orlando Calabrese on her walls, striking his signature pose: One leg up on a slat-back chair, a thin brown Nate Sherman cigarette in his hand, wearing a gleaming white tuxedo, a black bow tie blooming under his long, sharp chin, his eyes beckoning with coal-glowing warmth. The picture said: I'm your fairy-tale prince, and I know *every* dream you ever had.

Orlando Calabrese was dressed now in a casual sweater and tight-creased gray slacks that fit his behind just perfect. When he walked up to the receptionist, she dropped her pencil and gazed up at him with moony eyes.

"Doris, you know if Bones is around?" Orlando said, drawing on his brown-paper cigarette. "I need to talk to him."

"Um, yes, Mr. Calabrese, he is." The receptionist kept gazing up at Orlando, then she pointed at the Darlingettes. "These little girls here are waiting to see him."

Orlando turned to Esmé, Grace, and Annette. He flashed a smile that caught the sunlight flowing in from the transom above the door. Esmé saw he had the creamiest mocha skin she'd ever seen. "You pretty ladies don't mind if I just go have a word with the boss man, do you?"

"No, Mr. Calabrese," Annette said.

His smile brightened. "You, darlin', can call me Breeze."

Annette was buzzing so with delight she sounded to Esmé like a honeybee. Esmé herself was trying to keep her cool and barely succeeding. She kept moving one leg over the other. All the time there was a rampant tingling down under her lime-green dress.

"Doris, just call Margie, tell her I'm on my way back."

"Yes, sir."

"I think I'd take *him*," Esmé said to her friends as they settled back to wait. "If I ever got the chance."

"We don't get called back in to see Mr. Chapman, you ain't gettin' *any* kind of chance," Annette told her.

For twenty minutes more nicely dressed people bustled

past, looking busy. The Darlingettes just sat there. Esmé thought to bug the receptionist again but expected it wouldn't do any good. She'd just get scorn back. She walked over and did it anyway.

"Are you sure our message got through, Miss?"

"You heard me."

Esmé leaned down and said sotto voce, "Sweetheart, what you got stuck up your ass?"

The receptionist looked up startled.

Esmé leaned closer. "Think about this, Dorrr-issss." She hissed the woman's name. "What do you think will happen if we ace our audition with Bones, he cuts a disc on us, and it takes off up the charts? You think that through yet?"

"Ain't gonna happen," the receptionist said with utter conviction.

Esmé was taken aback. "Why not?"

"Just ain't." Pinched little smirk. "You'll see."

Damn, Esmé thought. Now we got this little twerp throwing hexes at us.

"What'd she say?" Grace asked.

Esmé shrugged, said, " 'Should be any minute.' "

It was fifteen minutes later when the door swung open and a short-haired, harried-looking woman came out, looked them up and down, and said, "Darlingettes?" Big nervous nods all around. "Very good. Right this way. Mr. Chapman is ready."

Bones Chapman was an immediately imposing presence, not because he was tall or particularly elegant, but just the opposite. He was short, with wide shoulders and no apparent waist. His build was that of a day laborer; his muscles pronounced even through his custom-cut mohair suit. Chapman had a broad forehead; his jaw was square, his nose crooked because it had been broken more than once. He came on fast, on the tips of his toes, and moved with uncommon quickness and certainty. His personal power, and it was full on you, was that he was right there in front of you . . . and beside you, and half behind you, too. Bones Chapman had you covered coming and going and you hadn't even had time to think.

He had a great, warm smile, though, which he turned on the three teenage girls, disarming them. All thoughts of the bitchy receptionist fled.

"Darlingettes. Like the name. Which of you thought of it?"

"We all sort of did," Esmé said, because she was standing a foot or so before Grace and Annette. "One day we were playing dolls on my mother's stoop, and we'd just got back from this Bette Davis movie, and we were acting it out, and I started calling Grace and Annette 'Dah-ling. . . .' "

"*Daahaalinnnng,*" Annette said, drawling out the syllables with a hint of her Alabama accent and twirling a finger in the air. "Daa-haa-haa-linnnng—"

"We were just like, ah, twelve then." Grace gave Annette a quick look. "We just said, 'Aren't we the Darlings.' It was just playing. Then when we started singing, well, there was the name waiting for us. We added the 'ettes.' "

"Just playin'?" Bones said. "That's all any of us are doin' here, girls. Just playing." A pause, then under his breath he said, "Life or death playing."

Esmé nodded at him; she got it.

Bones spoke up through his wide, glowing smile. "And you sing like—"

"Like . . . little 'ettes,' " Annette said, with a look back at Grace.

Esmé stepped forward again. "Like a charm," she said. "Are you ready to hear us?"

"No time like the present." Bones had already turned and was leading them through narrow, wood-paneled hallways. It was an amazing place: piano chords, saxophone trills, sweet violins poured out of every room, undercut by the furious clacking of typewriters.

As the three girls followed Bones, Grace gave Annette a

stinging finger-flick on her bare back, and Annette whirled and kicked Grace. Esmé, appalled, hissed silently, "Stop it!"

Bones took the girls down a flight of stairs to the basement. There were two heavily padded doors there.

"That's our Studio 1," Bones said, "where we cut our hits." There was a small, fogged-glass window in the door, and Esmé stood on her toes to look into it. The air inside was thick with gray smoke, but she could make out a room crammed with musicians wearing felt hats, gray and brown suits, loosened ties, most of the men with smoldering cigarettes, some drinking from short glasses. Microphones loomed down from booms like cranes. In the back of the room behind four thick silver mikes, barely visible through the smoke, were the Daisies; Esmé recognized them from a photo on a 45 sleeve she had. The four girls had large beehive hairdos and wore matching silver sheaths that glowed through the fog. They moved toward the mikes together in step, then back, then up again. Through the door a churning beat leaked, topped by the girls' dulcet voices.

Esmé felt in her soul a yearning to be in that room as powerful as anything she'd ever known.

"And this here's our practice studio." Esmé hesitated at the small window of Studio 1, but then Bones led them into a small, acoustically tiled room with a cigarette-scarred upright piano. He sat down and ran his fingers out of habit in a quick arpeggio over the keys, rippling teardrop-shaped notes into the room. "Now what I usually do is just have you sing, without backing. I want to hear your voices, how they blend. That all right?"

"No problem," Esmé said, concentrating. She was glad they couldn't hear anything from next door in here. She gave her friends a quick look to see if they were settled. Annette was brushing her hand through her hair one stroke after another, and Grace kept licking her lips. She didn't know what was getting into them—nerves, she guessed. Hoped that was all it was, though friction had been building between the straitlaced Grace and the wilder Annette for a while.

"What do you want to sing?"

"What would you like us to sing?"

"You know any of my songs?" Some of the early songs on FDL Bones had written.

"Of course, Mr. Chapman." This was Annette, evidently recovered enough to throw a hip vamp at the record label man.

"*The Long Story of Love*," Esmé said. "Ladies?"

Grace and Annette slipped to Esmé's side, the three of them did a dip-of-their-hips downswing, then came up with a sultry, bopping harmony of *oooh-ooooohs*. Then Annette stepped forward and in her high, soaring voice sang,

> *It's a story that comes and goes,*
> *A story of joy, story of woe*
> *A story longer than we'll ever know*
> *The story of love, your and my love*

The Darlingettes had practiced countless hours after school, and all of every summer, intense play/work interrupted only by a long stay Esmé had had the year before in Chicago, where she'd stayed with her long-lost father, the blues singer Heddy Days. There'd always been an easy harmony between the girls, and they'd polished their singing to where they could make their three voices sound like one. They swung through the rest of the tune, then took a smooth glide toward Bones, who was giving them a big smile.

"I like that. You do that song different from the Daisies, a little more soul. Little rougher. What's your name?"

"Annette. Annette Brown."

"And you're the lead singer?"

"Actually, we all sing leads to different songs," Grace said. "Annette goes high, I go sweet, and Esmé here, she goes loooowwwww."

"*Looowwwwww*," Esmé sang, mimicking her friend. She

gave her hair a flirtatious shake. "*I goooooo loooooowwwwwww.*"

"Range," Bones said. He'd set his thick buttocks on the edge of a table. "Nothing wrong with range. O.K., who's next?"

They'd worked out every possibility, and Grace stepped forward and said, "Let me do *All of Me*." They'd arranged this standard with a doo-wop backing, which Esmé and Annette fell into with a snap of their fingers. Grace was right: Her voice was sweet, and when she sang the tune, the *All* she was referring to took in her and her heavenly presence.

"Nice," Bones said. "The Darlingettes, hmmnn." A quiet second, then, "O.K., that leaves you, I guess."

"I'm Esmé Hunter," Esmé said, "and as you heard, I go *loooowwww.*" She cracked a wide grin, saw Bones grin back. "Can go high, though, too. O.K. if I do *Someone to Watch over Me*?"

"Gershwin's great, sure."

The girls did this classic straight, Esmé's voice smoothing into the lovely words, Grace and Annette hitting just a hint of jazzy lilt behind her, Esmé riding their steady orchestral bop yet putting her sweet, smoky voice over it. The phrasing of the song was all her own; she caught the rich emotion, the need and the challenge in the words, and was wholly true to herself throughout.

"Bravo!" Bones cried when she was done. "You girls— you girls've got the stuff, I can tell."

"The—"

"The stuff—the true stuff."

One by one, the girls beamed. "We do, we do," Annette said. Everyone was laughing.

"So—" Esmé finally said as the laughing died down and no other words replaced it.

Bones took a deep breath, rasping through his chest. A very deep breath. Esmé felt herself tense.

"O.K., I love you girls. You got the pipes, got the style—

love those popsicle dresses—and you got the looks. So what's the problem?" A long pause. Esmé thought: What problem? "Well, this is gonna sound stupid, but there is one basic problem: You're . . . girls."

"*Girls?*"

"The only thing I'm looking for now is a guy group. I'm top-heavy with women." Bones gave them a pained grimace. "If I had half a brain I'd just sign you and hold on to you, wait till things change, market's different, our roster gets filled right—I'd do it in a second if I was smart. If I could—"

"If you—" Esmé started to say.

"There's just two things I need," Bones interrupted, that chest-rattling deep breath again. His voice was more serious, respectful; Esmé knew he didn't have to tell them any of this business stuff. "I need myself a big, big hit . . . the right kind of hit, too, one that doesn't burn too fast. Gotta smolder slow first."

The girls waggled their heads. Grace said, "We can give you a hit. We know it!"

"But you don't see. I don't have the, um, resources even to get another girl group going right now. Gotta go with what I have."

This wasn't making any sense to Esmé, though she'd admit if asked that she didn't know a thing about the record business, not that she wouldn't want to learn. But this—this was a turndown, wasn't it? And it just didn't make any damn sense.

"And what's that second thing you need?" Esmé said, her jaw tight.

"Oh, that you can't help me with either." Bones kept the pained grimace on his wide face. "I need one more Cravatte."

"One more—"

"You know the Cravattes, right?"

"Of course," Annette bubbled. "We just bumped into them, out there."

"Well, like I said, nothing you can do about them, but I need four of 'em. Gotta fill out a sound. Need a higher voice, one that can soar over Otis, Mitch, and Robert."

"You ever think of a girl?" Esmé said boldly.

"In a guy group?" Bones shook his head. "Don't think I could sell it."

"What about the Miracles?"

"I hear you. But Smokey and Claudette are married, it's a whole other thing. You know, it's not just the music, it's . . . everything else." A strong smile, then a sigh. "You don't know all it takes to run a record label, girls." A shake of his head. "You just don't have a clue."

"So, with us—"

"We'll keep in touch. You got the stuff. The genuine stuff." Bones started to usher them to the door. "I'll be in touch, I know it. Just have to be ready to take on another girl group." A lighter smile. "Hey, you're young, and we're just getting going. There'll be plenty of time."

"Plenty of—"

"Plenty, plenty of time. Girls, I promise."

And with that the Darlingettes were back on the big lawn.

✳ ✳ ✳ ✳ ✳

THE BUS TOUR was set for two weeks, and Bones Chapman knew they were nowhere near ready. Would they ever be? Was the tour even a good idea? It wasn't in his nature to have doubts, but doubts he had. A tour through the South, then up the Eastern Seaboard; a busful of Fleur-de-Lys artists playing one-nighters in gyms and rec halls and roller rinks— wherever Bee Williams could get 'em booked. A logistical nightmare, and that was even if he could get the bus rolling.

There was trouble in the FDL family, too. There were the Daisies, their premier girl group, who had already broken the Top 10, but since then lead singer Maisy Columbine had been acting up and demanding the star treatment. She'd been dropping hints for months now that since she was the Voice of the Daisies, and since her name was such a "purr-fect" rhyme, well, wouldn't Maisy and the Daisies go down better?

Now Maisy was saying that she didn't want to ride on the tour bus but wanted her own car—just for her and Pinky, this nasty little Pomeranian she'd gone and dyed pink. Unbelievable! She kept believing she had special access to Bones, and, well, trouble was, there'd been a few weeks a year back when she had. Bones winced at the thought. It was those saucery eyes and her cooing baby-doll voice. But she was just too crazy. One night she was the lovey-dovey, lap-sitting sweetheart of anyone's dreams, and the next night, hell, the next minute, she was pitching frying pans at you like Bob Feller.

Bones winced double. He felt bad for the Daisies; could tell they felt Maisy had notions in her head like stirred-up bees. Maisy's latest: She'd agree to their wearing one outfit onstage, then come out in something different—shinier, slinkier, more glamorous—as the three other girls' eyes rolled.

Still, Maisy was the singer who had cracked the Top 10— the only Fleur-de-Lys group to get that high—and she knew it. Funny thing was she didn't even have the best voice. That would be Priscilla Bondrais, who went deep, and dark, and pulled out gospel melismata that shivered your backbone. It was actually somewhat of a fluke that Maisy had grabbed the lead on *My Kind of Man*; she'd been first in the studio that night and had worked up an arrangement with Candy Wilson, the bandleader, that to Bones just seemed right. Once she was in front of the group, Bones knew, not even one of them atom bombs could get her out.

He slammed a fist down on his desk. Nope, no way could she take that perfumey little mutt with her, and no way she'd have her own car. She was on the bus—they were *all* going on the bus.

O.K., what else? Oh, the Cravattes. Bones's forehead pinched. They just weren't working as a three-man male group; not enough range, not rich enough in the harmonies. Like he'd just told those pretty young Darlingettes—awfully sweet, and talented, but too young . . . and girls—he needed a high tenor to rise over the boys, and he needed one soon. He had a great song just waiting for 'em, *Let the Doorbell Ring*; hot new song, Bones cowrote it, which meant FDL would hold publishing, too—and damn, he couldn't get it to sound right in the studio yet. Needed—*needed*—that fourth voice.

He'd put the word out, seen dozens of songsters in silk jackets, twirly mustaches, Jheri curls that glowed brighter than the full moon, and not one of 'em had jelled. A group was a funny thing—every piece had to be just right. That's what that Robert Warwick kept saying, and he was damn . . . picky. Well, Robert was the group leader, and he had to be up onstage every night with whomever they chose, and it was true, Bones himself hadn't been blown away by any of the guys they'd seen. . . . But still, with Robert, everything seemed difficult; lately they'd been knocking noggins a lot, over arrangements, release dates, whatever came up. That boy had ambitions, they were clear as sunshine, but Bones had all the responsibility, and time . . . time was growing late. It was Bones who had to get *Doorbell* in the can, pressed, and out there so it was moving up the charts before the bus took off—if it took off.

Call Bee. He was reaching for the black handle when the phone rang, jarring him. Bones picked it up, saying, "Yes, Margie?"

"Um, it's Doris, Mr. Chapman, from the front desk. Sir, I have a Mr. Clark on the line."

"Mr. Clark?" That was a pretty common name. He knew a Rummy Clark in Chicago and a Willie Clark from St. Louis. "Did you get a first name?"

"Oh, Mr. Bones, I'm sorry. Let me check with him."

That Doris! She was his sister's husband's niece, and he'd promised Ramona he'd hire her. Maybe it was a mistake making her receptionist, she just filed her nails all day and talked on the phone to her boyfriends. Still, she was exactly the right age for FDL's music and she had a good ear. She'd even rescued a Cravattes B side once, got it made an A with her comment that every time she heard it, her feet started dancing over the floor. That was the record that charted as high as 38.

"He says his name's Dick Clark. From Philadelphia?"

Ah, Bones thought, Sweet.

"Hey, Mr. Clark," he said when the phone clicked over.

"Mr. Chapman." The voice on the other end was boyish, balloon light, but with a subtle cut to it that made Bones keep his wits about him.

"What can I do for you, sir?"

"You know I don't usually call people myself, Mr. Chapman," Clark laughed. "I have many minions for that."

That was a curious word. Bones said, "Minions?"

Over the phone Dick Clark cackled. "Yes, minions. I love that word. You know what it means, Mr. Chapman?"

"I do, yes."

"It means," Clark continued, "I snap my pretty little fingers, and they jump. You get your people jumping, Mr. Chapman?"

Bones laughed out loud. "Never high enough."

Clark laughed on his end. "Well put. Anyway, I wanted to let you know how much I like that new Daisies record, *Man Alive*. It's tearing things up here in Philly."

"Thank you, sir."

"Think we can get those sassy young girls on *Bandstand*?"

"I wouldn't see why not."

"Very good. How soon can you get 'em here?"

"Well, we're sending everyone out on a tour, leaving in a couple weeks." Bones shuffled papers on his desk, pulled out the often scribbled over itinerary. "Should be in Philly in—" how was Dick Clark going to take this? "—a month or so."

"We were thinking sooner." There was a quiet but vivid trace of impatience in Clark's voice.

"Well, sir—" Damn. This was *American Bandstand*. Bones knew only too well that that show made hits. So far of all his groups only the Daisies had been on the show, and after an appearance in '63, their sales spiked. Still, the tour was all set to go, and breaking the Daisies away from it to get all that glory—hell, as she'd see it, singling out Maisy Columbine— what would that do to the tour's morale? Might as well sink it before it got started. That's what Bee would say, and she'd be right. "*Man Alive*'s just coming out. Don't you think there'll be more of a cry for it in a few weeks?"

"We're booking now, Mr. Chapman." A pause, then Clark said, "Perhaps I should put you on with one of my min—"

"No, no, that's O.K. Just what I'm thinking, sir, is we got new wax comin' out on all our groups, hot *hot* new tunes. Here's what I'm thinking: The whole FDL Soul Cavalcade's gonna be hitting Philly in a month, all our groups ridin' them new hits, so instead of just having the girls, maybe you could put on a whole FDL segment. Get the Cravattes, Mary Hardy, Orlando Calabrese—"

"I don't know if—"

"Let me offer you this, Mr. Clark," Bones interrupted. He was thinking fast. "You know how much I respect you and your organization. And I want the best show you can put on, absolutely. Now we're sending our boys and girls all around the South and the Eastern Seaboard, we're gonna be promoting the hell out of all of 'em, so what I'm thinking is, well, you hold off for now on the Daisies, and when we get to Philly, we bring the whole troupe by. It'll be one humdinger of a show. It'll be—"

"Mr. Chapman, here, I'm going to put on my assistant, Miss Ross, now."

"Mr. Clark, just a second. Here, let me make you a deal." Bones kept thinking, wheels spinning fast as race cars. "You hold off like I'm sayin' till we get to Philly, and O.K., we put on anybody with a Top 20 song. Nobody hits the Top 20, we don't bother you; but we get the Daisies, Cravattes, Orlando, maybe Mary Hardy up there, then they all go on. That show, all them Top 20 hits, it's gonna be a ratings hit. You know it."

Silence on the other end.

"Mr. Clark?"

"You're a gambling man, aren't you, Mr. Chapman?"

"Call me Bones, sir."

"O.K., Bones." A dramatic pause. "Top 10."

Bones sucked in his breath. "Top . . . 10? That'd be four groups from one label for only 10 possible—"

"O.K., Top 15, but I want a Number 1 out of it, too."

"Local Number 1?"

"National," Clark said with a tight clip. *Billboard.*"

Bones sighed. "Deal."

Clark said, "Good enough, Mr. Bones. And you call me Dick. O.K., let me put Miss Ross on now. I'll tell her we'll go for your . . . deal. What're those dates again?"

Bones squinted at the itinerary. Hard to make out, but it looked like: "May 7," he said. "We're playing the Civic Auditorium that night."

"That's a Thursday. O.K., May 7 it is. And, Bones, you want a piece of unsolicited advice?"

"Um, certainly, sir."

"Get yourself a fourth singer in those Cravattes. They sound a little thin."

"I was just thinking that . . . Dick."

A slight hesitation, then Clark said, "Stick with it, Mr. Chapman. Stick with it. You got a good sound. O.K., we'll be seeing you on May 7—or we won't." A laugh. "Bye."

Bones sat back with a smile. Damn! he thought. Dick

Clark calling him personally. Maybe this damn record thing would work out after all.

Clark seemed to have his number, too. Bones was a gambling man, yes, indeed, and he liked this crapshoot. One month to get a Number 1. One month to put as many groups of his as he could in the Top . . . well, he knew if he got the Number 1, he could stretch the other groups at least to the Top 20. Then a glorious show on *Bandstand*.

He dialed his phone, Bee's number. She picked up immediately.

"Bee, baby, guess who I just talked to."

"Dick Clark."

Bones blew air out like a tornado. "Damn, no secrets around this place, is there? How'd you hear that?"

She didn't even answer his question. That was the thing with Bee Williams, she was all good business. Bee was his righthand woman, a strict churchgoer he could trust with his life—and his money. For some reason she was devoted to him, even with all his . . . sins. She seemed to look right past them. She'd started with him when she was a girl, back when FDL was putting out jazz sides. She'd graduated from a downtown business school and the next day simply walked into the FDL offices (same location, but it was Bones's home then, too) and started going through his paperwork. By the time he noticed her, she handed him a sheaf of file folders and said, *Here, boss, everything's under control now*.

Now she said, "We going on his show?"

"Yes indeed."

"When?"

"A month."

"He's calling that far in advance?"

The other thing about Bee, she really had his number.

"I made a little . . . deal with him."

"Uh, huh." She quickly got the full details out of him. "Well, boss, I can handle the tour, don't you worry." That was Bee, not only was she setting up the Soul Cavalcade, she was going along as den mother, group leader, and chaperone. Bones guffawed. Bee was at least half Marine drill sergeant—those lusty young kids'd never know what hit 'em. "But we might not want to tell the kids, stir 'em up too much."

"Good point."

"Yeah," Bee went on, "and you got your work cut out, too."

"I know. Hell, even ol' Dick Clark knows. Filling out the Cravattes."

"Keep at it." Bee hung up.

✳ ✳ ✳ ✳ ✳

ESMÉ HAD TO GET the pants to fit. The pants? Yes, the pants. Everything else was perfect, but the slacks were too long—they dragged over the heels of her thick black shoes, scraped the ground, made her look sort of bumbling and tramplike. She put a blank grin on her face, then twirled her fingers like she was playing Charlie Chaplin. A quick smile to herself.

She'd had the idea right there on the lawn in front of FDL studios, and set right to work. The clothes had come from a secondhand shop on 10th Street, and as she regarded herself in the mirror now, she was impressed. The suit jacket fit her shoulders perfectly, and the open-collared BanLon shirt hung straight down with no telltale bulges (though the hospital tape she'd used on her breasts was a little itchy; she'd have to find something better). The sleek beaver fedora rode her forehead like she was Daddy Cool. (She had enough hairpins under it that if she walked past a big enough magnet, she'd glom right to it.) But the pants . . . the damn pants was draggin'.

On her way home she thought more about her hair. If her ploy worked, she'd have to cut it—yeah, she'd have to. She took a long, whistling breath. It wasn't that she was particularly vain, and it wasn't that her hair was that long, but she knew she couldn't get away with wearing a hat all the time. So the curls would have to go. Maybe a nice medium-short cut, keep a hint of style. . . . Well, she'd worry that if she passed her audition.

A long sigh. *If* she passed the audition. That's what she was worrying about when she got home and her mother greeted her with an "Esmé, look at you. What're you doin' in that suit? What're you got up as?"

"Nothing, Mom," Esmé said, walking through the well-swept hall. "Can you just help me with these pants?"

"I asked you a question."

"Oh, just something me and the girls are doin'. With our singing."

"The singing again?" Mrs. Hunter's beauty parlors often kept her late into the evening. She was home today after a doctor's appointment, nothing serious.

"I just thought you could trim the pants."

"For the singing?"

"Yes, Mom!" Esmé pouted.

"And not for the college applications like we talked about?"

"I'm working on that too."

"I let you go to that Chicago last year, and—"

"I know. I said I'd be applying." Esmé sighed. "And I will be."

"When?"

"Mom, you know I love singing. There's something I gotta do—"

"Wearing men's clothes?"

"Mom, please, are you going to help me, or do I have to go find some tailor with pins in his mouth?"

Mrs. Hunter was a big-fronted woman, with two chins now but the memories of being young and gorgeous. "Maybe you should put some pins in *your* mouth, see how you sing with that," she said. Esmé looked hard at her. Mrs. Hunter cocked her well-plucked right eyebrow. And like that both women cracked up.

The next morning Esmé woke powerfully unsure of herself. Me, a man? What am I thinking?

But the longer she noodled the notion around, the more she saw how great it could be—if she could pull it off. She was all charged up to run right back to FDL, but figured that she should wait a bit, practice her deception, and also give Bones Chapman more time to forget the girl who had just sung for him.

For a week she spent each afternoon in her new getup. She went to the movies and boldly used the Men's room, slipping carefully into a stall; nobody said a word. She went to a local batting cage and slapped around some balls; well, maybe she hit like a girl, but nobody called her on it.

But she truly didn't know she was ready till she went to the downtown Grand Ballroom, where in her deepest voice she asked a series of lovely ladies to dance; and though not all of them accepted, nobody stopped and shrieked, Who are you? What are you doing? No, arm in arm, she moved across the floor, all the time thinking, Oh, my God, this is going to work!

The next day she waited till her mother headed off to her main beauty shop, then bound her breasts and pulled on her man's suit, appreciating the way the cuffs rode the tasseled loafers she'd picked up at Thom McAnn's, clipped back her hair again, snapped the brim on her fedora, and headed on out.

It was Doris again at the reception desk, and Esmé approached her warily. The receptionist was chewing her pencil and dithering over more of the sheets of scrawled lines, but when she looked up at Esmé, there was a quick-glow smile on her face that went off at Esmé like a flashbulb.

"Hey, sugar," she said, eyebrows up. "I'm Doris. Can I help you?"

"I'm hear to see Mr. Chapman." Was her voice low enough? It was still unnatural to speak this way, and Esmé felt like she had big marbles rolling around in her mouth. "Mister Boooones [rattle, rattle] Chapman."

"Sure, handsome." Glance down at a large kid-skin-covered book. "Do you got an appointment?"

"I'm here to try out for the Cravattes. I heard Mr. Chapman's looking for a tenor."

"You heard right." Doris lit up even brighter. "Tha's all we're hearing 'round here, gotta fill out the Cravattes. Got the tour comin' up, gotta fill out the Cravattes." A lingering appraising glance. "You sing good as you look?"

Esmé laughed. Hey, this was easy. A smile. "Hope so."

"Well, let me buzz Mr. Bones and we'll all find out."

Doris pointed Esmé to the same seat next to the big potted plant. Like the time before, beautiful men and women walked through the foyer, dressed to the bloody nines, laughing, chuckling, humming under their breaths. As before, this place, the FDL lobby, seemed to buzz with all the excitement Esmé could imagine.

She was so lost to her own swimmingly grand thoughts that she didn't notice Doris beckoning to her.

"Sir." The unexpected word went right past Esmé. "Sir!" A loud bark that broke through Esmé's reverie. "Mr. Chapman is ready for you now."

Esmé got up, and Doris briskly waved her to the thick, mysterious door. "By the way," the receptionist said, "what's your name?"

"Esss—" Esmé bit her tongue. God! She hadn't thought of a name. Quick, quick. "Um, Eddie—Edward."

"Edward what?"

She'd used her real full name the day before and figured that saying "Hunter" might raise more questions than she wanted. She thought of her real father's name, Days, and that's what came out.

"O.K., Eddie Days, good luck."

"So, it's Eddie?" Bones Chapman was waiting right inside

the door for her. "Hi, I'm Bones." He stuck out his thick hand, grasped Esmé's with a meaty, all-encompassing tight grip. She tried to give her firmest squeeze back, then held his eyes for a second, then a second longer, waiting for him to . . . but no, there was no trace of recognition or anything else out of the usual. "Sorry to keep you waiting, son."

"No problem," Esmé said in her low, rolling-marbles voice.

"Well, I'm pretty busy—you can imagine—but I can give you as much time as you need to audition. O.K.?"

"Absolutely."

"Good. Here, let me take your hat." Chapman reached out to her—

Esmé heard her breath get sucked in. "If you don't mind, I'm more, um, comfortable with it on." She touched the smooth beaver pelt. "All right?"

"Like Frankie, eh?" Bones shrugged. "No problem. Come on, right this way."

Esmé in her suit and her loafers followed Bones along a corridor, left, right, then into a small room dominated by a large walnut desk and a tall-backed leather chair. "This is my office," Bones said. "Thought I'd just hear your voice in here. O.K.?"

Esmé felt her hands shake. She was nervous as could be, but she knew she had a fine voice—well, a fine women's voice—but she'd told Chapman on the way here that she sang high for a man, and he said cheerfully that that was just what the Cravattes needed, which Esmé of course knew but didn't let on. So here they were. "You want me just to sing?"

"Just to hear the quality of your voice, Eddie," Bones said. "You know, I'm not great shakes as a singer, that's why I got into this end of the business, but I can carry a tune." In truth Chapman had been a member of the Four Clubs, an early '50s vocal group that didn't make it out of the 78 era. "I'll lay down a bottom, you just come on up over it. O.K.?"

Esmé—Eddie—nodded. Chapman started right in with some doo-woppy *shoo-be-doos, shoo-beee-deeeees,* which Esmé recognized as from *In the Still of the Night,* and on the perfect beat she came in with the verse. Her voice warbled nervously for a second, then, like a boat just launched, righted itself. Chapman's *shoo-be-doo-bees* were smooth as silken seas, and Esmé sailed right above them.

"Nice," Bones said, and there was true appreciation in his voice. "You been singing long? How come I haven't heard of you, Mr. Eddie Days?"

"I did a little work in Chicago," Esmé said, which wasn't quite true. "Not so much here."

"You from the Windy City?"

She shook her head. "No, no, Detroit born and raised."

Bones smiled. "That's the way we like 'em. Here, let's go with another song. New one we're working on, called *Let the Doorbell Ring.* Wanna see how fast you pick it up."

Esmé raised her large eyes.

"It's a genuine test, Eddie, but this is a *real* audition, and I got me a real situation with the Cravattes. A *real* situation." He moved around the desk until he stood right in front of Esmé. "O.K., let's go."

Bones clapped his hands, then sang the melody to the new song: *"Baby, fall into my arms / I'm right here before you. . . ."* He did it slow and not as high as the song was supposed to be—even as he sang, he kept pointing up with his thumbs—but to her joy, Esmé knew just where the tune was going and got it right away. It was a natural melody, and it felt smooth and soulful to her. She let Chapman's first go-round pass by, then joined him note for note on the second, and waved him silent halfway through the verse. There she was, in the office of the head of Fleur-de-Lys Records, singing a cappella, her voice as naked as if she'd just left the bath, and that's how she felt: shimmery, wet, sleek as a seal. She nailed those notes, spiked 'em, and came back for more.

Chapman moved back, sitting on the edge of his desk, and Esmé sang and sang. "What's the second verse?" she stage-whispered instead of catching her breath, and as Bones spoke the words to her, she immediately dropped them onto the notes now so vivid to her she could see them hanging in the air like bright slashes of color. Same thing with the third and final verse, and she knew she'd aced it. Bones didn't say a word, just looked at her with a curious, sharp smile. Finally, almost imperceptible, a tiny nod, then: "Come on, Eddie, right this way."

Back along the corridor, then down to the basement, to the two heavy quilted-Naugahyde-covered doors. Over there was the room she and her friends had auditioned in the day before, but this time they went left, into Studio 1.

Esmé was holding her breath. The room was so full she couldn't take in everything at once. There were large hanging speakers and wall baffles, music stands and boom microphones. But what filled up the room were the people. There was the whole band from the day before, big-shouldered drummer, zoot-suited electric bassist, a guitarist, a piano guy with long, be-ringed digits in front of a chipped-wood upright, and even a small string section, two violas and a violin, each guy hipster cool, little beatnik goatees on their chins, more than one wearing a fedora just like Esmé's as well as dark glasses. They were all smoking like crazy, and now she was in the middle of the fog. When she got to the center of the room she found a big-bulbed microphone on a stand, and arrayed around it the three Cravattes: tall, bearded Mitch Williams, sloe-eyed Otis Handler, and the shorter Robert Warwick, focused and intense behind his black-rimmed glasses.

Esmé finally let her breath out. "All this was here while you were auditioning me?"

"Nothing less," Bones said with a smile. Then: "Actually, we've been rehearsing that new song *Let the Doorbell Ring*, getting ready to put it on tape. You came at just the right time."

She shook her head. No, it was way too much to take in at once. She stood aside and heard Bones say, distantly, as if he were speaking in a wind tunnel, "Guys, this is Eddie Days—and he just might make ours. I just heard him upstairs, and he's got a sweet, sweet voice. Just what we need up top, I think. Mitch, move over, let him in to stand next to you."

Esmé, who was supposed to move, just stood there. The room swirled and tilted and fun-housed like mad.

"Eddie?" She blinked. "Eddie?"

"Um, yeah?"

"You're right there next to Mitch," Bones said. Then: "You don't know the guys yet, do you? Eddie, this is Mitch Williams, he's the sport of the group, right Mitch? The sportin' man." Mitch Williams had a hand large as a baseball glove, and it swallowed up Esmé's, as well as half her wrist. Up close he had cloudy, unsettled eyes, but his smile through his black beard was large, friendly, sound.

"And this here is Otis Handler. We call him Oat. He's the lovah man in the Cravattes. The lov-aah-aaah man, even though he went and got himself married." Bones guffawed. "Still, it's a good thing you ain't a chickie, he'd be all over you."

Otis blushed but still lifted an eyebrow in a gesture that said, *I won't admit it, but you know it's true.*

"And then we got our little genius here, Mr. Robert Warwick. Robert here wants to write songs and produce 'em, right, Robert?" Robert Warwick looked down, his gaze avoiding Esmé's. "Oh, yes, he's also a shy boy. Right, Robert? Likes to hide behind his big black specs." Esmé felt the tension between Chapman and Warwick. The boy might by shy, she could tell, but he wasn't any kind of pushover. Keeping his head down, Robert lifted his brow enough for his striking hazel eyes to look up; he gave Esmé a gentle handshake.

"A pleasure," Esmé said loudly. She was coming back to herself. As astonishing as it was to be here right in the Fleur-de-Lys studios, with the Cravattes and a cooking band, she quickly was understanding that in idle moments and day-dreams she'd been just here a thousand times before, and she was beginning to feel more and more at home.

"So let's get to work," Bones said, moving to a small glass-windowed control room off the studio. "Eddie's a quick study. I got him up on *Doorbell* upstairs. Eddie, this is an Otis Handler lead, he's got the bedroom voice to put it over, but I want you to find a harmony with the other guys. Then on that final line of the verse, *"So let the door . . . bell . . . ring,"* you double Otis up an octave. I want it to float, guys—" Bones fluttered his fingers lightly over his bull-like head "—butterfly, but-ter-fly."

The band dropped into the down beat, and Mitch Williams and Robert Warwick, the tall cup of cocoa and the squat mug of intense java, swooped up to a mike and lay down a floor of *ooooh-ooooohs*. Esmé, sensing her cue, stepped up a few seconds later and joined them. This was of course the first time she'd sung with the real-life Cravattes, and she was curious how her voice—her male voice—would blend with theirs. After a half-hesitant warble, it fit perfectly—honey down a jar. She wasn't the only one curious. She saw Bones eyeing her closely, and not the least, her new groupmates, Mitch, Robert, and Otis, hanging back for the lead to kick in. The way she read their faces, they weren't ready to commit themselves yet, but they weren't scorning her; no, far from it, and as she rode the ups and downs of the *ooohing* background with them, she felt herself fit tighter and tighter. It's like she knew where they were going, no, even easier than that, it was like they were a big truck on the highway and she was simply caught, confidently and gracefully, in their slipstream.

Otis Handler stepped to his own mike, the strings swelling behind his entrance, and lay down into the verse: *"Baby, baby, you gotta fall into my arms / Here I stand, I'm right here before you / I'm right, right, right here fo-ooo-orrrr you / So let the . . . door . . . bell . . . ring."*

And, yes, Esmé was there with him on the final line, doubling Otis easily, the wispy curl atop his low smoky voice, and they both held that word *riiiiinnng* until the violins swept in and carried the harmony away.

Esmé felt tingles, yes she did, up and down her neck, even along her arms. This was . . . better than the Darlingettes. This was the big time, real musicians, real music. She was thrilled.

Verse two, then a string-section bridge, during which the three other Cravattes fell into dance moves—step forward, step back, spin, bow, then as one step forward again—that Esmé could only stand back and admire. These boys had it, cool as ice, but smoking! But she had it too, and she felt in her hips the same moves they were making a moment after they made them. This was going to work out! This was where she was meant to be, in the mother-jumpin' Cravattes. How amazing was that? But Esmé wasn't going to question it; there was too much music to be made.

Bones liked that first take, didn't much like the second, and kept them at it through seventeen more till he said, "That first one was the freshest, let's go with that one—no, let's take it again tomorrow. Eddie, you'll have a chance to sleep on it all, right? I saw you moving there, you're gettin' in the groove." Bones stood, clapped his hands. "O.K., everyone, back here first thing tomorrow morning. And don't forget, the Soul Cavalcade rolls in two weeks. That's two short weeks. Got it?"

Nods all around Esmé. She was thinking, Soul Cavalcade?

"So you'll be ready?" Bones said to Esmé.

"You mean I'm—"

"Yeah, you're in. Congratulations."

"Well—" Before she could say anything, the three other Cravattes came up and shook her hand vigorously. She was overjoyed, of course, but confused in more ways than she could understand.

"The Soul Cavalcade?" she finally said.

"Bus tour," Robert Warwick said, standing next to her. "Bones is sending the whole lot of us out on tour."

"On a—

"Big bus. We did a short one a year ago, but now we're hitting half the country. It's an—" up went his eyebrows "—experience."

"Yeah?" What Esmé was thinking was, On a bus? Where we'll all be living together, higgledy-piggledy? A sigh. Could she conceal her true identity? Could she keep making it with the group? And then at least one pleasant question: Would *Doorbell* be a hit?

It was as if Robert read her mind. "That's why Bones is working us so hard. He wants *Let the Doorbell Ring* on the charts by then, so we can perform behind it."

"I guess."

"It's a lot at you, isn't it?" This Robert Warwick had a way about him, a way he seemed to understand her without her doing anything or him even half trying. Like he really could read her . . . well, at least some of her. She made a note: *He* was the one who could blow her masquerade.

"It's my dream," she said, even deeper than she'd been speaking—nerves. "Man." That last word sounded phony even to her ears; false jivey. She'd have to watch it. She understood now she could comport herself in her masquerade almost naturally, but if she became self-conscious, well, this Robert Warwick would be all over that.

As he was now. "Yeah, maaaannnn," he said, then laughed. Esmé blushed, took a deep, anxious breath and held it. But all Warwick said was, "Hey, Eddie, see you tomorrow. We'll nail *Doorbell* then, right?"

Chapter One

Friday, April 17, 1964—Pittsburgh

"O.K., HERE ARE the rules," Bee Williams said into the megaphone she held with one hand. She was at the front of the reconditioned old Trailways, and as far as she could see there were laughing, squealing . . . children, popping up like Jacks- and Jills-in-the-Box, bouncing around the bus like caroms, just one wild mess of postadolescent energy and abandon. How'd she ever get into this? Anything could happen with these . . . babies. Well, Bones had drafted her to watch over them. Why? Tight smile to herself. Because she was the only real grown-up at FDL Records. "The honest-to-goodness, can't-ignore-'em rules!"

Not even one person paying attention. Bee sighed. O.K., who would help her on the bus? This Trip Jackson, the bus driver, who was at least her age? Just look at his . . . goatee. Like some ghetto hipster, some H. Rap Brown like she read about in *Ebony* magazine. And that name, Trip Jackson, where did that come from? She didn't know if she could trust him to even get them where they were going, let alone have him help her look after this mass of panting, squirreling . . . entertainers.

What about the older guys set up in the back of the bus, the musicians already grouped heads-low around an upended waste basket, tossing out cards and currency—yeah, right, a lot of help they'd be. Indeed, the only other grown-up she could see now was the short one of the Cravattes, that Robert Warwick, who though only 20 could act 45, with his serious, almost spooky diffidence. (She didn't yet know anything much about the newest member of the Cravattes, Eddie Days, though he had a full-lipped, fine-featured prettiness about him, which in Bee's experience meant he'd be all over the ladies.) But Robert, though she knew she probably wouldn't get any trouble out of him, might not be much help either.

No, keeping these children in line was all her responsibility. And in truth she wouldn't have it any other way.

In the hand not holding the megaphone she gripped a metal yardstick, and she rapped it against the metal rail behind the first row of seats. "Listen up! Now! Quiet!"

Rap, rap, rap. The sharp sound flew like a shot through the bus but barely dampened the chattering energy. *Rap! Rap!* A few heads looking her way, then a few more. *Rap! Rap! RAP!* O.K., that was better.

"Now, family, we're going to be on this crate for two months." She waved with the yardstick at the bus interior: the sagging seats, the frayed luggage racks jam-packed with instrument boxes and suitcases, the dented aluminum window frames, the scratched bluish glass you could barely see out of, the smell of long-stabbed-out cigarettes and ancient sweat. In one of its incarnations the bus had hauled high school football players around Michigan; in another it had run bored housewives to Chicago for theater parties. "Those are gonna be long months. We have 21 performances, in 18 cities. Might not sound like much, but if you were on our tour last year, you know it is. A lot of road. A whole lot of possibility for trouble. You know how they spell trouble?"

Bee paused. "They spell it M-U-S-I-C." A few laughs. Even the guys in the back were looking forward now. Good—the babies weren't supposed to hate her, they were just supposed to respect her.

"All righty, Rule Number One: There will be no fraternization between members of the opposite sex."

Groans all around.

"That's the main ones. Boys, keep your lines to yourselves. Girls, keep your hands to *yourselves*." She reached out with her ruler. "That means you, *Mr. Orlando Calabrese!*"

Heads spun toward the singer. Orlando just lifted his shovel chin a little higher and chuckled.

"O.K, Rule Number Two: There will be a nightly curfew, and it will be honored—by everyone." Bee looked around, glum faces. She gave them her brightest, most ironic smile. "Now the curfew won't be a problem to make, since most nights you're all gonna be sleeping right where your purty little fannies are now—pardon my French. But on nights when we're sleeping off the bus, you got one hour to get back to your rooms. That's one hour after the final ovation. And if you follow my rules, you will have energy enough to put on a show worthy of an ovation. Got it?"

That hadn't cheered anyone up. Bee got mostly silence.

"Now, family, for you first-timers, we have us our band traveling with us. They're already in the back of the bus, and they already got a game going—don't think I'm not noticing." Bee touched her nose. "Nothin' gets by me, got it? Anyway, we got us musicians, which means we got us poker, and even I know there's no earthly way to keep a drummer or sax player from the cards. But—and here's Rule Number Three: For the rest of you, no playing cards with the band."

A few laughs, but Bee was in dead earnest. She was about to go on with Rules Numbers Four Through However Many She Could Come Up With, but the bus's door opened, and there was Bones Chapman walking up the three steps.

"Righty, here's the final rule." She made sure Bones was right next to her, hearing this. "We have to remember at all times that we're representing Fleur-de-Lys Records. We're its stars, children. People are paying good money to come see us, and we got to do everything we can to put on the best show we can—and to represent Fleur-de-Lys Records as best we can."

Bones moved up right next to Bee as her voice rose.

"We got things to prove to America, important things they got to know about us. And that means, Young Ladies will be Young Ladies, and Young Gentlemen will be Young

Gentlemen. That's our final rule, and you can bet your bottom dollar that I'll be letting all of you know just how it is Young Ladies and Young Gentlemen behave."

The troupe brightened. There was true passion among these poverty-born, projects-raised souls to be just that: true Young Ladies and Young Gentlemen in the new America their music was helping to birth.

"O.K., and now here's our boss and guiding light, Mr. Bones Chapman."

Hoots, hollers, applause, and cries of "Huzzah, huzzah." Bones slipped around Bee, who took her place in the first seat, and stood there, happy, blushing a little, as the tribute shouted on.

Finally, he said, "I just have a few words for you all. First, do everything Mrs. Williams here says. Right?" Well, Bones's eyebrows were lifted just a trace, and the *Yeah, yeah, sure, sure*s that rang out just might have had a touch of facetiousness to them. "Second, what Bee said was quite eloquent." A tip of his head to her. "But we all have us another mission here. You all saw the sign on the side of the bus when you got on, right? What's it say: NUMBER 1 EXPRESS. That's why you're here. Never yet in the history of Fleur-de-Lys have we had a Number 1 record. The Daisies, they got us to Number 9, and with a bullet, but they never hit Number 1.

"But that's why we're sending you out. We're going to do whatever it takes to get us to Number 1!"

Loud cheers, like you'd get at a football pep rally.

"Now we got us an extra burden, just as Mrs. Williams says. Don't know if you all know, but *Billboard* changed the way it does its charts last November. They got rid of that R&B chart, and now it's just one chart for every record. That means we're competing with the white people. Now I'm not worried, just means we gotta try extra hard.

"Good news is we been workin' hard, and we got new product on all of you. The Daisies are comin' on strong with

Man Alive, the Cravattes got *When the Doorbell Rings*, as well as their fine new singer, Mr. Edward Days—" a host of generous clapping for Esmé "—Breeze is lookin' sharp with *Our Hideaway*, our young Mary Hardy's got that new song we all know's gonna burn up the charts, *Sugar and Spice*, and you Shags, back there in the corner, you've gotten positively raucous with *Men on Fire*.

"Now any one of you can take that wax to Number 1. You all got the potential. So what I'm saying right here and now is, first performer to break FDL's cherry up there at the tippety top, well, we're talkin' a brand-new Cadillac."

"Boss," Mitch Williams called out, "that's one Caddie if we do it? You gonna force me to share my driving with Otis, Robert, and Eddie here?"

"O.K.," Bones said, laughing along with everybody else. "Whoever gets that Number 1 record first, *everybody* responsible gets a Caddie. How's that?"

Huzzah, huzzah, huzzah.

"I just hope it's Mary here. Mary, you old enough to even drive yet?"

"You give me a Cadillac, Mr. Chapman," Mary Hardy said. She had a heart-shaped face, touches of baby fat still, but eyes that didn't miss a thing. "And I'll get me old enough real fast."

Laughter rocked the bus.

"So that's it. The race is on. There'll be another surprise, too, if you move them discs, but, well, that'll remain a surprise." Bones smiled, thinking about how he'd foxed Dick Clark. "So the better you do onstage, the more people gonna go right out an' buy your record, they're gonna tell their friends, and the friends are gonna call the radio, and the radio gonna play it more, and more people are gonna go buy it—and you're gonna get to Number 1 and get that Caddie . . . or Caddies.

"Now I'm not comin' with you, gotta tend the home fires

here, get those records out there so they can be bought. But I want you to know I'll be flying out to meet you from time to time. And when I do, I want nothing but good reports from Mrs. Williams here. Bee, anything else to add?"

Bee lifted her megaphone again. "There'll be more rules as I think of them, don't you all worry."

Groans everywhere.

Bones was smiling. "We're all winners, don't you forget that," he said. "And . . . where's this bus going?"

"We're blasting off, boss," a cry rang out.

"And where we blastin' off too?"

"To Planet Number 1!" more voices cried

"Planet Number 1—made of gold records." Bones smiled wide as he started to get off the bus. "O.K., Trip, launch this sucker. You gotta be in Pittsburgh tonight, right, Bee? Good luck, be well."

With that—and a huge cough of exhaust—the Number 1 Express rolled out of Detroit.

＊ ＊ ＊ ＊ ＊

ESMÉ WAS SHARING a seat with Mitch Williams. He was right next to her, his meaty hips only an inch from her own thin ones, unless the bus swayed and he pressed right up against her. She was in the thick of his heavy, smoky man-smell. (As soon as the bus took off, at least half the people on it lit up, including Mitch; Esmé didn't smoke.) She was also aware of his muscles, the way they seemed to flex automatically beneath his silk sport coat even when he was resting; his beard, inches from her, as black and nubby as the brush on the end of an Electrolux; his jaw, thick and U-shaped; and most of all, his height, leaving him scrunched up in the bus seat, looking terribly uncomfortable. There had to be six-plus feet of him. (Esmé was five-eight.)

She felt so dainty, so womanly next to him. Couldn't everybody see right through her? She kept expecting some-body, probably that Robert Warwick, to cry out, *Hey, you're not Eddie Days, you're a girl!* But nobody had. She guessed she'd put herself together right.

She addressed her masquerade in order. First, there was the haircut she got right after the audition. She'd gone into a barbershop near a high school, red-and-white-striped poles out front and combs swimming in blue liquid, and said, "Give me a boy's cut."

The old barber, squashed stogie deep in his mouth, mumbled, "Pretty thang like you?"

"I'm in a play—Shakespeare play—over at the high school, and Mrs. Demeter said I gotta do this. Make it as nice as you can, just make me look like a boy."

Next, her smell. It was called Anvil, the aftershave she'd bought at Woolworths, and to Esmé it smelled like just that: rough and tough, pounding, sparking metal on metal, with subtler traces of horse barns on rainy days, musty wool blankets, and a high, redeeming whisper of that moment when your fingernail digs into an orange's skin. Anvil smelled like men if anything did, and Esmé doused herself in it every morning.

Her voice, which was everything. To her delight her voice was doing the job, just as it had from the beginning. So Eddie spoke a little high—that was the point, just what the Cravattes had needed. So sometimes she sounded to her own ears like a whiny girl; everyone seemed to be taking her enough for granted that they didn't really hear her voice any longer at all, except when it counted, soaring smooth above Mitch, Otis, and Robert.

O.K., her bosom, not that there was as much there to worry about as she'd like, but there was . . . enough. The hospital adhesive tape she'd started out with was clearly unworkable, so she'd headed to the drug store, then the hardware store, then the five-and-dime, and bought everything plausible she could find. She tried other kinds of tape, but even one that held her down just fine, the first time she peeled it off to go to sleep, she screamed like a chicken being plucked. Next, ribbon. A bold red-sheen job that dressed her up like a Christmas present but kept slipping as she moved; when she felt her nipples poke out through the silky fabric, she knew that wasn't going to fly.

Gauze! Gentle, cottony, and lightweight. Yes, perfect. She easily wound it around her upper torso, careful it didn't pinch, and at night she would tie the end around a doorknob and, laughing all the while, spin herself free.

Her wardrobe. Well, that's where the fun was. She put on her secondhand suit and fedora and went out shopping for real. She bought another suit, sleek gray sharkskin with slit pockets—in the mirror she was just the pip! She also picked up shirts, a couple Perry Como–like sweaters, baggy cotton briefs, ridiculously patterned argyle socks, and a pair of Italian boots like she'd seen on Orlando Calabrese. Indeed, the solo singer was her model as she shopped, though she was careful not to get anything exactly like he wore. But when it was time for the bus to take off she had a suitcase full of men's apparel, and just one skirt and blouse set, with stockings and heels, hidden in the inner flap just in case.

In case of what? She didn't really know. She was Eddie Days now, the brother she'd never had, the male singer the Cravattes were dying for, the voice that *When the Doorbell Rings* was released gave it that little extra oomph: The record had debuted on the Billboard charts at 78, and with a bullet. The second week it was up to 42, still with the bullet. And then the bus took off.

"Ever been to Pittsburgh?" Esmé asked Mitch. For the most part, Esmé had learned, Mitch didn't talk a lot; he seemed uncomfortable around words, even when he was singing them. He was the bass man and preferred backup nonsense *ooo-eeees* and *wooos*. Otis, dreamy-eyed and passionate, dropped words like flowers, each one a lady-loving gift. And Robert Warwick? The impression Esmé had was that if you got him started talking, you wouldn't get him to stop—

words like a gushing brook, silver and quick. *If* you got him started. Esmé couldn't put her finger on it, but there was often something distracted about Robert, as if his head were up in the clouds. Sometimes he'd disappear right in front of you. Still, he seemed nice enough, and friendly. Esmé liked them all, though she was acutely aware that she was the new guy—yeah, the new *guy*—and that her groupmates were still checking her out. Fine. She didn't mind their taking their time, and she was happy to lie low, be a little careful herself. Most of all, she didn't want her secret to be discovered.

"Couple times," Mitch said. "Nice town."

"Never been there myself."

"Nice town." Mitch gave a nod, then turned his eyes to the back of the bus. They'd been under way for about an hour, and after the initial high spirits had died down, everyone had settled in for the ride. For most of the troupe that meant sleeping, reading magazines, puffing away on the smokes that already clouded the bus's interior, or simply gazing out the window. For Candy and his boys in the back it meant snapping out cards and shoveling in bets.

"You play?"

"Play what?"

Esmé laughed gently. "I could say an instrument, but way you're looking, I meant cards."

There was a little dusky yellow in Mitch's eyes as he turned to face her. "I sort of got me a promise."

"Oh, yeah?" A raised brushy eyebrow. Esmé had stopped plucking them.

"Promise." Deep rumbling tones from Mitch. "*Promise.*"

"About what?"

"Not to gamble in Ohio."

"In Ohio?"

Mitch sighed, heavy air, like a truck settling after a long road. "Had me a little experience there once, in Canton. Better to not go into it."

"Ohio, eh? What about when we hit Pennsylvania?"

Mitch raised his thick eyebrows and laughed. "Then you're gonna have yourself one whole seat to stretch out on. Heh!"

"It's not that bad," Esmé said, and she'd been glad to find the bus wasn't uncomfortably crowded. There seemed to be a tacit order to things. The musicians had their games in the back, and then came the Shags, who Esmé didn't know that much about. They were five men, and they had recorded for half a dozen R&B labels before FDL picked them up. They were older than the other performers, early thirties, seemed to keep to themselves, and right off ensconced themselves next to the musicians; Esmé thought of them as part of that scene.

Next up were the Daisies, well, three of the girls, Priscilla Bondrais, Linda Strong, and Annie Sylvester, also far back in the bus. (Maisy Columbine had set up alone in the front, across the aisle from Bee Williams.) That left some empty space in the middle of the bus. Mary Hardy sat there, on a whole seat by herself (though Esmé had already noticed how Otis Handler had landed right across the aisle from her, turning his head in her direction more often than not). She and Mitch were next up, with Robert a seat farther on but across the aisle, also by himself. In front of Robert was Orlando Calabrese.

Ah, Orlando. She'd bumped into him nearly every day at the FDL offices, where she was rehearsing nonstop with the Cravattes; Orlando would always be gracious, give her a friendly nod, ask how work was going, say how much he liked the group's sound with her on top. But that was it. She'd look up at him with wide eyes, her hip in her drainpipe pants canted a touch, this beguiling—face it, she was flirting with him; how could she not?—but he just didn't respond.

That kept bugging her, even though she knew he was just seeing her as a *guy*. Esmé remembered those nights alone in her bed gazing up at the poster of Orlando in his lemon sweater, that slight, secret, saucy smile, his fine eyebrows (Esmé was sure he plucked them), his thin, well-turned nose, long chin, the high Cherokee cheekbones—and, damn, he really did look better in person. Even here on the bus she couldn't take her eyes off him. And she kept thinking there should be some kind of eye contact, a recognizing spritz, a hint of a promise of more to come, because God knows there was on her part.

She wondered what he was thinking right this second. His head was tilted against the glass, and it looked like he was staring out blankly, though she couldn't actually see his eyes. He did look a little forlorn, or maybe that was Esmé just reading into his empty face. She thought about moving up and sitting next to him, but the moment didn't seem right.

That left Maisy Columbine. She had already struck out her own territory, setting her makeup case beside her so that nobody would sit next to her and placing herself across from the chaperone so that nobody would want to. Esmé didn't know what to make of this Maisy Columbine with her big, round Betty Boop eyes. Maisy Columbine with the exaggerated curls to her hair. She'd overheard Robert quip to Otis, "If they put into our clothes budget what Bones gives Maisy for her hair, we'd be the sharpest-looking men around." (And of course the Cravattes already *were* the sharpest-dressed men around.)

Esmé had heard the rumors, of course, about Maisy and Bones, but everyone said that if there'd been anything there (other than Maisy's storytelling), it was way in the past; and here Maisy was heading off for a month without the boss anywhere in sight. No, Maisy up there walled in tight seemed pretty complete unto herself.

Esmé's gaze floated back to Orlando. He'd turned his head away from the glass, and now she could see his full face. She feasted a moment longer on it: his cool, untraced forehead, striking aquiline nose, manly jut of his chin, mouth just made to kiss. She licked her own lipstickless lips. And his eyes. She saw them clearly. They were milky, with an unusual bluish tint, and they looked more alive right now, bright, intense, focused forward. Esmé again tried to get into his head, this time following the course of his gaze. He was just staring straight ahead to the front of the bus, nobody up there but Maisy, Bee, and Trip the driver.

Maybe, Esmé thought, he's simply looking through the windshield, trying to see where they were all going—peering into the future. Maybe . . . just maybe . . . he's seeing me.

✶ ✶ ✶ ✶ ✶

PITTSBURGH, P-A! The bus swept along the wide, wind-capped Monongahela River, and there loomed the tall, silvery-stoned downtown buildings at the river's fork. Trip glided them through city streets crowded with rush hour, and then they pulled up in front of a nondescript granite building with a sign that read MASONIC HALL.

Mitch stirred first.

"Where's the theater?" Esmé said.

Her seatmate looked puzzled.

"The theater we're playing at tonight?"

"Oh," Mitch said, "I don't think we got us a legitimate house tonight. I think we're doin' the hall here." Esmé frowned. "No, it'll be fine. We play all kinds of places. This one's O.K. And don't worry, it's gonna get better."

Everyone was gathering themselves, shuffling off the bus. Maisy, no surprise, was first off. When Esmé stood, Orlando was right there in the aisle. He graciously said, "After you, Eddie." That voice! Esmé smiled a big thanks and went ahead of him. Outside the bus everybody was bunching by group, the rest of the Daisies going over to Maisy, the Cravattes gathering next to a flagpole in a wide concrete court afront the hall, Orlando and the rest of the Cavalcade standing about. Bee Williams pulled out her megaphone and said through it in that mechanical, tone-crunched way, "We

Behind them the band was setting up. Bunny Alexander plugged in his Fender bass, and deep notes rattled the wooden stage. A moment later, Robert Warwick came over.

"Robert, hey," Orlando went. Esmé nodded.

"What do you guys think?"

"Seems all right," Orlando said.

"How about you?" Esmé asked.

"Oh, we'll rock 'em, not too worried. Sound in the place is going to be awfully bright, though, unless we really fill it up." Robert Warwick's gaze was darting around the room.

"Bee said we were selling it out," Esmé said.

"There's selling out, and there's . . . selling out." Robert smiled. "Tickets are going at the door, too. We'll see how many we get."

"What about our position?" Esmé asked.

"You mean, in the lineup tonight?" Esmé nodded, then Robert shrugged. "I know we're gonna be movin' up."

She laughed. "That's what I think."

"Not at my expense, eh, Robert?"

"Nope, nope, not yours, O." Robert's eyes clearly fell on Maisy, primping now in a large mirror that one of the twins, Bart or Bert, was holding.

Esmé watched Orlando closely to see how he reacted to this bit of teasing, but there was no readable expression on his face.

Robert turned then and looked right at her. "I suspect you're a little nervous."

Esmé didn't answer at first. She wanted to be careful. "No more than you might expect." A tight smile. "First night with you all."

"I've been watching you," Orlando said, giving Esmé a long look with his sweet, hooded eyes that sent a startling shiver through her. Then he said, "You got the moves down, the songs. You'll be fine."

"Hey, thanks." Esmé brightened.

Behind them the musicians kept warming up, John Smith on guitar falling in, James Motion rattling his drum kit and tuning his snare, the two sax players, Henry Jackson and Norris Rowland, blowing exploratory scales. Bee, at the front of the stage, said into her megaphone, "Shags? Shags to the front. O.K., let's get this rehearsal moving."

Cotton Wilson, a.k.a., Cotton Candy, the piano player, was the de facto leader of the band; he was the eldest member, with dustings of silver through his black hair. When everyone was tuned, and the Shags in position, he lowered his hand on the downbeat—and the rehearsal kicked off.

A first-night celebration dinner followed, in a classy black-owned joint named Smothers on the far side of town, the whole troupe ushered into a rear room, where three women in starched black-and-white uniforms and pointed white caps waited at their attention. The long table was already set. Bee Williams took the end seat, closest to the door. Bee had stomach trouble, and everyone on the bus had discovered she liked her rest stops, which made travel a little pokey but broke it up nicely, too. The rest of the troupe filed in, group by group. The four Cravattes took the flank under a window. The clock had just kicked over to Daylight Savings Time, and it was still bright day outside. Esmé saw streets lined with painted wood row houses, boys in the street playing stickball and girls jumping rope, groups of wide-skirted women with their hair up trading news. Normal life. She looked around the room at the FDLers and smiled. Show folk. She was so thrilled.

Bee rapped her knife against a water glass. "Attention, family, attention," she called. The room was sputtering with high spirits, and it took a few minutes until everyone was almost quiet. Behind the diners the waitresses stood next to trays filled with wide platters of food. The luscious smells of roast pork, chicken, corn, greens, mashed potatoes and gravy, and bubbly orange macs and cheese suffused the room. Noses couldn't help but twitch in delight.

"Now this is our first show tonight, and I'm happy to see how up for it everyone is. Cotton told me he thinks the rehearsal went great, and I'm sure the show'll go better." Smiles all around. "I want to stress again, though, how important this tour is for all of us. This is our big chance to put Fleur-de-Lys Records on the map. Our chance to—" a pause there, while the stern-faced woman searched for the right word "—to af-firm our identity." Esmé, hearing this, looked at Mitch Williams sitting next to her, not knowing quite what Bee meant. Mitch didn't notice her look, but Robert Warwick caught her eye and gestured silently, *Later*. "To present a . . . a united front to the world.

"Now I can't stress how important it is for all of you to follow the rules. I gave you some rules for the bus, now I got some for the show tonight—and *every* night.

"O.K., Showtime Rule Number One: You'll all be prop-er ladies and gentlemen at all times. If you ever—*ever*—have a question about how to behave, well, that's why I'm here." A self-satisfied smile.

"Rule Number Two: You will be prompt. Shows start when they start, and everyone will be in the theater at least half an hour before showtime. That's not when your part of the show goes on—" a quick glance down the table at Maisy Columbine, who looked to be staring off into space "—but when the Fleur-de-Lys Records Spring Number 1 with a Bullet Tour begins. Got it?"

Mumbled yesses down the two rows of hungry diners.

"Rule Number Three: There will be *no* fraternization with the audience after the show other than *ap-pro-priate* fraternization. This is all important. Now Mitch, what's appropriate fraternization?"

Esmé looked to the bearded bandmate next to her, who with his wide mouth was silently turning over the two big words.

"Mitch!"

"I don't know, Miss Bee."

The chaperone frowned. On the other side of Esmé, Robert Warwick held up his hand.

No one could miss Bee's sigh. "O.K., Robert."

"Appropriate fraternization, that's when you wear a letterman sweater and get together with a bunch of guys and drink too much, right?"

Chuckles all around, but Bee was not amused. She turned to Esmé. "Eddie, I know you're new, but you seem to be smart and have common sense about you. What do you think appropriate fraternization with the audience is?"

All eyes on Esmé. She took a deep breath, lowered her voice. "Signing autographs?" she said meekly.

"Signing autographs!" Bee gave out her biggest, though still tight smile. "Yes, indeedy! Signing autographs. And making sure anyone you speak with knows the name of your record and that they can find it in stores tomorrow. And?"

Silence around the table.

"Anything else? Mitch, you know what we're talking about now? Otis? Jerry? Buzz?"

All the named men shook their heads. Next to Esmé, Robert had brought his fist to his mouth and was stifling a near-silent guffaw.

"Gentlemen, there is no . . . other . . . form of . . . appropriate . . . fraternization. None. You shake those sweet young dollies' hands, you give them an autograph if they ask, and that is that. Then we all leave. We'll be sleeping most nights on the bus, as you know, and the bus will be leaving punctually. Mitch, you do know what *punctual* means?" All eyes on Esmé's dour bandmate.

"Means we ain't goin' nowhere."

"It means . . . why do you say that?"

" 'Cause if the tires on the bus be punctual, then we ain't goin' nowhere. Right? Am I right?"

Everyone exploded in laughter. Bee tried to regain order,

but it was impossible. First the band, then everyone else began banging their silverware against the table and crying, "Food! We're starving! Feed us! *Foooo-ood!*" The all-proper waitresses started moving then, bustling about with platters heaped high with the wonderful-smelling grub.

"O.K, you all, eat up. You aren't going to be eating this good every night, believe it." Bee laughed, then sat down. "So enjoy yourselves now," she added, and the room quickly filled with all the noises of a happy repast.

On the way back to the Masonic hall, Esmé took the seat next to Robert Warwick. When the bus was rattling noisily along, she bent her head over and said, "It sounded like there was something else in Bee's bonnet—" the pun surprised her, and she chuckled; Robert smiled back "—well, when she was giving her speech. 'Affirm our identity. United front to the world.' You know what she's gettin' at?"

Robert brought his head around so he was only inches from Esmé. She smelled her aftershave, Anvil, and was glad she'd ladeled it on. From Robert she smelled a clean, flowery fragrance that smelled light and good. "I've heard a few rumors."

"Rumors?"

"About the business end. You know, Bones doesn't tell us much of anything about the business—sure as hell doesn't tell me. But most everybody don't care 'long as they keep getting the chance to record and a few dollars in their pockets for new threads. But I—"

"You pay attention." Esmé gave a nod. "I've noticed."

"Yeah, I do. Much as I can, at least."

"And?"

"Well, there've been rumors since the beginning of Fleur-de-Lys about where Bones's money came from. Some say he cut some . . . unusual deals."

"What do you think?"

"What I hear, all the ownership now is between him and his sister and brother—least the ownership that matters."

Esmé nodded. "But what's bothering Bee now?"

"I'm not sure, but feels like something's going on. Possible somebody's got some unwanted interest in FDL—"

"Interest? What do you mean?"

"I'm not sure."

"Do you know who it would be?"

Robert shook his head. "Don't know that either. I don't know who, and I don't know what they're trying to do, or what exactly they're aiming at. Just that something's worrying Bones."

"Does Bee know?"

"You never know how much she knows, but whatever it is, you couldn't get anything out of her."

Esmé noodled this around. "So what are we supposed to do?"

After a minute Robert sighed. "For now, just what Bee said, I guess: 'United front.' I take that to mean we all put on the best show we can."

A wave of nerves hit her, and Esmé winced in spite of herself.

"You ready?" Robert asked.

A moment's pause, then Esmé leaned toward him and said firmly, "Bring it on."

✳ ✳ ✳ ✳ ✳

BOY, THE PLACE filled up fast. Esmé had stuck her head out from the makeshift curtain hung from the two walls and the overhead basketball hoop at 7:15, and there were only about 20 people in the room. At 7:45 the place was crowded—just like that. At least 1,500 men, women, even kids, strewn unevenly on fold-up chairs and rising up the sides of the hall in pullout bleacher seats. At 7:55 they started clapping. At 8 on the nose, hoots, foot-stomping, and cries of "Get it goin'!" "Breeze, we love you!" "Daisies! Daisies!" even "Come on, Cravattes!" rang through the room.

The Cavalcade performers were at the edge of the stage,

eager to get going, but Rags Doheny, the emcee, held them back. He was a curious-looking man, with a lopsided patchwork cap that hung over half his face, and even stranger, a lopsided face that sagged on the side away from the pulled-down cap. His eyes were uneven, left higher, right lower, and his mouth sliced down at an angle. One eye was even noticeably larger than the other. Rags was like his cap, as if he'd been put together from odd parts. His shoulders were too wide, his chin too small. It was hard to tell how tall he was: Some people found him shorter than they were, though that wasn't the case; and others found him taller, though they had inches on him. The great thing about Rags was that when he was onstage, he was always in motion, so all these off-center body parts were in a jumble, like he was stirring himself up— an eggbeater up there, a whirligig. You couldn't take your eyes off him, and that was the point.

"Make 'em sweat," he always said with his rolling tongue. "Make 'em be *dyin'* for ya!"

At long last, Cotton Candy and the band took the stage, fell right into a bass-heavy rumba beat. The curtain was still closed, but the music was loud, and the crowd burst into applause then stood up and danced. "Go, go, go!" rang out. Esmé watched closely from behind the makeshift curtain. She could see the wooden stage actually buckle and thump on the downbeat. The band was blowin'! A fat woman and a skinny guy in an even skinnier tie erupted from the rows of chairs and boogalooed down the aisle up to the front of the room. Hoots and hollers, more "Go, go, *go*'s!"

Like that Rags took the stage, in front of the drawn mauve curtain. He was a Pied Piper in motley before the worn velvet backdrop.

"All right, all you catsters and chicksters, we're here, we're hot, and we're ready to rock . . . you . . . away. This is the Fleur-de-Lys Spring Number 1 with a Bullet Tour, and this is our first stop, Pittsburgh, P-A!" Loud shouts from the crowd. "That's right, let's hear it for Pittsburgh." More cries skirled up.

"O.K., O.K., now we got the truly happenin' acts in the business with us tonight. We have ... the Shags. We have Mary Hardy. We have the Cravattes. We have ... Mister Orlando 'Breeze' Ca-la-brese. And we have ... the glorious Daisies."

Shouts rang out after each name, building wonderfully through the hall.

"And now I think I know what you want. Tell me, you want to ... dance!" The mauve curtain started slowly sliding aside. "Yeaahhhh." "You want to ... rock and roll!" The audience could see the band now. "*Yeaahhhh.*" "You want to ... rattle your soul." There it was, almost all the way open. "Yeaahhhh. Yeaahhhh. *Yeaahhhh,*" from the crowd.

"All riiiighhhht!" Rags spun his arms. "That's what we're gonna do. We're gonna make your soul start shakin' like a baby's rattle. Heh, heh, heh.

"And to start us off, the magnificent Shaa-aaaa-aaaaags!"

The curtain was all the way back now, and the five Shags in their matching steel-colored sharkskin suits leaped and jumped onto the stage, spinning dervishly, then settling in front of the row of three microphones. Bright yellow and red lights poured down on them. The band pounded out an up-tempo beat, and the group was off on their recent release, *Men on Fire*:

> *Some men come on smooth, slick and cool as ice*
> *Other men swear they're gonna treat you nice*
> *But when we come at you, baby, we're one hundred*
>   *percent desire*
> *We're the men with the gasoline, the men with the*
>   *lighters*
> *We're ... the Men on Fire.*

They were, they were. As many rehearsals as Esmé had seen and been through, nothing prepared her for the wild excitement these old guys cranked up on the wooden stage in this rec room–meeting hall somewhere in Pittsburgh. It was Roman candles and fireworks and it was all in front of her. She felt dizzy for a second, and another nervous tremble ran through her: She'd be up there soon. But there was no time to worry. The Shags finished up *Men on Fire*, played another equally rousing tune, then Mary Hardy moved into the now blue spotlight. Mary was a demure 18-year-old wreathed in ice-blue rayon satin over midnight-blue chiffon, with matching shoes. She stood in front of the microphone a little nervous, like a fourth-grader giving a report to her school, but when she sang, a pure, sweet yet soulful alto rang out. Her new song, *Sugar and Spice*—"*I'm sugar and spice* [bop, bop, bump, bump] *and everything nice*"—was her first, and that was Mary to a T.

Mary Hardy sang two more songs, softly, even decorously, and though the audience hung on every note, Esmé could tell they were ready to kick it out when Mary left the stage. Rags sprinted up and said into the booming mike, "Give little Mary a hand. That's good, that's good. O.K., our next group needs *nooooo* introduction. They're FDL's premier male singing group, and here they are in a way you've never seen them before. Ladies and gentlemen, I present to you the fantabulous *four* Cravattes."

James Motion was laying down on his toms, and there was Mitch, Otis, and Robert sprinting ahead of Esmé onto the stage. She felt an anxious twitter, but there was no time. She had to hit that second microphone at the same moment Otis and Robert did, and so she kicked along in her Italian boots, feeling the swish of men's suit fabric between her legs, reminding herself in the intensity of the moment to not do anything weird like curtsy if they got an ovation.

Maybe not yet an ovation, but the audience was clapping, then slapping their hands in time to the rumbling tom-toms. Otis, Robert, and Esmé lifted their legs high, running in place, just as they'd rehearsed it. Mitch, in contrast, was the picture of calm before his solo mike. As she jiggled up and down, Esmé tried to focus on the audience before her, but it was just a standing, clapping blur. She couldn't in truth concentrate on anything.

Had she had one more second to think about what she was doing, she would have known it was all impossible, would have run from the stage in spooked nervousness. But the show was a runaway train, and Esmé could only hang on. *"When you call my name,"* Mitch sang alone, four feet from the rest of the group, and they echoed, *"caaalllll myyyyy naaaaaaaame."* *"When you join the game."* *"Joinnnn the gaaaaaame."* *"When you say we're playin' / I say I'm not stayin' / 'Cuz you hold all the cards, yes, you do, you hold all the cards."*

This was their up-tempo opener, *You Hold All the Cards*, and Mitch boomed his smoky whiskey voice, Otis laid down the bass, Robert filled in the middle, and Esmé cautiously, carefully sent her high tenor harmonies soaring over all of them. The chorus went: *"Baby, you can hold 'em / you can fold 'em / but, baby, how come you always know how to win?"* and as she chimed in on the word *win*, she felt a dazzling pop, like a flashbulb going off. This was her moment. Her free-floating smart-girl self-consciousness melted away, and in its place she was only a swaying, harmonizing singer—a male singer. Could anyone else feel the change? There she was, Esmé become Eddie, a true Cravatte, and the whole group— *her* group—just laid that song *doooowwwn!*

This was the best sensation she'd ever known. A huge smile burst on her face, and it was all she could do to stay in step, not let her voice take off completely.

Unlike the other acts so far, the Cravattes had four songs, and they built to their charting hit, *When the Doorbell Rings*. After *You Hold All the Cards* came *My Sympathies* and *When the Arrow Hits the Heart*. Esmé just swung through them. Then there was the familiar downbeat to *Doorbell*, and to Esmé's joy, the audience applauded wildly at the first few notes.

When they were done the hall rang with cheers. Esmé's forehead was glisteny with sweat; her legs felt curiously weak, as if she'd run a long race. There were she, Robert, Otis, and Mitch bowing. There was Rags coming on to introduce Orlando Calabrese. There was Orlando looking straight at her and giving a thumbs-up as he passed them as they ran off the stage.

"Let's hear it again for those Cravattes," Rags said, now center stage again. "And now we're coming up on the FDL man of mystery. Yes, you little ladies out there, you know who I mean. This is the man with the BMOC looks and the alley-cat moves, the shining face of the boy your mama wants you to marry, and the backdoor smile of the man you be dyin' to run away from home with. The man with the voice that sings to God and the voice that starts 'em jukin' down below. Oh, yeah, this man, he's church and carny, Sunday morning and . . . Saturday night. Heh, heh, heh."

Cheers and oogling cries from the crowd, mostly the women.

"So, O.K., here we are, it's Friday, and if I don't introduce him soon, the whole week is gonna go by. So without no further ado, I give you Mr. Orlando Calabrese!"

The tall, elegant singer loped to the stage, and though Orlando took the mike shyly, keeping his eyes straight down at the ground, there was a magnetism about him that kept the audience's eyes on him—certainly Esmé couldn't look away. He did a smooth, floating set to cries of "We love you, Breeze!" his voice strong throughout, his presence blooming as he ran through his songs. He finished strong with his new tune, *Our Hideaway*:

> *I pray*
> *We can sta-aaa-aaaay*
> *For more than a daaaa-aaay*
> *In our hi-iiii-daaaaaaaa-waaaa-aaaaaay*

His hooded eyes loomed over the mike, his smile teased

and provoked, and it wasn't far into the song that gasps of pleasure burst like tiny bubbles on the surface of the crowd.

Oh, my, Esmé thought from where she stood in the wings. His sweet, crooning voice fell like velvet across her skin, leaving vivid tiny prickles in its wake. And . . . damn, he's not just doing it to me, he's doing it to all of the women. She felt a curious jealousy then, followed by worry, as if the way that onstage she'd so confidently become Eddie Days of the Cravattes might slip away from her. No, she admonished herself, there can't be any place for feelings like that.

Then Orlando was off the stage, and the four Daisies swept on.

Compared with Orlando's shy, punctilious performance, the Daisies were the circus just pulled into town: The trapeze artists, elephants, and clowns all cavorting in one ring. Nothing demure here. "How y'all doin' tonight?" Maisy called into the microphone as the other Daisies—Priscilla, Linda, and Annie—lined up behind her. "I want to thank old Rags, our emcee, for all his introductions tonight, but I also want to thank him for not even botherin' to bring us out here, because he knows—and y'all know, too—that we Need No Introduction." A quick laugh to the clapping from the audience, then a pirouette back toward the band. "We're the Daisies, and, of course, I'm Maisy—" she chimed the rhyme "—Columbine." More polite laughter. "Oh, yes I am.

"Now we're gonna be wrapping up the show tonight, and that's 'cuz we got the hit. And we got the hit 'cuz you all *bought* the hit. *Man Alive* it's called, and, man alive, we're gonna do it for you now in thanks and tribute to all of you who went down to the Woolworths and handed over your eighty-nine cents—of which you'd be surprised how little we actually get, heh, heh—and took that record home and spun it for your family and your friends and got them to march on down to that five-and-dime, too, and then all of you sendin' it skedaddlin' right up the charts. We love you for that, don't we, girls?" A look back at the Daisies, shuffling calmly in place. "Girls?" Louder, sharper.

Priscilla Bondrais in her well-coiffed head stepped to the mike and said in her rich, throaty voice, "We do, we love you all." It was interesting to Esmé how sincere Priscilla's voice sounded after Maisy's intro, and yet there was something else in the backup singer's tone: how she subtly let the audience know that *she'd* never flirt and beg so shamelessly for anyone's love.

With a quick flash of her eyes Maisy stepped in front of Priscilla then said into the mike, "Well, we do—we just ahh-dore you all." She fluffed down her skirt, a puffy lime-green number that contrasted with the rest of the group's lemon-yellow sheaths. "O.K., O.K., enough talk. Enough, enough, *enough*. We be here to sing for y'all." A spin again toward Candy Wilson. "Maestro, they're all a waitin' for us. Girls, you ready? O.K., O.K., hit it!"

The band churned and choogled, and the backup Daisies did tight little steps in perfect unison. When the beat was easy and smooth, Maisy stepped forward and started the song. She had a high, breathy voice, but it worked; it slipped right into your head and was instantly memorable.

> *Man alive, I love that man*
> *Man alive, I love that man*
> *I love him in the mornin'*
> *'N' I love him with no warnin'*
> *Man alive, I lo-ho-hove that man*

Ooooh-hoo, sang the backup ladies. Step, step, the Daisies hit their perfect gliding moves. Maisy shook her head of wild curls and sang her panting tune. It was the kind of act that looked at any moment to career into excess but never did. Yes, Esmé thought, those girls got it, too. And along with everything else she felt a sharp note of pride that she was associated with Fleur-de-Lys Records, that she was part of all of this.

When the Daisies finished up their set—and did *Man Alive* again, as their closer—the whole troupe went back onstage for the final tune, an old gospel hymn, *The Road Is Wide, the Light Divine*. Each act traded off vocals. The rousing piece went on and on, voices swelling on the chorus, everyone swaying back and forth, linking arms—Esmé, next to Orlando, felt his arm slip lightly around her; to Esmé's other side was Maisy Columbine, and she felt her arm go around her own waist, too, until Maisy moved to the front and grabbed the last verse.

At the final chorus everyone on the stage bowed, their linked arms making one swoop; and on the floor the audience hooted and yelled. Everyone was standing and clapping. It *was* an ovation.

Out came Rags in his motley, saying into the mike, "Thank you, thank you. The whole Fleur-de-Lys family thanks you from the bottom of our hearts. We love you. We lo-ho-hove you. Good night."

As soon as they left the stage, Bee Williams was there to lead them to the bus, then try to spirit them all quickly on. There was a line of young women in colorful party dresses along the way to the bus, calling to the groups. "Otis," one cried, then, "Mitch—Mitch Williams!" The two members of the Cravattes stopped to chat up the fans, and Esmé hung back, curious. These fans were striking young women, with amazing hairdos, curls built on curls like an array of birdhouses one on top of the other. "Orlando!" shouted a clutch of them, and she saw arms reaching out as Calabrese went by. Esmé was watching him closely, too. Orlando had his cool, unknowable smile on his face, and while her bandmates were right up in front of their cooing fans, the solo singer kept a few steps back. With a thick black pen he carefully signed autographs for the girls who could reach that far.

"Eddie!" A cry came right at her. "Eddie, Eddie Days, over here!"

Huh? It took Esmé a second for this to register. Then she turned and faced a woman who . . . could have been her. The woman was about the same height, with a similar light-cocoa skin and pretty features. She wore an aqua and yellow crepe dress with a pleated skirt, and she was pert and eager, though the look on her face was dreamy, absorbed. "Eddie, Eddie, you were great!"

Maisy Columbine was right next to Esmé, smiling in a way Esmé knew she shouldn't trust. "Hey, your first fan," the singer said. "Go on over to her."

Esmé felt frozen.

"Comes with the job, sweetheart." Maisy's plucked eyebrow was lifted; she was giving Esmé a saucy smile. "One of the nice things." Then a deep moué. "Trouble is, it's just ladies out here." A slight flip of her shoulders. "Lucky you."

Esmé still didn't know what to do. The fan was smiling widely, with a look ripening into *come hither*.

"Hey," Maisy said, keeping her eyebrow up. "Go for it. I would." She came up next to Esmé and whispered in her ear, "What're you waiting for?"

Esmé, swallowing deeply, awkwardly, walked up to her doppelgänger.

"You were soooo good tonight," the woman said in a voice that struck Esmé as being not unlike her natural one. "I just love the Cravattes."

"Thank you," Esmé said, deep as she could.

"And they've just taken off since you joined. I love *Doorbell*, especially your voice on it. Most girls can't tell the difference 'tween you men, but I can. And, oooh, those high notes just give me the *shivers*." The girl threw her body into a shimmying shake.

Esmé took a step back. "Well, thank you again." God, was she blushing? She looked over at Maisy, who was batting her eyes and laughing.

The fan was looking right in Esmé's eyes. Then she

leaned forward and took her hand. Esmé felt something cool and metallic. The fan leaned closer, and Esmé recognized her own favorite perfume, Star Shine, before she'd had to start wearing that Anvil cologne. A soft whisper: "Can you get away tonight?"

What was that in her hand? Esmé looked down and saw a key, attached to a paper tag with an address on it. She blushed more deeply. The fan looked so hopeful, and finally Esmé leaned in and whispered to her, "I'd like to, sugar, but we have to get on the bus now and go to Virginia."

"Tonight?"

"Right now." This was going to be Esmé's first all-nighter on the bus, and she was half looking forward to it for the adventure, and half wondering how well she'd sleep.

"Well, Eddie." The fan batted her eyebrows. "You got my key now. Next time you're in town—" She licked her lips. "You know, I'll be waiting for you."

Maisy was still over there, chuckling. "Come on, Eddie, we got us a bus to catch. Bee's about to split her bonnet."

Esmé gave a final smile to the fan, who did a subtle but unmistakable bump and grind right there on the sidewalk. As she walked away, she saw Mitch reluctantly pull away from his fan, but not until he'd leaned in close, gave her a full-lipped kiss, then slipped a hand up the back of her wide skirt. The fan shuddered at his touch, quaking against him right there.

"Yeah," Maisy was saying to Esmé and Mitch as Mitch came up, "you men get all the ladies, that's for sure. At least the E-Z ones. Some of us ladies are a little more . . . particular. Know what I mean?"

Mitch rolled his eyes, but Esmé was simply thinking about the oddness of being propositioned by a woman who reminded her of herself.

"No, don't you worry none about Maisy Columbine," the singer went on. "Maisy don't need no Eeeee-Zeeeee pickin's.

Maisy likes it when there's a little . . . sport in it. You know what I mean?"

Something in Maisy's voice caught Esmé then. Was it, as the old schoolyard quip had it, a promise or a threat? And who was she talking about? Esmé watched Maisy's eyes closely. They were looking right . . . at . . . her. No! Was that possible? Come on! Esmé knew she was a good-enough-looking guy, but Maisy Columbine? Come on! But without really holding Esmé's eyes, Maisy's saucy gaze swept quickly past Esmé and over her shoulder.

It was Bee coming up on them, waving her arms, beckoning everyone along. "Bus leaves in *two* minutes, family," she called out. "Two minutes! You not on that bus, you just got yourself another record company." A smile. "You can call it Steeltown." Arms fluttering. "Hustle, hustle, children. Hustle, hustle."

"She means business," Maisy said softly. "Come on, Eddie, Mitch, let's go."

Chapter Two

Saturday, April 18— Richmond, Va.
Sunday, April 19— Raleigh, N.C.
Monday, April 20— Columbia, S.C.
Tuesday, April 21— Charleston, S.C.

WELL, ESMÉ THOUGHT, at least I found out I can sleep on a bus. Although that first night out of Pittsburgh nobody bedded down at all, except for Bee Williams, who once the bus was under way went out like that.

Even before Bee was asleep, the musicians had moved to the tail of the bus, upended their instrument cases, uncapped a couple bottles of Old Gentleman whiskey, fired up their Tareytons and Salems, and laid out the cards. After a few bored minutes in her seat watching the lights of Pittsburgh disappear, Esmé sauntered back to catch the action. Mitch Williams was already there; he sported a Vegas-style green eyeshade, and his sleeves were rolled up as if he meant business. Around him were James Motion, Bunny Alexander, Cotton "Candy" Wilson, Henry Jackson, and Norris Rowland. The only band member not playing was the guitarist John Smith; he sat in his seat with his own golden bottle of the Old Gent perched between his raised knees.

Esmé had little knowledge of cards, growing up without a father in the house or brothers, and so she wasn't sure what game the men were playing or even how it was going. Instead, she watched faces. It was Mitch she observed most closely. What she knew of him in the group, he was often distracted until he went before the microphone, when he would always pull out a spot-on vocal. The rest of the time it was hard to get a fix on him. He had that thick beard he seemed to hide behind, as well as his distant eyes. But right here, dealing cards beneath his green eyeshade, he was razor-focused, snapping off cards crisply, bantering with the musicians, all the while his fingers futzing around his own held cards, leaping at the next chance to throw one down. She'd never seen him more truly alive.

The rest of the musicians were their usual laconic selves, hunched behind their porkpie hats and smokes, sipping their thick-bottomed glasses of Old Gentleman and watching the shuffle go round. Esmé watched for a while then got bored. She looked around for the rest of the Cravattes. Otis Handler was with Mary Hardy, neither of them talking, their heads settled comfortably back on the bus seat. And Robert . . . where was Robert Warwick?

She walked back down the aisle. The bus had a run of overhead lights, now off, but also had individual lights above each seat, most of them off, too. She saw shadowy bodies curled into each other, blankets pulled up over necks, difficult to make out who was who, though none of them looked like Robert. There was a bent pair of knees, and as she got closer, she saw that Robert was scrunched up in his seat, head back against the side of the bus, the light on above him, a slender book in his hands.

"Hey," she said, perching on the edge of the seat across from him. "What're you reading?"

"Eddie, hey," Robert went. Then: "Oh, nothing."

"I'm curious," Esmé said.

"Just a paperback war novel." Robert shrugged. "Passes the time."

Esmé leaned over, trying to catch the title. She made out one large word, gold embossed on the cover: *Poems*.

"It's poetry."

Robert clutched the volume to his chest. His large milky eyes swam with amusement behind his thick black glasses. "Busted," he said.

Esmé laughed, as far back in her throat as possible. "Who is it?"

"You wouldn't know."

"Oh, yeah? Try me."

"His name's Keats. John Keats. He was—"

"English, last century." Esmé remembered with fondness a poetry class she'd taken at Miss Penny's Finishing School. "Proper ladies will properly know the classics," Miss Penny would pronounce, and Esmé was lucky, her teacher, Mr. Dobbs, actually made the poems fun. "*Ode to a Nightingale*, *Lamia*, *Ode to Melancholy*—"

Robert lifted his eyes. "I'm impressed."

"No, I'm impressed," Esmé said. "This is for your lyric writing?"

"It's because ... well—" Robert gave a shy smile. "Because I love words, love playing with them. Love—yes— love putting the best words I can into songs."

Esmé looked at him intently. "So how come we're not doing any of your songs?"

Robert shrugged. "Ask Bones."

"He's heard them, right? What's he say?"

A sigh. "He thinks the words—well, what he says, a good song's all about the beat. 'You got to get the beat right.' " Esmé leaned toward him, ready to agree with that. Robert held up his hand. "I don't argue with that either, God knows. But I keep thinking, Why stop there—"

"You get a good beat, plus good lyrics, you got a great song."

"And they will be great." Robert sighed. "Just got to keep at it."

"You'll do it," Esmé said firmly.

A smile. "Thanks." Then a cool appraisal. "Maybe I'll write you a song."

Esmé blushed. "I'm just the tenor harmony."

"Oh, I don't know. I think you could carry one of our tunes." Robert leaned closer. "I think it might give us a new angle on things."

There was something in this Robert wasn't saying, and Esmé looked closely at him but still saw no indication that he was in any way seeing through her disguise.

"I'd like that," she said. "I'd do my best."

"Consider it done," Robert said. He was smiling at her then, and she found herself smiling back at him—a smile involuntarily much larger and brighter than she intended. Esmé felt comfortable enough in the moment to change the subject.

"What can you tell me about Maisy?"

Robert rolled his eyes. "The NAP?'

"The—?"

"Negro American Princess."

"Oh!" Then Esmé laughed. "Yeah."

"What do you want to know?"

"Well, she—I don't want to think too much into it—but she, well, after the show she gave me this look—"

"She was coming on to you?" Robert gave Esmé a sly, conspiratorial smile.

Esmé gave her head a short shake. "Wouldn't want to go that far."

"You never know, though. She might've been. You're a handsome enough man, and Maisy, well, she's got a record—"

"What do you mean?"

Robert shook his head then, pulled back a couple inches. "I shouldn't go talking—"

"Robert—"

"I don't like to gossip—"

"Robert!" Was Esmé sounding too much like a girl here? She couldn't help it, she wanted whatever dish she could get on the Daisies' singer.

He sighed. "Maisy, well, she gets around. Definitely not a one-man gal, you know what I mean. Seems to want to work her way through the FDL men, starting with—"

"Orlando?"

Robert shook his head. "No, Bones."

"Really?"

"That's what they say, yeah."

"But how about—"

Robert quickly shook his head. "Not me. I'm too . . . short for her or something. Good thing, too."

"No, I meant—" She paused. "I mean, what about . . . Orlando?" She couldn't help herself, that's what she wanted to know.

He gave his head a short shake. "I never heard nothin' yet 'bout him and Maisy."

"That's good." Oops, that just came out of her.

"What do you say that for?"

Esmé gave a quick, she hoped noncommittal shrug.

"You know," Robert went on, "if Maisy did give you that look, well, could just be 'cause you're new here."

"More I think about it," Esmé said, wincing, "less I'm sure that—"

Robert leaned his head in close. "Just keep your wits about you. You don't want to get involved with that woman." He laughed. "Only man deserving of her, he's wearin' red, got horns, a pair of cloven hooves—"

"The Bride of the Devil," Esmé said, laughing. "Hey, might be a song in that."

Robert leaned back, then started singing softly, *"You better listen to me, what I say's on the level / That woman you're lovin', she's the bride of the devil."* Just like that he'd come up with his couplet.

Esmé heard words in her head, spoke them: *"You say you want a true love, well, who doesn't / But the love you think you're seein', it's—it's—*no, can't get the rhyme."

"The love you think you're seein', it's the love that . . . wasn't." Robert winced. "No, that ain't gonna work. Still, Eddie, you had us on the right track."

Esmé beamed. She had fooled with a few songs before

alone, but this was close up and fun. "Maybe we can work more on it later."

"Absolutely," Robert said. "Let's see what we can come up with."

They were silent then, Esmé for one enjoying their easy camaraderie. She leaned her head back against the bus seat and listened to the silence. She was drifting off to sleep when she heard a loud "Ooooh!" come from a few seats ahead. It was a woman's voice, and she added, "Where you goin' with that mangy hand?"

Only mumbling in return, then a man, one of the Shags, guy named Jerry a few rows behind Esmé and Robert, called out, "Yeah, man, where you think you be goin' with that disgustin' . . . main-gee . . . hand?"

"Hey, shut up!" This was obviously the man next to the girl who'd just cried out, and Esmé recognized the voice: the Shag they called Buzz because, unlike any other man on the tour, he had razor-short hair.

Laughs up and down the bus.

"You gonna make me, Buzz?" Jerry said.

"Yeah, you and whose mother?"

"*Quiet!*" The word snapped from the front of the bus. It was Bee Williams. She'd gone from sleep to awake faster than the bus could go from zero to 20, and now she started walking down the length of the bus aisle. "Don't you know this is lights-out, sleep time?"

Grumble, grumble, but everyone settled down. Robert gave Esmé another conspiratorial smile, and she returned it. Then she again set her head back against the seat, and to the softly lulling run of the bus down the highway, she quickly fell asleep.

✳ ✳ ✳ ✳ ✳

ESMÉ COULDN'T BELIEVE the trees down here. They positively . . . drooped, like they were crying. And so shaggy. They looked like out-of-control 'dos, like—a curious thought—that

British group that had been burning up the charts all spring, the one they called the Moptops. Everywhere they went she saw Beatles haircuts lining the roads.

They'd played Richmond, Va.; Raleigh, N.C.; Columbia, S.C.; and now they were pulling into Charleston. The pace was more than she expected. After the excitement of the first show in Pittsburgh—and the first night on the bus—the whole crew had been groggy as they pulled up to a roadside café for breakfast. The exhaustion lasted the rest of the day, though Esmé was surprised how well everyone burned it out for the show that night, in the Mosque Auditorium in Richmond. Back on the bus the next night, Bee with her megaphone called out, "O.K., family, I'm going to sleep now, but you all can carry on any ol' way you want."

Yeah, right. As cramped as it was in the bus seats, the exhausted troupe quickly fell out and slept like stones till morning.

By now as they headed into Charleston the crew was beginning to pace themselves, well, more or less. The musicians in the back seemed to exist without sleep, without much of anything except their cards and their smokes and their Old Gentleman. As for Esmé, Maisy hadn't paid her any mind the last couple days. Nothing from Orlando, either. He was keeping to himself, in a quiet kind of sulk, as Esmé interpreted it, though maybe he was just feeling shy and withdrawn these first few days on the road.

The general idea was to spend every third or fourth night in a motel so everybody could sleep in a bed and grab a shower, and tonight was to be the first motel night. Esmé was looking forward to it as an ocean-bound castaway prays for a palm-ringed island. After the show the Cavalcade lingered longer than usual signing autographs, but then Bee bustled up and pushed everyone up the steps and onto the bus. "Children, children," she cried, her arms akimbo, "come on. We got you all a special treat tonight. It's spelled B . . . E . . . D . . . S!"

The Oak Tree Motel, outside of Charleston, separate wood cabins in two facing rows (with a drooping oak tree between them), a little rundown, but not perilously so. A short, beetle-browed man with fold after fold of black skin came out with a passel of keys jangling in his hand and let the performers into their cabins one by one. There were two single beds in her room, which she entered right behind Mitch Williams.

She was nervous. This was going to be the first night she'd ever spent with a man in the same room, and her worry was not just because of her disguise, though that was most of it. So far she'd been able to avoid urinals at rest room pit stops, and fortunately the bus had a toilet in the back with a door that even though it didn't swing tight, closed enough that in the dark—the overhead light was burned out—kept her private. But tonight she'd be taking off her clothes, wearing pajamas, and sleeping—with a *man* only five feet away.

Enough! She bucked herself up, then went to the bed to her right and uttered, "Mitch, wow, this is gonna be heaven."

Mitch walked around his bed as if it were a wild thing.

"Mitch?"

"It's awful tempting," the tall, bearded lead singer said.

"That it is."

"And I got me a belly full of that turkey and dressing that says sleepin'."

"Hey, I'm willing to turn in right away," Esmé said. Facing Mitch, she kicked her feet up, leaped backward, and bounced about on the narrow bed. The mattress was soft but not too soft; her head fell back and floated on the pillow. "I feel like I could sleep a week."

"*Awful* tempting." Mitch was standing at the end of the bed, and now the way Esmé saw it, he was looking at it as if it were his freshly dug grave.

"But?" Esmé leaned up and pulled her heavy shoes off and let them fall to the floor with a pleasing plunk.

"But I'm down my pay for the next month."

"Down? You mean the poker game?"

"At least the next month. I'm into Candy."

"He's taking your money?" Esmé said sleepily.

"Every penny he can."

"So?"

Mitch didn't say anything for a moment, then looked toward Esmé and said softly, "I gotta go. You have yourself a good night." He pulled the door quietly shut behind him.

The first thing Esmé did was undo her gauze breast harness—tight, uncomfortable thing—then take a cooling shower. Even so, and exhausted as she was, she just couldn't sleep. She tossed left and turned right, then flipped back and forth all over again. She wasn't really thinking about anything that much, just not feeling her bones settle. Finally, she got up.

It was 1:30 on the clock. She pulled on a casual pair of pants and a shirt, then pulled a crew-necked sweater over it. Even though the air was warm, she wanted to be careful about showing too much. She clicked open the door and went into the night.

There was a partially rusted metal chair outside her door, under a yellow insect light nonetheless swarming with long-winged bugs, and Esmé settled into it. From a cabin about 50 feet down from hers she could hear gambling noises, intense, concentrated silences followed by loud whoops and cries of men's voices, and saw a warm yellow light creep out around the closed blinds. Looked like everybody's blinds were shut tight, and Esmé sat there, wondering what all was going on behind them. Everyone sleeping? She sort of doubted that. This seemed like one hyped-up group of young people— finally, tonight, sprung from that endless bus.

Something caught her eye. A movement, quick, furtive. Someone else was out. It was a heavily humid night, but not that dark; an orangish light rose up from somewhere— seemingly everywhere—and turned the ground a curiously glowing black while it cast the cabins into quick, sharp relief.

There—someone running between cabins. Could be anyone going anywhere. Esmé drew a deep breath, settled back in her chair, softly shut her eyes. A second later she was startled: Somebody'd sat down right next to her.

It was Orlando Calabrese.

"I couldn't sleep," he said in his low, soft voice. "How about you?"

"Um," Esmé mumbled. Orlando was the last person she'd expected to see. "Um, nope, not a wink."

"You'd think, here we are, finally settled in a real motel, and we could just tumble off." Orlando shrugged. "Guess not."

"I was just tossing and turning." Esmé felt a curious tingle using these words with Orlando.

"Got it." The solo singer looked out into the night. "Might be easier if we were like those guys—" a nod toward the gamblers' den "—wouldn't need sleep at all."

"I don't get it," Esmé said, agreeing. "How do they do it?"

"One of the mysteries of the road." Orlando shifted then, and grew silent. She heard him take a deep breath, but instead of saying anything, he simply held out his hand. There was a mysterious flat, pucklike object in it. "Hey," he said in a voice falsely bright, "want to try one of these?"

"What is it?"

"Haven't seen one of 'em since I was a kid. They call it a Moonpie. Cakey thing, with marshmallows."

Esmé looked at it closely. "Looks like something you'd find in a cow pasture."

Orlando gave out a little laugh. "Yeah, now that I'm older, gotta say I suspect it don't taste much different, but when I was a boy—I grew up my first twelve years in Alabama—we'd live and die for these things. Cost a nickle, used to spend all of a summer's day going round begging pennies off people. We get enough of 'em, we headed right down to Mr. Garfinkle's store and bought us Moonpies and Co'Colas—"

"Co'Colas?"

"That's what they call Coke down there. Boy, Eddie, it's all coming back to me."

Esmé reached out and took the offering from Orlando. She could feel a dull, flat chocolatey cover. She took a bite. Yeah, it wasn't great—tasted like congealed library paste between chocolate-iced cardboard. "I think I'll stick with my Baby Ruths."

"You was always in Detroit?"

"Yeah."

"You like it?"

"Sure. How about you?"

"Oh, yeah." But Orlando sounded half-hearted, distracted. "Yeah, of course." A long silence followed; to Esmé it was clear that he wasn't ready to pursue anything that personal. Also clear to Esmé that what was on his mind was something other than Moonpies.

Finally, he shifted in his chair, cleared his throat. "Listen, Eddie, I wanted to have a word with you."

"A word?"

"A little . . . well, clear something up."

"O.K." Esmé's fingers nervously dug in tight to the arm of her metal chair. She had no idea what was coming next.

"It's about Maisy." Orlando stretched out his hands, fingers folded into each other. "I've noticed that, well, she seems to have some eyes on you."

"Oh," Esmé exclaimed, startled that someone else had seen what she wasn't sure was even the case. "Are you sure?"

"I have a pretty good eye for Maisy. And, no question, she's got at least one eye on you."

Esmé shook her head. "That seems pretty—"

"Well," Orlando stopped her. "What I really want to know is, Do you got eyes for her?"

Esmé knew she had to be careful to say the right thing. If she simply uttered the truth, that she couldn't stand Maisy

Columbine, that might insult Orlando, who, she was picking up clearly, dismayingly did seem to have eyes for her; but if she expressed any interest in Maisy at all, she could lose Orlando as any kind of comrade or friend. She took a deep breath, then said, "I think anything between Maisy and me would just be . . . impossible."

"Why?"

Esmé reached over and put a friendly hand on Orlando's shoulder. He was wearing a thin knit polo shirt, and she could feel his skin right through it. This might have been the sexiest move she'd ever made, and he'd never know it.

"Orlando—"

"Call me Breeze." Orlando ruffled his shoulders. "Everyone does."

"Um, Orlando—" Esmé couldn't bring herself to use the nickname. "Listen, you have nothing to worry about with me and any girl—"

"Any girl?" Sharp curiosity.

"Um, on the tour, I mean." What was she saying?

"What, you got a lady back home?"

"I'm—" She was flustered, that's what. She saw no easy way out, so she simply answered his first question again. "Orlando, you just don't have to worry about me and Maisy. I swear."

He leaned back and regarded her, his strong chin high. "And I can trust you?" She was close enough to him to feel the sigh run through him.

"Yes."

"Man to man?"

"I swear it," Esmé said.

Orlando leaned back, brought his arms together, folded tight over his chest. He looked to be in quiet pain.

"So, tell me," Esmé said gently, close to his ear. "What about you? Do you have eyes for her?"

Orlando looked off into the soft, fat night. Esmé kept her

gaze on him till, there—there again somebody was stealing furtively between cabins. She tried not to look in that direction, to hold her eyes on Orlando. She saw thoughts spin and tumble through his mind. "I don't know what to do," he finally said.

"What do you mean?"

"I—I can talk to you?"

"Of course." Esmé's voice was so soft and comforting that to her ears it sounded like her true womanly voice. Orlando didn't notice anything, though, and seemed relieved by her tone.

"I've just—I don't know why, and half the time I think it's insane—but there's something about her that . . . gets to me. She looks—you know, maybe it's just 'cuz we're down here—but I keep thinking of Miss Washington, this teacher I had when I was a boy." Orlando's eyes were bright. "Man, I had the hugest crush on her. She—she looked a lot like Maisy, with those giant eyes, and now . . . now Maisy, she—" he had his head lowered now, almost buried in his hands, and he spoke in the tones of confession "—well, there's something about her that . . . like Miss Washington . . . that makes me think she can really see me. I mean, Miss Washington, I'd be in the back of the class and start to daydream out the window, and she'd go, 'Orlando, quit your lollygagging!' " He winced. "She could nail me just like that. And . . . something 'bout Maisy, well, she . . . I think she understands me."

"What does she understand?" Esmé said in little more than a whisper.

Orlando hung fire, then said back softly, "You see, I don't exactly know. That's one of the reasons I got eyes for her."

Esmé took this in. She wasn't sure what Orlando was saying, and found it amazing that he was confessing to her at all. He had seemed so together, so manly perfect when he was simply a pinup on her wall; but now here was the true soul right by her, speaking man to man to her, letting out his. . . .

"The funny thing," Orlando said, interrupting her thoughts, "is that she don't seem to have eyes for me at all."

"You sure?" Esmé was trying to remember if she'd ever seen Maisy flash one of her carnivorous glances toward him.

He nodded. "I get nothin' from those big, beautiful eyes—"

"You sound like you got it bad."

Orlando sighed. "You're a guy, you gotta know what I'm tryin' to say."

That startled her; Esmé didn't know what else to do but nod.

Orlando just shook his head. "You know that song by Smokey? The one where the guy knows he doesn't dig the chick, but can't help but really love her—"

"*You Really Got a Hold on Me*. Love that song."

"That's it, that's just what it's like."

"Well," Esmé reached over and patted his hand; she felt Orlando flinch at her touch. She quickly added, "You know now you don't have to worry about me."

"That's a . . . relief. But it don't, excuse me, it don't make things that much better. I still can't get her eyes on me."

Oh, Breeze looked so forlorn. Esmé was seized by the greatest compassion. "Maybe I could do something," she impulsively said.

"You?"

"I could, I don't know, go speak to her for you?"

Orlando recoiled. "I don't—" He visibly shuddered. "What good would that do?"

Esmé shook her head. "I'm not sure." But wild thoughts were spinning through her head. Yes, she *would* do something; she was liking this all too much, being with Orlando, having him talk openly with her, his needing her. She couldn't just shrug and say, Good luck. There must be. . . .

Orlando had leaned back and was taking the last bite of his Moonpie, but Esmé beckoned his head toward hers. And though she wasn't sure exactly what she could offer right then, she felt such need that she had to say, "Orlando, I have an idea."

"What is it?"

"I—I don't think I should say now. It's just coming to me."

"But—"

"I'll be . . . careful. And it might take some time." And there it was, a less crazy thought spinning through her head, and it seemed . . . plausible. "I think I can help you."

Orlando was all sad eyes and a wan smile. "Really?"

Esmé nodded, then sighed herself. "I damn sure hope so."

✳ ✳ ✳ ✳ ✳

WELL, *THAT* WAS flat-out embarrassing. Orlando put his hand on his forehead as he lay in his bed. It was a little clammy. Did he really say too much to that sweet new guy Eddie? He did, didn't he? And now Eddie, eager young beaver, was going to help him with Maisy—if that was possible. He winced. A good idea? His only answer was the way his cheeks burned. He got like this sometimes, when he let things out that he knew he shouldn't—all hot and anxious and troubled.

A hissing sigh through his tight lips. Not that Orlando was ever *not* troubled. He'd had a tough life, raised by an uncle and aunt down South, both a little too quick with the razor strop, then shipped north to Detroit when he was twelve. Up there he basically lived on the street, getting by any way—with any kind of help—he could. Those cold snowy nights on the Avenue, the tin-drum fires, the guys with haunted eyes and maybe, just maybe, an extra blanket.

Ugh. He shuddered even now to think of it. Thank God for Bones Chapman, who'd found him in a youth choir and saw his potential; Bones who'd simply come along and saved him.

He was looking down at his long legs, at his fingers floating in the air. Sometimes he was such a mystery to himself. He knew women found him gorgeous, the high cheekbones, fine

Indian nose, strong jaw, and he was the coolest dresser—just check out those slick linen slacks, the tumbly-soft lemon cardigan—but though he could see what others loved to see, he could never see himself clear at all. He knew what he had to be, though. What was that phrase: a ladykiller?

He gave out a bitter laugh. Oh, those ladies—sometimes he did want to kill them. Just the way he wanted at times to kill Maisy, just stab something into those huge, radiant eyes. . . .

Well, that was a horrible thought. Still, it was those eyes, even more than her resemblance to Miss Washington, that brought out his feelings for her. Not exactly love, just more this sense he had that somewhere behind those huge eyes she could truly see him—see so far into him that maybe Maisy could see his deepest secrets.

The secret that he truly didn't know was there.

He shook his head sharply. What was he thinking? Was that the reason he had eyes for Maisy, that only she could understand him even more than he understood himself?

The sweat was on Orlando now, the way it often came at night, and he wasn't sure he'd get to sleep at all.

And that led to the usual final question: If Maisy could see that far inside him, did he really want to know what she'd find out?

✳ ✳ ✳ ✳ ✳

WELL, THE FIGURES were good—damn good! The bus tour was selling out most every night, even midweek, and even in places like Columbia, S.C.; and record sales for all the groups were spiking in the days after.

Bones Chapman kicked back in his leather chair, put his feet up on the walnut desk, then lit up a cigar—a fat Cuban, from a prerevolution stash he'd held on to—and blew out a thick corona of gray-blue smoke. It clouded joyfully over his thick-haired head. This was still the great thrill of running his company, that he could put his feet up on his desk and enjoy a true smoke just like any old big shot down the road at Ford and G.M. It was even better, because he was the sole man in charge of Fleur-de-Lys Records. He didn't have pesky stockholders out there voting on what to do. He didn't have distant aunts and uncles worrying their picayune investments, just his brother and sister. And, best, he no longer owed any more money to the guys he'd had to reach out to when he was running his jazz label in the mid-'50s and so vividly saw the future: black music for teen-aged America, *white* America.

He thought of those old backers now, the guy at the Chevy plant who knew guys who knew guys who knew guys with deep pockets. The loan shark guys and pension-fund flunkies not too particular to get their hands dirty with Negro business. The weasel-browed guys who carried their lunch in a paper sack and sat there eating it, right in your office, stinking of liverwurst, before they threw down the greenbacks and left.

Thank God that was over, all the money paid back, the obligations square. All the creepy guys off plying their dark trades elsewhere. No, ownership of Fleur-de-Lys Records was nice and tidy now: He owed nobody nothing, and he and his brother and sister held every damn share.

So where was the trouble coming from?

A long sigh, and Bones lowered his feet from the desk. A problem had come up with the disc jockeys out there. Bones knew full well that if you didn't keep the jocks happy, didn't keep 'em in new Caddies and college funds for the twins, your records wouldn't get on the air; and if nobody heard *Man Alive* or *When the Doorbell Rings*, nobody'd buy it. Nobody called it payola anymore since the congressional investigation five years back; nobody called it anything. It was all a lot more carefully handled. It was, Just make sure the boys were taken care of. And it wasn't even asking to get a song played; the payments were just there to get you . . . considered. Bones knew, as every record man did, that you couldn't buy a hit—hits came from only one place: the damn grooves—but you still had to grease your way to getting a great song a fighting chance.

So what Bones had been hearing lately was crazy: That his competitors weren't just pushing their own records, but that someone was pressuring the jocks *not* to play FDL discs. What? The whole idea seemed ludicrous, as if FDL's songs were so great they'd take somebody else's down? A nice thought, but still. In the record game everyone fought it out together. Just as you couldn't grease Janie Q. Public to buy your tune if she didn't want to, you sure as hell couldn't keep her from buying the disc if she did. Well . . . couldn't keep her from buying it if she heard the record and loved it, and had enough money in her purse, and found it at the Woolworths. That's the other way FDL was getting hit. There were stories that discs supposed to be distributed were getting dumped off the sides of roads.

No clear-cut evidence yet, nothing definitive, nothing close by—these were rumors filtering up from far-away places like Arkansas, Arizona, Virginia. And nothing that ate into sales much, far as he could see. Just . . . rumors.

Or was he just being paranoid? Paying stations *not* to play his records? To what purpose? FDL always got along well enough with everyone, and Bones didn't think he had any out-and-out enemies, though this was the record biz, which meant, of course, he had competitors with few scruples. But what good would it do them to have FDL sell a few less records? How could that make their own releases get any closer to Number 1?

His eyes brightened; he took a long puff of his Cuban and let the smoke curlicue before him. For Bones, that was what it was all about. From when he was a kid fighting it out on the Eastside streets, through his ambitions as a football fullback—when his gifts proved good, but not good enough—to those soul-messing years on the assembly line, where no matter how hard you worked you couldn't stand out, couldn't be anything more than just a sore-backed, angry cog in the damn wheel. Yeah, even when he'd started FDL as a jazz label he really only had one goal: Get to Number 1. Wasn't going to happen then; *had* to happen now. Puff, puff, puff. Push one of those new records, Mary's *Sugar and Spice*, say, or Orlando's *Our Hideaway* or, most likely, the Daisies' *Man Alive* right up there to the tippy top. Go waltzing in on that ol' *American Bandstand* himself, introduce his acts—his Number 1s. That would shut all kinds of people up.

Yeah, he could taste it—taste that Number 1 record. Puff, puff, puff! And it tasted damn good. Get to Number 1, and he wouldn't have to take any crap anymore from *anyone*.

Chapter Three

Wednesday, April 22— Macon, Ga.
Thursday, April 23— Atlanta
Friday, April 24— Mobile, Ala.
Saturday, April 25— New Orleans

ESMÉ HADN'T FOUND any opportunity to help Orlando with
Maisy, the tour had been such a mad rush. The morning after
her talk with him she'd tossed and turned until Bee Williams
came banging on her door at 6 a.m.—what was with that
woman? But the tour had to roll, and that evening they gave a
show in the Macon Auditorium, all swank suits, swirling skirts,
and snappy rhythms, then right back on the bus to Atlanta,
then later that night on to Mobile, Alabama. Everyone including Esmé was exhausted, like the walking dead.

But, thank God, tonight they were going to be sleeping
in another close-the-door, lie-down-on-your-stomach, take-
a-hot-shower-in-the-morning paying establishment—this
time an actual hotel, on Rampart Street in New Orleans, on
the outskirts of the French Quarter. Esmé had heard about
that place all her life, and she was thrilled.

The bus was running over a long, long bridge, over some
kind of lake, the New Orleans skyline glittering silver in the
distance. Robert Warwick, again next to Esmé on the bus,
said, "This is one of my favorite cities."

"I bet," Esmé said, looking out the window. She turned
toward him. "You've been here much before?"

"Back in the late '50s, I sang in a group put together by
this genius guy down here, Dave Bartholomew?" Esmé
shook her head; didn't know the name. "Nothing like that
New Orleans sound," Robert went on. "They got this back-
line rhythm: *Oom-poom-poom-pah-doo*."

Esmé pursed her brow.

"Oh, you've heard it," Robert said to her. "Guys like Fats Domino, Ernie K. Doe?" Esmé smiled, remembered laughing at K. Doe's song *Mother-in-Law*. "You know," Robert went on, "I wanted to get a little of that rhythm into some of the FDL stuff, but Bones just didn't get it. Said it sounded too slow."

"Slow?"

"It's not slow at all, it's just the way the beat seems to stop time. You know, put you so far into the beat that it isn't a beat any longer, just a place you are where things move in their own way."

"I'd love to hear some of it."

"Maybe we can get away after the show."

"If I'm not too exhausted."

"Yeah, that's right, it's Bed Night."

"Bed Night indeed, but, yeah," Esmé said, "let's try to get out."

They nailed the show. New Orleans might have its own great music, but the girls in the audience with the wide-skirted big-polka-dot dresses and the boys with the 'do rags back over their heads stood up screaming at the Shags and didn't stop through Mary Hardy, the Cravattes, Orlando, and the Daisies. Maisy, who'd told everyone she had family down here, was even more out front than usual, batting her big eyes and shaking her shoulders in that way that said, Boy, ain't I the sexy one. Ain't I the one they're hangin' their eye-balls on. Ain't I the goddamn peach!

All the while in the background Priscilla Bondrais, Linda Strong, and Annie Sylvester sailed through their smooth-movin' grooving.

Robert wasn't the only one with get-away notions. Though everyone but Maisy—she had plans to go stay with her aunt—followed Bee onto the bus to get back to the hotel after the show, when it pulled up, nobody went in; they just broke into groups and hit the narrow, iron-balconied streets of the Quarter. Otis Handler and Mary Hardy tagged along with Esmé and Robert.

Even though it was 12:30, the narrow streets were full of people. Kids who couldn't've been much over eight tap-danced in front of upturned high hats in the middle of the street, old guys busked blues on street corners, passersby weaved from side to side clutching huge cups foaming over with pink alcoholic brews.

Otis was off buying everyone drinks when a white guy in a crew cut lurched toward Esmé and flipped his gumbo right at her feet. She recoiled, and the crew-cut guy and his frat-boy pal stumbled away without even an apology.

"Asshole," Otis called after him. He said it loud, and even though the frat boys were half a block away, they turned around.

"What you say?" the sick boy's friend called out.

"I said you about threw up on my friend here. Said you're an asshole."

This was stopping traffic now, a black man yelling at a white boy.

"Come on, Pip," the friend said. "We gotta get that nigger."

"Otis, come on," Esmé said, taking her bandmate's hand. "It's all right."

"Yeah, Otis, what're you doing?" Mary said.

But Otis, with Robert beside him, held his ground.

The two boys had turned around, but they were a long half a block away, and as they started back, their steps were slow and weaving; and then about a hundred feet away the first boy, Pip, flung his arms around a sculpted iron lamp and threw up again, this time all over his shoes. He was bagged, there was no way around it. Otis watched him with his hands on his hips, then he took Mary's arm and said, "Pathetic. Fuckin' pathetic."

"Otis, don't use that word." Mary gave his arm a tug.

Otis just looked back, a quiet fury on his face.

Esmé had heard the story about Otis. He was usually the gentlest, kindest of men, but things were getting difficult for him. He was married back in Detroit, with four kids, but there'd been something going on for a while with Mary

Hardy; and now that they were on the Soul Cavalcade together, they were inseparable. But news had just come from home that Otis's wife was hearing rumors. She was a sweet, churchgoing woman and was loath to believe distant tales, but it had come to Otis that she had nonetheless taken to her bed with a fever. Otis was such an upright guy that this news shook him to his soul. His heart was torn, and he felt he should go back to Detroit. But he loved Mary, and he knew he had to make it through the tour for the rest of the Cravattes. So he was torn. It was all his fault, of course, except that he really did love Mary and was sincerely thinking of a divorce, except he hated the idea of that. And what about his kids? The whole thing was a horrible mess, and ever since Esmé had heard about this from Robert a few days back, she'd seen the pressure getting to Otis.

They were able to get him into a club, the Dew Drop Inn, where a rubber-rhythmed horn band was smoking away. Drinks were served. Otis sat quietly, his arm around Mary's shoulders. Robert and Esmé sat across from them.

"So what're you going to do?" Robert asked. He and Otis were close, and this was not too forward.

Otis sighed. "I really don't know."

"You really could go back, dear," Mary said. "Just go up there and settle it."

"Not in the middle of the tour."

"I don't know," Robert said. "We could pull through as a trio for a few days. Right, Eddie?"

"It wouldn't be the same," Esmé said, "but we could manage."

"But I don't even know what I'd do."

"Talk to her, dear, tell her about us straight up. Tell her we want to get married."

Another long sigh. "Yeah, I could do that."

"But—" Robert said.

"I can't. Not right now. Myrtle'll be all right. She's got

her mother . . . hell, her mother's just 'bout moved in. It's some crisis world up there." Otis winced, then added quietly, "It'll be all right."

"For how long?"

"How much longer's this goddamn tour?"

"Little over two more weeks. We're almost halfway through."

"Seems like we've been on it for a year," Mary said.

"Amen," Esmé said.

"I've never had such a good time." Robert took a sip of his rum and Coke. "Truly."

"Oh, man," Otis went.

"Making music every night, living close like this. I think it's like camp. I read about camp when I was a boy, but never got near one. Bet it's like this, everybody piled on top of each other. No—"

"No secrets," Mary said. "Robert, does everybody know about me and Otis?"

"I don't think anybody cares," Robert said. "They got their own agendas going down."

"Yeah, like Maisy Columbine. What's with that girl?" As Mary Hardy said this, she looked over at Esmé.

"Don't ask me," Esmé said.

"I heard she's been makin' eyes at you."

"Maisy makes eyes at every guy," Robert said. "You know that."

"Not at Orlando." Mary slid closer to Otis, hung tighter around his neck. "What's with him?"

Esmé heard herself sigh. "He's got some ideas about Maisy, seems like. He knows they're misplaced—"

"*Misplaced* ain't the word for it."

"And she won't give him the time of day."

"That's the natural truth." Mary yawned just then, but stifled it. "Wonder why that is. Orlando's a nice-looking man—" Otis Handler glanced over at her. "Come on, Oat, you can't stop me from lookin'!" At this Otis if anything appeared more wretched.

"What I heard," Robert said, "was that Maisy had some serious kind of crush on Orlando when she was just a knock-kneed girl in the projects and he was already signed with FDL. She being Maisy made this crush clear, but Orlando didn't even notice her. Something like that. Then she got her Maisyness together and joined the Daisies, and they got signed, and—well, it's a different story now."

Esmé looked right at Mary, then asked, "How much of it's true about Maisy and Bones?"

Mary, unlike Robert, went at the question like red meat. "Well, you know," she said with a raised eyebrow, "don't hurt none to sleep with the boss."

Robert gave out a loud snort.

"This was awhile back, though," Esmé said. "Nothing going on now, right?"

"You put Maisy on the bus, Bones back in Detroit, and, yeah, nothing going on on the bus." Mary laughed. "But I do think whatever it was is over. Robert?"

"It's over."

"But that's got something to do with Orlando's . . . interest?" Esmé asked.

Mary laughed. "Who knows how men think."

"Oh, Mary, I think you got a pretty good idea." Robert smiled. "You're always surrounded by 'em." He glanced around the square table. "Like now."

Esmé's ears stayed up. She was trying to think it all through, but she still couldn't see why Orlando was hung up on Maisy, his confession about his schoolmarm aside. Couldn't he see she was bad news? Why wouldn't he just let her go off and, in Robert's great phrase, stew in her Maisyness? "I don't get that, why Orlando'd be comin' at her now."

"Because she's the big star." This was Mary.

"Or because she simply won't let him have her." This was Robert.

"I don't know." Esmé thought about the man who'd

appeared before her that late night at the motel. That wasn't just some kind of payback or general frustration; this was a man who was soul-rattled. "There must be something else."

"If there is, I don't know it," Robert said, brightening. "And as you know, I know most *everything* 'bout this ol' bus tour."

"I wish you didn't," Otis said.

"Doesn't everyone." Robert gave out a large smile. "Come on, anybody want another drink?"

✳ ✳ ✳ ✳ ✳

ESMÉ WAS a little lit up and Otis Handler looked wasted, though both Robert and Mary seemed sober enough as they walked the few blocks to their hotel. It was about 1 a.m., and the night clerk was behind the desk.

"Hey, sugars," he said as they came in. "Y'all with the Soul Cavalcade?"

"Sure are," Mary said. "This is Otis Handler, Robert Warwick, and Eddie Days."

"You're the Cravattes!" the clerk said, his voice skirling up into a falsetto. "Oooh, I love your music. I looo-hoove your music!"

The desk clerk was dressed, well, singularly. He was wearing a tuxedo shirt with a pearl neck pin but no tie, an undertaker's jacket with tails, and a pair of sand-colored trousers with leather sandals. What was most notable was his makeup, scatters of silver glitter across his high-cheeked ebony skin, and his turban. The turban was a hefty-looking purple silk with gold brocade, wound high up over an already breathtakingly tall forehead. Then there were his eyes: They were big as half-dollars, colored a green-sparkled hazel, and were flying high now in joy and amazement.

"And don't forget Miss Mary Hardy," Robert said with a smiling laugh.

"Oooh, Mary, Mary, I love you, too!" The clerk was wiggling like a newborn puppie. "Every time *Sugar and Spice* comes up on the transistor I got me here, I go, 'Ooooooh, ooooooooooh, weeeeeeee!' Sister, I shake to that song." And the desk clerk started singing, "*Sugar and spice, and everything nice / I just love the way you taste to meeeeee....*"

Everyone laughed, even Otis, who managed a hiccuped chuckle. Esmé was thinking, Well, this *is* New Orleans.

The party took their keys and squeezed into a teeny elevator that rattled up the five floors to their rooms. Esmé was bunking with Mitch Williams again, and was not surprised to not find him in their room. She kicked off her heavy shoes, stretched out her legs, rolled her shoulders. A long day, and she was tired all over. But she was feeling pretty good, though her head spun just enough that she had to steady herself on the neweled bed post. How many of those damn drinks did she have? Well, less than Otis, that's for sure. But more than Mary. And certainly more than Robert. Ooooof! Esmé wasn't used to drinking, and it was making her feel a little sick. And she suddenly had to pee something fierce.

The bathroom was down the hall, shared by the whole floor, and when she got to the Men's, she found it occupied. The Women's was next to it, and quickly glancing around, Esmé slipped into that. She started to unbuckle her suit pants when she saw there was no toilet paper. Damn! How was she going to wipe herself? And what if any of the girls needed to use it later?

She peeked her head out the door, nobody in sight, the Men's still locked tight. Down the hall she saw the elevator remained on her floor. This'll be easy, she thought, and scampered in her stockinged feet over to it, then took it down to the lobby.

"Well-ell-ell," the desk clerk said, his smile stretching like a rubber band. "This be an honor all over again, Mr. Eddie Days."

"The bathroom up there," Esmé said, "it's out of toilet paper. I was wondering—"

"Sugar, don't you worry. Here, I'll be right back." The clerk disappeared through a hanging-cloth-covered door, a sand-colored image of a lion patrolling the veldt on it. Esmé looked around the small lobby. Nothing special: a couple tape-mended Naugahyde chairs, a floor-standing chrome ashtray, a stack of *Look* magazines, but a big, fresh bouquet of flowers on the edge of the check-in desk. She leaned over and gave them a smell. Hydrangeas and pea pockets.

"You like flowers, sugar," the clerk said. He had a roll of white tissue clutched to his chest.

"Sure," Esmé said. She held out a hand.

"Now you can't be in that much of a hurry, darlin'."

Esmé did a double take.

"I'm Ezquevez, at your service." The turbaned, glitter-faced man bowed. "That's Ez-que-vezzzzz. Just the one word. That's all the name I need. And you're that dreamy Eddie Days, ain't you?"

"Um, yes." This was getting curious. Esmé brought her hand to her chest.

"You be that *hiiiiigh* voice in the Cravattes, true?" Ezquevez said. He was coming around the desk now, still holding the toilet paper close to his chest. The clerk was whippet thin, and his chest looked, under the fancy coat and white tuxedo shirt, to be almost concave.

"That's me."

"Oooooh, I just love it when you come in on *Doorbell*. Molly-golly me! You know, first time I heard that voice, I said to myself, Any man sing that high and that beautiful, that's a man I'd like to get to know better."

Esmé finally got it: This Ezquevez guy was coming on to her. She knew she made a pretty man, but. . . .

Ezquevez reached out and ran a manicured and painted— what was that color? Some kind of deep-night purple— fingernail across her cheek. "Now, sugar, I just know what kind of man you are. Ain't I right?"

"Um," Esmé said, backing up a step. "I don't think you do."

"Way you sing? Sugar, you can't fool ol' Ezquevez!" And he moved another step closer to her. She got his smell now: gardenias, rich and fulsome. After all those drinks she almost gagged.

Ezquevez reached back and set the roll of paper on the edge of the desk, then took Esmé by both shoulders.

"I—I really don't think you do," she got out.

"Oh, no, sugar, I can tell—I can *always* tell." Ezquevez gave her a sly smile. "Always know which way the Breeze blows, know what I mean?" He fluttered his sparkly eyebrows. "Even if *you* don't know it yet. Even if this is the first time you ever met a boy like Ezquevez." A wide wink of his glittered eyes.

"No," she said. God, her head was spinning. She'd drunk too much, and now this guy was . . . no, she just had to laugh. His interest was flattering, in its way; more so than the bobby-soxers who chased her after shows. This guy was an original, and in dead earnest. But. . . . "I mean, I do know what you mean, at least I think so, Mr., um, Mr. Esmévez—" Good God, did she really say that? "—but you, um, you have me all wrong. Truly."

"Sweetie—" moving even closer to Esmé "—how do you know anything till you give Ezquevez a try? I guarantee you, you give Ezquevez a try, you'll never look back!"

"No, um, no," Esmé mumbled. Half of her wanted just to lie down so her head would stop spinning, the other half wanted to laugh uproariously. "No, you see, you aren't that wrong—"

"That's what I'm saying, baby—"

"But, it's . . . just . . . that—" No, she couldn't tell him, could she? She'd sworn to herself that she couldn't tell a soul, that if the truth ever came out, even in the most innocuous way, it could twist and snake around and bite her down the way. But it was *soooooo* tempting.

"Listen, Mr. Eddie Days, all you gotta do is promise me you won't bolt your door. That's all you gotta do. It ain't like you'll be saying yes, you know what I mean? You just won't be saying no."

Esmé lifted her sleep-heavy arm, started to say, "I'm just going to—"

"I know what you're thinking, what about night prowlers. Well, banish that thought! Only Ezquevez knows your room, darlin'. You go back there, get into that ol' bed, just got to promise me you won't bolt the door. You can lock it—locks'll keep out them night prowlers—but I got me a key, of course I do." A blithe laugh that jangled the eyebrow glitter. "Now you just don't go bolting the door. All right, sugar?"

Esmé wasn't worried about this guy, he was so slight, his bantam, concave chest and his ridiculous turban, and she knew that if there was any trouble, she'd just call out to her fellow Cravattes and they'd pitch this guy through a window. She sighed and said, "Please, just give me the toilet paper."

Ezquevez picked it up, held it out, then flirtatiously pulled it back.

This was getting annoying. "Oh, come on, please."

"Not till you promise. No bolts on Eddie's door tonight. You can even go to sleep, that don't bother me—I like that. Sugar, I'll sneak into your very . . . dreams."

"No, Ezkeevezzzz—" What was his ridiculous name? "Please, just hand over the toilet paper." Her feet did a little dance.

"You're laughin'."

"No, I'm not." But Esmé was giggling.

"You *are* laughin'!"

"Oh, please, please," and as she said this, she reached out and grabbed at the toilet paper. Ezquevez pulled it back, then did a quick sashay around it, and the next thing Esmé knew, he'd planted a thick, wet kiss right on her lips.

He pulled back, a confused look on his face. "Sugar, what—"

She lunged again for the tissue, wrested it from his hands. The clerk gave it up without a fight. He put his hands on his hips and stared at Esmé.

"Sugar, there's something ... something you're not telling me."

"I'm telling you I need some toilet paper," Esmé said, laughing out loud now. She felt oddly flirtatious herself. "That's all I was *ever* tellin' you."

"But you're not—"

Did he get it? He sure looked like he was thinking something like the truth. Esmé couldn't help herself; holding the toilet paper roll securely, she leaned in and whispered to Ezquevez in her real, girlish voice, "I'll leave that bolt open, sugar. And I'll be in that bed, with nothin' on. And I just know I won't be able to fall asleep, just waitin' to hear your key go slippin' into my lock."

The clerk stared at her, his jaw fallen, his hands planted firmly on his hips. As she turned to go back to the elevator, Esmé saw him squinch up his nose and mouth, then go "*Ewwwwww.*"

Hah! She laughed all the way up to the fifth floor, finally—*finally*—peed, wiped herself, then headed back into her room. First thing she did after she closed the door was slam the sliding bolt closed. She even shook the door. No way anybody could get in.

After she lay down, she thought of Mitch, wondering if he might be coming back sometime before she woke up. Probably not—he usually gambled till the bus took off. But if he did, he'd just have to bang on the door. Her head spun, and she was near to passing out, but before she did, she let out a huge chortle. Esmévez indeed!

Chapter Four

Sunday, April 26— Shreveport, La.
Monday, April 27—Jackson, Miss. (Free day)

A WHOLE DAY OFF! How long had the Cavalcade been on the road? A year? Five? Seemed like it. (This was the 11th day, but the first with no show planned that night.) And they were in a motel again, this time in Jackson, Mississippi, where there was a show the next night, but . . . not a damn thing to do till then.

Esmé was tucked into her bed, the sweet, springy bed, alone in the room; as usual Mitch's bed was empty, as crisp as the maid had left it that morning. (She still wasn't sure when, if ever, he slept.) The motel was surrounded by pines, and their sap-rich scent filled the room. She drew it in—you never smelled nothin' like this in Detroit—then let out a long sigh, stretched out her arms, turned a glowing face up to the sunlight slipping through yellow curtains over the double-paned windows. Aaaahhhh! She could lie here all day.

Which meant she flinched something fierce when the loud rapping came on the room's door, followed by Bee Williams's bark: "Up and at 'em, gentlemen. Bus is about to leave!"

Esmé panicked. Bus? What bus? Had she slept through a whole day? Two days? Missed a concert? She scrambled up in bed. God, what if Bee came in, she'd see the famous Cravatte in her pajamas, her breasts poking through the thin material, her hair tumbled just like a girl's.

"Gentlemen!" Rap, rap, rap.

"Oh, Bee, it's just me, um, Eddie. Mitch isn't here."

"Figures." Then: "Come on, bus is going."

Esmé was still racking her brain. "Bus is going where, Bee?"

"Just like you Cravattes. Can't remember the noses on your faces." A pause. "Come on, it's almost noon."

"Noon?" That meant Esmé had slept at least 12 hours. "But it's our day off. Where we going?"

"Picnic, sugar. Now put your sweet ass in gear, get on out here. Don't wanna hold everyone up."

Esmé sprang out of the bed, thankful she had an all-night-gambling roommate. She whipped through her morning routine, taking off her pajama top and spinning the gauze around her breasts, then putting on a slickly pressed pair of black linen pants and a pink-and-black silk shirt with two pockets, not by the breast but down by the waist—no Cravatte, indeed, no member of the Soul Cavalcade, would be caught even on a day off dressed anything less than to the sparklin' nines.

The whole troupe was in the center of the motor court waiting for the bus. Bee had a Brownie in her hand and was trying to arrange a picture.

"Maisy," the chaperone called, "don't hog the front. Let the other girls in." Maisy Columbine, wearing yellow pedal pushers ironed sharp as razors, hair up in a higher beehive than anyone, was vamping and laughing in front of everyone else. The other Daisies were lined up off to the side, next to the Cravattes.

"Maisy, hey, back here." This was Orlando Calabrese calling out. He was in the back row, rising over the shorter Robert Warwick and Otis Handler in front of him.

"I ain't goin' to the back," Maisy said.

"I'm not saying go to the back." Bee had a sharp glower on her face. She was holding the Brownie by the strap, swinging it by her side. "Just let the other girls in in the front."

Esmé, standing in front of the semicircle of fellow performers, saw Orlando glance down, clearly hurt. She felt her heart go out to him.

At that moment Maisy called out, "Eddie, hey, you come

stand by me. You're just the right height, you'll complement me well. Come on!"

The three Daisies stood in their spots, trying not to show any emotion. But Bee was shaking with exasperation. Finally she said, "Suit yourself."

Esmé, thinking fast, called out, "Sorry, Maisy, I think I better be in the back with the boys." She moved quickly over next to Robert, Otis, and Mitch, and right in front of Orlando.

Maisy, pouting, settled down, and Bee fiddled with her camera.

"Hey." Esmé turned and whispered to Orlando. "You O.K.?"

"Sure," he said, though his lips remained tight.

She's not worth it, Esmé yearned to say, though she knew this wasn't the right time or place.

"O.K., O.K., let me just get the picture." Bee raised the boxy brown camera to her eye. "Maisy, you do what you want, just don't screw it up."

Bee leaned forward, squinting into the viewfinder; everybody stood a little taller, flashing their widest smiles, Maisy's the brightest (and her eyes popping the biggest); and after she clicked the shutter, Bee called out, "Just one more." The whole troupe preened again, the shutter clicked, and when Bee said, "O.K., that was good, but I think I'd like just one—" well, nobody listened to her; they all broke formation, laughing and chasing each other over the lawn like schoolkids just given recess.

As they were getting onto the bus, Orlando leaned over to Esmé and said, "Eddie, can you sit with me?" Esmé nodded yes immediately, though all the way to the park, beyond one simple request, Orlando didn't speak at all.

The Soul Cavalcade car, driven by Rags Doheny and carrying Bert and Bart, had gone on ahead to the municipal park in Jackson, and when the bus showed up, everyone found concrete picnic tables festooned with gay red-check-ered tablecloths and pots of fresh-picked flowers, along with bowls of potato chips, mayonnaisey-rich potato-and-egg salad and vinegary cole slaw, and platters of glistening brown pork barbecue next to gold-toasted buns. Buckets of icy beers held down the table ends.

"God, I'm starving," Esmé said to Orlando when they were standing before the delights.

"So let's dig in," the tall gentleman said, letting Esmé fall into the line before him.

On the bus, Orlando had asked for a private moment with Esmé. Now, their plates full, Orlando pointed out a big rock across an open meadow and suggested they eat there.

Settled on the hard-stone outcrop, and half the food devoured, he said, "I wanted to thank you for not going over to Maisy when she called to you."

"You don't have to do that."

"I don't understand her, I righteously don't." Orlando sighed.

Esmé gave him a sympathetic smile, then fought back the urge to take his hand. She was a man now and men didn't do that.

"I don't want to be made a fool of," Orlando said emphat-ically. "I really don't." Esmé knew enough not to say a word. "I'm just afraid I can't help it," he added.

"I don't—"

"I know, I don't understand me either." Esmé looked up at Orlando and saw his heavy eyebrows, his downcast eyes. "I just keep havin' eyes on her, even when I'm not seein' her."

Esmé heard herself draw in a breath. "I was thinking of that night awhile back—where were we?—that first night we had a motel. Talking with you."

"I was thinking of it, too."

"I said I thought I could help you." Esmé shifted uneasi-ly on the gray rock. It was suddenly impossible to get comfortable. "I'm afraid, Orlando, I might've just been talking through my hat." She smiled up at him, and then let out an involuntary low guffaw. "And you know, I wasn't even wearing one."

Orlando smiled. "Thanks anyway."

"But I'd like to help. I'd do what I could, but—"

His eyes brightened. "Something's gotta happen. I mean, look at me. All the girls love me. They adore me. I ain't had any problem with the ladies before. You've seen it, right, Eddie?"

"You're a dreamboat," Esmé said, just as dreamily as possible—and the second the words were out, she blanched. She quickly added, down and dirty, "Man."

Orlando didn't seem to notice anything. "Can I be frank?" he went on.

"Frank?" His tone had changed, and the word unsettled Esmé.

"You're not, like—I mean, I know, she called you over to stand with her, and you didn't go. No, you came and stood by me, and I—well, that meant a lot." He pulled in a couple quick breaths. "But, that wasn't just—I mean, like, you know—" He hemmed and hawed, and finally screwed up his courage, saying, "There's nothing I don't know about what's goin' on with you two." Quick darting glance straight into Esmé's eyes. "Is there?"

Esmé shook her head, then spoke fast, like a quick stream of water hoping to allay his burning. "No, nothing, Orlando. I swear." She felt his shoulders relax, then she went on. "I honestly don't know what she wants from me. She hasn't said a word. I know, she did that thing at the picture taking— made it seem like there's something—but damn if I know what it is." As she spit out the curse word, she gave her shoulders a swaggery shake.

Orlando brightened. "Well, Eddie, you know, you're kind of a dreamboat yourself." He winked, and Esmé blushed; and then Orlando was blushing a little, too. "I mean, if a man like me can say that." A nervous guffaw. "Oh, you know what I mean."

Esmé stretched, felt her spine go straight. "Orlando, I can swear to you again, I'm not interested in that woman at all."

The tall singer was holding his breath, and then the air whistled in one long stream. "Wish I could say that," he finally said.

It was so sad she couldn't help him; she really wanted to. But of course she didn't actually *want* Orlando to hook up with Maisy Columbine—seemed like deep down, he knew it made no sense to be with her either. That Smokey line came to her again: "*I don't like you, but I love you.*" Her eyes went wide. She had a sudden . . . yeah, that was it. What a great idea! She didn't actually have to *help* Orlando get Maisy, she only had to make him not want her.

She started thinking furiously. Could she talk him out of his infatuation with the singer? A quick shrug: She thought back to her obsession with the blues singer in Chicago; no, she knew too well the blinkered ways of the besotted. Well, then, what if she showed him how two-faced and dismissive Maisy was? But . . . he already knew that. And yet—yet maybe he didn't know it quite well enough. *Hmmmnn.* A swift nod to herself. Yeah, the more she thought about her idea, the more sense it made.

"Breeze, listen, I meant it when I said I'd help you. I'll do anything I can."

"You mean it?"

"I meant it before."

"But—"

"I think I got an idea." Esmé gave him a determined smile. "All I need's a good opportunity." She stood up, flushed with a sudden enthusiasm. "Come on, let's pack up our lunch and get back with the others."

✳ ✳ ✳ ✳ ✳

THE GOOD OPPORTUNITY didn't take long at all. When she and Orlando were back at the picnic table, Maisy Columbine came up to Esmé, a fat piece of devil's food cake on a flower-ornamented paper plate in one hand, a beer in the other. The beers, Bee Williams had made it clear, were for the band, maybe the male singers, not the young ladies—but there Maisy was, belting one back.

"Want one?" she said, holding out the Falstaff bottle.

Esmé didn't particularly like beer, but she right away smiled and accepted. "Please," she said in her deepest voice.

Maisy vamped down to the end of the table, pulled a water-slicked bottle from the icy bucket, and when she got back to Esmé, handed it to her, then ran a finger along Esmé's cheek. The finger was freezing cold.

"So, Eddie, I've been wanting a few words with you for a while now." Maisy batted her perfectly curled lashes at Esmé in an amazingly blatant way. Maisy's eyes were even larger up this close, huge white saucers, and, Esmé noticed now, she hardly ever blinked; it was weird, her brows looked propped up by invisible toothpicks, her eyes bright white orbs shining out. "Seemed you were always back in the bus with one of them Cravattes." Maisy flickered her eyelids at Esmé, and it was like the moon had winked. "I think, sugar, you've been duckin' me."

Esmé shook her head. "That's not—"

"Duckin' me." Maisy clearly liked saying this, the three syllables tripping from her smirkingly. *"Duck-in' me."*

Esmé had to laugh. She took a step toward Maisy. This was all part of her plan. "Well, I'm here now."

"Big boy!" Maisy's eyebrows fluttered. "Come on, Eddie, drink up." She pulled down half of her beer in one gulp, then leaned a shoulder toward Esmé. "So you want to ask me to take a little walk?"

Esmé made a bow. "Maisy Columbine, would you do me the honor of letting me escort you on this fine afternoon?"

Esmé had heard this someplace, in a movie, maybe *Gone with the Wind*? Could she get more cornball? And did Maisy buy it?

The lead singer hooked her arm by her side and let Esmé thread hers through it.

As they left the picnic Esmé saw Orlando, sipping his own beer, standing off to the side. She glanced at him, then winked, trying to let him know that this wasn't what it might look like. He looked away before she could be sure he understood.

The park they were in had signs that read COLOREDS clearly posted around where they were picnicking. Off in the distance were well-manicured baseball diamonds, concession stands, even what looked like a small amusement park with motorized rides. In their section were these tables, a mangy ball field, and the outcropping of rocks. Esmé led Maisy—who now seemed ready to be led—over toward the rocks, up on a small hillock surrounded by shaggy lindens. Up there in the trees, they found sudden privacy.

"Well, Mr. Eddie Days, you certainly work quick," Maisy said in her light, flirtatious voice. She spun on her flats and set herself right before Esmé. There went the eyebrows again. Maisy was close enough that Esmé was hit by a flood of strong perfume: She recognized Chanel No. 5. "But I want you to know, darling, no matter what you might've heard: I'm not easy."

Yeah, right. Esmé had the quick thought that she should really be taking notes here. Maisy was already showing moves she'd never even imagined. "I would never think that, Maisy. Never."

"Well, good. Now that we got that settled, what do you want to do?" Maisy was up on her toes and half out of her shoes, which flapped loose below her small, pretty feet. Her lips were ready to be kissed.

"Enjoy the view?" Esmé squeaked out.

Maisy held her straining-forward position, tilted like a

carved mermaid on the bow of a ship, then stepped back. "What view?"

"The beautiful skyline of . . . whatever this city is."

Maisy laughed, a loud chortle. "It all gets to be a blur, don't it?"

"I think we're in Mississippi," Esmé said. "You can tell that 'cause of those signs."

"Can you believe that?" Maisy said with a quick, blithe anger. "We're nothin' but 'coloreds' to them."

"It's another world down here." Esmé shook her head contemptuously.

"It just burns me so," Maisy said, her voice deeper, raspier. She had a sudden bright, wild look in her large eyes, and Esmé, to her surprise, found herself pulled into the other woman's commanding energy. "Hey, let's do something about it."

"What?"

"Don't worry, hey, come with me." Maisy was already walking down the far side of their hillock, along a path through the lindens and bushes.

Esmé didn't hesitate. She was no less angered by the segregation, and now that they were on their way to a direct challenge, she knew she would have come up with doing this too; though she had to hand it to Maisy to be fully cocked enough to run right into the heart of it.

When they got past the full curtain of shrubs and bushes, Esmé pulled up and said, "Look, Maisy, there." In the distance, about a football field away, was a fenced-in area, and as they got closer to it, they made out a sign that read PETTING ZOO. Maisy skipped ahead, and Esmé, as manlike as she could, ran after her.

At the gate to the small zoo there was a sign that said WHITE ENTRANCE, and when the two women got to it, they simply walked right in. The whole zoo was a couple hundred feet square, divided into slapdash pens separated by lanes covered with dry straw. Most of the animals were walking free through it. There were chickens, ducks, lambs, goats, a couple of blond-maned ponies, even an ostrich. Moving among them were a couple dozen families, all white, most with small children.

There was notice of the black couple, heads lifted, gazes sharp at them, but nobody said or did anything. The petting zoo had this overall sweet, innocent ambience; as she strolled through it, Esmé was feeling like a girl again—though of course she walked like a man. She and Maisy approached a lamb, and as she ran her hand through its matted wool, she felt more relaxed and comfortable—yes, just as if she were nine or ten again, off on a Sunday idyll with her mother.

"This is great," Esmé cried, her voice fluting up girlishly in her enthusiasm. Maisy looked over, a glance of curiosity. Esmé bit her lip. Got to be more careful. She almost repeated the words *Really great* in a deeper voice, but knew instinctively that that would sound phony. Instead she just petted the fluffy lamb.

Maisy's hands were deep in the lamb's wool, too, and something about it gentled her. Though her eyes were shining, they were actually less round and astonished than onstage; here they shone in a quieter, softer way. A striking, all-consuming innocence rose off her. She's a funny woman, Esmé was thinking. I know she's totally calculating and ready at any moment to dance with the devil, but still here we are, and she's got us flaunting the NO COLOREDS sign and at the same time she's just like a little kid; truly is, she's not faking it, her innocent eyes, heady, uplifting spirits. . . .

Then Maisy's hand found its way into Esme's. It was Esmé's right hand, and she fought a recoil and just left it where it was, deep in the lanolin-soft wool, the other woman's fingers fluttering down the tender crevices between her own. That was also her plan, getting as close to Maisy as she dared—as a man.

Maisy kept her eyes away from Esmé, and so there was nothing but the gentle hand-holding between them; yet that was charged enough to become the sole focus in her head for the longest of moments.

When the two women left the lamb, they walked hand in hand.

Maisy was curiously quiet as they strolled the straw-covered paths. Esmé wondered what Maisy was thinking; she wondered, also, what she herself was thinking. The ostrich, its tall thin head bobbing uncertainly above its long, mottled neck, waddled by; and by a goofy leap, she thought of Orlando. There was something gawky, too, about him, though you'd have to be around him for a long time before you saw it. Hmmmph. Just that nervous thing about Maisy, the way he needed her own help. . . .

Back to her plan: She leaned over and gave Maisy a light kiss below her ear. The singer shivered, squeezed Esmé's hand more tightly.

They were by the goats now. There were three of them, basically kids, their hair not yet wiry and rough. A couple of little girls with big bows in their blonde hair were already petting them.

"You know, sugar, this is awful sweet being here with you," Maisy said. "I've been thinking about it for the longest time."

"Me, too." This was it: time to make her move.

"And?" Maisy was all expectation. Her face was bright the way it had been when she was waiting for Esmé to kiss her; but it was more than that, her whole body yearning up and outward now. Esmé thought of golden-brown dough starting to rise in a bowl.

"And what?"

"Well, I told you I wasn't easy, darlin'," Maisy said, though her eyes spoke differently. "I really meant it."

"You're saying?" Esmé was puzzled a moment, then she

got it. She said in her deepest, most rumbling voice: "Maisy, you want to go somewhere we can be alone?"

"Now, now sugar. Didn't I just say—"

"But Maisy," Esmé said in her lowest voice, "you're makin' me all . . . jumpin down there." Was that O.K.? Did men talk that way?

They must, because there was quick, bright triumph in Maisy's eyes. She squeezed Esmé's hand tighter, then let out a long, guffawing whoop. Maisy slid up closer to Esmé so their bodies were touching; their womanly curves bumping alarmingly together. Esmé took a quick step apart but squeezed the other woman's hand.

Maisy turned Esmé's hand over in hers, then, flashing her eyes, said, "What're you sayin', mister? You know I'm not that kind of girl."

"Well, um—"

Maisy picked it right up. "You're thinkin' I'm going to go somewhere with you right now?" She took Esmé's hand, fluttered her fingers over it. "Go and lie down with you?"

Esmé's head started spinning.

"Just go someplace right here in the . . . daylight? Like over there, back under those trees?" She flicked her eyes outside the petting zoo to a deserted copse of trees. Her hand left Esmé's and ran along her hip. In spite of herself, Esmé felt a tingle.

O.K., this is it. Time to make her move for Orlando. She tried to get her breathing under control, then took a step back, away from the other woman's hand. "Maisy, I have to ask your help." Her tone was notably less flirtatious.

"My—"

"It's a promise that I made, to a friend." Esmé gave her her sexiest guy smile, which, God knows, probably wasn't even as sexy as the goats in front of them, though Maisy didn't seem put off. "About you."

Maisy's long, thin brows went up, then curled down. "I don't understand."

"It's Orlando." Esmé spoke quickly. "He's been, well, I was new to the Cavalcade, you know, and he went out of his way to make me feel comfortable." She paused to gauge the other singer's reaction, but Maisy gave up nothing. "I feel I owe him."

"And—" Sharp, scratchy tone.

"And—" No, there was no way to do this other than just say it. "Do you know he has eyes for you?"

Maisy was silent, her bulb-bright gaze dialed down. "I'm not aware of that." She spoke coolly.

Esmé believed that like. . . . But what she said was, "It's a secret, but—"

Maisy stiffened. "I don't understand why you're tellin' me this. Especially right now!"

Esmé took a step back, almost stepping on a baby goat, who scurried quickly away from her. When she spoke she was blushing—a true blush, it just rose out of her. "Well, it's just 'cause of this promise, and what I feel I owe Orlando."

Maisy folded her slender arms before her chest and stepped back. "And what does this have to do with me?"

"Well, this is awfully, well, it's terribly . . . awkward. But, you see, if Orlando didn't, well, if he weren't interested in you anymore, then I wouldn't feel—" Esmé winced, and that was genuine, too. "Well . . . there wouldn't be nothin' worryin' me." Did that make any sense at all? "You understand?"

Hand it to Maisy, vague as Esmé was being, the singer picked right up on it. "Not that I ever gave even one minute's thought to making that man fall in love with me, but now you want me to make him fall *out of love*?"

"Um, that's it, yeah."

Maisy's spirit suddenly fluttered; up flew her eyebrows. "Darlin', I gotta say, I'm good at a lot of things, but makin' men fall outta love with me, well, don't know if I've ever bothered to learn me that."

"Oh, Maisy, I'm sure you'd be the best." Esmé could barely keep back a snicker.

Maisy laughed. "Oh, I'm sure you're right." A sly smile. "Couldn't be too hard, big dumb ol' lug like that." Her brow curled. "Breeze, eh? Hmmmn. Might be sort of . . . fun."

Fun? Breaking Orlando's heart? Esmé sighed.

"So, how do you think I should do it?" Maisy said, brightening.

"Oh, I'm sure you'll think of something."

Maisy pursed her brow and let a stream of no-doubt devilish thoughts run behind it. Finally she said, "Oh, I'm sure, you sweet man, that you're right."

During these last words the two of them had strolled away from the goats and found a puddle of water with a few geese swimming in it. One of them honked as they came up.

Then there was another honking sound. A heavyset woman with a spun confection of blonde hair piled in a tall beehive, half askew like the leaning tower of Pisa, came up to them and said in a sharp bark, "You—and you—you don't belong here!" She had her hand out, swinging her pointing finger between Maisy and Esmé.

Esmé was startled, but Maisy whirled right on the woman, saying, "Who're you talking to?"

"You and your kind." The woman sniffed. "Don't you read no signs?"

Esmé got it now. She stepped forward. "No, we didn't read *any* signs."

"Well, that don't matter none, we don't 'low your kind in here with the animals. Least not when we's here."

"I don't understand," Maisy said, moving toward the woman. Up close, she had wide continents of red splotches floating in the curdlike white sea of her face. "What do you mean, our kind?"

"Nigras."

Esmé felt that word like a punch in her jaw; she flinched,

then felt bad about having reacted at all. Maisy wasn't so circumspect.

"You bitch," she said right in the woman's face. "You have any idea who we are? What we do? I'm Maisy Columbine. You know who that is, or are you just too fuckin' stupid? The Daisies. Maisy Columbine of the Daisies. *Man Alive*? I sing the goddamn songs you toot along to in your goddamn trailer with your goddamn snot-nosed kids."

At Maisy's loud voice a crowd began to form around them. Every last person was white, families with their kids.

The bouffanted woman stuck her hand out hesitantly, then with a clear flash of appalled anger on her face, she swung an open palm at Maisy. She was slow and ungainly though, and the singer pulled back.

Esmé stepped forward and spoke firmly. Her voice never sounded so low, so strong. "Listen, we have every right in the world to be here. And you have no cause to do anything about us except let us be."

"Harold!" the woman cried out. "Harold, where are you? The Nigras are giving me sass."

Up came a rail-thin, shock-haired man in a yellow seersucker shirt. He had a tall forehead and wire-rimmed glasses. He was chewing something in the side of his mouth, probably tobacco.

"Harold, do something!"

"Betty Ann, what's wrong? You're scarin' everybody."

"Can't you see what's wrong?"

"I see some people enjoyin' the zoo," Harold said. "What's wrong with that?"

"But they're Nigras!"

"Where you from?" another woman with a wide bowl of chestnut hair said, pushing forward.

"I told you," Maisy said, not giving any ground. "We're the Fleur-de-Lys Soul Cavalcade. From Detroit. Detroit, Michigan."

"You see," Harold said, "they's Northerners. They plumb don't know no better." He smiled at Esmé and Maisy. "You enjoyin' our zoo?"

Esmé laughed out loud, she couldn't help it, then said, "We were, yeah."

"Harold!"

"Then you just go right on ahead," Harold said. "Betty Ann, leave 'em be. They ain't Nigras, they're from up North."

"Oh, no, we are . . . Nigras," Esmé said. She was standing as tall as she could. "And, yes, we're from the North." She moved up so that now she was in the blonde woman's face. "But if we had the . . . the serious misfortune to live among you people, we'd still come here. Those times you could push us down, they're over—way over."

With that Esmé took Maisy's hand, and the two of them walked off slow and easy together. They dawdled by the ostrich, a big, nasty bird with a long, jutting beak, all the time shooting sweet secret glances between them.

Twenty minutes later, on their way back to the picnic, Esmé said, "So we're good on Orlando?"

Maisy skipped ahead a few steps, then turned and gave her a quick, undisclosing nod.

✳ ✳ ✳ ✳ ✳

GIVE THE FLEUR-DE-LYS PERFORMERS, already playing a show a day, their first night off in eleven days, and what do they do? Sleep? Write a letter home? Catch that recent blockbuster *It's a Mad, Mad, Mad, Mad World* at the Bijou? Simply take a quiet, moonlit walk through the streets of Jackson, Mississippi? Not on your life. Everyone wolfed down dinner at the rooming house Bee had booked them into, then they dug up a nightclub and went to shake it all down.

The place was the Tip-Top, a large club down a narrow street in downtown Jackson; it was a half-uptown, half–down home joint fronted by a neon sign of two martini glasses winking at each other. In an earlier life it had been a burlesque theater, the Variety, a name still in faint paint behind the neon glasses. Bunny Alexander, the bass player, had played the Tip-Top when he was running the chitlin' tour through the South, and he said that the musicians were hot, the liquor cheap, and the atmosphere great. What more could anyone want? Bunny phoned ahead, and when the whole Soul Cavalcade pulled in about 9:30, the red carpet was already out.

A tall, top-hatted gent named Sass Carpenter ran the club, and he came right out to the sidewalk with his diamond-encrusted walking stick, rubbing his hands delightedly and saying, "O.K., this is one night we's all gonna remember. I'm right now declaring this Fleur-de-Lys Records Appreciation Night. The drinks are on the house, the band is all yours, the crowd's been gatherin' all day and they're sittin' right in your palms. And . . . y'all can do anything you damn well please."

Up went the shout: *Hooray!* What could be more fun than to sing and play till dawn?

The Cavalcade band crowded up next to the house band on the stage, which though small magically expanded so all the guys had a place to sit or stand. The FDL band led off the first vamp, and the house guys were right with 'em, and though there were two drummers, two bass players, two piano men, and an exaltation of guitarists and horn players, everyone swung along as one.

The Cavalcade singers had taken seats saved for them in the front. The club was big enough that the patrons in the back were dissolved in smoke and darkness. After the band blasted through a couple of opening instrumentals, Rags Doheny took the stage. He cupped his hand over his eyes and looked around, then said, "You know, I can't believe we's all here tonight when we should be sleepin', but here we are, all your favorite performers: Mary Hardy, Orlando Calabrese, the Daisies, the Cravattes, and, to start us all off tonight, like they do every night, the fabulous Shags."

On rushed the five older men, kicking high and smiling.

"Now," Rags went on, "this ain't no performance night, this is our night off—hope our friend Sass made that clear." Rags hung an open palm behind his ear and waited till somebody called out, "Maisy. I love you, Maisy!"

"Well, that wasn't what I thought I'd be hearin', but it's O.K. by me. Long as you all know we're not putting on our regular show tonight. We're gonna make this one up as we go."

"Get on down!" someone called out. Then: "Love y'all." And: "Long as that long, slow Breeze sings, I be happy."

"Oh, he will, and the Daisies will, and Sweet Mary, too. And even though this stage looks pretty tight, well, I think we have enough room for the Cravattes to shake their eight ol' legs." Rags pulled out one of his trademark handkerchiefs and mopped his brow. "But like I said, we're gonna start off everything with our dancin', prancin' friends . . . the Shags." And because it was a private club, and their night off, Rags moved close to the microphone stand and repeated the word *shag*, each time bumping suggestively against it. "Shag! Shag! Shag, you doggies. *Shag!*"

The five Shags leapt and spun and whirled and kicked and attacked that stage like a line of eggbeaters. They sang like they were truly *Men on Fire*, and were dripping with sweat when their set was done. So was half the audience.

The Cravattes had a table to themselves, and Esmé was sitting back, enjoying the show but also keeping her eyes on the table next to her, at which Maisy and Orlando, along with the three other Daisies, Bee Williams, and the bus driver, Trip Jackson, were sitting. Maisy and Orlando were a couple seats apart, and so far Esmé hadn't seen Maisy do a thing toward Orlando, though she kept seeing the tall singer steal glances at Maisy. Esmé shook her head: No accounting for love and affection, is there? Then: Would *Maisy* make her move to make Orlando fall out of love with her tonight? Had she figured out how to do it yet? Or maybe she was just waiting till after the Daisies performed.

Which happened soon enough. First, Mary Hardy went up and sang a couple of ballads, then the Cravattes did a short version of their set, then Orlando crooned, and finally the Daisies kicked it for all they were worth. For all Rags had said, it was more or less the regular to-do, because that was what they knew. But because it wasn't work—actual, paying work—and they were in a club, where the free drinks were flowing, by the time Maisy and the girls finished up, everyone was feeling damn sparkly.

"O.K., O.K., that was pretty much what y'all gonna see tomorrow, you come out to College Park Auditorium—that is, that was our regular show," Rags said, taking the stage behind the pert singer. "But we ain't gonna stop now, are we?" He turned to the band. "You guys got more in you?"

The bass rumble-tumbled, drums rolled, horns *toot, toot, tooted*. "All right, nice, *niii-hiii-iiiice*. You boys be cookin' up somethin' mighty sweet. We gonna spread that music out over y'all in a little jam."

The band started playing instrumentals. Esmé noticed that after the Daisies' set Maisy hadn't come back down from the stage. Orlando had gone right to his seat, so her disappearance had nothing to do with him; it was just that the lead singer was nowhere to be seen.

This was curious. Esmé leaned over to Robert Warwick and said, "Hey, any idea where Maisy is?"

Robert glanced up with a look that said, Why do you care? Then he shook his head no.

The band boiled through its final piece, and right then a short, mustached young man, with wonderfully smooth light-cocoa skin and wide, pretty lips, walked up to the microphone. He wore a sleek tuxedo with a silver tie and a top hat, just like Sass Carpenter's, canted at a sharp angle over his forehead. He walked with an exaggerated strut but came up to the microphone like he owned it.

Who was this? All eyes front. Some local guy?

"Gentlemen," he said into the mike with a smile and a wink, "*Smoke Gets in Your Eyes*. Ready," and he proceeded to count out a downbeat, which the surprised-looking musicians quickly picked up.

The voice was high, sweet, with a thrilling vibrato, and . . . familiar. Really, who was this? He was good, really good, and Esmé thought he'd be a real discovery if he was just a local talent. She leaned over to Robert again and said, "You have any idea?"

Robert turned to the stage, then shook his head. "Interesting voice. Guy who plays here regular?"

"I don't—" Esmé kept staring. The thin eyebrows, the full lips, the wide eyes, the cut to the young man's cheeks . . . *ohmygod!* It was Maisy. Damn! Maisy Columbine dressed up as a man!

So that's where she'd gone. Backstage, and, yes, the club had once been a vaudeville house. Esmé's eyes lit up with a sudden great idea.

Was anyone else getting it? Maisy kept singing, trying to get her voice low and sultry, but it held up and sounded not unlike her. All eyes in the club were on the stage, and she/he was wowing them. Did anybody realize who it was?

"Robert," Esmé said, tapping her friend, "it's Maisy."

He quick-shook his head, cocked his eyebrows, peered closer. "God, you're right," he said with a breathy rush. "Wow."

"She must've gotten the costume from backstage."

"Yeah." He gave his head another shake. "Look at her, she does a great guy. You think anyone else has figured it out yet?"

Esmé gave a quick shake, then put her finger to her lips and said, "Don't say nothing. Let's see how long she can play it out."

Maisy finished up *Smoke*, then slid into *That's the Man I Love*. This was curious. She was a girl put up like a man singing a song she did smashingly as a girl. Did it work? Well, the crowd hung on every word. But . . .look, Maisy's up to something. She was clearly directing the song right at Orlando, and, Esmé's hand flew to her mouth—Maisy had taken the mike from its stand and was down off the stage, moving over to the tall singer.

"He's the man / The only man / He's the man I love."

Maisy in her mustache ran her hand over Orlando's head, down his neck, teasing his collar, the top button of his black silk shirt. Esmé read the appalled look on his face: There's a boy here, he's singing a girl's song at me, and *fondling* me? Yet she was surprised that Orlando didn't get up or move.

"The man . . . the man . . . the man I truly, truly love."

Maisy was all over Orlando, and as she/he crooned the final note, she leaned down and gave him a kiss. There was a frightful grimace on his face, but also, Esmé saw, a curious impassivity. She was a little surprised at the way he simply sat there and took it.

What is Maisy up to? Is this her way of getting to him? Very, very strange. Then Esmé, inflamed with her own idea, gave Robert a wink, left the table, and ducked through a door behind the stage. Behind her the band kept choogling. She was in a corridor leading back to a warren of small rooms. The second one she went into had upright cabinets with colorful costumes splashing out of them, and she went to the box hung with glorious women's dresses. She scanned them quickly for one her size, pulled out a sleek pink number with a frilly neck, held it up before her, decided it would probably work, and lickety-split slipped into it.

Her hair was still man-short, but there behind her were three plastic heads with wigs on them. She liked the one with long copper hair and pulled that on. A moment in front of a floor-length mirror—God, how long had it been since she'd seen herself as a girl?—and then she was out on the stage, heading toward the microphone.

Maisy was back up at the mike, playing with her fake mustache, having left Orlando in his seat, visibly embarrassed. She shook her shoulders, leaning into the mike, finishing up her song. And whose high, dulcet voice was joining hers? This pretty girl with the long reddish-black hair? Moving in and harmonizing with her? Taking another step closer and . . . kissing Maisy on the lips?

Hah! Esmé laughed to herself. Now it was Maisy's turn to be startled. She jumped back, her mouth twisting sour, but then she must have thought, O.K., I don't know who this girl is, but she thinks I'm a guy. So, hey, why not? Because the next thing Maisy did was move in close to Esmé, put her arm around her, and join her in a final chorus. Their voices, Esmé's soaring high—what a liberating feeling to sing as herself!—and Maisy's, trilling higher than she looked, blended sweetly, and when the song feathered down into its end, Maisy leaned over and gave this pretty girl another kiss . . . though it was only a discrete peck on the cheek.

The audience loved them. Esmé curtsied, then bowed; Maisy stood tall and looked on approvingly.

And Orlando? Where were his eyes? He was still looking at Maisy, the man who'd come down and plopped into his lap. That was strange.. Esmé batted her eyelids at him. Vamped with her shoulder. Was staring right down there straight into his eyes, trying to . . . oh, yes, there, she caught a spark.

"Hey, sugar," Orlando said, standing, "mind if I come up and sing a duet with you?"

Who stepped forward first and said, "Sure"? Maisy, of course, her hands on her womanly hips, her legs short in the tuxedo pants, her fake mustache starting to slide just a little. . . .

Esmé slipped behind her and whispered, "Maisy, your mustache is falling down"; and as Maisy's hands flew to her lip, and her mouth dropped open in astonishment that this mystery girl knew who she really was, Esmé stepped in front of her and said into the mike to Orlando, "I think our voices would go very nicely together. You're that dreamboat Orlando Calabrese, aren't you? Please, please, come on up."

But who was he going to sing with, the girl whom he knew as a man but who now looked like a beautiful girl or the beautiful girl he professed he had eyes for who was now dressed in the spitting image of a man?

Was there a moment's hesitation? Not really. No, all eyes were on the three of them, and so, when the band fell into the old Shirley and Lee duet *Feels So Good*, it was Esmé in her dress who Orlando went up to.

Easy as that they started singing, and, Oh, yeah, it felt . . . so . . . good.

Though Esmé sure loved being with the Cravattes, this singing with Orlando was a whole other thing. For one, she was so close to her true voice, as swooping and dulcet as she could make it, and the freedom to blast off into soprano range was exhilarating. But then there was Orlando's honeyed tones next to hers. She'd thrilled at his voice when she and her Darlingettes had heard it on the radio, and she loved it each night backstage after the Cravattes' performances; but this was the first time she'd had his mellow, plangent tenor so near to her, breath close, a voice of power and gentle restraint, hitting the notes soundly, then working them, kneading them, coddling them—getting as much out of each phrase as there was to be gotten.

And yet he was leaving room for her. That was the true pleasure, that for all Orlando's restrained but vivid power, he never crowded her. His voice was a gentle presence under her. The image of an Arabian magic carpet came to her, soft, pliant, woven carefully with lambent images, and gliding beneath her as easefully as a dream through the very air.

Yes, it felt . . . so . . . good, and as she and Orlando traded verses or trilled their voices together during the choruses, she knew she'd never felt so full and complete before.

The audience was clapping loudly. The handsome man, the cute girl, the remarkable harmonies—the applause rolled back through the club, then rolled forward again.

Orlando leaned over, flashed his eyes, then whispered in Esmé's ear. "You were beautiful," he said. "Beautiful and amazing." Then he kissed her.

Her hand went to her chest. She felt lightheaded, actually swooned. Orlando saw her falter and reached around to support her. And everyone in the audience kept on hooting and shouting and laughing.

Rags Doheny took over the mike. "I think I'm gonna call Bones tonight and tell him to get his lard down here and sign this girl. Baby, what's your name? I might be just the lowly emcee, but I think you and Orlando should be cutting tracks together."

"Um, I'm . . . I'm Doris," Esmé said.

"I'm Orlando Calabrese." He turned and gave her a small bow.

"I know," she said, curtsying back. It was all so sweet. Orlando beamed.

"Well, Doris, you done good," Rags said into the mike. "And I mean it, I am going to tell our boss, Bones Chapman, all about you. Sugar, make sure we talk before the night's over."

Esmé blushed with pleasure, then nodded. Orlando was nodding, too, a bright encouragement she'd never felt from him before. When she was . . . Eddie Days. She sighed. This wasn't going to work out, was it? She wasn't Doris or even Esmé but Eddie Days, and a Cravatte to boot. Still, maybe there was some way, just for tonight, that she could. . . .

But there, as if on cue, was Maisy, still in her man garb,

moving back up to the mike, pushing Rags aside. She turned to the band, gave them a beat, and as they vamped behind her, she simply stood there, staring into the room. Esmé and Orlando were off to her right. She wore her top hat and tails proudly and fired a furious, half-smirking glare out at the audience.

"You know, there's nothing as sweet as a man and a woman singing together, is there?" she said. Esmé stole a glance up at Orlando, who was staring down at her. "Not at all like two *men* singing." She shook her head. "Nobody wants to see that. You got nothin' but men, you need yourself a whole group, sort of like our Cravattes, right?" Maisy hooked a glance at Esmé, who took a protective step closer to Orlando.

"No, you don't want two men singing some *love* duet, there'd be something . . . funny about that." Maisy turned and faced Esmé and Orlando. "That's why Breeze here, he had no choice but to go for the pretty girl. Yeah, give Breeze a choice in front of people, he's always gonna go for the girl. Right, Orlando?"

Orlando looked unsettled.

"But you all out there," Maisy went on, touching her mustache, "you remember what your mommas told you? How you can't always judge no book by its cover?"

Esmé could feel the heat of the whole audience on the three of them at center stage. Uh-oh.

"Yes, she did, I'm sure your mommas told you that. It's good advice. Watch!" And with that she leaned over and pulled off Esmé's copper-bright wig.

Esmé grimaced, looked to Orlando for help. But the tall singer was simply staring at her now, his eyes wide and startled.

"And you see," Maisy went on, "you wipe off some make-up, and our little songbird Doris here, she turns right before your eyes into . . . Mr. Eddie Days. Hah!"

You could hear it, the sharp intake of astonishment, roll

back through the cavernous room; and then after a long pause when Esmé realized the moment could turn any direction possible, the audience erupted into laughter and cheers. "Go, Eddie, go!" someone up front called out. "You're one bewitching laaa-dy," somebody else shouted from the back. "Wanna come sit with *me*?"

Esmé only had eyes for one: Orlando. His eyes were huge, his forehead damp. He seemed to get it now: He'd been smooched by a mystery man (Maisy), then had just been singing a passionate love duet with . . . Eddie from the Cravattes? Up went his eyebrows. Of course even without the wig, Esmé still made a pretty good-looking woman; her hair was revealed as its short black nap, but her cheekbones and lips still held their makeup, and her natural hip curves, slipped into the pink dress, were unmistakable, at least to her.

But everyone knew her as Eddie, and that's who they saw now.

From the audience Otis Handler called up, "Eddie, what're you up to? Why in drag?"

Esmé shot a glance at Maisy, whose smirk was consuming her whole face. "Because it's dress-up night," and with that Esmé reached over and ripped off Maisy's mustache.

Maisy's hand flew to her lip; her jaw dropped. Then Esmé snatched away Maisy's top hat, and her black hair tumbled down.

"Maisy?" Mary Hardy called up from where she sat next to Otis. "Is that you, Maisy?"

Now Esmé held the widest smile. Maisy looked flustered, but only for a second—she *was* Maisy Columbine, after all— before she said, "There's a whole wardrobe back there. I thought we all needed us a little fun."

Oh, look at poor Orlando, he looked as if his head had been spun around half a dozen times. This guy who had kissed him was his own would-be sweetheart . . . Maisy Columbine.

Then another surprise: From behind the stage came six women, caked heavy with makeup, all teetering on high heels, wearing sheaths that bulged and rippled in curious places, all of them wrapped in feather boas and sporting high-flying Carmen Miranda hats.

The women moved into place behind Maisy and Orlando (Maisy, pushing in to sing with the astonished Orlando, had elbowed Esmé to the side of the stage) and started kicking up their legs like Rockettes.

This time the joke was clear to everyone, and when the line of chorines with the telltale late-night shadows stubbling through the pancake started backing Maisy and Orlando in a deep-bass doo-wop, the audience hooted. Even Esmé, her ears burning, had to laugh. She easily made out who they were: her friend Robert Warwick leading the five Shags.

As Maisy and Orlando swung into the song *How High the Moon*, Esmé tried to get back to Orlando; but all the while Maisy hogged him, her breathy Betty Boop voice spritzing its high candy all around the steady fountain of Orlando's mellow tenor. Esmé had her number now: As Maisy the girl, she was making damn sure Orlando stayed with her—line by line, verse by verse, his eyes warm, his arm tight around Maisy, the music swaying their bodies together.

The night spun on. After Robert and the Shags turned up in drag, anything was possible, and in short order Esmé was witnessing events that spun her world upside down. There was Mary Hardy sitting in Otis Handler's lap, sprawled all over him, her tight skirt hiking up her primly stockinged legs. Look, Bunny Alexander on bass was playing with a toilet seat hung over his head, and the two sax players, Henry Jackson and Norris Rowland, had stripped down to their shorts, baggy ones that flapped loose over well-turned legs, yet they kept blowing up endless magical conjurations on their light-catching instruments. Someone had gone to Esmé's table and pasted a playing card on Mitch Williams's forehead, and he, all those free drinks to the wind, didn't even know it was there; Esmé, amused, just let it go.

Then, wonder of wonders, Bee Williams and Trip Jackson made it out to the dance floor, shaking it with all the gusto their middle-aged bones could muster. They stayed out there forever, it seemed, and when the band went into a ballad, Bee tucked her head into Trip's shoulder and they waltzed the floor to applause and astonished laughter.

A little later, Priscilla Bondrais of the Daisies took the stage. She was a stunning woman with long, almost straight red-tinted hair and full lips. She started singing a bluesy song, *She Stole My Sweet Man*, and her voice was so richly timbred, yet meaty and soulful, Esmé couldn't help thinking that she was in church, but not any old one—the devil's rectory itself. Priscilla hit melismatic notes that tumbled magnificently over each other like benighted angels floating in the air. She was scorching the stage, and riveting the audience, and Esmé had the quick thought that at any moment a jealous Maisy would storm the mike and pull it from her backup's hands.

But, wait, Maisy was nowhere to be seen. Esmé looked left, looked right—she was gone from the stage, gone from the Tip-Top.

Then it hit her. She'd been so caught up in the crazy fun she hadn't noticed that Orlando was no longer there either.

Chapter Five

Tuesday, April 28—Jackson, Miss.
Wednesday, April 29—Memphis

BEE WILLIAMS BROADCAST the news on the bus: Bones
Chapman was flying down from Detroit. The boss would be
there for the show that evening in Memphis.

There was a quick buzz up and down the aisle. Finally
Robert Warwick piped up: "Bee, so why's he coming?"

"Because he loves you."

Up went a dozen heads, tilted doglike to the side.
Hmmnnnn.

"No, really," Maisy Columbine said.

"I don't know nothin' about why Bones does a thing,"
Bee said, "but he said all along he'd be makin' a trip or
two to see you." She clucked her tongue. "You ask me, it's
about time . . . way you all was carryin' on the other
night."

"We was just having fun." A few different voices said this,
half plaintively. Nobody'd slept all that night, though they
caught some shut-eye in the Jackson motel before the show
there. Now they were on the bus to Memphis. Hangovers
were still in effect.

"Well, you'd better get your act together, the big man's
gonna be there tonight in the audience, and he's gonna want
to see you all perform."

"Anything wrong with our show?" Robert called up to
the front.

"Yeah!"

"Listen," Bee's voice clucked. "Let me just give you all a
word to the wise. I talked to Bones last night, and though he
didn't say nothing specific, I could tell something's buggin'
him." Bee held up her hand. "Now I don't know what it is,

but there be something in his head. And I bet we're all gonna find out what it is."

"What do you think it could be?" Esmé said to her seat-mate, Robert Warwick. They were sitting in the middle of the bus, their usual place. Around them were the Cravattes, Mary Hardy, and behind them the band. But there was one major change: To Esmé's huge consternation, Orlando was up front with Maisy, where he'd been yesterday, too.

Robert shook his head. "We're near selling out all the shows, performing great. I don't know what he could be worried about."

"Records?"

Robert shrugged. "You think Bones Chapman lets me see any of his sales figures?"

"Bee makes it sound sort of serious, though." There was a definite note of strain and worry in Esmé's tone, and Robert picked up on it immediately.

"You O.K.?"

She nodded quick. "Sure." But she wasn't; it was Maisy and Orlando, together since they'd gone off together after the impromptu performances two nights back. What had Esmé done? It was her plan that Maisy go with him only to get him *not* to love her; and here the two were, thick as pirates. After the Tip-Top everyone had taken the bus back to the motel except for Maisy and Orlando. Where had they gone? They both made the show the next night, and right on time. Tongues were wagging, of course, but nobody actually knew anything; and Esmé as Eddie was careful not to look too obviously concerned.

But against her better judgment she was.

"Well, we'll find out when Bones gets here," Robert said. "Other than that, we just get up there every night and kill 'em like usual."

Esmé nodded again, but faintly, her thoughts again her own. She kept seeing Orlando's face when Maisy had tugged

Esmé's wig off. He'd gone immediately blank, and pulled back from Esmé in a way that felt to her like a bandage being yanked away. She'd been so close to him, their singing so inspired, so dreamy. The night had been so like a dream . . . then a nightmare. She winced just thinking about it. After Maisy had pulled off her wig, she'd fought to hold Orlando's eyes, but when he looked at her, it was as if she were something shocking, a freak, and she had to turn away.

And why? All because he thought she was a guy.

By the time she'd turned back, Orlando and Maisy were singing together. There hadn't been a chance to talk to him after that, and what could she have said? No way could she give away who she really was. So she'd had to face Orlando's scorn as well as Maisy's playful derision—or was she just imagining this? The question had struck her this morning: Had Maisy been playing her, just as at the petting zoo she thought she was playing Maisy?

But to what end? Why would Maisy have flirted so strongly with Eddie Days if she really wanted Orlando? She knew Orlando was moon eyes about her; she could have had him in a wink.

And now she evidently did. What burned Esmé most was that from everything she could see it was her own doing that had made Maisy discover Orlando in a whole new way—in just the dreamboat way Esmé saw him.

Damn! Well, there was no hope in brooding about this, no hope at all. There their heads were, eight rows up, not exactly touching, but not far apart. Esmé remembered Orlando's smell from their duet, his smoky, wet-leaves man scent as he leaned in close. Even all these seats back she could almost taste it.

＊ ＊ ＊ ＊ ＊

THERE WAS A CRACKED, beer-stained upright piano behind the stage of the Memphis City Auditorium, and after the sound check, when everyone else went off to dinner—a sort of anxious dinner, with Bones expected at any time—Robert Warwick stayed behind to work on a song. He'd been writing for the last year, at first fumbling efforts not as slick as the tunes spun out by the staff boys Bones had put together in the back room, but now Robert believed he was getting the hang of it. The lyrics were flowing, mostly boy-girl stuff, just like every other hit, but now they were taking interesting twists.

The song was called *My Eyes Go Wide*, and he sang the first verse he had now:

> *You're sunny as a parfait*
> *Perfect as a summer's day*
> *You make my eyes go wide*
> *With surprise and delight*
> *Every time you . . . walk on by*

He liked the first two lines, the way *parfait* became *perfect* in the next line, and wanted to keep up that kind of wordplay. No reason you couldn't have a little fun with a song. He started to sing, *"You're sweet as an apple pie / And I love you, no lie."* Ugh. That was off. *"You're sweet as banana cream/ And I . . . I see you in my dreams."* Jesus, even worse. He winced, then took a deep breath. Maybe he was hurrying things. He knew with writing, simple as most lyrics were, you had to be patient, wait for the right line to come—you couldn't force anything.

But he was racing now. Why? Because Bones was coming. And Bones Chapman, even though he'd hired Robert for the Cravattes, hadn't yet let them record any of his songs. Even the not-bad ones. Even the ones that the rest of the group said cried *Hit!*

Robert wanted the perfect song to move the boss with—the *parfait* song. Wanted to have him come in and Robert could go, "Hey, Bones, got a new one the group likes. Can we sing it for you?" Wanted Bones to shrug a half-aggrieved O.K., then sit back quietly as the boys did the song, his eyes growing lighter as the Cravattes churned their way into it.

Wanted Bones to wrinkle his heavy brow the way he did, then stroke his chin and say, "Robert, I don't know why we ain't done your material all along. That's a great song. That song's a Number 1. I want the boys and you in the studio *today*."

Yeah, right—fuckin' in my dreams. Robert didn't know why but Bones Chapman had never seemed to take Robert for anything more than just the short guy in the Cravattes— well, with Eddie in the group, no longer the only short one—but the guy who was just part of the dancing line behind Mitch's or Otis's lead singing.

Did Bones just not see him for who he was? Was the boss blind in some way? Was it 'cause Robert was so young? It couldn't be personal. Robert had never done anything to cross him, ever, though with Bones you never quite knew; he was a prickly, moody son of a bitch. A real . . . sourpuss.

Try that: *"You're sweet as a cherry tart."* Nice. Good play there, sweet as something sour, but not sour at all. That's a grabber. And the second line? Well, don't get too tricky, give the girls who'll hear it on the radio something *smooooth* they can hang on, something like: *"Your smile goes straight to my heart."*

Well, yeah! He sang the verse to himself, fingers rippling over the piano keys.

> *You're sweet as a cherry tart*
> *Your smile goes straight to my heart*
> *You make my eyes go wide*
> *With surprise and delight*
> *Every time you . . . walk on by*

Nice. Two verses. O.K., time for a bridge. He played some different chords on the piano. The song was in C, and Robert ran up to F, then G, dropped down to an A minor, then back to C—pretty conventional but strong for a bridge here. He started singing:

> *Early in the morning, only one thing that I hear*
> *Just like that: Sweet words are in my ear*
> *There're sweet words right in my ear*

Could that be it? Just like that the bridge was done? He gave the lyrics a long, angled look, sung them soft under his breath—damn, they held up. They were . . . *sweet words right in his ear*.

All right, only one more verse. Concentrate. Gotta get this song right. Gotta have it nailed and in the pocket before Bones gets here, the sourpuss son of a bitch. Gotta come up with something to make him see me as I really am.

✴ ✴ ✴ ✴ ✴

THE CRAVATTES WERE UP there singing. Nobody had moved in the order, and they still came on third, after the Shags and Mary Hardy and before Orlando and the Daisies. Swoop, dip, turn, walk, dip, swoop, swoop. All four of them were lined up doing the Cravattes' signature moves, hitting each step, swinging through *Doorbell*, rows of young girls swaying in unison in their seats, long-legged couples up and dancing in the aisles. This Memphis crowd seemed with it, almost exactly half white and half black, and the whole Cavalcade was giving them a great show, spot-on professional and joyous—and then the whole tenor of the air changed. Esmé felt it strongly as she rolled through the moves with the other guys, the way they were being watched was different, more intense, darker somehow, and their expectations of the audience, as if mercury in a thermometer, suddenly spiked.

Bones had arrived—that had to be it. Esmé knew this, and then clearly the rest of the Cravattes did too, dipping their hips deeper, hitting their marks tighter, reaching deep and shaping their honeyed harmonies with even greater richness.

As they left the stage to grand applause there he was: short, stolid, his heavy shoulders and thick neck, almost-shaved head and deep eyes. Mitch walked right by him, Otis greeted him with a quick handshake, and Robert hung back a little, surprisingly nervous but with a tough, defiant look in his eyes. Esmé, still the new guy, wondered if he even remembered who she was.

"You guys were solid," Bones said softly. He had that way sometimes, when he'd speak so quietly you had to really lean in to hear what he said. "Solid."

Robert looked like he was going to say something, then thought better of it, and he just walked on. Esmé was wondering if this was a compliment. She gave Bones a smile, then started after Robert.

"Eddie, hey," Bones called.

"Mr. Chapman." Esmé had gotten good enough at her new name that when somebody called it out, she always turned toward them.

"Bones, please."

"O.K." Esmé felt herself blush nervously. "Bones."

"I hear you're fitting in fine. You like the boys?"

"I love 'em," Esmé said without hesitation.

"And you're all . . . happy?" A tilt of his heavy-browed face.

"We're doing great shows, Mr. . . . Bones." Esmé smiled up at him. "How's the record doing?"

"Oh, fine, fine." Chapman was looking away from her now, already distracted. "Well, Eddie, keep up the good work." And he was off.

Orlando was on the stage now, in his buttoned cardigan sweater, holding the mike carefully, singing into it with his eyes closed, his Indian cheeks sharp, his voice as soulful and seductive as ever. Esmé felt her usual confused rush of emotion. Then she saw Bones looking stageward, too, his brow knit as he watched Orlando. Had he heard yet about Orlando and Maisy? Could that be the reason he was here? And if he had, would he do anything about it?

"So I saw you talking to him," Robert Warwick said, coming up to Esmé. "What'd he say?"

"Nothing much." Esmé shook her head. "Just wanted to know if I was happy—we all were happy."

Robert gave her a close look. "What'd you say?"

"I said, 'Sure.'" There was something in Robert's eyes. "We are, aren't we?"

"Happy? Absolutely. We're all happy."

"Robert?"

"It's nothing." Robert looked down.

"Robert?" He kept his gaze down, his thick black glasses sliding down his nose. She knew she wasn't going to get anything out of him. "So, why is Bones here—you have any idea?"

Up came his eyes. He'd talk about that. "I'm hearing rumors—"

"Is it Maisy and Orlando?"

Robert gave her a curious look, then shook his head. "I don't think so."

"Really?"

"Eddie?"

Now Esmé shook her head. "Oh, it's nothing."

"No, it's something bigger. A direct threat to FDL—"

"A threat?"

"Somebody's messin' with our distribution—I heard that." Robert shook his head.

Esmé raised her eyebrows. "This is more than you knew when we started out?"

Robert nodded, then said, "But I don't have anything else." He shrugged. "And I don't think Bones is going to be telling me more either."

"Want me to try to talk to him?" Esmé spoke with muted alarm.

"Wouldn't do any good." Robert shook his head. "But, you and me—let's keep our eyes on it."

Esmé stuck out her hand impulsively, and Robert shook it. He patted her on the back. "We'll keep talking." Then he walked away.

Which left Esmé standing there, watching Orlando finish up his set. He gave the audience a deep bow, then skipped from the stage and beelined toward Maisy, who was preparing to follow him with the Daisies. That was a kiss, wasn't it? On Maisy's cheek? Or did it land smack dab on her mouth?

✳ ✳ ✳ ✳ ✳

BOY, YOU LET THE CHILDREN out to play, no telling what kind of mischief they'll get into. Bones should've known. Although he trusted no one more than Bee Williams to keep things in order, he guessed there were too many of the little ones for even her to control.

He was sitting on a plush burgundy-velvet settee, looking through the window of his way-up-top suite in the Peabody Hotel. He had a good view down Union Street to the gray-green Mississippi, and he was watching it closely. At first glance the river wasn't moving at all, but when you looked long enough, you could see ripples and little spinning eddies on it. The longer he looked, the more he was getting a rhythm off the river; it was slow, thick, a little gooey like your feet stepping through mud—quite a different beat from what they cooked up in the Motor City—and he was trying to turn its easeful undulations into something in 4/4 time he could take home with him when he heard a knock on the door.

"Come in," he called. The door swung back tentatively. "I'm here, Bee, it's all right."

"Yes, sir." Bee edged into the room. She must know he was steamed. Good. Good to see the redoubtable Bee Williams nervous.

Bones looked at his watch. "I've been here in Memphis only six hours, but I've heard an earful of troubles." He looked at the older woman closely. She held a blank poker face. "We have to talk."

"Can I sit down?" she said. Bones had gotten up from the settee to welcome Bee, and now he beckoned her to a chair. He sat across from her. "Well, sir," she went on, "I don't see it that way. I think everything's going great."

Bones tilted forward. "Bee, listen, I put you on this

because I knew I could trust you—I needed someone who wouldn't give me shit." He leaned even closer toward her. "So what's really goin' on?"

"I mean it, Bones." She was getting some of her color back. Strict as Bee was, Bones had found you utter a swear word around her, she perked right up. "I think the tour's going great so far. We're making all our shows, the kids are playin' their hearts out, and everybody's getting along well enough—" Bones began to speak, but Bee held him off: " 'Well enough,' I said."

"Granted, we ain't had any disasters." Bones shrugged, gave her that. "But I'm hearing we got some potential problems brewing."

"Potential?" Now Bee leaned forward. Their heads were just a few feet apart.

Bones nodded. "Problems brewing."

Bee ruffled her feathers. "And you don't think I know about 'em," she said in her sharpest tone. "I'm letting 'em slip me by? Is that it?"

"I just want to—"

"O.K.," Bee said. She stood up then, pulling up a wave of air with her; Bones felt it flutter under his chin. She started pacing back and forth right in front of Bones, each step more determined. "The boys in the back are gamblin' up a storm, and even smokin' some reefer, but you know well as me that the real crisis would come if I tried to stop 'em. Right?"

Bones took a second, then nodded. "But what I hear about Mitch—"

"He's losing big-time. But Mitch has always lost big-time. Boys know that, and that's why nobody ever puts the squeeze on him to pay up. Mitch's gonna go to his grave owing every soul he's ever known, and that's just God's truth. But that ain't a problem."

Bones sighed. How come this woman always had this

effect on him? Wasn't he the boss? Still, he couldn't keep back a smile.

"And what about—"

"You're gonna ask me about Mary and Otis? I know you are. You want to tell me to keep 'em apart?"

"Um, Bee, I'm worried about—"

"Otis's marriage." Bee was pacing vigorously now. "You don't think I am? But that's why I'm not making too much of it. This is the road, Bones, and you know what happens on the road. What I'm tryin' to do is keep word of it from getting back home." She stopped, put her hands on her hips, and glared at her boss. "You ain't been tellin' anybody anything, have you?"

He quick shook his head. Damn this woman!

"Well, let's hope nobody else does. Only two problems I see with them. One, we try to break 'em up, and then we got Oat maybe not hitting his steps so good with the Cravattes, and we got Mary up there bawling her eyes out and not being able to sing at all. Or, two, we got Naomi comin' down from Detroit trying to save her marriage, so she'd think, and walkin' into a hornets' nest. Then trouble would really start." She stuck out her head like an irate chicken, then said, "Next?"

Bones puffed out his cheeks, held his eyes open wide. He didn't say anything; realized he didn't have to.

"You're also thinking about Maisy. What the hell's she doin' with that Orlando Calabrese? Well I can tell you flat out that I don't know, but it ain't what it seems. This is Maisy Columbine, right? Maisy don't care nothin' 'bout no one's hide but her very own—you know that. Maisy's playin' him, maybe playin' somebody else, too."

Bones had heard that Maisy and Orlando had been sitting together, but he hadn't made too much of it. All this was news to him. "Playin' him how? And for what?"

"The situation's pretty new," Bee said. Her tone had

changed; she had the boss coming to her now, and she knew it. "Just the last two days. I haven't got it all untangled yet, but I'm working on it."

"What do you think?"

"I think Maisy's got a game on." Bee raised an eyebrow. "You know anything?"

Bones shook his head. "Not that I'm aware of." No, anything with Maisy and Orlando was a mystery to him. Though he felt certain he'd be hearing from Maisy again about changing the group's name. Get something in her jaws, she shook it and tore at it like a wild pup.

"Well, don't worry, boss, I got 'em all pretty well locked up now, though, you know, there might've been some sneakin' round before Jackson. I got me two eyes, I ain't got a hundred."

Oh, yes, you do, Bones almost said. Instead he simply smiled. Well, that pretty much took care of it, and—he looked at his watch—in only five minutes. There was, of course, the other issue, the large shadow weighing on him, but Bee couldn't be any help with that. "Well, that's good," he said. He stood up. "I guess I shouldn't've worried."

Bee lifted her thick-curled head, gave Bones a sympathetic smile. "I know, sir, you got other troubles."

"Other—" Bones lifted his chin carefully. "What do you—"

"I've been hearin' things around. About NRC, what they're doing to our disc jockeys. Gettin' 'em to not play our—"

"You said . . . NRC?" Bone's voice lifted. Was it possible that Bee was putting a name to his faceless worries?

"You say that like—" Bee hesitated, then said through a light smile, "You know, boss, you oughta get out of Detroit more often."

Bones didn't smile back. He sat right back down. "Bee, no jokes. You sure it's NRC doing this to us?" He stared straight at her. "Come on, you gotta tell me everything."

Chapter Six

Thursday, April 30— Nashville

NRC. BONES WAS MORE than a little surprised. NRC was the acronym for the huge National Recording Company, though nobody called them anything but NRC—the white-face, "white shoe" (with gold tassels), and boundlessly deep-pocketed company from New York. Along with RCA and Capitol they'd ruled the '50s charts, but now RCA had Elvis, Capitol had grabbed the Beatles from VeeJay (after playing *Ed Sullivan* a few months back, the so-called moptops looked to be huge), and NRC had . . . Theresa Beaver. Guy Loman. Paris Muffin. Little Evie Stone. And the always thrilling, if somewhat geriatric, foursome: The Four Flops.

Bones let out a tight laugh. Well, that might as well be their name, those boys were so clueless; even if they were black, they were still piping up like the Platters. He knew NRC was getting desperate for a hit, but they were still play-ing catchup with R&B and rock 'n' roll. Bones had heard they'd approached Barry Gordy at Motown, but Motown was just too big these days, with their handful of Number 1 songs—including Mary Wells's *My Guy* right there atop the *Billboard* chart as Bones sat here in Memphis—and Gordy sent them packing. FDL, though, had no Number 1 yet—just all their bubbling, churning potential—and so NRC had come around to talk to him.

That was two months back in Detroit. In came this young white guy named Rick Lapidus, with his slicked-back hair, slinky mustache, cloud of lavender aftershave, and a pinkie ring that'd put your eye out. Lapidus was total fast-talk New Yorker, and he spritzed out NRC's offer. Hey, baby, dig this: New York–quality studios, better distribution, smoother payments to disc jockeys. Bottom line (Lapidus seemed to love the phrase):

more hit songs, more Cadillacs. (Bones saw the words behind his eyes: You know how you people love a new Cadillac.)

Bones had been patient with Lapidus, explaining that what made FDL work was that it was local, family. He knew everyone, and they all felt comfortable. Their offices weren't some fancy tower but an erstwhile family house. They got their own sound out of the studio in the basement, and they had their own relationships with the deejays around the country. So they were a little weak on the West Coast and in Texas, they still sold plenty well even down there. No, Bones didn't see what letting NRC in would get him. (And it wasn't just letting NRC in, it was making a deal with them that, he was sure, would lead to their calling all the shots.) There's a lot of talent out there, he said to Lapidus as he showed him the door. He was sure NRC could find their own artists.

And that was that. He didn't hear anything more from Lapidus or anyone at NRC. Put 'em out of his mind, even when the deejay troubles started—they were a big, important, white company. Hell, their main offices were in Rockefeller Center! How could they be up to such underhanded tricks?

Bee swore they were: She'd heard it direct from deejays who had shown up backstage in Atlanta and New Orleans. Any actual evidence? Bee shrugged, said, "How would I have that?"

But Bones needed more. He started pacing around his suite in the Peabody. It was 1:30 in the morning, a Wednesday night. Late for some people, but for others he knew . . . no different from high noon.

He quickly dialed one of his oldest friends in the business, the disc jockey the Magnificent Murgatroyd. Murgatroyd was the late-night man in St. Louis, and Bones got put through right away.

After he'd heard Bones out, the deejay in his wondrously deep, rumbly voice said, "Yes, Mr. Bones, that's the way it be."

"You're sure it's NRC? They've come to you?"

"They've come to me."

"Shit!" Then quickly: "And?"

"I kicked those white boys out on their alabaster keesters." Murgatroyd let out a hearty laugh that cracked like an earthquake.

"But not everyone has."

"Oh, no. Those white boys got them that *white* money. You know the kind? Smells like perfumed toilet paper—before it gets itself alllll dirty."

Bones's head was spinning. "This is huge." A short sigh. "I'm going to need some evidence."

A pause from the Magnificent Murgatroyd.

"Murg? Do you have anything?"

"I don't, no."

"But somebody else?"

"Well, Mr. Bones, you know that cash, it don't leave much trace of itself. Even after it gets dirty—'specially then."

"All right." Bones was trying to keep his head clear through his growing rage. NRC had money, experience, lawyers—whatever they needed. And what did he and FDL have? Just talent and drive. "O.K., this is all good to know."

"And Bones—"

There was something in Murgatroyd's voice. "There's more?" Bones said.

"Maybe."

"Shit!" Bones took a deep, angry breath. "Murg, listen, put the phone down for five seconds, all right?" Bones took the phone from his ear and whapped it against the oak end-table over and over, sharp raps through the room. Then he put it back to his mouth. "O.K., what?"

"What in hell was that?"

"Nothing. Murg, what else you got?"

"Well, Mr. Bones, I don't know if I give this much credence, you know, it seems awfully. . . ." Bones could just see Murgatroyd's big-shouldered shrug. "But still, I've heard a word or two that, well—"

"Murg, please!" Bones, tempted to crack the phone against the end table again, instead just clattered his nervous nails against the receiver.

"Well, that they're goin' at, um, making a run at—" Bones could again feel the Magnificent Murgatroyd shrug his massive shoulders "—um, one of your own."

"One of my—"

"Your performers."

Bones gulped. One of his own people? One of the *family*?

"They're making a run? This is going on now?"

"Maybe not. I just—"

"No, you heard something." Bone was gripping the phone furiously. He had to know more, and asked point-blank: "Who is it?"

Murgatroyd spoke carefully into the phone. "I don't know who, Bones, and I don't know how far it's gotten. This just be something I heard."

"Jeeeeez." Bones let it out now, a long, unsettled sigh. The news had kicked the air out of him. Who could it be? He spun through the whole FDL roster: the groups back home, the Corvelles and Penny and the Thoughts—no, probably not them, they weren't big enough. Had to be someone on the bus tour. Mary Hardy, no, too innocent. The Shags—not enough upside with them. What about the Cravattes—could it be one of them? That Robert Warwick, who was always bugging Bones for producer credit on a cut, his ambition bright as tattoos on his skin? Hmmmn, possible. Orlando? Not likely. How about the Daisies? Bones lifted a sharp eyebrow. His first, strongest thought was Priscilla Bondrais. Bones knew she was unhappy with Maisy's carryings-on, and that Priscilla was sure she was the better singer—hell, she probably was—and could carry the whole group itself. Would she be open to NRC's blandishments? The second banana wanting to swing the whole bunch herself? Could be. Then of course there was Maisy, making no bones about wanting her name out front. Could it be her? But why would she take up with Orlando if she was going to take a powder on the whole troupe?

"You figure out who it is?" Murgatroyd said softly.

"I can't, Murg. Could be a few people, logically, but might not be no logic."

"And it might be nobody. I know you run a happy family up there. Might just be a scurrrrr-ri-lous rumor—accent on the *cur*."

Bones sighed. "Well, thanks, my man, for the heads-up."

"My pleasure." Murgatroyd's sincerity came through the line. "And sorry you got troubles, bro."

"I do, don't I?" Bones said softly, more to himself than to his friend. Then: "Well, when the hell haven't I?"

✳ ✳ ✳ ✳ ✳

THE SONG WAS DONE! Took Robert the bus trip from Memphis to Nashville to work up the last verse, but he had it now. He always got this hot, beaming glow on his forehead when he finished a new song; stood up and swooned around the backstage room with a delightful dizziness. That was it. Nailed it. *Bang bang bang!*

The show wasn't for another hour, and Robert was desultorily strumming the chords to *My Eyes Go Wide* on a guitar he'd borrowed from the show band's guitarist, John Smith. The Cavalcade was playing at Nashville's Fairground Coliseum, a big venue with a spacious if spare concrete dressing area behind the stage—a luxury even if it did smell faintly of pigs.

"What's that?" Esmé said. She'd drifted over to Robert from a table filled with the worst sandwiches any of them had ever eaten; what was it, Spam and peanut butter? Fried bananas and mayonnaise? The rest of the Cavalcade were off in other parts of the room. "Sounds nice."

"New song."

"Really? Bravo, Robert." Esmé clapped her hands as Robert smiled. "So, what's it called?"

"My Eyes Go Wide."

"How's it go?"

Was he ready for someone else to hear it? A moment's hesitation; it was his new baby. But this was his good pal Eddie Days. "Sure," he said, then began to sing softly so nobody else could hear, catching the syncopation easily on the f-hole guitar.

> *You're sunny as a parfait*
> *Perfect as a summer's day*
> *You make my eyes go wide*
> *With surprise and delight*
> *Every time you . . . walk on by*
>
> *You're sweet as a cherry tart*
> *Your smile goes straight to my heart*
> *You make my eyes go wide*
> *With surprise and delight*
> *Every time you . . . walk on by*
>
> > *Early in the morning, only one thing that I hear*
> > *Just like that: Sweet words are in my ears*
> > *There're sweet words right in my ears*
>
> *You're smooth as a soda pop*
> *And you're good to the very last drop*
> *You make my eyes go wide*
> *With surprise and delight*
> *Every time you . . . walk on by*
> *Every time you . . . walk on by*
> *Every time you . . . walk on by*

"Clever," Esmé said. "Bouncy. Yeah, I like it. Got a place for me in it?"

"Want to try a harmony?" Esmé nodded. "Let's see. How about on the refrain line."

drops bounced off the windows, and the bus's wheels were spinning through pools of mud. "And Bee seems really anx—"

"No, that's crazy," Robert said. He gave his head a quick shake.

But Esmé was hit by sharp quivers of anxiety, and they weren't all about Bones's flight. "And Orlando—didn't he tell you he and Maisie'd be back in plenty of time for the show?"

Robert nodded, then looked at his watch again. "They should be here."

"They're not."

Bee walked past at that moment, calling out into the capacious room, "Five minutes! You hear me, ladies and gentlemen, we have five minutes."

Robert snapped to attention. "Eddie, you ready?"

Esmé drew in a deep breath. Like that all her worries receded in her mind's eye. It was simply all about the show now; that's all that mattered. "I am," she told her fellow Cravatte. "Let's go."

* * * * *

BONES WAS ANGRY at himself. He probably should've taken the bus along with the troupe, and then he certainly should not have caught the wink from the chambermaid with the tight blouse and the dusky voice who wanted to audition for FDL Records right then and there, enough past check-out time so he actually had to pay up for another day. Damn! After it was clear that Ruth or whatever her name was couldn't sing worth beans, he still had to leave money with her as "consolation"—though of course it was Bones who had been consoled, right out of his shorts in the tile bathroom, Ruth on her knees scrubbing more than the floor.

So he was sure he'd missed the goddamn plane, which was the last one of the day. Except that there was a huge storm in Memphis, and the plane had been held. The ride was the bumpiest he could remember, his stomach doing loop-de-loops, but after a jarring landing the prop plane taxied sweetly to the gate. And there: Bert—or was it his brother, Bart?—was waiting for him with the company car.

The Cavalcade was playing the Fairground Coliseum—"Place smells of pig!" Bert said in the car; and it was Bert, Bones had simply asked—and as Bones walked in, he heard Mary Hardy's dulcet voice over a fairly crappy P.A. system. She was singing, "*Sugar and spice, and everything nice*," which meant she was finishing up her set with her new song, up to Number 23 now. And climbing . . . if those fuckers at NRC didn't shut down his markets on him.

Not too bad. He'd just missed the Shags; the Cravattes to come next, then Orlando, and finally the Daisies. The closer he got to the stage, the better Mary was sounding. He was picking up less sound from the P.A. and more of the live band. Those boys can cook. Like that, Bones felt the tingle in his fingers, the quick-step in his feet—and he was right there.

"Ohmygod!" He heard someone cry out, then knew it was Bee, her usually guttural voice lifted to a high-pitched sandpapery shout. "Bones, Bones, is that you?"

"Hey." All he had to do was stand there and let her rush up to him.

"God, we was worried." Bee's palms met at her chest in involuntary prayer. "You O.K.? Plane ride all right?"

He smiled his most innocent smile. "I just got hung up a little in Memphis, a little unexpected business."

It was clear that Bee's relief over his appearance overrode whatever carping she might've had, which was good, except now it left him feeling even guiltier. He was pinching his legs together as if that were somehow mollification for his delinquency.

"Well, I'm real glad you're here. We got us a problem."

"The sound?" Bones said. "It's not very good, is it?"

Bee looked at him with her head tilted slightly as if she wasn't quite hearing him. Then: "No, this is a real problem."

"What?"

"Maisy and Breeze."

"You told me all about them yesterday."

Bee dug in her heel. "I didn't tell you nothin'!"

"What do you—"

"They're gone."

"They're—"

"Bones, they're simply not here. Gone, gone, gone." She told him quickly the last day's developments, and how Maisy had insisted the two of them have their own dinner and then hadn't come back. "No word, nothin'."

Bones was astounded. He also knew right away just what this meant. So it was her. Had she really taken Orlando along? Was that possible?

"We have the Cravattes all ready to go," Bee was saying, "but after that, I don't know what we're going to do for the show."

Bones gave his head a shake, snapped to. "We get the Cravattes to sing a few more songs, move the evening along. Then Orlando—" He shook his head "—all right, he ain't here. But for the Daisies. . . . Priscilla's O.K., right?"

"Of course."

"We'll put her on lead. She knows Maisy's parts, doesn't she?"

"I'm sure she does," Bee said. "But people expect four Daisies. And I'm not sure Priscilla can put over all their songs—the ones where Daisy gets breathy, you know, that's not Priscilla."

"She'll do the best she can." Bones spoke quick and tough. "We'll *all* do the best we can." He took a step back. The remarkable news was settling in.

"I have an idea," Bee said, taking the step forward to match Bones's step back. "We had this . . . this night the other night, um, well, our night off, and we all sort of—"

"Bee, what *are* you getting at?"

✳ ✳ ✳ ✳ ✳

ESMÉ'S HEAD SPUN. What were they asking? She was standing there with Bones Chapman and Bee Williams, and even though the Cravattes were expected onstage in less than a minute, Bones was speaking fast, and Bee was echoing him with her own urgency; and she couldn't tell if they'd figured out her disguise or not. Didn't sound like it, but. . . . She decided the best thing to do was just stand there and choose her words carefully.

"You know all their songs, don't you?" Bee said.

"All our songs?"

"No, Eddie, the Daisies' songs." This was Bones.

Esmé turned to him. "Um, I've heard 'em enough. Yeah, I guess."

"And the girls like you, well as I know," Bee said, then pursed her brow. "Nothing secret goin' on there?"

"No, of course not."

"And you want to help us out in any way you can?" Bones was standing awfully close to her. His wide body and forceful presence smothered the air around her.

"Yes, of course." Esmé gave a quick smile. "I'm still not exactly clear what you're asking, though."

"Haven't you heard a word we're saying?" Bee said emphatically.

Bones smiled, eased away from Bee. "I heard that you were awfully persuasive that night in Jackson—and it was fun for you, right?"

Esmé gave a tentative nod.

"Then we want you to dress up like a girl again. We want you to be the fourth Daisy."

"Dress up like a . . . girl?" Could they actually be asking her to . . . dress up as herself? A wild smile burst onto her face. "I'll do it—I'd love to do it." She grasped Bones's hand. "Oh, you have no idea."

Then she was off, falling into line with Mitch, Otis, and Robert as the audience erupted at the Cravattes' trademark smooth, swinging strut onto the stage.

Chapter Seven

Friday, May 1—Pensacola, Fla.

IT DIDN'T REALLY SINK IN until the next morning: FDL had lost two of its star acts, poached by NRC; they were in the middle of a tour to sell records that were getting sniped at by NRC; and Bones was sure Maisy and Orlando would be releasing songs any day now . . . for NRC. Songs that with the huge company's money behind them could be chasing his off the charts.

Would that really be possible? He had contracts with his singers, of course, and the paper tied them up tighter than a tourniquet. But he'd never had to defend a contract before, especially against deep pockets like NRC's, and he was concerned. He knew stories of big labels going in and just vacuuming independents dry, and there was never anything they could do about it. He made a note to call his attorney in Detroit, Abe Gritowski, and go over things.

But as he sat here in his hotel suite in Nashville, what really got to him was the way he believed FDL was family, and two of its favorite sons and daughters had run off on him just like that. Did Maisy hate him that much? Orlando? Or was it just the money—and the promises of those shiny white faces with their pretty, whiter-than-white teeth?

He gave his head a sharp shake. Well, the show had to go on. And actually the night before hadn't been too bad. There'd been a few audience cries of "Where's Breeze?" but Rags kept things moving, and right after the Cravattes, the new Daisies swept out to huge applause. Could the kids tell it wasn't Maisy but instead Priscilla up front and that Cravatte, Eddie, dressed up like a girl? Not so Bones could tell. The crowd clapped at the hits, shouted out the names of B sides, and gave the girls a standing O at the end. How had

Priscilla done? Her voice was rich, her moves smooth, and she rose fully to the occasion.

So, good. He'd just take things as they came. The bus had left the night before for . . . where was tonight's show? Oh, that's right: Pensacola, on Florida's Panhandle. Bones had been through Pensacola, and he remembered . . . bugs. Bugs big as finches, loud as Aeros. Bites raising pink Himalayas up and down his arms and legs.

Could he get out of it? Sure, he could just turn tail and head back to Detroit, say business was pressing there, which of course it always was; but in truth, the real business was right here on the Cavalcade. He trusted Bee to make the show go on, but he knew it would take all he had to hold morale together as it sunk in that Maisy and Orlando had betrayed them.

There was a knock at his hotel door. He was in The Carillion downtown, and he'd stashed the twins in a motel across town, telling Bert to get him up. At least he thought it was Bert—damn, he still couldn't tell the boys apart—so when he called out, he smeared the vowel so it could rouse either of them. "Baeaerrrt? That you?"

"Hey, boss, you ready to go? We got us a long way ahead of us."

Bones looked closely. O.K., he was wrong, it was Bart. Then he saw the other twin out in the hallway. Oh, no, they both would be driving him, and he'd never be able to tell which one it was. Right then he decided to say not a word the whole trip.

"Just getting up, Baeaerrrt. You and your brother, go get some breakfast in the hotel restaurant, put it on my room tab."

"Yes, sir."

It was going to be a long, long drive—400 miles or so, which would take all day. Bones winced. He'd looked into flying, but there was no scheduled flight, and no way he could get a private plane from Nashville to Pensacola, especially as a black man, short of actually buying one.

"Baeaerrrt, before you go, you know we're gonna have to eat some miles today—eat some big miles. Let's say we roll in thirty?"

✳ ✳ ✳ ✳ ✳

THEY WERE ALREADY on a train to New York. You had to say this about NRC, they didn't waste no time. No sooner had Maisy made the agreement with Rick Lapidus, the mustached A&R man, than he'd made arrangements to meet her in the lobby of the Caravelle Hotel downtown and send her on her away. Maisy couldn't wait to go. The deal was simple: She'd be MAISY COLUMBINE in BIG letters on the album cover, over a full-face picture of herself. (She imagined one of those sexy black-and-white close-up jobs, like that of a siren movie star, Audrey Hepburn or Sophia Loren.) Nobody else behind her, no sharing anybody's name. Lapidus assured her that NRC had a studio and a famous producer all set to go in New York City. All she had to do was show up.

Boy, did Lapidus's jaw drop when she brought in her little surprise.

"Breeze," he said. "Wow. Hey, man, I'm a huge fan of yours. It's a pleasure."

Maisy stood back then, cast a sharp glance the slick record man's way. O.K., it was one thing that she was bringing along a little . . . bonus; it was something else if this Eye-talian was going to plumb go ga-ga over Orlando.

"Can I ask what—"

"He's coming too," Maisy said. Oh, the light inside her was bonfire bright. "It's my little surprise, Rick. Orlando here wants to make it on the big label, too." She stepped in front of the tall singer. "Thanks to me."

She loved the boy's smile then, sort of snaky but respectful. "Maisy," he said, "whoever named you named you right. You truly amaze me."

"I think we could put Breeze on a couple cuts, you know, announce he's left FDL, too, and he's singin' now with me."

"Well, we'll look into that, sure. Have to see about the contracts. You guys know offhand if Breeze signed when he was underage, like you did, Maisy?"

They both looked at Orlando. He'd been quiet through all the A&R fireworks.

"Um, I was nineteen."

"Well," Lapidus said, his arms flapping enthusiastically. "There're always ways." He stuck out his hand. "So, Orlando Calabrese—hey, big man, how you doin'?"

Orlando gave a quiet nod but declined to shake Lapidus's hand. The A&R man didn't seem to notice; he just swept them both up and got them to the train station perfectly on time.

On the train now Maisy looked over at Orlando. She was sitting tight next to him, her head on his shoulder. He seemed to like this fawning girlfriend thing, and Maisy never minded doing it; she knew from long experience how effective it could be. "Hey, sweetie, you getting hungry?"

Orlando had a habit of sitting absolutely straight; it seemed odd to Maisy. Somewhere along the line somebody must've beaten posture into him like it was hell's fire. He was ramrod tight now. "I don't think the club car's open yet," he said.

"Hey, I'm Maisy Columbine. Don't you think they'll open it for me?"

They were still below the Mason-Dixon Line, and Orlando looked as if he had his doubts.

"Oh, they will." She moved her head off his shoulder. "You don't believe me?"

"I'm actually not that hun—"

"But you don't believe me? You don't think I can do it? That I'm not big enough of a star?"

"Maisy, I never said—"

She jumped up. "No, this is a challenge, Mr. Man." She winked saucily at Orlando. "You just sit here and let's see."

Wasn't much of a challenge, really, since Maisy had already had an . . . encounter with the dining car's maître-d'. He was another tall black man of military carriage, but with sharp, hawk eyes that immediately caught Maisy's when they'd boarded the train. Hours back she'd left Orlando to go to the Ladies' and just happened to bump into the maître-d'. She made sure he recognized her, then asked him about menus and special dishes and meal times; and when he'd said he had to look something up in his office in the back of the dining car, she'd followed him in there and made it clear that if he made a move, she wouldn't resist. He'd made the move.

The maître-d's name was Clarence, and she found him in his office. He looked up, gave her a faint smile, then went back to the papers.

"We need something to eat," she said.

"We?"

"Oh, I'm travelin' with another gentleman." She laughed. "You didn't know?" No, it was clear Clarence didn't; he looked a little shocked. "But it's mostly . . . business." She threw a dismissive glance over her shoulder. "He's another singer. Orlando Calabrese?"

"The Breeze is here?" The maître-d's eyes went wide. "Here on this train?"

"Um, yes." Maisy found herself wincing. "He's, um, traveling with me to New York."

"You know, Breeze's song *Lover Man*, that's my theme—" Clarence blushed. "I mean, that man means a lot to me." He stood up, though he had to stoop slightly in the small, rattling room. "Can you introduce us?"

"Can you open up the dining room?" Maisy heard the petulance in her voice, but was glad Clarence didn't seem to mind. No, he was beside himself with the idea that stupid old

Orlando Calabrese was here. Jeez. Was it going to be this way all the way to New York? And what about up there?

"Oh, sure, sure. Come on, y'all, I'll do it right now."

When Maisy went back to tell Orlando that it'd been a piece of cake, they could go eat now, he said, "Really, I'm not hungry," then she'd said, "Well, turns out the maître-d's a big fan of yours."

"He is?"

"Huge fan. Maybe even a bigger fan of you than of me." Hah, fat chance, but she enjoyed watching Orlando's face light up. "Come on!" She reached down and gave the big lug a yank. "I said we're going to eat, and we're going to eat. Just follow me."

✳ ✳ ✳ ✳ ✳

ACTUALLY, THE DRIVE turned out to be relaxing. They'd been on the road for too many hours to count, and Bones was a little dozy. The good news: The two boys were pretty entertaining. They kept spatting in a comic way about their parents—which parent loved which twin best. As far as Bones could tell, Mom went for Bart and Dad for Bert, or was it the other way around? It was all rather complicated and seemed to shift every few miles. "No, no," Bart would insist, "she stuck *your* hand into the hot oil!"

"No she didn't, where's the scar?" Bert fired back. "And it was you Dad threw off the roof!"

Bones tuned it out. As they wove through the hay ricks and shanty shacks and crying trees, maneuvering around the backfiring tractors on the two-lane road, he felt calmer than he'd felt in weeks. He'd called Detroit, gotten Abe Gritowski, and sicced him on the case. And under the timeworn theory that the best defense was a good offense, he was also formulating his own attack against NRC. He knew how to do it, too: more great music. Bones took lube jockeys down at Ford and teased-hair girls from the projects and turned them into singing heart-throbs. He'd done it before, and he'd just do it again.

Which didn't make him one iota less pissed off at Maisy and Orlando for breaking his damn heart.

He sank back in his seat. This was a really long drive. The roads were even worse than they were in Michigan, which he thought amazing, since up North the winter cracked pavement like it was overcooked toast. Bart was a pretty good driver, but he'd been at the wheel for an awful long time.

"Hey, Bart," Bones said across the front seat.

"I'm Bert, boss."

"O.K., Bert, listen I'd like to drive some."

"You sure, Boss? Bart and I are doing great."

"How long we been on the road?"

"Oh, six hours or so. T'aint nothin'."

"Well, let me spell you guys for a while. Here, pull over over there, in that turnout."

Bert shrugged but said, "Okeydoke, Boss. Anything you say."

It was fine being behind the wheel; much better, Bones was thinking, than being merely swept along as a passenger. He was loving the way the DeSoto was ripping down the road. It had horsepower to burn. Yeah, this was great. Nothing like being back in charge.

Dusk came as they crossed the Alabama line into Florida. They were still on two-lane roads, but everything was flatter here and hotter. Bones kept the gas pedal down, and each time he blew past a slower-moving car, he felt jazzed. Lot of wild, wild horses in this buggy. Down went the pedal, zoom went the DeSoto. There was something peaceful in the quiet of the land, a way it drew him into himself, made everything manageable. The faster he drove, the more clearly he saw the future coming clear in front of him—the way he could make all his problems work out.

The road swung west in Florida, and across the Panhandle the setting sun bloomed huge across the horizon, a brilliant golden-orange light that swelled the whole sky.

Beautiful, and so quiet. Bones dropped the sun visor but didn't slow down. The road was basically straight, and why not just keep gunnin' along it?

The slow-poking tractor pulled onto the two-lane from the dirt road right when the sun was flat in Bones's eyes. The big machine was painted yellow, near the same color as the sun, and Bones didn't see it till a spark of sunlight flared off the top of the tractor's open-hooded engine. He yanked the DeSoto to the left.

But it wasn't the tractor, it was the muffler-dragging Ford station wagon with the old married couple heading home from a day shopping in town. The Ford was laden down with grocery bags and in the back a new yoke for their mule. It was bearing down in the other lane, and the driver of it saw the tractor and then the DeSoto swoop around it. He was a man named Mr. Sanborn, and his reflexes weren't what they used to be. He saw he couldn't go to his left because the tractor was there, so he yanked the wheel of the Ford to the right, but he couldn't get far enough that way in time.

Tires howled. Metal shrieked. Then the stillness of the land returned.

Chapter Eight

Friday, May 1—Pensacola, Fla.

THE NEWS HIT the Cavalcade right before they went onstage in Pensacola, and everyone was stunned to silence. Bart Jones made the call from a pay phone, and he kept running out of change, so he had to ring the Civic Auditorium three times before he got to Bee Williams and was able to tell her the full story. There it was: Bert, in the front seat, was dead; Bones, driving, was in the hospital, barely alive; and Bart, who was in the back, besides being in shock, had a broken arm and slashing painful contusions.

"Where are you?" Bee said.

"We're in Pensacola, I think."

"You're *here*?"

"They took us—" Bart was suddenly overcome with tears. "Took us round and round. Even drove us past one hospital, but the ambulance wouldn't go there." Bart sobbed wildly. "Bert, he was still alive, Bee, he was in my arms in the back. But he—he didn't make it."

"I'm so sorry, Bart." Bee fought to keep a steady tone in her voice. "So sorry. And don't you worry, we'll take care of everything. Now about Bones—"

"They have him in a room, it's sort of dirty, Bee, and he's just lying there. They call it a coh-maaa or something."

"Coma. Jesus." Bee was starting to hyperventilate, but fought that back. "Can you get me a doctor to talk to?"

"I don't know if they even got doctors here. Bee, this is one sorry place. That first hospital, it looked all bright and new, but they said it wasn't for our kind." Bart's voice skirled up into hysteria. "Bee, I don't know where we are."

"It'll be all right. Trust me. Bart, just go put on somebody with a uniform."

A nurse finally came on the phone, confirming Bart's rattled story and giving Bee the hospital's address. The show was to go on in half an hour, and though Bee planned to keep the news from the troupe till after their performances, she had to tell somebody, which was Rags Doheny, and after that word leaked out.

"Let's pray," Rags said when everyone was gathered together. They all clasped hands, and the emcee led them in a somber prayer that began "Dear Father, please shine Your light of mercy down on our three friends tonight. . . ."

Then it was curtain time, and the band took the stage, kicking furiously into their opening tune, and the Shags ran out, falling into line and jumping all over *Men on Fire*.

Mary Hardy seemed particularly broken up with the news about Bones and the two others. Otis Handler was by her side as the Shags ran off in a flurry of churning legs and arms, then pulled up silent and grim as soon as they were off the stage.

"You can do it," Otis said to his lover.

"But Otis—"

"Go out there and sing it just the way you always do."

Mary started to sob.

"Oh, baby," Otis said, pulling her to his chest. "It's gonna be all right. It is, it is. Just sing it the best you can. Break their hearts, Mary."

She did. Her signature tone, plaintive and self-possessed, deepened into true pathos.

Somehow the troupe got through the show. Everyone tried to fight back their tears and lose themselves to the music.

When the final song was done, Bee came up to where Esmé was standing with Robert Warwick. "Robert, I want you to come with me," the chaperone said. "We've got to go find Bones."

Robert said, "Sure," then turned to Esmé and said, "Eddie, you want to come, too?"

Esmé nodded quickly. "Can I change out of this ... dress?"

"Can't you wear it?" Bee said hurriedly. "Trip's found us a car and wants to get going right away."

"Sure," Esmé said, but it was strange, as delighted as she was to be onstage as a woman as the fourth Daisy, she was now so used to being in pants and a jacket that she half-tripped over her high heels.

"Here," Priscilla Bondrais said, coming up behind her. "I have some flats you can borrow."

"Thanks."

In the car Trip was driving, Bee sat next to him, and in the back were Robert Warwick, Esmé, and the bandleader, Candy Wilson. Trip had his usual way with roads and drove them straight to the Pensacola Mercy Hospital. It turned out to be a low-slung stucco building that was once a match factory. They pulled up at what looked like a loading dock then walked through a sliding steel door into a dimly lit waiting room. There was one prominent sign: THIS HOSPITAL FOR COLOREDS ONLY.

There was nobody there. Low-wattage lightbulbs hung overhead without shades, and the light in the place was a murky yellow-white. Four or five brown-Naugahyde chairs with tufts of cotton puffing out like Kleenexes ringed a scarred wooden table; the seats were straight out of an old barbershop. The floor, water-damaged, buckled and tilted. The five Cavalcaders stood stunned in this dreary place until Bee noticed activity down the hall.

They found a doctor there, a man easily in his mid-70s with large, milky eyes and three chins. He had a stethoscope dangling loose around his neck.

"We're here for Bones Chapman," Bee said, taking the lead. "We understand he's in a coma."

The doctor took his time answering. He looked Bee, Trip, Robert, Esmé, and Candy Wilson up and down, muttered a few indistinguishable words to himself that Esmé made out to be "Show folk," then said more or less clearly, "Mr. Chapman is stabilized."

"Is he going to be all right?" Robert asked.

"It's too soon to say, son—" the doctor spoke molasses slow "—but as I just informed you folks, he's stablized."

"And that's good?" Trip said.

"It's good."

"What do we do now?" Esmé said.

"Well, dear, I suggest you just sit yourselves down and wait."

"Can we see him?" Robert was starting to pace back and forth in the narrow corridor.

"You kin?"

"Um, well—" Bee started to say, but Robert interrupted her, saying, "Yes, this is his wife, Bee, and over here's his, um, his daughter, um, Doris." Robert winked at Esmé. She stepped forward in Maisy's dress and found herself almost curtsying, but knew that that would be inappropriate. She told herself: O.K., I'm Esmé again, or Doris, whatever—but a girl again, not Eddie. But it was just so odd wearing a dress in public.

Esmé and Bee followed the doctor back into a room so crepuscular she could barely see. There was a bed—actually, it was more of a cot—and on it with a sheet pulled up to the bottom of his chin was Bones Chapman. Some hoses and pipes ran into him. His skin was a crepey gray under the black, his eyes barely flickered. There was one nurse by his side.

"He's just lyin' there," Bee said.

"That's what a coma does, ma'am," the old doctor said. "Makes you just lie there."

"But he's going to be all right?" Esmé said.

"Well, daughter, he may or he may not. We just gotta ask for the help of the Lord."

Esmé sighed. When they left Bones's bedside, she took Robert's arm and steered him down the hall. "We have to get him out of here," she said.

"I know. Gotta get him into a better hospital."

"Can we do it?" The whole trauma was catching up with Esmé and she felt a little dizzy.

"We have to," Robert insisted.

"Yeah."

At that moment they saw Bart walk into the hospital's waiting room, and they ran up to him. They got the story out of him as well as they could. It was the ambulance drivers who wouldn't take Bones to the best hospital in Pensacola and drove him and Bert instead to this ramshackle Negro establishment.

"The drivers, they said they wouldn't admit Coloreds there," Bart said.

"Did you argue with them?"

"I—I don't know. I yelled. My brother was dyin'. Mr. Bones, he looked to be dyin' too. They just took us here."

"Let me get on the phone," Robert said. "They have a telephone in this miserable place?"

"Over there, Mr. Robert." Bart pointed out the door to a phone booth in front of a gas station across the street.

"Good, God!" Robert sighed, then started toward the door. "Doris—Eddie, I mean—come with me. I have some ideas. We're gonna make this work."

What Robert did was call the local Baptist church, where he found the Negro pastor; Robert told him who they were and what the problem was, and the pastor had an ambulance dispatched to them posthaste. The attendants were black, and though they didn't want to move Bones while he was in a coma, Robert was determined, waving his arms and shouting at the top of his lungs, and they very gingerly lifted Bones onto a gurney, then wheeled him out of the hospital.

Robert and Esmé went with him in the ambulance, the other three Cavalcaders following in the car.

Where they ended up, the lights were bright, doctors and nurses bustling, and to their surprise nobody stopped and said anything about Bones or his helpers being black; they just wheeled him in and went to work on him. Esmé, Robert, Bee, Trip, and Candy waited in a proper waiting room. It was a sad situation all around, and Robert said to Esmé that he'd hated having to make the call to move from the Negro hospital, but they'd all seen how grim it was—and they had to do everything possible to save Bones. Esmé agreed that there wasn't any other way. "Yeah," Robert said. "It's a shitty thing."

Esmé took his hand.

Robert laughed then, though it was tight-grimaced.

"What?" Esmé said.

"Nothing."

"Robert, what?"

"It's just that—" what was this, he was blushing a little "—but you make a pretty good-looking girl."

"Thanks!" Esmé exploded in surprise and exasperation. She yanked her hand back. "God, Robert, what if I said that about you?"

"I know, I know." Robert shook his head. "Sorry."

Finally a young white doctor came out to talk to them. "Everything's as good as it can be," he said right off. "Where he was, they did all the right things. But you're right, it's probably better that he's here. We can keep a good eye on him."

"And—"

"And I hope we'll be having some good news for you. But Mr. Chapman sustained a serious injury to his head and spine. We don't know when he'll regain consciousness."

"But he will?"

"I'm a doctor, not—" He caught himself. "I can't make promises. But I think there's reason to believe it will turn out all right."

"How long do we wait?" Bee said.

"It's a deep coma." The doctor gave them a professional smile. "As long as we have to." He turned to go. "I'll keep you informed, of course."

All five stood there for a long minute until Trip Jackson said softly, "What do we do now?"

And not one of them had an answer.

Part Two

Chapter Nine

Saturday, May 2—Jacksonville, Fla.
Sunday, May 3—Spartanburg, S.C.
Monday, May 4—Columbia, S.C.

SHE WAS UP ONSTAGE dueting with Orlando, moving into the mike at the same time, their bodies in sway to the music playing silently, and each time they swung forward she'd catch a corner-eyed glimpse of him, and he'd look more like some kind of bird—his head was actually a bird's head, or maybe a bird mask, with a long black beak and tight, pointy eyes. The bird's head rose out of his swank tuxedo jacket, and it looked like Orlando, with his long nose and high Indian cheekbones, even as it was somewhere between a crow and an eagle.

There were other birds on the stage with them—the band was penguins—and there, right behind her, was a red songbird with a breathy voice and a comically sleek figure. Esmé knew it was Maisy, who else, and she was poking her pointed beak in at the microphone and trying to push Esmé aside. Esmé, who was nothing but a girl again, but a bird girl, a starling, hissed, "Scoot!" at Maisy, but she was persistent. Still, Orlando was singing only with Esmé, and the song was going great. The audience loved it, and . . . look, they were all birds, too, orioles, robins, and woodpeckers, fluttering in a crystal-blue sky before the stage, which was itself built high up in a huge tree. . . .

When she woke up on the bus, her shoulders pinched, her head aching, the dream shredded away like fine lace.

As her eyes adjusted, she took the whole bus in fresh. They'd been on it almost two weeks, and it was a disaster. All the cigarette smoking had permanently grayed the air. The underlying smell was of dead, fetid tobacco, mixed with the piquant residue of night sweats and bodies washed most often only by roadside washcloth baths. Not only Esmé, for the obvious reasons as the fourth Daisy, but all the women had taken to wearing long-flowing wigs—there was just no way to daily wash their hair. Floating above the base smells were traces of week-old gardenia perfume, vaporized lighter fluid, floating gray motes of cigar ash, and the bouquet from the heavily distilled Old Gentleman the musicians in the back swirled day and night in their paper cups; topping off the whole miasma were traces of sweet, sticky hair spray spritzed every morning over their piled-high, performance-ready coifs.

Though Bee tried to get everyone to keep the bus picked up, there were always soda bottles rattling between the metal chair legs, as well as lipstick-stained cigarette butts cast underfoot, sprouting shreds of brown tobacco. The ladies on the bus had thrown decorum to the wind pretty quickly, and filmy drying undergarments and taupe stockings flew from the overhead racks, so thick it was like walking through a bra and panty forest. (Nobody asked why there was no gentleman's underwear in sight, the best answers too disturbing to calculate.) Dresses that needed to be kept well-pressed hung everywhere, and half of the windows let in light only through yellow or green rayon chiffon; during high daylight the interior of the bus felt a little like being in an aquarium. Now at night, though, the only light was from the tiny flashlightlike bulbs set above each seat as night lights. They cast out small yellow penumbrae that floated distinct from the night air around them; it was visible where the light ended and the dark began, the whole effect like a torchlit cave with shadows deeper than sin itself.

Something had happened to the bus's frame, and the floor seemed to tilt some. The Naugahyde-covered seats were as hard as ever. The bus's interior walls were an institutional green, and to Esmé's amusement, Robert Warwick had been scratching perpendicular lines into the paint, then crossing them like a prisoner counting off his days of confinement.

This is what Esmé woke into from her dream, and saw clearly for a fleeting moment. The vision took a moment to register after her airy, bird-light dream. Then a second later she smiled and closed her eyes again. As rank as the bus was, it had become to her nothing but her blessed home.

＊ ＊ ＊ ＊ ＊

THE TROUPE HAD PLAYED a show that night in Spartanburg, South Carolina, and it was an uninspired affair. Worry over Bones in his coma, grief over Bart's death, and the wisps of news floating in from Detroit were enough to dampen any performance spark; the Shags, Mary Hardy, the Cravattes, and the Daisies (Esmé again doing double duty) had run through the show, but for the first time Esmé could remember, everybody couldn't wait to get off the stage. Then it was back on the bus, where things just got worse. It was a trip to nowhere.

Robert Warwick was up front talking to Bee, and finally he had an announcement.

"We're going to cancel the next show," he said. "We're scheduled to play Columbia, South Carolina, where we've already been. Tickets haven't been moving as fast as we'd like, and I think everybody needs a night off while we wait to hear about Bones."

Bert in his grief and wanting to keep busy had volunteered to stay behind in Pensacola to keep watch over Bones and phone twice a day with updates. But nothing had changed. The boss was in stable condition, the doctors said, and they remained confident. But he was also completely beyond consciousness.

"Do you think that's a good idea?" Henry Jackson, the tenor sax player, called out from the back.

Robert lifted his chin and said, "It's only one show, so we can catch our breath and figure out what to do next. We're playing Washington, D.C., the night after, and we'll do that gig." He cast his gaze around the bus. "Everyone agreed?"

General nods and muttered O.K.'s. Robert nodded, gave a quick pat to Bee's shoulder, then took the seat next to Esmé.

"I think that was a good idea you had," he said to her, "bagging Columbia. Any others?"

Esmé shook her head. It was easy to suggest canceling the Columbia show; obvious how strung out and anxious everyone was. But she was no less in the dark as to how to go on as anyone else. "Have you heard anything more from Detroit?"

"I've called but can't get Bill Sylvester or Hermione on the phone."

"Hermione?"

"His wife." Robert smiled. "Everyone calls her Mrs. Bones."

"I didn't know he was married."

"I'm not sure he always knows he is, too."

"But she's in charge now, this Mrs. Bones?"

"She says she is, yeah."

"And . . . she's ducking you?"

"I don't know what to think," Robert said.

Esmé took this in. "And there's nothing more from Maisy and Orlando?" Robert nodded. "Do you think they even know?"

"Oh, I think so, yeah," Robert said. "I think everyone in the business knows. Especially NRC."

"More than just stealing Maisy and Orlando?"

"I have some feelers out." Robert's eyebrows went hooded. "It's hard being on this bus, I can't call anybody, and nobody can call me, but when we get to Columbia, I'll hit it hard. I'll get more."

"Stick with it, Robert," Esmé said.

"Yeah." And the short singer gave a deep nod, then was lost behind his thick black glasses to his own thoughts.

✳ ✳ ✳ ✳ ✳

WHEN THE NEWS came about her husband, Hermione Chapman was in a Detroit nightclub, the Golden Slipper, with her bosom pals Beatrice and Tony. (She didn't know their last names.) The club owner, Mike the Barnacle, had heard the news from the radio and had come up to Hermione sitting deep in a banquette, a line of lime-green daiquiri glasses before her, and said he had some bad news.

"You're not cutting me off, Mike, are you?" Hermione had a way speaking when she'd been drinking that was just a few decibels too loud. (Beatrice and Tony were just as loud, which is why none of them noticed.) Hermione wore a powder-blue mohair-soufflé dress that hugged—some might say pinched—her wider and wider curves, a long yellow Parisian silk scarf around her neck, and shoes with heels so thin and high that when she walked there was always worry that her ankles would buckle and she'd tumble like a felled tree. She never did, though, which was part of her mystique; sober or drunk, she'd sail unscathed through situations subtly treacherous or otherwise, like a cartoon cat running a gantlet of bare-fanged dogs, dancing cleavers, and cyclone-spinning slat-backed chairs.

"Um, no, Mrs. Bones." That's what everyone called her. At first they'd done it behind her back, but since her husband had become a real player in Detroit (and was known to everyone simply as Bones), Hermione began to encourage the appellation; would even use it herself in situations in which her own redoubtable powers weren't garnering immediate attention.

"You wouldn't dream of that, would you, Mike?"

"Not with you, Mrs. Bones. But—" Mike the Barnacle

was a big guy, with stevedore arms, squished into a monkey suit.

"You can send over some more drinkies, though, if you'd like," Hermione interrupted.

"Well, Mrs. Bones, I'll be happy to do that, but I must have a word with you. There's been some . . . some bad news. I think I should tell you in private."

"Private?" Hermione liked to think all men wanted her. She also liked to think that her husband would kill any man who actually propositioned her, which is why no one ever did. They just didn't have the manhood.

"In my office." Since Hermione wasn't immediately moving, he added, "It's about your husband."

"He's not cutting us off again, is he, Hermione?" This was Tony. He was thin and epicene, with a high-pitched voice that sounded like a squirrel's. Beatty, even larger than Mrs. Bones, had a huge moon face and little chocolate-drop eyes. "The snake!"

"It's not that." There was something about the club owner that was unsettling Hermione; an obsequious hand-wringing quality that didn't make sense in the context of the Golden Slipper.

"Then out with it, Mike!"

"I think . . . in private—"

"What are you hiding? Out with it—right now!"

"Well, Mrs. Bones, you see, the radio is saying that there's been a, a car accident. . . ."

That was three days ago. Hermione spent a couple of sleepless nights worrying that Bones would die; well, not worrying so much that he'd actually expire as that she'd stop being Mrs. Bones, with all that came with it; though she did her damnedest, she could never forget how she'd been a dime-a-dance girl when she'd met Bones eighteen years earlier, not that she really owed him anything. Still, she couldn't help but worry that FDL Records could fall apart without him; and without the record label behind her, who knows how she'd end up.

She'd stayed in contact with the Florida hospital, but evidently nothing had changed since the accident, and up here in Detroit she couldn't quite tell from the doctor's tone which way things were going to go. She knew she should probably go to Bones's bedside, but Florida was so far away and Pensacola not easy to get to; it would take at least two or three days. Besides, hospitals were always so grim, and, in truth, what was he actually doing there besides just lying about unconscious?

What she was telling everyone was that she had to keep track of FDL's affairs, which was only partly true since William Sylvester III, the white guy who did the label's finances, had day-to-day authority and was keeping things moving. But then the phone call had come the day before.

You couldn't say Mrs. Bones knew a whole lot about the record business, but she certainly knew NRC. Many of her favorite singers, like Paris Muffin and Little Evie Stone, were on the label. They had offices in Rockefeller Center in New York City (they used the famous Atlas statue on their labels), and their records blanketed radio from coast to coast. Their promotion was seamless, none of this hit-and-miss under-the-table stuff that Bones was no doubt up to that she just didn't want to know about. No, NRC was class. FDL . . . well, it kept her in silk, which was something, right, even if performers like the Shags and the Cravattes were a little . . . boisterous. (And then there was that Maisy Columbine and her fellow tramps the Daisies, a woman Hermione, for damn good reasons, couldn't abide even hearing about.) But when the call came from Captain Bryant, the head of NRC, she was all ears.

Captain Bryant was properly concerned. He spoke in a slow Southern accent, topped off with some Long Island WASP. "I understand that there's a very good chance Bones'll pull through."

"We're praying, Captain Bryant." Hermione was feeling all puffy around her eyes, not from worry over her husband so much as a late night at the Slipper the night before. "We surely be." Then caught herself: Did that sound too . . . Negro?

"We surely be prayin', too," the Captain said.

Hermione pinched her big eyes. Did rich white people actually talk like that?

"Sir?"

"Yes, darling."

"It's got me . . . all upset."

"I can imagine."

"Can you?"

"Well, so much is up in the air. Your whole . . . livelihood." She heard Bryant clear his throat. "That's the right word, isn't it, Mrs. Chapman?"

"I hadn't really thought about that."

"Your husband has a fine operation there, dear. A fine, fine company. It's a firm anyone would be proud to own."

"You think so?" She liked that word *firm*; it sounded so grown-up, so unlike the real FDL.

"Oh, yes, very, very proud. And very, very, how shall I put it . . . grateful. To own FDL, that is."

"Grateful?"

"Almost beyond your imagination, darling." A laugh through the phone. "Unless you have the imagination that I think you have. Then it just might be a dream come true."

There was a long pause then while Hermione tried to figure just what Captain Bryant was getting at.

"Grateful, eh?"

"The kind of grateful, darling, that you can take to the bank."

"The bank?"

"Any bank you choose."

Mrs. Bones found herself leaning forward. "Please, Captain, I can call you Captain?"

"By all means, darling."

"Well, Captain, you wanna be tellin' me more?"

✳ ✳ ✳ ✳ ✳

THEY WERE BACK IN Columbia, and it was true—it was a huge relief not to have to perform this night. The show the night before in Spartanburg had been the worst ever. Not only was the whole Cavalcade reeling over Bones, but when they'd gotten to the Memorial Auditorium, they'd found a rope line running up the center aisle, the black audience on one side, white on the other. Robert in particular flipped. He and Bee went to the promoter, who simply said that that was how things were done in Spartanburg. Robert threatened to pull the whole show if the rope wasn't lifted. The promoter, a florid-faced man named Ricky Water, said, "That ain't never been done."

Robert, wound up, said, "Do it now."

Ricky Water just smiled and said, "We'd have ourselves a riot, we lifted that rope, Mr. Warwick."

"I doubt it."

"Oh, yes, we would. And Sheriff here wouldn't countenance no riot."

The two men stood forehead-to-forehead until Bee said, "Robert, let's just do the show tonight—we'll just never come back."

Robert stood his ground. Esmé was nearby, taking all this in.

"Robert, I'm going to overrule you," Bee said.

Ricky Water just stood there smiling broadly. Finally, Robert simply had walked off.

"I don't know, what would Bones have done?" he said to Esmé backstage.

She shook her head. "I don't have a clue."

"I don't—" Robert shook his head. "Damn! This whole thing has—" Then he walked away from her, going off to a corner to stand silently.

The show was sloppy, half-hearted. The audience loved it

anyway, though it was surpassingly strange to look out and see nothing but black faces to the left and white ones to the right. To the Cavalcade's credit, there were almost equal numbers of fans on each side. The show ended with the Daisies. No one had the heart to gather onstage for the usual rousing gospel climax. And nobody said a word as the troupe trundled onto the bus.

Bee had called ahead and worked up a motel for the Cavalcade, and when they got there—cabins set in piney woods; big bugs buzzing around dingy yellow lights—it seemed as if everyone immediately sacked out. Esmé sure did. There'd been a change in sleeping arrangements, though. Robert Warwick had worked it out that they'd be rooming together. She'd had no trouble rooming with Mitch Williams the nights they'd been in motels, mainly because he was off all night gambling and was never there. With Robert things might be trickier. She figured that if he was in the cabin, she'd just go into the bathroom, put on her men's PJ's, brush down her hair, try to get the lights out, then climb quickly into her own bed—and hope for the best. A good plan, but unnecessary: Robert wasn't in the room. She hadn't seen him since they'd gotten off the bus.

Her head hit the pillow and she flicked out like a lamp. The bird dream was back, but different. This time they were at a zoo—a huge, complicated version of the petting zoo in Jackson—and Esmé was a tiny hummingbird with feathers buzzing invisibly. She and Orlando and Maisy were in a cage. Orlando kept flying against the sides, his head and beak poking through, wings batting against the iron bars. Maisy hovered above him, a wicked gleam in her BB-sized eyes, floating slowly back and forth; odd as it seemed, in Esmé's dream Maisy was laughing. Esmé herself was so small she could actually flit in and out of the bars. She was frantic over Orlando, who kept banging and banging against the cold iron. There she was in front of him outside the cage, and then above and behind him; and all the while she couldn't do a thing to help him.

She woke with a loud gasp when the door to the cabin clicked open. "Ohmygod!" she cried in quick-seizing terror. For a second, she didn't know who or where she was. Her breathing whistled like a runaway train. "God, who is it?"

"It's just me. Ed—Eddie, are you all right?"

Oh, no! I shouted out in my girl voice.

"I'm sorry, I was having this strange dream." She slowly lowered the pitch of her voice, hoping Robert didn't notice. "I was—there were—Orlando and Maisy were in it, and we were all birds in this cage—"

"Sounds curious." Robert was quickly inside the room. He carefully locked the door behind him, then went into the bathroom, not to use it but just to take a look.

"What're you doing?" Esmé said.

"We have to talk."

"Robert?—" She immediately jumped to the worst possibility.

"Maybe we should take a walk. I don't want anybody around."

"What is it?"

He sighed loudly. "We're in trouble."

"More than—"

"A lot more. Come on, get up, throw on some clothes." Robert headed toward the bathroom again, this time to use it. "There's a creek down there behind the motel, we can go along that."

At least she wasn't busted. When her friend was safely behind the bathroom door Esmé jumped up and pulled her trousers over her pajama bottoms, then tugged a V-neck sweater over her pajama tops. Her breasts were unbound, and she'd have to hope Robert didn't notice.

In the sky was a half moon, bright enough to cast the path beside the creek with enough silver light for them to walk without worry.

"So what is it?" Esmé said when they were a quarter mile down the path.

"I've been popping dimes and quarters into this stupid phone all night," Robert said. His hands were thrust into the pockets of his sport coat, almost punching through the cloth. "O.K., here's what I've found out. NRC has made an offer to buy FDL. They're—"

"Buy it?" Esmé lost a step when she heard this; skipped to keep up. "How can they?"

"Like vultures. With Bones in his coma, they're swooping down on Mrs. Bones."

"They can get her to—"

"It's complicated, that's the best thing going for us." Esmé heard that "us" and was quietly pleased. "She's trying to get Bones declared legally incapacitated—"

"Can she do that?"

"A good question. I'm not a lawyer, obviously. But as long as he's in the coma—"

"Right."

"In any event she's acting like she controls the company, and if she sells it fast enough, well, would we be able to go up against NRC's lawyers?"

Esmé nodded. "She has the right to sell it?"

"No—not all by herself."

"That's good, right?"

Robert nodded, then said, "The plan if Bones is declared, um, incapacitated is that Mrs. Bones holds forty percent, and Bones's brother and sister split the last sixty."

"That is good."

Robert sighed. "It's our only hope."

"What're they like?"

"I've never met them, don't know that much. Octavus,

the brother, is a preacher in Detroit. Ramona, the sister, is a high school teacher."

"And they'll have to agree to any deal—"

Where they were, the path was running right next to the creek. The gurgling water was so loud Esmé couldn't hear what Robert next said. "What?"

He beckoned her away from the water and onto a side path. They were deep in shadows here; Esmé could barely see his face.

"I don't want to shout. O.K., what I think Mrs. Bones is trying to do is lock in a deal with NRC before she goes to Bones's siblings. I do know she hasn't made the deal yet. A team from NRC in New York is going to Detroit to talk with Hermione, but I'm sure they'll take her back to New York to finish the arrangements. They'll want her away from everyone else, and they'll want all their guns."

"So we have some time."

"Not much."

"What can we do?" Esmé heard her own breathing now, jumping quick and barely controlled from her chest.

"Well, here's what we have against us. One, we have Bones in that goddamn coma. As long as he's lost to that, he obviously can't help us. Two, we have Hermione eager—that's what I heard, she's eager—to sign the company away. And—"

"And three," Esmé said, "NRC already has Maisy and Orlando. That's gotta be a big one against us, right?"

"Sure. It takes away from the value of Fleur-de-Lys, even makes it look like the company is already going down—that NRC isn't preying on us but riding in on a white horse to save FDL."

"Jesus."

"Yeah," Robert said.

"O.K.," Esmé said, her brain whirring, "here's what I see. One, we hope Bones gets out of the coma; that'd solve everything."

Robert shrugged, meaning he wasn't that certain. What he said was: "But we can't count on that."

"We can pray," Esmé said. "And we will." Robert nodded. Esmé moved right along. "O.K., two, the family. What you're telling me is that, ultimately, Mrs. Bones needs either the sister or brother to sign any deal."

"Yes."

"Will one of them do it?"

"I don't know—that's something we gotta find out more about, just what Octavus and Ramona think—"

"Exactly," Esmé said. Then: "So what else can we do?"

"Here," Robert said. He was already standing right next to Esmé in the dark night, but he moved even closer. She picked up his smell; it was both sweet and tangy—and a little ripe, from everything he'd been through. But not unpleasant. "I have another idea," he went on. "I want to know what you think."

Chapter Ten

Tuesday, May 5— Washington, D.C.

FINDING A RECORDING STUDIO in the nation's capital wasn't so easy, but there was a blues scene in the northside of town, and Robert after asking around turned up a makeshift place on First Street in a second-floor warren above a dry cleaners and a fish fry. The floppy-hatted, greasy-mustached guy who ran it, name of Brandy Watson, a name *not* shortened from Brandon, called the place Trident, and there was a crude drawing of the three-pronged instrument that looked remarkably like the Fleur-de-Lys insignia. A good omen?

The smell in the one-room studio was enough to knock you over, the heavy glistening fried oil of the fish joint and the acrid chemicals of the cleaners in an unholy mix, peppering the air, coating your skin, making your nose itch. But the sound in the room worked. The carpet was shabby, soundproofing on the walls came from nailed-up egg cartons, and the glass to the minimal control booth had a jagged scar-like crack running right through it; but when James Motion set up his drums and whacked the snare, and Robert got the crisp, snappy sound printed on tape, he knew that the place was going to turn out just fine.

They set up the band in a far corner, squeezed in so tight Bunny's bass head was right under In Motion's nose when he reached out to hit his ride cymbal, and Henry Jackson and Norris Rowland were playing their horns so close together it was like they were Siamese twins: two bodies, two arms, two horns. They set up Esmé in front of a ribbon mike right in front of the band. There wasn't going to be any of that new-fangled stereo here; Trident's philosophy was simply get everything miked, play it all at once, and slam it onto one track of tape.

They were doing Robert's new song, *My Eyes Go Wide*, the one he'd played for Esmé a week back, that he'd wanted to try out on Bones before the accident. That was Robert's idea for them: Record the catchy song with Esmé singing it, or at least her as Eddie. She knew the song was a clear hit, and it didn't take much to persuade Robert to at least let her give it a try.

So there they were, Esmé in her best men's suit to set the right tone, the band putting the final polish on their loping, bouncy arrangement—she loved the floppy quality of In Motion's drums on the song, a bass and snare with skin so loose they thudded more than rang; and yet James was able to turn the kit's weaknesses into the song's gentle, thumping groove. *Bang!* and he just had it.

Robert was behind the cracked glass, calling out, "Take One," and everybody clanged up the opening hook, then Esmé sang in her best men's tenor, *"You're sunny as a parfait / Perfect as a summer's day. . . ."*

At the end of the song the horns lifted and swung, and James crashed down a final downbeat—it was a wrap. The performance had felt . . . pretty good.

There was no room in the control booth for more than one person, so Robert turned the playback speakers around and boomed the take back into the room. Everyone listened silently.

"Nice," Cotton Candy Wilson said from the tiny Farfisa organ, the only keyboard the studio had. "James, you really swung that."

In Motion nodded, said, "Bunny, you were perfect in the pocket with me."

"Yeah, you guys have it," Robert said. He had a single finger up by his ear and looked even more contemplative than usual. "What about Eddie?"

"Sounded O.K. to me," the guitarist John Smith said.

"He swung it sweet," Cotton Candy said.

"Gentlemen?" Robert opened his arms and got grunts and nods all around. "Eddie?"

"I think it was all right. I think I can do it better." Esmé gave a tiny fly-away smile. " 'Course I'd probably always think that. How 'bout you, Robert?"

"Something—"

"What?" Esmé leaned forward.

Robert gave his head a vigorous shake. His black glasses slipped cockeyed down his nostrils. "Something, I don't know, maybe it's the key."

"It feels O.K. to me, though I could take it higher." Esmé had been singing down, where she always sang as Eddie, and as usual she did it fine, though like a baseball switch-hitter who was better lefthanded than right, she knew it wasn't her best voice; that was her as herself, a woman, of course.

"I'm hearing something—no, this is a little crazy."

"What?" Esmé said again, encouraging him. She had a sudden intimation where Robert was going, and wanted to make sure he got there.

"Who's singing the song?" Robert said. A couple funny looks from the band: Isn't that obvious? "You know, in the song."

"Some guy who really likes his girl," John Smith said. " *'My eyes go wide, every time you go walking by.'* Like that."

"Yeah, but is it a guy?" Robert said.

"It's Eddie singing it," Bunny Alexander said. "And, yeah, *'You're sunny as a parfait'*—whatever the fuck a parfait is?"

Laughs all around.

"That's sort of my idea," Robert said. "I keep seeing a girl's eyes go wide, and I keep thinking it's cool if she's saying, 'You're sunny as a parfait,' which, you clown, you know is a kind of sundae—"

"Oh, I thought it was a Monday," Bunny came right back at him.

Everybody laughed louder.

"Ice cream, you moron."

"Robert, you scream, I scream, then we'll all scream for—"

"O.K., man." This was John Smith, interrupting Bunny. "So where do we get a chick to sing it?"

"That's what I'm thinkin'. You know, Eddie's been doin' that double-duty thing with the Daisies. I think he could hit it as a girl. Eddie?"

Esmé said with delight, "Sure, boss."

Robert caught the wink in her eye. "It wouldn't be any trouble? We could take it up a key or two."

"Let me see." Esmé as herself started singing low the first couple lines. "I think we go down a step, step and a half, and I sing it an octave up. That'll sound like. . . ." and she sang the first verse again, soundly in her best range this time.

Robert started nodding determinedly halfway through; then he said, "Any problems with you guys?"

"Falls into A like a charm," Candy Wilson said.

"O.K., let's do it."

It did seem odd to Esmé to sing as herself without the camouflage of Maisy's left-behind clothes, but so much of what she'd been doing the last few weeks since she'd walked up the wide lawn of the FDL building had been strange and confusing that she just took the session in stride. She needed four takes until Robert and she and everyone else agreed they'd cranked out a surefire *girl* hit. By then she was beaming and smiling more than she could ever remember; and it was a woman smiling out from her suit coat, and she didn't notice, or, if she did, she simply didn't care.

"I love it," Robert said. "This is just what I wanted. Thank you."

"Thank *you*," Esmé said from the bottom of her heart.

"So whose name's it going out under, boss?" John Smith said, and Esmé noted this second use after hers of the word *boss* applied to Robert. She knew he deserved it, and was glad the band was seeing that, too.

"Well, we put it out as Eddie Days, nobody's gonna know *what* to do with it." Robert turned to Esmé. "You got us a girl's name you'd be comfortable with? Should we go with Doris?"

Esmé had an answer ready. "Um, I have this . . . cousin in Detroit—I ever tell you about her? She's this really good singer?" She hadn't actually said anything of the kind to Robert, was just inventing on the spot, but the songwriter was polite; he gave a half shrug, waited.

"Well, it was funny, Robert, when I was singing just now, I was thinking of her—some. I've been thinking of her all along when I get up and pretend to be a girl with the Daisies, but with *Eyes Go Wide*, well, it was like I was singing it all in her voice." Esmé shrugged. "That make sense?" Robert nodded, and Esmé nodded enthusiastically back. "Well, so why don't we just use her name. I'm sure she wouldn't mind."

"What is it?"

"Um, Esmé. With an accent—one of those funny French things—over the second E." She made a small flick of her pointer finger in the air to illustrate it.

"She have a last name?"

Esmé blanked for a second, then quick said, "Of course she has a last name, it's Hunter." She shrugged. This was more revealing than she wanted to be. "But if the song's goin' out with me singing it, how 'bout we just call it Esmé. Draw it out a little, Ess-maaaaay? Just the one name, you know."

"One name?" Candy Wilson said. "Isn't that a little full of itself?"

Robert lifted his head. "Yeah, but nobody's done it, have they? Just put out a record under one name? I mean, I say Etta, you know I mean Etta James, but she's still Etta James. Same with Dinah—she hasn't given up Washington yet. This will be the next step. *Essmaaaaay*—Eddie, I think it's a great idea." A quick frown. "You're sure your cousin won't mind?"

"Oh, it's her fondest dream to have a record out, I can guarantee that. She'll love it."

"O.K., then," Robert said. "We got the show in an hour, so I'll get *Eyes Go Wide* pressed tomorrow." He lifted his forehead. "And when it does hit, come on, guys, tell me, what does this song have written all over it?"

"Number One!" the band cried out.

"What was that, guys? I can't hear you."

"Number One!"

Robert laughed brightly. "O.K., then, everyone, that's a wrap. Brandy, here, I'll pay you the rest of what I owe you, just rewind me the tape. All of you, you did good today. I'm proud of you. Now you got the rest of the day off . . . least till the show tonight."

✳ ✳ ✳ ✳ ✳

FINDING A RECORDING STUDIO in New York City was no problem whatsoever, especially if you were NRC and owned one whole complex yourself and regularly booked two others. Today's session was going down in Ambassador Studios on 52nd Street, populated at 10:30 this evening with sharp-looking (if a little long-faced) studio musicians; Rick Lapidus, NRC's new producer; and NRC's just-signed, hot new duo, Maisy Columbine and Orlando Calabrese—MC&OC as the session sheet had it. The session had been scheduled for noon, started only two hours late because Maisy hadn't shown up on time, and had been going on all day since.

"O.K., gentlemen, from the top again," Lapidus said into the P.A. from behind the control room glass. He sighed loudly, then ran his hands through his brilliantined black hair, then wiped them on his tight, black Italian wool-blend pants. "Maisy, how you doin'? You still with us?"

"Just fine, Mr. Rick."

"Breeze?" Lapidus said.

Mr. Rick? Orlando was thinking. I know it's been a long day, but where'd that come from? What're we, back on the damn plantation?

"Breeze?" Rap, rap on the mike, a sound that crashed out of the P.A. speakers and made Orlando cringe. "You good?"

"Um, yeah, sure." But he wasn't good. For one thing, his damn boots pinched. He'd bought them just this morning from the $500 advance NRC had given him; they pinched horribly, and by now he was walking like he was crippled, which was not the way the Breeze chose to move on this earth. Not that anyone noticed. But the boots were nothing compared with what had been squeezing on him for the last four days, ever since he'd heard about Bones's accident.

He'd heard the news from a hotel bellhop who was an FDL fan and reeling from the shock. Orlando had called Detroit, got the horrible story confirmed. Then he'd told Maisy.

The news made her catch her breath—but that was it.

"You heard me, right?" he said. They were in Maisy's hotel room; she'd insisted on separate rooms, and Orlando's was on another floor.

"I heard you."

"And?"

"It's terrible." Maisy wasn't even facing Orlando; instead she was applying makeup in a large three-sided mirror over a polished wood vanity. She pursed her lips, put on lipstick, then dabbed some rouge on her cheeks. She fluffed her hair, and a bright light gleamed in her eyes. "What do you want me to say?"

He just stared at the back of her head. "Why are you doin' it?" he said softly.

"What was that?"

"Why are you—" Then he had second thoughts about asking Maisy this question.

But she'd heard it anyway. She spun around to face him. "Why am I doing all this? What's wrong with you, open your eyes! I'm doing it because I'm damn sick of struggling along with that two-bit operation, suffering the in-*dig*-ni-ties. You remember that bus. How crowded it was in there. All of us singing our hearts out but never getting any money—not even getting our songs to Number 1. You remember all that, right?"

"I'm just thinking about Bones."

"Yeah, and I'm sayin', what'd Bones ever do for you?"

Orlando found his heart in his throat. "He discovered me."

"Oh, yeah, that was hard. Where, oh, where can I find me a tall, beautiful man who sings like an angel and makes li'l girls get all wet inside?" She cupped her hand over her eyes, pretended she was up in a crow's nest looking for whale. "Where, oh, where could he be?"

"Nobody else did it."

"They woulda. They're doing it now." Maisy dropped her hand and put both hands on her hips. She was wearing an amazing peach dressing gown, all lace and organdy and flounces that amplified every motion of her own flesh. "Listen, it's terrible about Bones, and of course I'm upset. Of course I am. But, darlin', we got us a job to do here. A new life. A new label—"

"Shouldn't we maybe—"

"Listen, I know that Bones, he's made of hard rock. I'm sure whatever happened down there just shook him up a little. We do anything silly like go to him, hell, he'll be up and snorting before we get there."

Orlando simply sighed.

"Come on, Rick is taking us out on the town. I gotta finish getting dressed." Maisy stood back and gave Orlando a long look. He was wearing a tux NRC had given him the day before. It fit perfectly. "Hey, you're lookin' good, Mr. Long Legs." She went over to Orlando, tickled under his chin. "Come on, quit being so glum. We got us a great dinner comin' up, on NRC." A long, sly smile. "Then we got us dessert back here—on me."

In the studio now Orlando kept thinking about Bones, what he'd say about this NRC record date. It never would've gone so long; if FDL couldn't nail a hit right off, everyone went on to the next song and came back to the first one another day. But Rick Lapidus had had them going over and over their duet, *A Rainy-Day Love*, for the last eight hours.

"O.K., Take ... forty-three," Lapidus said into the booming P.A. "You all good? Come on, people, let's nail the sucker this time."

The violins swelled up, though a little sleepily, the drums came in rock solid—the hired guy was a stone pro—the piano hit its high-black-key, supper-club tinkling, and the guitar scraped its ninth and thirteenth chords high up the neck. The first line was Orlando's, *"Here I am inside, waiting all alone / The rain out there already soaked me to my bones,"* and he launched into it with all the polish and professionalism he could muster—just as he'd done forty-two times before.

Then Maisy came in. *"Here I am, dear, outside your door / The rain has soaked me right to my core."* She sounded just like Maisy Columbine, her voice as bubbly and pert as it had ever been with the Daisies. Her eyes were huge, her smile liquid, her tones playful—everything sounded great.

Back to Orlando. His voice was thick syrup, he could see the words he sang roll slow through his lips: *"I'll let you in, help you get dry / Build us a fire by and by."*

And then Maisy came in together with him for the final line of the verse: *"All we can do, when the heavens crack high above / Is to share / Our rainy-day love / Our rainy-day looohoooohooooove."* And there, as they had forty-two times before, they lost it.

It wasn't the notes, which they hit with precision, and it certainly wasn't their voices separately. It was just the tone they hit together. It had all the charm of sandpaper and broken glass.

The first time they'd tried to blend both of their voices, they'd jumped back as if they'd gotten an electric shock. Lapidus had immediately shut the take down.

"Whoa!" he'd said then. "You guys O.K.?"

They'd both nodded, somewhat sheepishly.

"What was that?"

"Um, I don't know," Maisy said, giving Orlando a glaring look. "Something just happened."

"Well, all right, you guys are the best. Let's just do it again."

The takes didn't always fall apart right when they came in together; sometimes they got through the first two verses and then, flying into the bridge in which they were to sing note on top of note, they would sputter out halfway through. Once they got to the end of the song, to the long note they held, *"Loooo-hoooo-hoooove,"* when Maisy collapsed into giggles.

"Maisy!" Lapidus cried, not able to conceal his stern tone.

"Oh, Rick, it just sounded sooooo goooooooood, I just . . . just lost it." She kept laughing, a little hysterically if you asked Orlando. "I'm sorry. Won't happen again."

"Well, all right, proves you two can nail it. Come on, let's keep going." That was about nine in the evening, an hour and a half ago. Everyone was famished, but Lapidus had made it clear nobody was going to break till they finished the damn tune.

"My throat is powerful dry, Rick," Maisy said now.

"You want another Coke?"

"Those Co-Colas ain't doin' it." There was a whole line of the green-glass bottles lined up on top of a guitar amplifier. And why did it take Maisy twenty minutes to go to the Ladies' room, and doing that what seemed like every ten or so minutes? "You know what I think will just do the trick, Rick?"

Lapidus didn't say anything.

"Darling?" Maisy put her pointer finger to the corner of her mouth, wiggled her hand in her best Betty Boop. She'd come into the session dolled up in a slinky gown with a fur around her neck (a personal gift from Captain Bryant, and even though it was May outside the studio she was wearing it everywhere; she'd made Lapidus crank up the air-conditioning). She'd also been wearing heels so high that she almost came up to Orlando's nose, but she'd shed the shoes hours ago—if only I could take mine off, Orlando thought—and was now standing on a stool to get height against her partner.

Lapidus looked through the control room glass. "Yes, Maisy."

"A sarsparilla."

"A what?"

"Sarsparilla. It's a soda, used to have 'em as a girl." Maisy beamed a girlish smile. "They make my throat feel soooo nice and tingly."

Lapidus tried to match her smile. "I don't know if we can find a—" He was brushing his hands over his jacket as if he were looking for lint. "Maisy, would this have helped earlier?"

"I just think it'll help now."

"A sarsparilla?"

"It comes from a root," Maisy said brightly. "The sars-parilla root."

"I'm sure it does."

"What's the matter, Rick?" Maisy stepped off her stool, took strides toward the control room. "You don't know where to get it? Oh, honey, isn't this New York City? Can't you get yourself any ol' thing just by snapping your power-ful record producer fingers? You ain't makin' me think we're back at dingy ol' FDL are you?"

The producer looked straight at her, his jaw down, then half turned away before Orlando caught him rolling his eyes. "Jimmy, go get Miss Columbine a sarsparilla." A pause, then: "I don't the fuck know. Try the deli down the corner." He turned back to the chanteuse. "Mind if we go after another take while we wait? Maisy?"

Orlando sighed. No, it just wasn't going to work. He didn't really understand it. He and Maisy had never dueted back at FDL, that was just Orlando and Mary, and the two of *them* had never had to do more than two takes to get wax. But he and Maisy were both professionals; why couldn't they get through this silly little song?

"Orlando!" There it was, Lapidus's voice booming through the P.A. again. "Maisy's game for another take before she gets her, um, soda. Orlando, you ready?"

"Yes, sir," he said. He stole a look at his watch: 11:15. His stomach growled. The violins sawed into their opening, the rock-solid drummer brushed his snare, and he stepped to the mike and started singing, *"Here I am, dear, outside your door. . . ."*

He found his manicured fingernails pressing bitingly into the flesh of his palms as he waited for Maisy to join in.

Chapter Eleven

Wednesday, May 6— Washington, D.C.

IT WAS A COUPLE OF HOURS before showtime, the whole
Cavalcade in their downtown hotel not far behind the
Capitol dome (Esmé, thrilled, could see it glow silver out her
window; remembered as a girl marveling over a model of it
in a pop-up book of American landmarks she cherished),
when shouting came from down the hall. It was 5:30 in the
afternoon, and the bus to dinner, then the Capitol Arena for
their second show there was scheduled for six. The yelling
was high-pitched and furious, and when everyone first heard
it, they shook their heads. That sounds like Mary Hardy,
people said to their roommates. Sweet Mary? That doesn't
make sense.

A moment later Mary and Otis Handler were in the
hallway.

"This is our chance," she was shouting at him. Her eyes
were wide and her thin nostrils flared. "This is a clean break."

Otis stood in front of Mary, his thick arms folded across
his chest, his chin jutted out. He was a patient man and knew
women; knew how to let them blow off all their fiery air.

Mary was blowing, like nobody had heard her before.
"Why won't you answer me? Don't you love me?" She stamped
her foot. "You been using words you don't believe? That's not
the Otis I know." Her voice swooped startlingly lower, a roller-
coaster car hurtling down the high hill. She touched his arm,
then went on cooingly, "Otis, *Oh*-tis, all the things you been
sayin' to me, well, darlin', now it's time to make yourself a decision on 'em. This is it. We have to do it now."

The big man didn't move for a moment, then he lowered
his head and shook it, like a horse in a paddock.

"What're you doin'!?" Up swept Mary's voice again. "I don't fuckin' believe you!" Nobody had heard Mary swear before, either, and everyone who was now settled behind doors cracked slightly open looked at their roommates and shook their heads. *"Otis!"*

"I can't, Mary." His head was so low now his dark eyes were hidden. "I just can't."

"What kind of man are you?" she shouted. There was more than a little hysteria in her voice.

"Not that kind, I guess." Simple words from Otis but they infuriated Mary. She reached out and threw a slap at his heavy head. She cupped him behind his ear, but he didn't raise his head, didn't move much at all.

Mary steamed a moment longer, then dashed back into their hotel room. Then she was dragging a huge suitcase down the thin-carpeted hallway. The corner of the paisley-cloth-covered bag bounced randomly like a wild rubber ball as she furiously tugged it behind her. They were on the fifth floor, and when she got to the elevator, she started jabbing at the brass button. Nothing immediately happened, and she poked her finger over and over at it. Then she started pacing wildly.

Finally, the elevator came. By then everyone on the floor was out in the hallway. Mary spun around and addressed them just as the elevator doors opened. "You're all losers!" Mary cried. "All of your stinkin' asses. It's over for you all, and you're too stupid to even see it." She yanked her bag inside the car. "Especially you, you goddamn Otis Handler!"

Then she was gone.

Now the Cavalcade was gathered in the hallway, moving a little tentatively, shaking their heads as you would right after a surprise thunderclap had exploded directly above.

Esmé got to Otis first, along with Candy Wilson, the bandleader, and Robert Warwick.

"What's goin' on?" Candy said.

Otis didn't say a word; he looked more shocked than anyone else.

"Otis?" Esmé reached out and touched him lightly on the shoulder. "Otis, what was she so worked up about?"

"And where's she going?" Robert said to the still uncommunicative man.

"I can't talk," he finally said, and slammed his way back into his own hotel room.

Bee Williams, who was staying on the third floor but had been waiting downstairs with Trip by the bus, got off the elevator, the one that Mary had just left by.

"Hey, what's goin' on here?" she cried. "All of you, we got to get goin'. We got us a show to do."

Nobody moved.

"What's wrong?"

"Did you see Mary?" Robert said.

"Mary?" Bee pursed her brow. "Was that *Mary*?"

"She and Otis had some kind of huge fight," Esmé said, "and she stormed out of here."

"I—I saw somebody rush past the bus, yeah. Thought it was Mary, but when she kept on goin'—" Bee bristled, pulled herself up straight. "O.K., what is going on here?"

Nobody spoke.

"I want answers right now. You said it was about Mary and Otis?" Nods all around. "O.K., where is he?"

Linda Strong of the Daisies pointed toward the tight-shut door. Bee went right up and rapped loudly on it three times. "Otis!" She rapped again. "Otis, it's Bee, come on out!"

Nothing.

"Otis, we got us a show to do. You come and tell me what's goin' on."

Still nothing. Bee grabbed the handle, twisted it right, then left. The door wouldn't open for her. She banged on it again, calling Otis's name. No response. The hallway was filled with Cavalcaders. Buzz of the Shags called out, "You want me to break it down?"

Bee stood back. She shook her head. "When that boy comes out, you send him to me. You hear?"

Abashed nods all around

"What do you think?" Esmé said to Robert as the troupe shuffled back to their rooms.

"I think that if we thought we had trouble before, we got more of the damn thing now." Robert raised himself on his toes, stretching, almost preening, though there was no pride in him, just an anxious energy. Even with him on his toes, his eyes were barely on a level with Esmé's. "Eddie, that's what *I* think."

✳ ✳ ✳ ✳ ✳

WHEN THE HALLWAY was clear, Robert went up to the door to Otis's room. He pulled a plastic card out of his wallet, turned so his back was to the door, reached behind him, jiggered the card in the door crack, then gave Esmé a wink. The door swung back. Robert slipped in, and Esmé tagged along.

"O.K., Oat, we gotta talk. What happened?"

The large-chested singer was on his bed, visibly distraught. His eyes were puffy, and he kept rubbing his nose. He was also drawing furiously on a cigarette. He didn't seem that surprised to see Robert in his room. "Like I told you, I don't want to say nothing about it."

"You gotta. We have the show, it's going on in—" Robert checked his watch, a large-dialed affair with a crystal that caught and flicked back the overhead light—"little over an hour."

Otis just lay there, his head hung low.

"Tell me this, Mary's not coming back, right? Not going to perform tonight?" No response. "Oat, come on, think of the rest of us."

The big man sighed. "She's not going to perform anymore—at all."

"She's—" Esmé said.

"Yeah, Eddie, she's gone."

"Jesus! Where?"

Otis breathed deep through his nose; both Esmé and Robert heard the air whistle in. "I can't say."

"Why not?" Robert insisted.

The big man's eyes teared. He sat there, his eyes glistening, looking so sad Esmé felt her heart ache.

"I just can't say." He looked up, his cheeks wet. "I—I promised her."

"Does it matter, Robert?" Esmé said. "She's gone—we have to fill her spot."

"How can we fill it this late? With who?"

"Then we go right around her. Talk to Candy, we can all work something out."

Robert blew out a slow stream of air. He nodded at Esmé, then turned back to Otis. "Oat, you gotta tell me, what did she mean when she said, 'What kind of man—' "

Esmé nudged Robert with a fast elbow then, and he looked over at her. She was shaking her head, thinking as loud as she could, Don't ask him that. Don't ask him why she said. . . .

Otis had heard Robert. He glowered at his fellow Cravattes, then said, straight at Esmé, "At least I'm not the kind of man who likes to dress up like a *girl*."

Otis snarled out the last word. Esmé looked at him; his eyes were sharp as knives.

"Not like some little pansy boy. Not like a nelly who can't *wait* to pull on his nylons."

Esmé took a step back, shocked at his sudden vehemence, but Otis followed her. Up went his fists. Fury twisted his lips. My God, is he going to hit me? Her own hands fluttered before her.

"Otis," Robert cried. "Otis!"

Esmé took another step back, balling her own fists. She'd won her battles back on the schoolyard, but that was against little kids—girls. This was a big, rageful man snarling crazily through his beard. For a second she could just feel it, the sting of his punch. She brought a hand to her cheek—

But at the last minute Otis pulled back. His fists unclenched and hung before him like lost birds.

"Dammit!" Robert said, jumping between the two Cravattes. "Eddie here is helping us." He shook his head. "What the hell do you think you're doing? What's wrong with you?"

But Otis was spent. He looked stunned. In a voice like a siren winding down he said, "Oh, God, I don't—don't know what I'm doing. Eddie, can you—"

Esmé stepped forward now and put her hand on Otis's shoulder. He quaked under her touch; seemed to shrink right before her. She knew he hadn't meant what he'd said; that losing Mary had simply shaken him to his soul. She looked at him now with nearly bottomless pity. "It's all right," she said.

Otis was hangdog silent, then he turned to Robert and said softly, "I don't know what got into me. I'm so—" Tears ran, and Otis buried his head.

Robert and Esmé looked from Otis to each other, and their thoughts were clear and in harmony: We'll simply forget what just happened. The problem is Mary's gone and the show's in an hour. . . .

"Listen, Oat," Robert said, "you'll be O.K., I promise. And we're fine, too—don't worry. Now rest a bit. But . . . we're gonna need you on the bus in twenty minutes. The Cravattes need you. You gonna be there?"

Esmé leaned toward her friend and put a hand on his shoulder. Otis lifted his eyes wearily. "I'll try, yeah."

"That's the trooper," Esmé said. "Come on, Robert, let's get everyone else ready."

✳ ✳ ✳ ✳ ✳

CANDY WILSON MADE the decision to extend everyone's act; fortunately, they'd been rehearsing extra songs anyway, since the show had already been decimated. This was never so clear to Esmé as when she saw the poster backstage at the Capitol Arena. Across the top in bright green writing it read:

THE GREATEST SHOW OF STARS FOR '64

THE FABULOUS FDL SOUL CAVALCADE

ALL YOUR FAVORITE ARTISTS

LIVE AND ONSTAGE!

Then below in big blobs of red and orange were the performers. Highest up, above a silhouette of the girls in line in their party dresses, Maisy Columbine stepped forward, her bubble hair poking into the words THE DAISIES. To the left was Orlando Calabrese, his smooth hair slicked back, his eyes moony and lusty at once; to the right was Mary Hardy, just a head shot, with her collar high up her neck, her teenage flip hairdo insouciant in its own little bubble of pink. In the middle of the poster were the Cravattes, full body shots with them in trademarked dance mode. Esmé saw herself second from the right, between Robert Warwick and Otis Handler. Below them with just head shots were the old guys, the Shags.

The poster near broke her heart. Look what had happened. Maisy was gone, Orlando—sweet Orlando—and now Mary Hardy. The show's lineup was simply the Shags opening, the Cravattes' rich harmonies second, and then to close it all out the Daisies (with Priscilla, Esmé, and the other girls trying to do their best). It must have crossed Robert's— maybe everybody's—mind to shut down the whole tour. But they were just heading into the homestretch, with this second date in Washington, one night in Philly, and then the final stop: three nights and one matinee at the crown jewel of the circuit, Harlem's Apollo Theater.

In the dankest of swampy Southern nights early in the tour Esmé would sit on the bus trying in vain to sleep, thinking, O.K., we get through this, we get to play the Apollo. She knew she wasn't alone. And she was glad that as weakened and grief-burdened as they were, the whole Cavalcade was pressing on.

"How quick can you change?" she heard in her ear as she stood there dreamily before the out-of-date poster.

"Excuse me?" She turned, and there was Robert.

"I'm thinkin', Eddie, how quick can you get out of your suit and into that, um, dress."

"Damn, you're right, I don't have Mary between us and the Daisies anymore."

"Should I have Candy do an instrumental or two?"

Esmé winced. "Well, one probably wouldn't hurt." She smiled at Robert. "It's the . . . panty hose."

He made a face.

"What?" she said.

"You and that dress." His fine features were all squinched up. "I don't feel at all like Otis, but I—I don't think I could do it." He grimaced. "No, I gotta say, I'm amazed how well you've adapted to, um, Maisy's clothes."

"The show must go on," Esmé said with a laugh.

"You're a trouper."

A smile. "Thanks."

Robert smiled at her, and then Priscilla Bondrais, down the backstage hall, started beckoning to him. He gave Esmé a nod, then got up to go solve Priscilla's problem, whatever it could be.

"Don't worry, Robert," Esmé called after him. "We'll kill 'em!"

Robert didn't turn or say anything, just walked toward Priscilla as fast as he could; but to Esmé's eyes, he looked alarmingly stooped and worn down.

* * * * *

THE FUNNY THING was that the show was better this night than in South Carolina, tighter, yet wilder and more impetuous; each act—though there were only the three, the Shags, the Cravattes, and the new Daisies—passionate and soaring. The band played furiously, the girl singers shimmied and koko-bopped, the guys strutted chins high and in perfect formations. The audience fell into the groove from the first downbeat, and their shouts and the clamor between numbers, even during them, were loud and heartfelt. Soul music, when hot and perfervid, is just that: music that rouses the soul . . . and on this night the faith was in the music, its own brilliant congregation; and more than entertainment, there was testifying in the hall, a swell of transported bodies shaking and shouting with so much abandon the floor shook.

"Wow!" was all Esmé could say when she and the Daisies finally sang their final encore, joined by the Shags and the three-member Cravattes (was anyone missing their dainty, high-voiced tenor on that churning stage?), and the whole troupe ran off the stage, breathless, skin glistening with sweat, hair tumbling out of sprayed perfection, wigs wobbling, everyone possessed by the magic and mystery that had just risen out of them and suffused the whole hall.

"That was something," Priscilla said next to her. "Was that the best damn show ever!"

Even Otis Handler was beaming. "Great job," Robert Warwick called to him, and Esmé, coming over in her borrowed dress and trying, as always, to walk that fine line of being a man dressed as a girl, forgot herself and hugged the big man, trying to reach her hands around her back.

"Eddie, come on," Otis went, but he kept his giddy smile. The outburst before the show was forgotten. Nothing even needed to be said. The music could always do that to them all.

But the high didn't last. The troupe returned to their hotel and quickly retreated to their rooms. Robert hung back in the lobby, but Esmé, still bunking with him, took the elevator to their room. She quickly changed out of her suit, putting on her man's pajamas and using the bathroom sink, slicking her hair back with water. She'd been keeping her

breasts pushed down with the gauze, then when she was supposed to be a girl, putting a bra on over the tight gauze and
filling it with tissue. She made it clear to the rest of the
troupe that it was simply tissue they were seeing lift the
bodice of Maisy's dress. In the bathroom now she took the
bra and tissue off, but kept the gauze in place under the loose
pajama tops.

She was in bed when Robert came in. He went right into
the bathroom. When he came out, he said, "Eddie, you
asleep?"

Esmé, under the covers, said she wasn't.

Robert sat down at the edge of her bed, closer than he'd
been before. He had something in his hands and held them
out.

"I found this in the bathroom."

Even looking closely, Esmé couldn't see a thing there.
"What is it?"

"Your hair." He held a thumb and middle finger out
pinched; there must have been a few strands there.

Esmé pressed her elbows tight against her side. "Um, my
hair?" she said as low as she could. She had one quick
thought: Could he be seeing something about my deception
. . . in my hair?

"You have to be more careful."

She shifted in the bed. "Robert, I—"

"Nobody told you?"

"Told me what?"

"About what can happen."

"With my hair?"

"Listen, Eddie, I know you're still pretty new here with
us, but we always have to keep in mind that we're stars. We
have a record on the charts. All kinds of things can happen."

"Robert, I—" Esmé shook her head. That was a relief,
him calling her Eddie, but she still didn't know what he was
getting at.

"With the girls. The fans."

Esmé gave her head a vigorous shake.

"I've heard stories," Robert went on. "Never actually happened to me—" a curious wince then, as if so short and fine-featured, he wasn't as sexy as his singing mates "—but it did to both Mitch and Otis, last time we were on the road. Girls snuck into our hotel rooms, got locks of their hair, and then did stuff to it."

"Stuff?"

"Hoodoo stuff." Robert carefully took the strands of Esmé's hair and twisted them into a ball with his fingers. He got up off the bed and headed toward the bathroom, then paused at the door. "Took their hairs and went home and hexed them."

"Hexed?" Esmé's voice rose. "Like how?"

"Turn their luck around. Get 'em in trouble with ladies—like what happened with Otis and Mary." Robert was moving toward the bathroom, his fine-featured face backlit by the light there. He had a faint silvery penumbra around his tight-processed hair. "Just turn 'em all around."

"Robert, do you believe that?"

Now he disappeared into the bathroom, then Esmé heard the flush of the toilet. "Hey, they swear on it," he said, coming back out.

"But do *you* believe it?"

"I believe—" A wary shrug. "I believe you can't be too careful."

Esmé was sitting full up now. She kept the covers as close to her neck as possible. "You know, Robert, we haven't talked all that much. I mean, personally." She cleared her throat. Is this how a guy would put it? She felt her cheeks tighten, then went on anyway. "Are you really scared of being hexed by your hair?"

"I know what you're saying, yeah." Robert stood looking at Esmé, hands on his hips. "But it's a wider, stranger world out there than anybody can think. And to have somebody messin' with me? Damn right I don't want that."

This caught at a well-buried question for Esmé. "Let me ask you—" she shifted again "—you got a girlfriend back in Detroit?"

Robert was moving toward the bed but now he stopped. "Sure I do. I'm a Cravatte. I got a lot of girlfriends." He lifted his delicate chin. "How about you?"

Esmé wasn't expecting that. "Um, no, I don't," she said. She made a bright face. "I don't have anyone."

"Then maybe we *should* be leavin' your hairs around." Robert gave out a tight laugh.

Esmé rolled her eyes. "So tell me about them. 'A lot of girlfriends?' How many is that?"

"Plenty." Robert had tilted his head up in a brazen way. "We're the Cravattes. You see how they come up after shows—"

"But I'm meaning somebody . . . special. You know, like one person."

"You got yourself a lot of women, then you sure got yourself *one* woman." Robert was speaking quickly. "It's logical. It's like . . . math."

"Robert?"

His eyes dropped, then he sighed softly. "I don't know, Eddie. I'm just awfully busy, you know." A deep frown. "But no, there ain't anybody special."

"Maybe you should be leavin' *your* hairs around, too." Esmé winked at him, but Robert didn't wink back. "But . . . nobody, Robert? I'm surprised."

He stood there stone still for a moment, then let out a long sigh. "Oh, I've had lots of—" He started out in his high, braggodacio voice, but then like a balloon the air just went out of it. "I don't know." Another shrug. "Most of the time, Eddie, I just think I haven't met the right—" Robert stopped speaking, no air left.

"What'll she be like?"

Robert grimaced and turned aside. "This is getting a little—"

"What, personal?"

Robert was silent.

"What's wrong with that?" Esmé said. Robert made a display of taking off his jacket, one arm extended, then the other. "Come on, you can talk to me. We're friends, buddies, aren't we?"

Robert winced, then lifted an eyebrow.

"Robert, you're a sensitive guy, come on." She was almost cooing at him.

"Sensitive, yeah, that's right. Lucky me."

"I'm not going to say anything," Esmé said, understanding now. This had to be the way guys talked about deep things like this, all bashful asides and tortured winces. "I'm not going to put you down, man."

Robert looked at her, half plaintively, then finally gave a light, forced laugh. "You mean, what do I dream of?" He winked at Esmé. "How about somebody who's *'Sunny as a parfait. Perfect as a summer's day.'*" Robert floated his tune lightly on the air.

Esmé smiled. "Well, yeah, as long as your eyes be goin' wide."

"But, seriously, well...." There was another tortured wince. "Um, somebody who ... understands me." Robert paused. "That sounds stupid, doesn't it?"

"Not to me." Esmé spoke with all her sincerity.

He waited a second before going on. "Well, also someone I can talk to, easily, think things through with." A private smile. "Just hang with comfortably, you know what I mean?"

"A girl who's like a friend, right?"

"A friend, sure, but a looker, too." Robert popped his eyes open, then leaned over and gave Esmé a poke in the arm. "Gotta be the looker, man."

"Gotta," she said half-heartedly. She knew she looked good, well, most of the time she knew it; just right then she was curious what Robert would be saying about her if she were dressed as herself—as a girl.

"So, how 'bout you?" Robert said quickly. "What're you looking for?"

Esmé thought about her recent romantic history, especially about a boy named Willie Lee Reed, a blues singer she'd had a huge but ultimately unrequited crush on in Chicago a year ago, in spring 1963. She'd fallen for that boy's energy, the magic in his blues-playing fingers, his chin-up cockiness; but when it was clear she wasn't going to have him, she'd also felt a wide sweeping relief—he was probably just too messed up for her.

She couldn't tell Robert about that boy, obviously. Then there was of course her crush on Orlando, which she couldn't tell Robert about, either.

"Well, um, pretty much the same things you want, I guess. Someone I can talk easy with." A vision of Orlando came to her then, and she said, "But of course, a good-looker, too. Some guy—um, girl." Esmé blanched at her mistake, hammered down the final word. "Some girl who has it, you know? The eyes." She was speaking fast and blushing. Had Robert heard her mistake? "I gotta thing for the eyes. Gotta be able to lose myself in their eyes."

"Sounds like you could've gone for Maisy." Robert had a bright, winking, sardonic light in his own orbs. "She's *all* eyes."

"And all teeth, too." Esmé laughed. "Like a vampire."

"I feel sorry for Orlando, a little."

"Oh, me, too."

They shared a good laugh together, then Robert said, "You know, Eddie, it's easy to talk with you—easier than with the other guys."

"Thanks. With you, too."

"Yeah," Robert said, "it's sort of funny. Find somebody I like to talk with, who seems to understand me . . . and he's my roommate." He shrugged again, this time louder and more vivid than before. "Hang in there, man, and don't worry. We'll find those women. They're out there somewhere."

Esmé just gave him a smile.

Robert started undressing then. He unbuttoned his tight pants and untucked the pink silk shirt with the wide, sharp-pointed collar that the whole group had worn that night. Out came the shirttails, then he unbuttoned the shirt. He wasn't wearing an undershirt, and his ebony flesh was nearly hairless. His chest had a slight gleam from leftover sweat from the performance. Esmé started to turn her eyes away modestly, then realized a guy probably wouldn't even be noticing.

Robert whisked off his pants. He wore tight, plum-colored shorts with white stripes down the side. Esmé couldn't help but notice the thick bulge at the front. His legs were also nearly hairless, thin and sleek. He didn't wear pajamas and just stood there naked except for his shorts.

"Are you going to bed now?" Esmé asked.

"In a minute." Like that, Robert dropped to the floor and started doing push-ups. He held his body board-straight, dropping his chin within an inch of the carpeted floor, then lifting his whole torso. Esmé had a perfect vision of his tight buttocks rising and falling.

"Whoooo, I needed that," he finally said. Esmé in spite of herself had started roughly counting; she'd left off at fifty.

"Lots of tension?" she said.

"You can say that again."

"I don't think I will," Esmé said.

"Will what?"

"Say it again."

Robert looked puzzled for a second. He had reached down and was moving his hand underneath his shorts, arranging things. This time Esmé couldn't help herself, she had to look away. "Oh," Robert said, "you're goofin' on me."

"Not really." Esmé dared to look back. Oh, no, he was still playing with his balls. "Just trying to lighten things up."

"God knows we need it." And there, he was done. He whisked back the bedsheets and threw himself under them, pulling them up to his neck.

"So, what's up tomorrow?" Esmé said, relieved.

"Bus to Philly. You ever been there?"

She shook her head.

"Got a lot to do. Get your record pressed up, for one."

That brought a slow smile to Esmé. "My record. Almost forgot about that."

"I have somebody I want us to see. Deejay named Longbone Martin. He's a power in Philly. Think I can get you in that dress, get you to come with me?"

"I'm there," Esmé said.

"Good." Robert clicked off the light between their beds, and the room was dark. "Night, Eddie."

"Hey, bro," Esmé said. "Good night."

Chapter Twelve

Thursday, May 7— Philadelphia

BEE'S FINGER TWIRLED the dial of the black telephone.
Now that they were in Philadelphia, it was time to call up
Dick Clark Productions to find out about getting the
Cavalcade on *American Bandstand*. She wished Bones were
here to deal with Clark, but he wasn't, and so she made the
call.

"Mr. Dick Clark, please," she told the receptionist. If
she'd learned anything in the music business, it was always to
talk only to the guy who carried the whole company around
in the tattered notebook in his back pocket—like Bones did.

"Who's calling, please?" High-pitched, nasal voice.

"This is Bee Williams from Fleur-de-Lys Records."

"Just a moment, please."

One moment, two moments—a flood of moments. Bee
was worrying she'd been cut off when there was a crackle on
the phone.

"Miss Williams, I'm Edith Ross, Mr. Clark's assistant."
The voice on the phone was pleasant and round-toned,
though with a steel-sharp snap to it. "How can I help you?"

"I wish it was Mr. Bones calling you, but you might've
heard about his accident—"

"We did, and we're very concerned," Miss Ross said, her
voice lower, softer. "How is he?"

"Still in the coma. No better, but thank the Lord, no
worse."

"He's in our prayers, Miss Williams."

"You can call me Bee."

"Bee."

Bee was used to dealing with men, all kinds of men, cigar

smokers, fat guys with gold chains, guys packing guns, but it was a little unusual to be talking to a woman in power. She liked it. "Seems that Mr. Bones had an arrangement with Mr. Clark that when we came to Philly with the Soul Cavalcade, we'd be on *Bandstand*."

"I'm aware of that, yes. I spoke with Mr. Chapman last month."

"Well, here we are!"

"Congratulations."

Yes, this dealing with a woman was a whole other experience. "And we'd love to come on your show," Bee said.

"Tell me, how long are you here for?"

"Only today. We're playing the Apollo tomorrow night."

"Oh." A long pause. "Well, it's too late to book today."

"Too—" Bee glared into the phone. "But I know Bones gave you the date. May 7. We had a deal."

"Yes, Bee, um, Miss Williams. But the deal was that you had to have Top 15 songs."

"We got 'em." Bee heard her voice ratchet up a few tones. "Top 10 songs. Cravattes up there with *Doorbell* at Number 9, Daisies at Number 5 with *Man Alive*."

"The Daisies? Maisy and the Daisies?"

Bee knew what this Miss Ross was saying. "The Daisies. Just them, the Daisies. Hitmakers!"

There was a pause on the other end, and then Miss Ross said, "Well, Mr. Clark tells me he also expected a Number 1 record."

Bee shook her head. Why was this woman giving her a hard time? Damn, it was supposed to be easier than this. "We're tryin', Miss Ross. And you lettin' us drop by today, that'd help us a whole lot."

"I'm sorry, but as I said, it's too late for today. Maybe if you'd called—"

"We've been all tied up with Bones's . . . and just getting the show. . . ." Bee thought fast. "O.K., here's an idea. How about we come down here again after we play the Apollo. It's only through the weekend. We could be back here on Monday."

A long pause.

"Or Tuesday. Any day next week."

Bee could picture Miss Ross's hand over the receiver. Then she was back. "I'm sorry, Miss Williams, but we don't have any place for FDL on our show right now."

"Right—" Bee snorted. "What're you telling me, woman?"

"Just that, Miss Williams. We respect FDL, yes, but we can't put you on the show. That's it."

"But why? There were promis—"

"I have to go now, Miss—"

"Wait! I don't understand." Bee was breathing fast, speaking fast. "We got one of the hottest labels in the country. We got really great performers out there in the country tearing up a storm. We got every damn thing you need, Miss Ross!"

"Goodbye." And with that the woman hung up.

Bee sat there, in a kind of shock. Had she approached this wrong? No, she was respectful but firm—only way to be. Had she said something off-putting? Of course not. Had FDL done anything to bother Dick Clark? What could that be? And why wouldn't a show whose bread and butter was hit artists coming on and lip-synching tunes turn down two Top 10 groups? Bee didn't get it. Why wouldn't *American Bandstand* be all over that?

Bee saw fingers—long, well-manicured, white fingers—stretching out. Could they reach that far? All the way to *Bandstand*? She pursed her lips and blew a long, worried breath into air.

✳ ✳ ✳ ✳ ✳

IT WAS ESMÉ'S first radio station. She'd seen pictures of broadcast studios, and they had her expecting a large, open room, gleaming with metal, a shiny aluminum board with lots of lights and switches, mikes on booms swooping down from the ceiling, rows of turntables, and piles of records everywhere. Well . . . the records were there, but everything else looked like one of her old teachers' writing studios: a couple of slat-back chairs, a wooden desk with only two microphones on it, two turntables, and one desk lamp with what couldn't be more than a 25-watt bulb. The deejay's room, as Robert and Esmé were ushered into it, was almost cave dark, and the man who stood up to greet them was as big and black as a bear.

Longbone Martin set a fuming cigar in a crystal ashtray that covered almost a quarter of the desk, then held out his plump, fleshy hand. Esmé let her own be swallowed up.

"Hey, how you doin', sweetheart?" the big man said. He wore a black cowboy hat with a hatband of hand-tooled silver disks, and Esmé was surprised to see in the dusky light that he was affecting other cowboy garb: a pair of black boots with red piping in the image of girls smoking cigars, and the hint of a Texan accent even though Robert had explained that Longbone was all North Philly. "Robert, you got yourself good taste in the ladies. Better than the one I last saw you with, eh?"

"Robert?" This was Esmé playing the girl, *enjoying* playing the girl.

"He means Bee," Robert said quickly. "I told you about that. We were on our first East Coast tour."

"Yeah, she was some fine piece of woman." Longbone snorted. "Sure there wan't nothin' between you two?"

"Longbone, please." Robert looked flustered.

"Here, little lady, you have yourself a seat." The deejay gestured to one of the slat-back chairs. He was in a large leather swivel chair, and he reached over and picked up his cigar again. "Robert, you too." Then he took a long puff, smoke cascading gray-and-white into the dusky room.

When they'd settled, Longbone reached over and pulled a 45 off a pile that stood at least three feet tall. That was three feet of thin round discs. The whole stack wobbled but didn't fall.

"Gimme a second." He moved his mouth right into his silver bullet microphone, then said, "All right, you hipsters and dipsters, this song is goin' out to all of you on this sweet Philadelphia night." Into the mike he spoke slowly, in a deep-rolling voice, like a stream meandering timeless down a high mountain. All trace of the Texas accent was gone. "It's *South Street*, by our very own Orlons. Rosetta, baby, I love ya, darlin'!"

The song that played asked the undying question of where all the hippist were hanging? The answer: Philly's own cheesesteak-lovin' South Street.

As the song bounced along through the large speakers suspended high in the dusky little room, the deejay turned abruptly toward Robert and said, "O.K., Mr. Genius, quiz time again."

Robert had been reaching into his bag for one of the copies of *My Eyes Go Wide* he'd had emergency pressed-up that morning. He looked up with a scowl.

"Don't make me that face, Mr. Smarty-pants." Longbone turned to Esmé. "Mr. Robert Warwick here, he thinks he knows his music. Last time I gave him a little test, and I'm gonna do it again. O.K., Roberto, what was the Robins' Number 1 hit?"

Robert lit up and said right away, "*Double Crossing Blues*, with the Johnny Otis Quintette and Little Esther." Quick smile. "Next question?"

"O.K., O.K. Gimme their next and last hit, and . . . what group did they become?"

Robert didn't miss a beat. "*Smokey Joe's Café*, and then with Jerry Lieber and Mike Stoller they became that great group the Coasters."

"Not bad, son. You been keepin' up on your history. I'm impressed."

Robert finally pulled out the white-labeled 45. But Longbone's attention had swung full-on to Esmé. She felt his eyes like headlights rushing at her.

"And who is this pretty little lady?"

Esmé, flattered, smiled and was about to give her name when Robert said, "This is Ess-maaay." That's how he referred to her, the drawn-out hissing *ssss*, the long *aaaay*. In truth, each time she heard him say it, she felt a little shiver run down her back. "She's our latest FDL artist."

Longbone took Esmé's hand, lifted it to his lips, and gave it a kiss. Robert gave Esmé a look she read as, Eddie, he's kissing your hand! She lifted an eyebrow. Then Longbone turned back to Robert.

"So what brings you to Philly, little buddy? I know y'all are playin' the Civic Auditorium, but I hear it's long sold out."

"We're here about Ess-maaay. She's got—"

"You talk, darlin'?" Longbone interrupted, keeping his eyes on Esmé.

"I do, Mr. Longbone."

"That's simply Loooonnnng-boooonne to you, sugar." A cloud of smoke accompanied his words. The way he drawled out his name made Esmé blush in spite of herself. "So, O.K., son, you got yourself a charming singer here. Ess-maaay indeed. No last name?"

"Well, I have one, of course," Esmé said. "But Robert here likes that way of saying it: Ess-maaay. We think it fits."

"Robert, I got me one question," Longbone said, whirling on the songwriter. "This ain't some made-up artist you're comin' up with, is it?" His voice was gruff. Then he turned and gazed straight on at Esmé. His look was so intense and knowing that she wondered what he could see. If she were masquerading as Eddie Days, she had the notion he'd be seeing right through her. But what was there to see through now that she was a girl again?

Robert looked alarmed, though, at Longbone's piercing gaze. "You willing to listen to her?" He held the fresh-pressed 45 in his hand, fanned it back and forth as if he were unconsciously trying to get a fire going. "Truth is in the grooves, Mr. Longbone." He smirked a little. "It's always in the grooves—now where did I hear that before?"

Longbone was silent a long moment, then he let out a loud, guffawing laugh. "I taught him that, sugar," he said to Esmé. A toot on his cigar, then he reached out and took the small black disc. "And there ain't nothin' truer."

The Orlons' rocking tune had run down on the turntable, and Longbone leaned back, flicked up another 45 off his stack—he held both Esmé's tune and the other record in his hand at once—and put one of them on the machine. As he did this, he turned to the mike and said in his deep radio voice, "O.K., Philadelphia, we're gonna take us a little trip now. Movin' out to Dee-troit. Got us a great song from there, a really hot, hot song—"

For a second Esmé held her breath; she sensed Robert doing the same.

"And it's called *My Guy*, by that Motown sweetheart, Mary Wells."

The room filled with the finger-snapping sounds of that current Number 1 song. Esmé's white-labeled disc was still in Longbone's hand. He gave the singer and the songwriter a wink as he turned his mike off.

Longbone had an old plastic RCA 45 player, with a perma-nent large cylinder on it, at the edge of his desk, and almost as if he were tossing a horseshoe, the deejay flipped the disc onto it. A slide of a button, and the brown arm lifted, the record dropped, and the needle fell. Out came Robert's slippery back-beat, Henry and Norris's horns, and then Esmé's—or Ess-maaaay's—whiskery voice. For half a minute there the song played in competition with *My Guy*; then Longbone turned down the radio song and just listened to *My Eyes Go Wide*.

It was terrifying to Esmé to hear her own voice and song going up against this proven Motown singer. She'd always liked Mary Wells, from her first hit, *The One Who Really Loves You*, to this new one that simply said, Hit! And yet— *Eyes Go Wide* didn't sound that bad up against it. Not that bad at all. In fact, it sounded damn. . . .

She looked over at Longbone, who listened intently for a few more seconds before his shoulders started twitching subtly to the beat. His expression was blank, but his gaze, Esmé could tell, was focused. When the song kicked into the bridge, he cocked his head back and lifted an eye, then clearly winked at Robert and Esmé.

Esmé's spirits flew sky-high.

Longbone seemed to know just how long *My Guy* was playing, and when it ended, he reached over and put another 45 on his turntable. *Eyes Go Wide* was winding down the chorus. When it was over, Longbone leaned back in his chair, then reached up and lifted off his cowboy hat. Esmé was startled to see that his head was totally shaved, a shiny black dome. It took her a second to hear what he was saying.

"Well, it's got the beat." Longbone waved his hat in front of his face, then set it back on his remarkable bald head. "Love the melody, and the words—hey, they're pretty clever. I'm not surprised, Little Robert."

Robert, though clearly trying not to, was bouncing in his seat. A big smile glowed on his face. Then Robert said, "And he sings it great, doesn't—" Did he actually say *"he"*? Esmé threw Robert an alarmed but amused look, and he recovered. "Doesn't she?"

"Well, yeah, I'd say so. I think *she* does." Longbone's thick eyebrow was cranked high. He threw Esmé a big smile. "Hey, I can tell you're a girl, even if Mr. Hit Record Producer over here ain't sure."

Esmé stifled a laugh, knowing it was at her friend's expense. But Robert was clearly thinking all business.

"So, you really like it?"

"Oh, yeah." Longbone leaned back. "I'd say it stands up nicely to that new Mary Wells."

"You mean it?" Esmé said.

"I don't say nothin', sugar, I don't mean," Longbone drawled through a puff of cigar smoke, and Esmé believed him.

"And you can help us out?" Robert leaned forward. "Like, give it a play on your show."

"Welllll—" There was a sudden cooling in the room. Longbone looked down at his cowboy boots. "I might be able to give you a play or two."

"A play or two?"

"Sure." A tentative smile. "We can do that. How about tomorrow?"

"I was hoping you could get it on the air right away, I mean, like while we're sitting here. You know, make a little production out of it. You'd be having the world exclusive, Longbone." Robert was nearly jumping out of his seat. "You could even interview her. You know, great new singer. I mean, it is great, isn't it? Ess-maaaay does such a fine job—"

Longbone held up the disc, looked at the blank label. "This is going out as a Fleur-de-Lys record, right?"

"Of course."

A long sigh. Robert looked at Esmé, who looked back. Something was obviously bugging Longbone, but neither of them could see what it could be.

"Well, O.K., I'm a man of my word. I said I'll be happy to give it a play. Couple times. Tomorrow. Maybe late at night." Longbone handed the 45 back to Robert, then reached over and dropped another one off his pile onto the official turntable. "Best I can do, folks." He gave them a tight smile. "Now if you'll excuse me, I got me a show to do."

He held the arm over the spinning disc, then said into his on-air mike, "O.K., you boppers and whompers, we got us somethin' a li'l different now. It's by that new beat group from England, been whistlin' up the charts. Oh, yeah, I know, they's white, and white people don't got nooooo kind of beat. But listen up, you cool cats and backdoor rats, this record, it jumps. Calls itself a little *Please, Please Me*, and if that ain't what it's all about, you pleasin' me, and, baby, *meeeee* pleasin' you, well I don't know why I'm sittin' here." The deejay dropped the needle, then sent out a high, chortling laugh over the Beatles' chiming voices. "This be the Looonnnng Booooooone . . . comin' straight and hard right at ya!"

✳ ✳ ✳ ✳ ✳

"SO, WHAT WAS that about?" Esmé said. She was in a rented car with Robert. They'd just left the WRMC studios and were on their way to the pressing plant where Robert had dropped off *My Eyes Go Wide* that morning.

"I don't know." Robert was at the wheel, and they were jouncing over the spring-weather-potholed streets of South Philadelphia.

"I mean, he really seemed to like the record. Why wouldn't he play it?"

Robert shook his head. "A lot of funny stuff going on."

Esmé raised her chin. "Do you think—"

"We really don't know," Robert said, interrupting her. "But I agree. It felt awfully . . . funny."

"Damn!"

"But Longbone did like the record," Robert said. "He wasn't faking that." He moved his head forward, peered through the curved window glass. "Now where was that place?" They were on a street of two- and three-story brick row houses. "I remember there were a lot of warehouses around. Shit."

"What's the address?"

Robert read it off the invoice.

"We don't have a map, do we?" Esmé said.

"Don't worry, I'll find it—I'm good at that stuff."

Spoken just like a guy, Esmé thought, though she kept quiet.

"So," Robert said, "I've been thinking. Want to tell me more about your cousin? The one you mentioned the other day."

"Esmé?"

"Essmay, yeah. The one whose name we're puttin' on the disc."

"What do you want to know?"

"I don't know. Whatever you can tell me." Robert was moving slowly through an intersection, looking to his left and right. He pulled himself up an inch or so to get a clear view. He evidently didn't see anything recognizable and slowly moved straight ahead. "What's she look like?"

"Good," Esmé said. And why's he interested in that? "She's a good-looker."

"Oh, yeah? Like what?"

"Um, well—" Esmé tried to conjure up this imaginary cousin, but went with the first thing she thought of. "She's, a, kinda got my chin, and her eyes aren't that different from mine, either—"

"You have nice eyes," Robert said, still looking intently down the street.

Esmé blushed a little. "It's a family trait. That and the chin." Without thinking she brought a hand up and touched her own chin. "My cousin's got nice long hair, sort of naturally straight. And a cute, pretty face."

"Sweet."

"Why're you asking?"

Robert didn't answer, instead saying, "This looks right. O.K., I'm gonna turn here."

They went down another block in silence, then Robert nodded to himself and said, "Yeah, I think I recognize these buildings." A sign on one read PALMETTO IMPORTS; the one next to it, DEROBERTI'S TOOL AND DIE. "Yeah, this is looking right."

Robert relaxed back into his seat. "So, O.K., tell me more," he said. "You said Essmay sings. What's her musical background?"

The choice, Esmé had figured out by now, was to start wildly making stuff up or just to describe herself. She thought: If I invent too much, I might get carried away and say something that'll come back at me. But if I stick to details about me, *my* own life, could I really screw it up?

"My cousin's sung all her life. Like I said, when I'm singing like a girl, I'm sort of thinking of her."

"Any professional experience?"

"Sure. She's in a group in Detroit—the Darlingettes."

Robert considered this for a moment, then shook his head.

"You haven't heard of them?"

"Nope."

Though she'd have been surprised if he had, this bothered Esmé. "They're really good. Three girls. With a great sound."

"I'm glad to hear that."

"You get home, you might want to audition them." Now why did she say that? That was crazy. There were no Darlingettes anymore; she had been the lead singer, and here she was already with the Cravattes and the Daisies, and with her own record as Essmay about to come out. Still, she did want to help her old friends Grace and Annette any way she could.

"That's a thought," Robert said distractedly.

His distraction annoyed her. "Did I tell you about Esmé's father?"

Robert shook his head.

"Well, it's a long story, but he's—he's the blues singer Heddy Days."

"Really?" Ah ha, that caught his interest. Heddy Days was well-known as the King of the Blues. He was based in Chicago but lately had been spending much of the year playing to enthusiastic audiences in Europe. In general the blues were hurting in these days of revitalized soul music and the incipient British Invasion, but Heddy Days remained the grandest of the classic bluesmen.

Esmé wasn't sure she should keep telling him more but couldn't help herself. "Yep. She didn't know him much growing up, but they got back together last year. You know about him, right?"

"Of course I do." Robert smiled. "I passed Longbone's test, didn't I?"

"Well, then."

"Well yourself." Robert had all his attention through the front window, but he said, "So that makes Heddy Days your uncle, right?"

"Um—" scramble, scramble "—yeah, of course."

"Cool." Right then Robert slowed the car, then turned into a driveway. The sign on the building read SOUTHSIDE RECORD SERVICES. "O.K., this is it."

Esmé followed Robert through an unmarked door, then down a long corridor into a room filled with cardboard boxes. There was a white woman there, her hair still in a Jackie Kennedy flip even though Jackie tragically was no longer First Lady, and she took Robert's invoice. They sat on torn vinyl and aluminum chairs, a floor-standing ashtray smelling fulsome between them.

"So, why so curious about my cousin?" Esmé said.

Robert wasn't looking at her but at what looked like some kind of nothing in the near distance. "Oh, just making conversation."

"Robert?"

"Eddie, nothing special. I just have a couple ideas—"

"Like—"

"Here they are," the woman said, back in the room and leading three black men with hand dollies. On them were 12 cardboard boxes.

Esmé's heart fluttered. There the records were. Robert was first to the boxes. He took the proffered razor blade from one of the hand-cart men and sliced open the top box. Out came a shiny black 45 disc. He held it up to the light, closely read the label, then passed it to Esmé.

There was the Fleur-de-Lys logo, the three-petaled iris in black over the red label. Below it was:

MY EYES GO WIDE

(R. WARWICK)

ESSMAY

Her heart leaped. She carefully held the plastic disc, noticed how the wax caught the light above; and there, wasn't that a glimmer of her own reflection in it? She had never seen anything so wonderful.

Robert, too, was bright with pride. They loaded the car with the boxes, the trunk and the backseat, too. Records were everywhere. It was on the way to the Civic Auditorium that Robert sprung one of his ideas, taking Esmé's breath away: How would she feel about going out before the audience tonight as Essmay—to try out *My Eyes Go Wide* in front of a real audience.

✳ ✳ ✳ ✳ ✳

WHEN ESMÉ AND ROBERT walked in on the rehearsal, they found a big surprise: Orlando was back.

He was standing next to a piano, with Cotton Candy Wilson at the keys, looking tall and grand and beautiful—at least as Esmé first saw him. He was wearing his trademark sweater and the tight-cut Italian slacks that accented every part of him below the waist, but as she got closer, Esmé noticed that the buttons of the sweater hung open, the shirt under it was faintly soiled, and his hair, usually close-cropped, was shaggy and in need of a trim. The expression on his face was diffident, even a little sheepish. Her heart went out to him. What *had* that Maisy Columbine done to him?

He said hello to Robert, then to Esmé, saying, "Well, yes, your eyes ain't lyin'. I am back."

"Great!" Robert said with clearly honest enthusiasm.

Orlando flashed a smile that could only be called demure, lifting his shovel chin so it was on the same angle as the collar of his Banlon shirt. "Is that you, Eddie, dressed like that?"

"Good to see you," Esmé said in her deeper man's voice. She was actually feeling quite stirred up but wanted to sound cool. "When'd you get in?"

"Just an hour ago. Took a train from New York. I hear you guys were off getting copies of a new record."

Esmé and Robert nodded, Esmé saying, "It's my first solo shot—wait till you hear it." And there it was, sneaking out: her flirtation voice, Come on, big boy, let me play you my new record. In her enthusiasm she sounded almost girlish. She told herself to cool her jets.

"I hear it's great," Orlando said. "And you're, like, faking some different voice?"

"Breeze, meet Essmay," Robert said, throwing an open palm toward Esmé. Orlando smiled, truly interested, but looking as if he was still pretty much in the dark. Robert went on: "Eddie here's recorded a song of mine, but, you know, it had to have a chick singin' it, and we were thinkin' how well he's doin' with the Daisies and all, and, well, it just came out with him as a chick." He cocked an eyebrow. "Fools me, I'll say."

"It's my God-given talent," Esmé said, smiling. "To sound just like a girl."

"A sexy gal, I bet," Orlando said.

And Esmé blushed.

"So y'all ain't mad at me?"

Robert blew a long stream of air out of his pursed mouth. "I don't think so, Breeze. We've—well, we can use all the help we can get." He stepped back. "So what did happen?"

Orlando sighed, raised himself to his full height. "Well,

Maisy and me, we went over to NRC—I guess you know that."

"Why're you back?" Esmé said.

"I don't—well, maybe they wanted her more than me. Hell, maybe she wanted them more than me." Orlando's face tightened. "But I also got really shaken about what happened with Bones." He shuddered. "People been tellin' me he's probably gonna be all right. That what you hear?"

"He's not getting any worse. Just has to come out of his—his situation." Robert made a pained face. "The doctors down there in Florida don't know when that's gonna be." A quick hopeful smile. "We're praying for him."

"Me, too."

"Did you hear anything more, Orlando, about NRC, what they might be up to?" Esmé asked.

"What do you mean?"

"He means," Robert said, clearly picking his words carefully, "that we've got more problems around here. Mary's gone—she stormed off a couple days back after a fight with Otis. And there's some indications that—"

"Oh, Mary's with them now."

"She's—" both Robert and Esmé said at once.

"With NRC, yep," Orlando said. He spoke with a curious enthusiasm, eager, it seemed, to offer up useful information to make up for his betrayal. "She showed up yesterday morning. Maisy had breakfast with her."

"Damn!" Robert muttered. He looked furious. Then he called toward the stage: "Otis!" The fellow Cravatte looked over. "Otis, hey, a second, man." When Otis trotted up, Robert said, "Do you know that Mary's with NRC now?"

The bearded singer's eyes popped. "You're kidding?"

"Breeze saw her yesterday. Right?"

Orlando nodded.

"Shit!" Otis looked down, did a shy shuffling step. "So maybe it wasn't about me that much at all."

"Shit. Shit. Shit." Robert's eyes were glaring, his nostrils fluted. He turned to Orlando. "You know, we've been hearing stuff about them trying to take over Fleur-de-Lys. You know anything about that?"

The tall singer shook his head.

"About them wooing Bones's wife—"

"I didn't hear nothin' 'bout Mrs. Bones, or—wait a minute." He scratched his long chin. "Maisy did say something. We were there, trying to cut this damn song, and. . . . Damn, what was it?"

Everyone was all ears.

"I wasn't paying much attention, she was—well, you know Maisy, she was all over the place. We were singin', and she was—" Orlando fell silent. Dark shadows flitted behind his eyes. Esmé's heart went out to him all over again. Then he brightened. "It was just something about Mrs. Bones, that she was . . . coming to New York. That's it. I didn't think nothing about it." His eyes went bright. "You think they're makin' a deal?"

"We think she is—trying to at least."

"Damn, you mean I might end up workin' for NRC after all?"

Robert and Esmé sighed. "We're doing everything we can think of," Robert said. "That's why we cut the side on Eddie—"

"Because?" Orlando interrupted.

"To prove that we can still do it. That we're going strong."

That stopped Orlando for a second. "So, Robert," he said, "you're making the decisions now?" There was a sharpening look in the tall man's eyes as he looked down at the shorter man.

Robert lifted his chin, didn't say anything.

"Robert?"

"It's not just Robert," Esmé said quickly into the whiff of tension. "I'm helping him, Bee, the whole Cavalcade. We're all pitching in to do what we can to save FDL."

Orlando held fire, kept his gaze on Robert.

"Hey, Orlando," Esmé said, feeling she had to do something. She spoke in her gentlest voice. "It was you who skipped on us. Remember?" Orlando turned toward her and set his shoulders. To Esmé's dismay now, it was she and Orlando who seemed to be squaring off.

"Eddie, it's all right," Robert said softly, moving between Esmé and Orlando. "We're just glad Breeze is back, right?" He reached over, clapped the big guy on the back. "Looking forward to anything he can do to help us."

"I'm still in the show, right?" Orlando said.

Robert held the tall man's gaze for a long, long moment. Then he spoke slowly, distinctly: "Absolutely, man. You're still in. Like I said, we need you."

Orlando took in a long breath, then he nodded. A few seconds later a light went off in his eyes. "Oh, wait," he said. "There was more to what I heard. Damn, what was that?" He squinched up his features, looked almost in pain. "Oh, right, Maisy said Bones's brother and sister was coming too."

"To New York?" This was both Robert and Esmé at once.

"Yeah."

There was silence all around, everyone lost in thought. Finally Robert spoke. "Well," he said. "Good thing that's where we're going, too."

✻ ✻ ✻ ✻ ✻

BUT FIRST THEY had the Philadelphia show to get through. Plans were quickly made to work Orlando back into the line-up, back to his old slot now right after the Cravattes, giving Esmé more time to dress as a woman. Robert was keener than ever on her going out as Essmay and singing *My Eyes Go Wide*. So tonight after the Cravattes nailed their set, Esmé ran off quick. She had a special reason to be so fast. She whisked on her taffeta-skirted dress and pink shoes and straight-haired wig, and rushed to the wings so she could catch Orlando out there singing *Our Hideaway*.

Yes, he still did it to her. His unlined forehead, wide, sexy mouth, that jutting—jutting just right—chin that said, Girl, follow me, I know just where we're goin'. (Even if in real life he didn't have a clue.) What girl wouldn't love the tall, elegant crooner, especially when he was at the microphone. His secret? He always had that ability to make you feel he was singing just for you, soft into your ear, private desires answered on his warm breath. Was he singing direct at Esmé? Well . . . of course not; to Orlando she was Eddie Days of the Cravattes. But as she stood there listening to him it was sweet as pie to think he was.

She was still standing there watching Orlando as he wrapped up his set. Then Rags Doheny took the mike: "O.K., all you music lovers out there, we got a real treat for you. I'm proud to introduce the newest member of our Fleur-de-Lys family. You don't know her yet 'cuz her record has only just come out, but you're gonna love her, I guar-an-teeeee it. Let's all put our hands together and welcome . . . Essssss-maaaaaay!"

They were applauding for her, her alone, as she moved into the yellow-blue spotlight. She looked over at Cotton Candy, and the pianist winked, meaning, Robert got us the charts, all you gotta do is sing for us. Be the best Essmay you can be.

And that, though nobody knew it, was simple as cherry wine. Esmé took the mike from Rags, fluttered out to the lip of the stage, wide-eyed and pert, then said in her real voice, "Hi, I'm Essmay, and I'm thrilled to be here tonight. I got a new song for you, written by my friend in the Cravattes, Robert Warwick. It's called *My Eyes Go Wide*."

And everyone's eyes did. Bounce, bounce, the band got the irresistible rhythm going, and right off girls in the audience were up in their seats, bopping back and forth, and then their boyfriends, clapping on the beat, setting down a firm foundation for her candy-striped vocals.

She sang the hell out of that song, sang it at least as good as on the record, sang it as good as she'd sung anything in her life, and when she was done, the applause was so great that Rags sidled out, hugged her to him, then lipped into her mike, "Ain't that song a hit? You all wanna hear that hit song again?"

They did. And the applause, loud at the beginning, only got louder as she ran through *My Eyes Go Wide* again.

"We're gonna do our best," Esmé said over the cheers when she was finished, "to get that little record into the stores here in Philly soon as possible. You go look for it, and call up your local deejays, especially a Mr. Longbone Martin at WRMC. Tell 'im Essmay said you should. That's capital E, S, S, M, A, Y—Essmay. Thank you."

Esmé ran off the stage, pulling off the wig she'd chosen for Essmay—a beehive she'd gotten from Priscilla Bondrais—and pulled on the one she used with the Daisies, a straight-hair flip that curled just above her shoulders. How different did she look? Orlando passed her as she was rushing back onto the stage and did a double take. "Do I know you?" he said, and as she ran past, Esmé called out, "I'm Maisy's replacement in the Daisies."

"Hey, baby, what's your name?" He was using his low, bedroom voice on her.

Hadn't Robert explained to him who she was? He'd told him that Eddie was singing as one of the Daisies, but maybe Orlando couldn't believe it or simply hadn't heard him right. Should she have a little goof on him now? But no, that was crazy. How many rolls could she play? But it would take awhile to explain again. She glanced toward the stage, where the three other Daisies were about to run out, then flashed the tall singer a big smile. "Um, oh, I gotta go."

As she hit the stage she noticed the Daisies' lead singer, Priscilla, glancing her way. There was an unusual intensity to her face? What was it? Curiosity over Esmé's talking to

Orlando? Anger? Or was it wholly something else? She shook her head. No time to worry this. Candy waved the downbeat, and the four girls sailed off into their first song.

✳ ✳ ✳ ✳ ✳

FROM THE STAGE during the Cravattes' act Robert thought he'd seen Longbone Martin off to the side. This was unexpected, and during the Daisies' set, Robert went to find him.

"Longbone, hey, it's Robert Warwick." The tall disc jockey was wearing his cowboy getup, hat, silver belt, boots. He was hovering beside a twist of stage ropes, looking out at the stage. "You didn't say you'd be comin' to the—"

"Shhhh," Longbone went, holding up a hand. He was looking intently at the stage, and Robert followed his gaze. "One terrific piece of woman, ain't she?" Longbone said. "Your idea to have Priscilla take over the Daisies?"

Robert half nodded, said, "Bones's—but I think it makes the most sense."

"Well, just let me appreciate her, O.K.?"

The Daisies were singing their hearts out. Priscilla with her striking face, long, swirling hair, and wide-hipped glory was taking her strong soul leads, but Eddie was right there in his dress and his wig to whisper his way through *Man Alive*.

When the group went on to its next-to-last song, Robert, curiosity burning, asked Longbone, "So, what'd you think so far?"

Longbone finally turned around. "I'm impressed, son."

"You mean it?"

The tall disc jockey leaned back and said through a quick smile, "Longbone don't say nothin' he don't mean."

Robert took that in, then softly said, "So what about Essmay's record? You play that yet?"

Like that, the air changed around the deejay. He stood silent a moment, then said, "Son, I wanted to talk to you about that." His Texas twang had disappeared. "I could tell you and that . . . that fetching Essmay, you was all keen to get your record on the air, and—" Robert started to interrupt, but Longbone held up his hand "—you got every right to be. It could be a hit, I know it—"

Robert brightened, then started to say, "We're really excited about—"

Longbone halted him again. It was easy for him to do this; he just swung his bulk around and carried a gamy, powerful air with him that stopped Robert's enthusiasm cold. "I also know you were wonderin'—" Longbone paused. "Well, what was goin' on with me."

"Yeah, we were—"

Up went Longbone's hand again. "Well, son, some of us radio men, we been gettin' us a little . . . pressure." The big man turned his eyes away. "Little pressure when it comes to FDL."

Robert stepped right up to that. "From NRC, right?"

Longbone didn't look particularly startled, but this did throw him off for a moment. "You know about that?"

"Oh, I know all about NRC. That they're trying to take us over. They poached Maisy Columbine and Mary Hardy, even had Breeze till he came back today." Now Robert held up a hand. "It also seems like they're trying to get control from Mrs. Bones."

Longbone Martin whistled. It was a deep, soulful whistle—a North Philly whistle. "Damn, that's more'n I know."

Robert, with the upper hand, smiled, all business. "So why aren't you playing our records?"

"It's not that we're not—"

"Longbone, come on, what're they doin' to you guys?"

"They ain't doin' nothin' to me," he said, stretching to his full height. "Not me. Just some of the deejays, and—"

"What are they using?" Robert interrupted. "Money?"

Longbone's eyes lit up for a second. "There's always money—"

"Then what is it?"

The disc jockey sighed. "I came here 'cuz I was feelin' a little badly."

"Badly?"

"About the record, and ... everything." Longbone looked straight at Robert. His eyes were fierce. "I love Bones Chapman, always have. He's a true pioneer, him and Berry, Don Robey at Duke, that Bearcat Jackson got hisself killed years back down in Memphis. Black men makin' records—damn!"

Robert held fire.

"I don't like to see what's happening."

Still silent, letting him spin it out at his own pace.

"There've been some—" Longbone swallowed his last word. "Not to me directly, some of the other guys."

"Physical threats?"

"I ain't sayin' nothing—"

"We're talking NRC," Robert said, eyes widening.

"I know, One of America's Most Respected Companies. I see the ads every day."

"And—"

Longbone took a long sigh. He glanced toward the stage, where the Daisies were finishing up. "Ain't I heard you guys got a big finale? Don't you gotta get back out onstage?"

"Longbone? Sir?"

"I just wanted to—" The tall disc jockey looked down again, hid his features from Robert's gaze. "Listen, here, y'all are headin' to New York City tonight, aren't ya?" Robert nodded, then Longbone held out a piece of paper. "Man I think you should talk to. Name's Devine. We used to work together in Cleveland. He's at WMAC now, program director there. James Devine."

Robert reached out for the piece of paper. On it was written in clear block type, THE BLUEJAY. 138 / LENOX.

"Might be some help, you go lookin' for him up there."

"Longbone?"

"Son?

Robert held the big man's gaze now, smiled. "Thanks," he said.

✳ ✳ ✳ ✳ ✳

ESMÉ WAS ONCE AGAIN sliding the black silk stockings down her legs, slipping out of the sheer-nylon-over-taffeta pink sheath she and the Daisies had worn onstage. Though she was used to quick-changing herself now, and indeed being Eddie Hunter had come to be second nature to her—there were things she liked about being a guy, the swagger, and the way she was so easily included in Robert's plans; and not least, that no man short of that Ezquevez ever bothered to look her up and down with his ravening eyes—she had to admit, yeah, that all this bouncing back and forth between being a man and a woman was getting to her. It wasn't that she ever got confused, well, not more than momentarily, it was that it was so exhausting—like living two or more lives at the exact same moment. Of course she wasn't alone in being worn out; the Soul Cavalcade was doing everyone in, all that sleeping on the bus nearly every night, not to mention all the problems they'd had: Maisy's leaving, Bones's accident, and now NRC coming after them all.

But the tour was almost over. The whole troupe had been saying for a week, Soon as we get to New York things'll be better. The end's in sight. Just gotta get our bones to New York City.

She was lost to these thoughts when Robert came in to the backstage dressing area. He quickly called the singers and the band together.

"Bee says the bus to New York leaves in half an hour." He cupped his hands together to make sure his words were broadcast through the large dressing area. "We're heading to New York—to the Apollo. Think about it, the Apollo Theater! You've all been doin' great, and we're gonna knock New York on its sweet ass."

Tired but heartfelt cheers rose up from the troupe.

"Before we go, I got one announcement. Eddie Days here, our most recent member, you all know he's been doing huge service. Not only singing with me in the Cravattes but putting on a dress—think about it, a dress—every night and going out as one of the Daisies.

"And tonight, what'd the man do? He took Mary's spot and sang—twice—our latest single, *My Eyes Go Wide*. I think we all should give him some special applause for workin' so hard."

Esmé was out of the dress and into her suit pants and man's shirt, but she still had on her girl makeup and the flip-haired Daisies' wig. She blushed as everyone around her clapped and whistled. "Way to go, Eddie," Priscilla Bondrais called out.

"So, Eddie," Robert went on as the tribute died down, "here's what I'm thinking. I'd like to take some of the burden off of you, get you back to double duty 'stead of triple."

Double duty instead of— What was Robert getting at? She felt a tightening in her chest. He must mean. . . .

"Do you think you could get your cousin here, the real Essmay?"

It took everything Esmé had to not clasp her hand to her bosom. Get . . . Essmay here? There was no Essmay!

"If she could fly in and meet us in New York, that'd be great. And if she's as good as you say, she can take over *Eyes Go Wide* tomorrow night."

"Um, I—"

"You look speechless," Mitch Williams, standing next to her, said.

"No, it's a surprise. I—I haven't talked to . . . to Essmay in . . . since we went on tour—"

"Tell her she'll be singing at the Apollo," Robert said.

"Oh, she'd love that." Esmé, caught in her tight beltless pants and her blooming black wig, blushed hugely. Was anyone even seeing her clearly anymore; that here she was: half man, half woman? "I'm sure of that."

"Well, call that girl up, tell her Fleur-de-Lys will pay for everything." Robert smiled. "Everything. Hell, tell her to go shopping first, put it on our tab. That'll get her here, won't it?"

Esmé felt suddenly faint. Who knew what this would mean, having not only to be herself but her cousin, too. Her head reeled, her breaths came sharp, and she had to reach out to the nearest person, Mitch, to steady herself.

"Eddie?" Robert said, all friendly concern. "You all right?"

She was hyperventilating, breaths whistling in and out of her mouth. She fought to catch her breath. Finally, she pulled herself together. "Sure, Robert," she said as emphatically as possible. She could see no way out. "I'll—I'll see what I can do."

Chapter Thirteen

Friday, May 8— New York City

AND HERE THEY WERE, Harlemtown, U.S.A.!

Rags, ever the tour guide, had run the bus into the city through the Holland Tunnel, and there, right in front of them, was the Empire State Building. He drove them up Sixth Avenue, pointing out 52nd Street, home of Birdland and a host of other jazz clubs. Then through Central Park until they hit the wide streets of Harlem. Virtually every face was black, and even though it was well after midnight, the streets were clogged on this warm May night. Even better: When passersby saw the bus sporting the FLEUR-DE-LYS NUMBER 1 EXPRESS slogan on its side, cheers went up, followed by cries of "Daisies! Cravattes! . . . Orlando, we love you!"

Although Bee considered it extravagant, Robert had said that with everything going on they had better treat the whole group well, so he'd booked them into the Hotel Theresa, known as the Waldorf of Harlem, at the corner of 125th Street and 7th Avenue. The welcome mat was out. The official hotel greeter, a tall man in a top hat and an out-of-date but still commanding purple zoot suit, went to meet the bus. "Welcome, welcome," he cried. "We're thrilled you're here. We can't wait for the show tomorrow night."

The lobby was marble, the chairs covered in velvet, and a midget bellboy in a tight burgundy monkey suit with gold epaulets and piping, and a gold-tasseled pillbox hat, led Esmé to her room. All the way he gushed about the Cravattes, how all he had to do was play *When the Doorbell Rings* and his girlfriend would lean down and give him a kiss.

"You have a girlfriend?" Esmé asked through a yawn. They were outside the door to her room. The little man had her two suitcases on each arm, and Robert Warwick's balanced on his head.

"Yeah, and she's six feet," the bellboy said with high-pitched swagger.

That pulled Esmé attention. The bellboy couldn't be four feet, if that. He'd barely kept her suitcases from bumping on the woven rug as she followed him down the hallway. "Six feet tall?"

The bellboy nodded his chin up and down. "It's like climbing Mount Everest. All in where you plant your feet." A quick wink. "Eddie, ya know what I mean?"

Esmé gave a silent wince. No, thank God, she didn't know what he meant.

The bellboy was clearly chatty. As he dropped the suitcases, he turned and said, "Yeah, my lady loves all that FDL music—loves it. You know what happens when I put on that Orlando Calabrese?" And without prompting, the bellboy popped his thumb into his mouth, then darted his tongue round and round it.

Esmé turned away. She was tired, she just wanted this bouncy leprechaun to go away, so she reached into her back pocket for her wallet.

He leaned in close to her and said in a whisper, "Hey, Eddie, you want to give me a real tip? I heard that new song today on WMAC, *My Eyes Go Wide*, new singer for you guys—Essmay or something?" The bellhop's eyes bulged. "Man, her voice made me start smokin', you know what I mean?" And he began to fan his lower parts with both of his small, wrinkled hands. "What's she look like? She that hot in person?"

Esmé, nonplussed, finally got out, "Um, she's, um, good-looking."

"Yeah?" His eyes grew larger. "She a big girl? How tall is she? She over six feet?"

It was all Esmé could do to just shake her head.

"That's O.K., no problem, no prooob-lemmmm," the

bellboy went on in his high, squeaky voice. "You wanna introduce me to her anyway? What room she in?"

Esmé had unintentionally pulled out $10 from her wallet, which seemed ridiculously high, but she so much wanted to get rid of the midget bellboy that she simply handed it over. In her most dismissive voice she said, "I don't know where she's staying."

"Hey, Eddie Days," he crowed, looking at the bill, "you is the best. Thank you, sir!" As he shuffled out the door, he called back, "You ain't gonna want for nothin'! Your every wish, my friend. Know what I mean?" Then as the door was swinging shut with the bellhop blessedly on the other side of it, he said, "I might just park myself right out here in the hallway so I can serve you better. My man!"

When the door finally fell shut, Esmé double-bolted it. She didn't know when Robert would be back—he'd gone off on what he said was "business"—but figured he could just pound on the door till she woke up and let him in. Either that, or right before she fell asleep she'd unbolt it—hope for the best from the bellboy and all Essmay's other fans.

She rolled her eyes. As she undressed she thought about how she still wasn't sure how to pull off Essmay's appearance. She'd been able to postpone it a day, pretending to Robert that she'd called her cousin in Detroit and she'd said she'd be thrilled to join the Cavalcade but needed a couple of days.

"We don't have a couple days," Robert said, clearly miffed.

"Well, she—"

"Can you get her here tomorrow?"

"I—I guess—"

"That's plenty of time. She could even take a train in that time. I want her on the Apollo stage with us rehearsing no later than tomorrow night." Robert moved brusquely past her. He had a lot on his mind, she knew, and didn't begrudge him his impatience.

"O.K., yes, I'll make certain of it. She'll be here tomorrow for sure."

So she'd bought herself a day. Now all she had to do was create out of thin air this terrific singer who was going to look like a cousin of Eddie Days, and, more remarkable, sound just like Eddie as "he" pretended to be a woman even though he was really Esmé pretending to be a man who, with everyone behind the curtain knowing and nobody in front of it having a clue, was pretending to be a girl—and, yeah, her head was spinning, too.

It had to end. But the good news from the bellhop was that *My Eyes Go Wide* was out and on the radio in New York already. (Though she did wonder how it had slipped past NRC's shady boycott.) She sang the first verse in a low whisper, *"You're sunny as a parfait / Perfect as a summer's day. . . ."* No, no reason to worry how the "real" Essmay will sound— she'd sound just like Esmé being Eddie being Essmay. That is, she'd sound just like herself.

But how she could turn up as this whole other person on top of her current masquerades, well, that sleight of hand was for now beyond her imagining.

✳ ✳ ✳ ✳ ✳

BUSINESS, INDEED, ROBERT thought as he walked the broken concrete sidewalks of Harlem, up 7th Avenue from 125th to 138th. It wasn't business, it was the damn salvation of FDL Records.

Robert was on his way to the Bluejay that Longbone Martin had directed him toward. It was getting near 4 a.m, which the greeter at the Theresa told him was closing time, though the top-hatted gent had added, "Of course, nothin' ever closes in New York City." The streets were still full of people this late, most of them dressed to the nines in flowery blouses and swaying skirts, mohair sweaters and razor-creased pants. Robert had the thought that everyone here was dressed not that different from the stars of the Soul

Cavalcade. Were people in Harlem actually following style points from the likes of the Daisies, Orlando, and the Cravattes? Evidence suggested they could be.

The Bluejay was a narrow, dingy joint with a long bar; indeed, there were only a few square feet of open room in the front before the bar ran determinedly down the rest of the room. Lighting was dim, mostly from leftover strings of Christmas bulbs behind the bar. The liquor bottles, though, cascaded in pyramids.

"Last call was five minutes ago, brother," the bartender, in a black knit skullcap, said. "Sorry."

"I'm looking for somebody," Robert quickly said. "I was told he liked to close the place." The bartender gave him a half-interested look, and Robert, pursing his brow said, "A gentleman named—" Robert looked at the slip of paper he'd been carrying with him "—James Devine."

The bartender hooked a thumb down to the far end of the bar. "Hey, Swiz, guy here asking about you."

There were three dark man shapes all the way down, all three hunched over, and Robert didn't think they were together. None of them looked up.

"Hey, Swiz, you entertaining visitors still?" The bartender threw Robert a glance, then rolled his eyes, meaning, You might be getting him a little late into the evening. "Swizzle?"

Robert headed right down, slowing behind each of the three broad-shouldered, slumped-over men until the bartender gave him a nod as he stood behind the middle one. "James Devine?" he said.

Up came a big, curly-haired head, around came a big-nosed, flat-cheeked, wide-lipped . . . white face.

Robert was startled. There was nothing in Devine's appearance from the back that suggested he was white; and Longbone hadn't said anything, either. Robert felt a tinge of nervousness, which he quickly was embarrassed over and tried to sweep aside.

"You're James Devine?"

"Who're you?" The voice had a black rasp and snap, but it wasn't really black. Devine seemed sullen, as the bartender had hinted, long gone into his cups.

"Longbone Martin down in Philly said I should look you up." Robert held out his hand. "My name's Robert Warwick."

The white man looked him up and down. "Longbone, eh?"

"Yes, sir."

"And you said your name is—" A slight slur to his words.

"Robert Warwick."

Up went a thick eyebrow on the whiteman's face. "Any relation to Robert Warwick of the Cravattes?"

Robert almost sighed; O.K., this was going to be easier. "That's me."

"Right, the one with the glasses. Well, well, good deal." Now that his eyes had become accustomed to the Bluejay's gloom, Robert could see that Devine was actually wearing a seaman's cap; under it, his hair, though in tight curls, was actually red. His face had a rough-skinned ruddiness, splotches of red and white over its expanse. "Liked *When the Doorbell Rings*. Was trying to give it some good play."

Robert hooked on two words, play and trying. "Longbone didn't say much about you, just that I needed to look you up. We just got to town, we're playin'—"

"I know, the Soul Cavalcade's comin' into the Apollo tomor—um, tonight. We're cosponsoring the show."

"And we are?"

"WMAC. The Good Guys."

"Longbone really didn't—"

"I'm Jimmy Devine, formerly the Divine Jimmy Devine, when I spun wax. Now I'm the PD."

Robert nodded.

"And what did Longbone say you needed me for?"

"You said you 'tried' to play *Doorbell*. What do you mean?"

Devine gave him a long look. "You better tell me more of why you're here first, brother."

Just then the bartender called out, "That's it for the night, gen'lemen. Closing time. We'll be open again at 10 a.m., and—" he gave out a hearty laugh "— I expect to see all of you here then. *Punctual!*"

"Saddest two words in English, *closing time*," Devine said.

"That means you, Swizzle, you and your pretty-lookin' buddy."

"Come on," Devine said. "No real problem. We'll just step ourselves around the corner."

Around the corner was an empty storefront with a whited-out window and a nondescript black wooden door. Devine had a lusty step, unburdened by weaving, and he went right up and rapped on a brass knocker: *Knock-knock*, pause, *knock-knock-knock*.

The door pushed open. They were in a narrow concrete walkway, a very faint bare bulb overhead. There was water on the ground, and Robert wasn't as lucky as Devine; he stepped into a puddle that quickly covered his shoe. "Damn!" he muttered.

"What?"

"Nothin'." They kept walking, took a right turn, then stood before a heavy metal door. Above it was the faintest of neon signs: DOOBY-DOO. Inside, the light was low, but Robert right off saw big pillows on the floor surrounding small tables rising like mushrooms, a candle in a netted bowl on each one.

A hostess, a black woman with long straight hair and elaborately painted makeup, walked up and gave Devine a cheek kiss, then turned to Robert. He was startled. The woman was very pretty, but she looked strikingly like Eddie Days back on the bus when he was dressed up as girl. Robert blushed. The hostess and Devine noticed. "This is a private club," the program director said. "A very private club. After we're done talkin', my friend, the sky's the limit." He gave Robert a genial smile.

They sank into the luxurious pillows, and drinks came immediately.

"O.K., Mr. Robert Warwick of the Cravattes," Devine said, actually licking his lips in anticipation as he held his glass of whiskey before him, "what can I do for you?"

Though Robert wasn't sure, he figured he had to trust this man, as quirky and inebriated as he was, so he told him the whole story, of the success of the Cavalcade, then Bones's accident, the rumors of disc jockeys being pressured, and what he'd been hearing about NRC coming after the company. Devine kept mostly a poker face, though there were flashes of understanding in his milky eyes.

When Robert was done, Devine said, "It's all true."

"It's all. . . ."

"Just as you have it, my friend. Just as you have it."

"They really are—NRC is intimidating people into not playing our records?"

"They're trying to, yeah. Don't always succeed. But . . . that's probably the least of it." Devine said this boldly, though it struck Robert that some of the bravado might be coming from his whiskey, and this curious place. "And, yeah, they've come at me."

"And—" This was Robert's big question, the only reason he figured Longbone would have sent him to this man "—can you give me anything to prove it?"

That quieted Devine down. He looked away from Robert, then at his glass of whiskey, then with eyes shaded back up at Robert. "Maybe."

"*Maybe?*"

"What did Longbone tell you?"

Robert shrugged. "Not much. Just that you were the man to see."

"And did he say why?"

Robert shook his head.

"Do you have any idea?"

Robert saw it now, there was a fine flame in Devine's eyes. It held a quiet fury and burned with astonishing precision. "No," he said.

"It's because I love the music. I love it." Devine was staring straight at Robert now, so intensely that the singer felt uncomfortable. "That's why I'm good at my job, I know the stuff, know your stuff, know it all. I feel it, and that feeling— man, that feeling is everything. I *am* the music. You hear me. I am the fucking music!" He threw back the rest of his drink, then beckoned to the skimpily clothed hostess for another one.

"I believe you," was all Robert could say. Would he call Devine possessed? More than drunk? The burning eyes. At this moment he would, yes.

"And I'm the goddamn *good* music. None of this shit, this fake shit they churn out. This crapola hire some session guys, get some skanks in the studio, copy what the real guys are doin'—none of that phony white shit." Devine's voice rose. "Can't fuckin' stand it. I might look white to you, brother, but I ain't white. I ain't! But they like me, all the honky honchos love me, they call me the White Brother, 'cuz they know I know my shit and yet they can get down with me. You understand?"

Devine was slurring words now. His second drink—well, second drink here in the after-hours club, but who knew how many at the Bluejay—came, and Devine took a wolfish sip.

"So I know the real shit, I play the real shit, I make the real shit happen—make hits. You guys at FDL, Motown, Stax—you guys got the real shit. Fuckin' NRC, they think they can scare the real shit away, and if they can't do that, they think they can buy it."

"You know about that?"

"Know about it? Fuckin' Captain Bryant calls me up, asks me to front for him. I turn him down. But I know about it, yeah. Everybody knows about it. How they grabbed Maisy

Columbine, then Mary Hardy. How they're makin' moves on Bones's wife."

"How much do you know about that?" Robert said as calmly as he could.

"Man, what you're worryin' about, some little intimidation, that's last week's shit. The new shit is they got Mrs. Bones here in New York ready to sign on the fuckin' dotted line."

"Damn!"

"Yeah, damn."

Robert leaned back. "So—"

"So you were askin' me a question. Something about some kind of proof." Devine's eyes danced; then he whispered, "Something like . . . a tape."

"A tape?"

"A little metal reel, brown plastic looped around on it. A tape, my friend. Some people . . . talkin' to me."

Robert got it. "Jesus!"

Devine burst into a loud chortle, threw back more whiskey, then started flapping his arms as if he were dancing. "Yep, I'm the Man. I be the ever-lovin' Man. I am the god-damn shits, my friend."

"What's on it?" Robert was breathing loudly, he was so excited. "On the tape?"

"Well, my friend, it is a real honor to meet you, I love your records. Jesus, here I am, talkin' to Robert Warwick of the Cravattes. Wonderboy of Fleur-de-Lys Records. Up-and-coming writer-producer, too."

Robert gave his head a shake; he didn't get this turn in the conversation. "About this tape. . . ?" he said softly.

But Devine was off on a new tangent. He gave Robert a big smile and said, "I hear you've been busy."

"Busy?"

"Got somebody new comin' along, worked her up all by yourself."

"What are you—"

"Hey, I told you, I am the music. I'm the ever-lovin' Music Man. You think anything gets past me?"

"You're talking about . . . Essmay."

"You don't think I ain't the first man in New York to hear *My Eyes Go Wide*."

This spooked Robert. How could copies even be in New York already? Far as he knew, the only ones so far were with him, and . . . a few guys in Philly. Like Longbone.

"You knew I was coming, right?" Robert said.

"Nope." Devine shook his head.

"But you got the record?"

"Record? You call it simply a record? I don't call the motherjumper a record, I call it a hit. A motherjumpin' hit!"

Robert couldn't help himself, he brightened. "You—"

"And you know, I started playing it—"

"You've—"

"Yep, on WMAC. Got my WMAC Good Guys all over that record. That record screams *Hit!* and nothin's gonna stop it!"

"But what about—"

"Fuck 'em!" Devine barked. Robert was silent as the program director stood up and shouted to the whole room. "I said, I'm Mr. Fuckin' True Music, and I say to the National Record Company, Fuck you!"

It took a long couple of minutes for Devine to calm down, then sit again on his lavender pillow. When he was settled and had taken a long, messy gulp from his drink, Robert said, "About that tape—"

Devine leaned across the table, his eyes suddenly hawk bright. "It's a tape I guarantee you nobody at NRC would want to come out. You understand me?"

Robert nodded.

"So, I have a little proposition for you, Mr. Robert Warwick. A way we can both help each other out. Everybody but those goddamn phonies at NRC." He lifted a red-haired eyebrow. "You game, my friend?"

There was only one thing for Robert to say: "I think, my friend, you'd better tell me more."

✳ ✳ ✳ ✳ ✳

WHEN ESMÉ WOKE UP, to brilliant May sunlight flooding through thin white-linen curtains, her first thought was, Wow, I'm in New York! New York City! This was a lifetime desire of hers, and she was unshakably thrilled to be here.

She looked over to the bed next to her where Robert lay sleeping. Before she herself fell asleep she'd relaxed and unbolted the door; Robert must've come in while she was out cold. He had a low, raspy but smooth way of breathing—not a snore, more a pleasant I'm-sleepin' buzz. She thought to wake him, but he'd been working so hard—looked like he needed the rest so much—that she decided just to let him be.

As she was lying there, soaking in the sunlight and hearing pigeons and jays wing-whirring and chirping out the window—imagine, birds in Harlem!—there came a light knocking on the hotel room door. Who could that be? That twisted bellhop? She ignored the knuckle rapping gently against the door, then wondered if Robert might be expecting someone. Should she get him up? He looked so peaceful. O.K., I'll just go and answer it myself.

The knocking came again, and she wrapped the blanket around her so there'd be no trace of her body, then patted down her hair into some semblance of a manly cut.

It was Priscilla Bondrais, looking perky and cheerful in a yellow sundress, bright against her golden skin.

"Hey, Eddie, I woke up with this idea. I—" Esmé yawned, then patted her hair down again. Priscilla noticed and said, "Hey, you growin' one of those Afros I've been hearin' about?"

"Um, not really." Those first words out of her mouth each morning, Esmé never knew what tone they'd have—whether they'd be truly male deep or a clear female grunt. This phrase sounded, well, she couldn't tell. "Just need me a haircut."

"Well, we can take care of that, too."

"Priscilla?"

"Oh, my great idea: I'm gonna take you downtown shopping." Priscilla shuffle-shoed joyfully through the doorway. "I mean, if you're really gonna be a Daisy, well, shouldn't you start wearin' your own clothes instead of Maisie's?"

"Shopping?" Esmé's head spun again. Shopping for. . . ? "Dresses?" she said.

"Of course dresses. Can't have you be a Daisy wearin' those sharp duds you wear in the Cravattes."

"You're going to take me shopping for . . . girl clothes?"

"Listen, sweetie, if you can fake 'em out on the stage, you can sure fake 'em out in a store. They'll never know you're a guy." Priscilla was giving her a big, saucy smile. Evidently the deception in all this was jazzing her up.

"You think—"

"Oh, come on, it'll be fun. It's New York, and I talked Bee into giving us some clothes money for you. Get yourself dressed—in your nicest dress, that is—and meet me downstairs. I'm gonna be getting some breakfast." A wink. "Come on, girl, do it!"

By the time Esmé hit the bathroom and turned on a hot shower she was as charged as Priscilla with the day's plans. Shopping, in New York! Macy's, Gimbles, Saks Fifth Avenue! When she got out and stood naked before the mirror, she thought about the gauze she used to bind her breasts, and she shuddered. She was so tired of that. Couldn't she—well, just for today, if she was going out shopping as a girl—couldn't she forgo that?

Robert raised his head as Esmé tip-toed through their room toward the door. He saw her, then gave his head a quick shake. "Who are—"

"It's me, Eddie."

"What're you doin' dressed like—"

"It's all right, just me and—" Oh, no. Her voice had started off as her own—she was that giddy—but she grabbed herself and tugged the next words down in register. "Just me and Priscilla off to have some fun."

Robert gave her a wink. "You don't know whose voice to use, do you?"

Esmé flushed. "Oh, Robert, Robert, I surely don't."

Robert laughed. "So, you and Priscilla?"

"Shopping—for girl clothes. For the Daisies." She gave what she hoped was a half-mortified manly shrug. "You gonna be around?"

"Not sure. I got a lot to do."

"Well, we'll meet up anyway later, you can tell me everything. But—gotta go now, Priscilla's waiting."

They cabbed to midtown, to Bloomingdales. Priscilla said that that was where they had the snappiest new fashions.

Esmé, dazzled by the racks of wonderful clothes, swooped up a handful, then walked out of the dressing room wearing a taffeta skirt that flared over her lovely legs.

"I gotta say, girl, you sure got the look." Priscilla was sitting in a plush chair in the young ladies' department.

"Girl?" Esmé winked.

"You sure could fool me." Priscilla lifted her hands up to her own chest and said, "How you get your bosom so full, Eddie, if you don't mind my asking?"

"One of my secrets." Esmé primped in front of the mirror. Yes, this dress was great on her.

"I'd say." Priscilla set her mouth just so. "Wonder what kind of man I'd make if I dressed up."

"You didn't get into any of that in Jackson, did you, when we all started putting on make-believe?"

Priscilla shook her head. "That was Maisy."

Esmé nodded. "Was I right what I was thinking about you two?"

Priscilla lifted an eyebrow. "And what might that be?"

"That you weren't, you know, the best of friends?"

"Oh, Maisy Columbine, I love that woman! All us Daisies

love each other to death." Priscilla said this brightly, too brightly, and Esmé understood she was using her interview voice.

"That bad, eh?"

"No, not really. We got along, long as me and Linda and
Annie knew our places. We were . . . backup singers, you know."

"I know." Esmé was feeling so relaxed with Priscilla now
that she was mostly using her real voice, just trying to take it
down a little. Priscilla didn't seem to suspect anything; she'd
been both Eddie-as-a-man and Eddie-as-a-girl for so long
now that she assumed everyone just saw her as both people
at the same time. "I'm not sorry she's gone, though."

"Someday somebody's gonna write a book about us, I
know it," Priscilla said. "So if I say now what I really feel, you
think it'll end up in that book?"

"You don't have to say anything else." Esmé turned and
saw a salesgirl holding up an ice-blue evening gown. "Oooh,
that's divine."

Priscilla spun her head and said, "It's beautiful. Try it on,
and if it looks great on you, maybe I can get the rest of the
girls to go for it, too."

Esmé smiled. This was maybe the closest Priscilla had
come to saying that she was now truly one of the Daisies—
sweet. In the dressing room Esmé hung the dress on the
hanger and stepped back to admire it. It truly was gorgeous,
with long satin panels and a low, scalloped neckline. It also
looked like a huge amount of work to get in and out of, and
the thought crossed her mind that what the girls really needed onstage was a dresser. Well, a couple more hits and maybe
she could get Robert or Bee to go for that.

She took her time taking off the taffeta skirt and silk
blouse, all the while admiring the blue dress. When she was
down to just her panties, she felt a tiny gust of wind at her
back and turned to see Priscilla pushing through the dressing room door.

"Eddie, I thought maybe you'd need some help getting

into—" Priscilla started to say; then she caught herself, and her eyes truly went wide. "Eddie? What the—? Eddie," Priscilla cried out, "you have breasts!"

✳ ✳ ✳ ✳ ✳

ON THE RIDE BACK uptown the two girls fell into a easy-going silence. After trying to hail a cab for 20 minutes, they'd finally been picked up—by a black driver with a floppy cloth hat who now darted through the Park Avenue traffic. Grand limestone buildings rushed past, each with canopies and uniformed doormen with gold epaulets that sparkled in the sun. Esmé was indulging a feathery fantasy about one of those apartments being hers; saw herself in that ice-blue gown, hem teasing the parquet floor, sweeping into an apartment that would do Astaire and Rogers proud. She was imagining herself dancing lighter-than-air around the room when Priscilla broke into her reverie.

"I'm looking at you now, girl—" a long trill to the word *girl* "—and I got this feelin' I know you."

"Know me—" Esmé turned to her new friend, crossing her legs in the capacious cab.

"Yeah, from way before. Esmé ... Hunter. From ... damn, you weren't in Christopher Columbus Middle School, were you?"

Esmé brightened. "Hey, yes, I was."

"When?"

Esmé took a deep breath. God, so much was going on, she could barely remember being a woman, let alone a knock-kneed 14-year-old girl. "Um, Eisenhower, that old, bald man was president—five, six years ago."

Priscilla bloomed a huge smile. "Damn, it *was* you. You were in the class behind me, but we had Miss Warren together. I can see it right now. You was a couple rows over." Priscilla closed her eyes a second. "You had these pigtails, they just sprouted out of your head."

"Right," Esmé said, laughing, "those pigtails."

"Yeah, and I remember they was always flying out from your head something wild." Priscilla's voice lifted, and her eyes half-closed. "Weren't you the girl always standing on her head, doing somersaults?" Esmé brightened at the memory. "Yeah, I can see you now. Legs going up, pigtails flying, your school skirt fluttering—damn, girl, I remember you was always flashing your white panties—"

Esmé was guffawing now. "I was some wild thing, I remember."

"You were!"

The girls fell into each other, laughing. After a minute Esmé said, "What I remember most are my braces—horrible, medieval contraption in my mouth." A wince at Priscilla. "You don't remember that? My mouth flashing aluminum all the time?" Priscilla shook her head. "Yeah, those braces. My mother always said to me, 'Daughter, you might look a sight now, but when you get older, you're gonna thank me. I'm gonna make you bee-ooo-teeee-fullll.' "

Priscilla lifted an eyebrow, then winked. "Well, she sure made you one good-looking man, I'll say that."

Esmé gave her a smile. She was trying to remember Priscilla. A few rows over, and . . . back three seats. "You had the straightest hair," popped out of her. "I can see it now. Just like your hair now, waves and waves of those super-fine black curls." Priscilla was smiling. "How'd you do that?"

Another lift of Priscilla's eyebrow. "A lady's got to keep her secrets."

"God, I was such a tomboy." Esmé sighed. "All I wanted to do was climb fences, get muddy, play cowboys and Indians with the boys—hell, I even collected stamps."

"Stamps?"

"Yeah, my mother didn't get it either." Esmé closed her eyes. "But I loved those little slips of paper, all those colors and funny writing, each one a . . . well, like a little peek into another world, some place wonderful."

"For me, sweetie, it was boys. Boys, boys, boys. Big boys, small boys—" Priscilla reached out a hand and wiggled her fingers "—boys right there in the middle." She guffawed.

Esmé took a deep breath, then spoke softly. "Yeah, I guess I was a little late with that. I had my books and my stamps and my . . . pigtails. I guess that must be why my mother sent me to Miss Penny's—"

"You went there? With all the stuck-up little pretties in their fancy pinafores—"

"Hey, Pris, don't hate me." Esmé's voice rose. "It was my mother's idea, and I didn't really like it."

"It wasn't Central."

"Oh, I'm sure it wasn't. Grace and Annette, girls I sang with in the Darlingettes, went to Central. I heard stories."

Priscilla nodded, then said brightly, "So what you doing for boys these days, Mr. Eddie Hunter?"

"Boys?" Esmé turned the word on her tongue. She quick-thought of the recent Shirelles song of that name: How when a boy kisses a girl, it's like a trip around the world. Well, yeah. Lots of world excursions she'd been taking lately! Then out burst a guffaw to match Priscilla's: "Oh, I been sleepin' with a boy every night, Pris."

Up flew her new friend's eyebrows.

"Been sleepin' with myself, darlin'!"

Priscilla rolled her eyes, and Esmé couldn't help but roll hers, too. There they were in the back of the lurching cab: Two girls giggling and goofing on each other. She'd never had a sister, but talking to Priscilla made her feel that way.

Priscilla reached over and took her hand. Her voice went softer, deeper. "Are you ready?" she said.

Esmé lifted her chin.

"For tomorrow?"

"Oh, right," Esmé said, swallowing. "Tomorrow."

Chapter Fourteen

Saturday, May 9— New York City

"IT'S MY GREAT PRIVILEGE," Robert Warwick said, standing in front of the fully assembled Soul Cavalcade at a rehearsal he'd had Candy Wilson call in the late morning the day of the second show at the Apollo, "to introduce to you the newest member of the Fleur-de-Lys Records family. She's our esteemed Cravatte Eddie's cousin from Detroit, just flown in for us, and she can sing up a storm." Applause started already, then built when Robert said, "We call her simply—Essmay."

Well, here goes, Esmé thought, and walked out on the stage as sexy and perky as she could. She was wearing one of her Maisy wigs, combed in a wholly new direction; and with Priscilla's great help, her makeup was changed enough so that, she hoped, she looked like somebody new to people who had already known her in one form or another for weeks. Now she was a girl, and only a girl, and that should have made it all go easier. But she was so used to being one refraction or another of her true self that instead of simply being the one true Esmé Hunter now, she found that becoming Essmay meant triangulating even further: Essmay was Esmé as Eddie as Eddie the Daisy as the cousin to that man as woman. Clear? Esmé wasn't sure even she was. A couple hours back she'd walked into the Theresa Hotel with an empty suitcase she'd bought on 125th Street, shaking off the imaginary dust of a long morning's flight, looking around all uncertain and asking for somebody named Robert Warwick, who, when he came down in the elevator, gave her a smile that said immediately, Oh, yes, you look perfect, then embraced her like his own long lost sister—and again totally took her at face value.

Now here she was onstage, everybody was joyfully welcoming her, and so she put one foot in front of the other and tried to make Essmay cute, bubbly, and every bit the star about to be born.

"Thank you," she said, pitching her speaking voice between Eddie's and Eddie the Daisy's, then trying to trill it out a little. "Robert here has been great getting this first single produced, and I'm quite thrilled to be stepping in now to sing it. I'm also overwhelmed to be part of such a fine family of performers." She let out her brightest, most beaming smile. "And I'm really sorry my cousin Eddie isn't here." She held up a hand, looked about her. "Eddie, you're not here, are you?"

No response—of course.

"Well, he said something about some special business. I just want you to know that I've always loved all of your music, and it's just fantastic to be here now." A look over at Priscilla: Am I going too far? But Priscilla gave her a quick wink, and Esmé knew she was O.K.

"Thanks, Essmay," Robert said, moving next to her. "Welcome again."

More clapping all around.

"Now the show went great last night, we put New York City on its ear—on its ear!" More applause. "And tonight we're going to have the real Essmay in the show, not Eddie stepping in, which is why Candy called the rehearsal. We just want to run through a few things quickly. Essmay, you'll be going on after the Shags. I think we'll just have you do the one song, *Eyes Go Wide*, tonight, and if the audience gets into it—and I'm sure they will—then Rags'll come back out and ask them if they want to hear it again, like we did with Eddie in Philly. Sound good?"

Nobody had any objection, and the rehearsal went smoothly. The Shags did their final song, Rags gave Essmay a huge introduction, and she sang *My Eyes Go Wide*—sang it fine, she thought, just like herself. Midway through, she looked over at Robert, who was smiling and, eyes closed, swaying to the beat; so he was happy. She saw Priscilla hold both her thumbs up. Then she caught Orlando Calabrese looking straight at her, his smoky eyes taking her all in. He had a sly, secretive smile on his face. It was a smile, the longer she looked on it, the warmer it felt. Her legs pressed tight together.

The rest of the group's rehearsal was mainly tightening up cues—in truth, it felt just like busy work—and everybody rushed through it so they could get back out into New York City and play.

Priscilla was first up to Esmé as the rehearsal wrapped.

"Well?" Esmé said.

"You got it," Priscilla said enthusiastically. Then she winked, adding, "Girl."

"It's going to be O.K.?" Esmé knew she really shouldn't be nervous, though she was.

"You're gonna knock 'em out tonight. Yes, you are, sister."

Esmé lit up in a wide smile. It was great having her secret shared—finally. Great also having Priscilla as a friend. They'd gone to dinner after the shopping trip, bags piled up around their table at a place called Sylvia's around the corner from the hotel. There Priscilla had insisted on hearing Esmé's whole story. When she was done, she leaned back and with a wicked smile said, "Well, I'm damn glad we got that straightened out. You know, Eddie—" a curl to her lips— "I was thinkin' I might be comin' on to you pretty soon myself."

At the Apollo now Priscilla took Esmé's hands and was holding them like they were the best of girlfriends when Orlando came up sneakily behind Priscilla. He brought a finger to his lips, *Shhhh!*, then squeezed Priscilla's waist with a quick pinch. Priscilla flinched, her fingernails unconsciously biting into Esmé's skin, then she spun around and cried out, "Breeze, what the—! Get your goddamn paws off me!"

Orlando just flashed his bedroom eyes. "Hey, sugar," he said to Esmé. "You got yourself one fine smile."

Esmé blushed.

"I just wanted to come over and welcome you."

"Hey," Esmé went. She was feeling unaccountably flustered; found herself trying to be as young and schoolgirlish as she could.

"You know who I am, right, darling?"

"Of course, Mr. Calabrese."

"You hear that, Pris? I do get some respect around here."

Priscilla's eyes were sparking, but she held fire.

Orlando rolled his heavy-lidded eyes back, bore his gaze down on Esmé. "Well, I want to say that we're all truly excited that you're here. That's a helluva song Robert wrote, and you—you're doin' it just fine."

"I appreciate that . . . sir."

"Sir?" Orlando let out a huge laugh. "Well, don't wanna carry this respect thing too far." He reached out now, and just as he had with Priscilla, took his fingers and pinched Esmé's waist. She jumped, both an inch or so in space—and a lot more inside her.

"Orlando, you animal!" Priscilla cried.

"Grrrr-roooaaaarrrrrrrrr," he went, making a noise somewhere between a bear and a lion. "Grrrr-roooaaaaaarrrrrrrrrrrrrr."

Priscilla swatted at him like you would at a bothersome fly, then turned to Esmé. "Come on, girl, let's get out of here."

Orlando kept up his deep smile. "Now, Essmay, girl, you want to come talk to me later about the ol' beast in me, well, I'm sure you'll be able to find my lair—"

"Jesus, Breeze, that's corny even for you," Priscilla said.

Orlando winked. "Yeah, but, darlin', you knoooow how well it works." He curled the corner of his mouth up at Priscilla, then patted Esmé's hand, gave her another quick wink, and sauntered off in his girl's-can't-get-enough-of-me way.

"Jesus, that man," Priscilla said when he was gone. She shook her head. "I swear, he's lookin' at you like you was a chicken just flapping around the yard."

"You think he's much different since he ran off with Maisy?"

Priscilla considered a moment, then said, "He's always been a wolf, you know, Essie, but, yeah, maybe there's a new, what, urgency to it all."

"Good thing I'm not really the innocent young Essmay, eh?"

"I'd still stay away from him." Priscilla was particularly insistent, and Esmé asked herself why. She hadn't thought this before, but she had to wonder if Priscilla had been involved with him at some point. Probably not; rumors were always rife around the Cavalcade, and she hadn't heard anything. Still, Priscilla had a reputation of being pretty private. She hadn't opened up much at all at dinner the night before.

"Good advice, I'm sure," she said.

"Very good." Priscilla erupted into giggles, then said, "So what's up now?"

"I think cousin Eddie had better come back from his 'special business.' Robert's going to need his help."

"You sure you're going to be in all the places you gotta be?"

Esmé rolled her eyes. "I damn sure hope so." She took Priscilla's arm. "You don't know what a relief it is, Pris, to have you know everything. If you're helping me, I think I can—"

Priscilla put her hand atop Esmé's then stopped her by saying, "I'm with you girl, all the way."

✳ ✳ ✳ ✳ ✳

ROBERT HAD A LOT of errands, downtown to get more records pressed up, to a distributor FDL used in

Brooklyn, and finally to the WMAC offices in Rockefeller Center. As he walked up Sixth Avenue, he saw a building with a black-onyx sign engraved with the letters NRC in gold above the entranceway. That caught up Robert's breath. It wasn't the same building as WMAC's, but it was just across the street.

Except for a few men in uniforms sweeping up around the buildings, he was the only black man in sight. He approached a ground-floor receptionist, who kept filing her nails while he stood there asking how to find the radio station's studios.

"We don't just send people up there without an escort," the woman told him.

"But Mr. James Devine told me to come by. He's the program director."

The receptionist, a red-haired woman with elaborately rouged cheeks, gave her nails a few last buffs, then lifted up a white telephone receiver. "Well, we'll call and see." Robert stood there, shuffling his feet. A moment later she looked up and said, "Mr. Devine no longer works at WMAC."

"He no longer—"

"That's what I said."

Robert leaned toward the woman, who immediately pulled back. "Can I talk—"

The receptionist gave a quick glance in the direction of a uniformed guard about twenty feet away, but then just said to Robert, "I'm sorry, but that's all the information they're going to give out. Mr. James Devine no longer works for WMAC."

What was this? Had Devine been fired? His drinking finally caught up with him? Or did it . . . did it have something to do with his playing Fleur-de-Lys records?

Robert stood there with his hands suddenly awkward before him. He looked again at the redhead and knew she wouldn't take even a little step further to help him, so he simply spun around and walked out of the granite building and stood in the heart of New York City with all the other tall granite buildings looming above him, trying to fight down the dark, reeling sensation deep in his gut.

✳ ✳ ✳ ✳ ✳

A COUPLE OF HOURS earlier Esmé had been in her man's suit walking across the street from the Hotel Theresa back to the Apollo Theater. A kid with nappy hair and a peach-striped T-shirt had a transistor radio up by his ear, waiting for the light, and from it came a sound curiously recognizable. Esmé stopped, listening to the thin, tinny noise, trying to make it out, when all of a sudden it hit her: She was hearing *My Eyes Go Wide*.

"Hey," she cried, "kid, can you turn that up?"

"What you want, mister?" The boy threw a snarky look at Esmé.

"The radio. I want to hear that song."

"You want my radio?"

"No, just want to hear the song."

The boy had a goofy grin. "It's a good song."

"Can you just turn it up?"

"It's up all the way, mister."

Esmé frowned. "Then can I just listen to it?"

"You mean, you really think I'm gonna give you my radio?"

"Please," Esmé said. "I think it's me singing."

The kid's eyes went wide: Oh, yeah! "It can't be you, mister. This is a woman singing."

Esmé shook her head. Duh. "I mean, I might be singing backup on it. I'm a singer, with the Cravattes." She pointed across the street at the marquee to the Apollo. "You know the Cravattes?"

The kid was truly broad-eyed by now, and all he said was, "You shittin' me. You ain't a Cravatte. You be too short."

Esmé laughed. "I am, son, I am. I'm not even the shortest. And that is me on that record, truth." She could hear enough now that she started singing along with it, her voice eerily harmonizing with the singer on the radio. The kid still looked dubious, but the wonder of what was happening evidently got the better of him because when Esmé held out her hand, the boy reluctantly held the transistor out to her but didn't hand it over. "My mama told me things," was all he said.

"Probably good things." The light had changed to green, and people were bustling past them. "That's O.K., I can hear it from here. Let me just stick my ear closer."

She leaned into the little yellow plastic radio and caught the fade of the song. She couldn't tell really how it sounded, but right then a disc jockey came on and said, "That's *My Eyes Go Wide* by Essmay, a hot new platter from the FDL label. Essmay, I like that. One name, that's got class, and that chickie's got the sound, too. I think this little platter's goin' right to the top."

"He likes it," Esmé said, mostly to herself.

"What you say?"

"I said—" She looked down at the young boy. "I said, he seems to like it."

"It's a happenin' tune, why wouldn't he like it?"

"This the first time you heard it?"

"No, they been playin' it all over WMAC all morning. I been hearin' it everywhere."

Esmé reached out and tousled the kid's thick hair, couldn't help herself. "Well, you keep groovin' on it," she said. "And get all your friends to buy it, you hear!"

Everywhere. She found herself after crossing 125th Street turning right, east, rather than toward the Apollo. She walked easily down the street, listening for music coming out of stores or more kids with radios, and it only took her half the block till in front of a open-fronted clothing shop she heard the jangly intro to her record, then her voice come on cooingly,

You're sunny as a parfait
Perfect as a summer's day
You make my eyes go wide
With surprise and delight
Every time . . . you walk on by

The speakers here were near as tall as she was, and the record had full extension, catching both Bunny Alexander's deep bass and her own breathy tones. And it sounded damn good.

Then a curious thing happened. Right after the bridge, *"Early in the morning / Only one thing that I hear / Just like that I got sweet words in my ear,"* the radio went dead and only static hissed out of the speakers. It was like one of those Conelrad system things for the nuclear bomb warnings. Esmé kept standing there, waiting for the song to kick in again, but finally the deejay's voice came on and said simply, "This is WMAC, home of the Good Guys. And now here's the new NRC hit by Little Evie Stone, *The Dog with the Diamond Collar.* Take it away Little Evie."

Esmé hooked her ears around the song, a number with way too much brass up front, but then it hit the chorus, *"Hey, big man, come on, show me a dollar / And I'll let you pet my dog with the diamond collar,"* and she just shook her head.

She was half-wondering what had happened to her record when she got to the front of the Apollo. There behind glass was a new picture. It was a slinky woman pretty much recognizable, and beneath it read ESSMAY. How the—? she thought.

Backstage only Bee was in sight, busying about. When she saw Esmé she called out, "Edward, hello."

"Hey, Bee, do you know where Robert is?"

She shook her head. "Said he had some errands." Bee was distributing a bag of fruit on a long table. "Where have you been?" Her voice went slightly more stern.

"Oh, a couple family things back in Detroit I had to deal with. I'm sorry I missed rehearsal."

"This is your first, right?"

"First?"

"First rehearsal you missed, or were even late for, if I remember correctly."

"Yes, ma'am."

"O.K., then we'll let this one go without a fine."

Esmé felt that same flash of shame she'd get whenever she'd be called up in front of a class and chastized. But what could she have done? "I'm sorry, Bee," she said. She was about to say that she'd swear it wouldn't happen again but knew she couldn't make that promise.

"How'd my cousin do?"

Bee smiled. "Everybody seemed to like her."

"And Robert?"

"Far as I could tell, dear." Bee put an apple down on the table. "But you'll have to ask him yourself."

Esmé nodded to herself. It was 2:30 p.m. She hadn't eaten lunch, what with pretending to be Essmay then changing back into Eddie, and the fruit Bee was setting out looked good. She walked over and took an orange. One last question: "You know anything about that picture of my cousin out front of the theater? She just arrived this morning, you know where it came from?"

Bee shook her head. She was arranging bananas. "You'll have to ask Robert, he handled that."

"Good enough."

She went off to get a proper lunch then take a walk through the shining May day, and when she returned, Robert was back.

"Hey, Eddie!" Robert was talking with a backstage sound-man, who was fiddling with a cable.

"Hey, Robert!" Esmé went over to him. "So, how was she?"

His eyes brightened quickly, and that was all she really had to hear. What he said was, "She's great."

"And she'll fit into the show?"

"I think so." Robert patted the sound guy on the shoulder, then turned his full attention to Esmé. "We'll find out tonight."

"Oh, I know she'll be fine in front of a crowd."

"Me, too."

Esmé walked over and picked up an apple from Bee's array. "Hey, what about that photo of Essmay out front. Where'd you get that?"

"Oh," Robert said, the sly look in his eyes Esmé really liked. "Took a chance."

"What do you mean?"

"That she'd look enough like you as a girl. We had some photos of you singing with the Daisies, just cropped the other girls out and touched it up a little."

"And?"

His thin mouth smiled. "I think your cousin's prettier."

Esmé fluttered her eyelids. This hit her . . . *damn!* She was jealous, which was strange. For a second she flashed red inside, then she remembered who and what she was supposed to be, and to cover herself said quickly, "Well, I damn well hope so! She is a girl, you know."

Robert winked. "I know."

"Robert?"

"Hey."

"Robert?"

"What're you askin'?" he said.

"Do you have a crush on my cousin?"

Robert was silent a moment.

"You do, don't you?" Esmé was unaccountably tickled by this, thought it was at the least an amazing joke. "Come on, admit it!"

"I'm not saying anything."

"Oh, you took one look at her, you sap, and you just went dreamy on her. *Hoo-eeee!*"

"I'm not admitting anything." But he kept smiling. Esmé

was so suddenly deep into the game of this that she wasn't thinking any of it through.

"You don't have to. Don't have to say a word. Wait'll I tell her!"

"You—" A shock of alarm in Robert's voice.

"Yeah, wait'll Essmay hears—"

"You do and I'll—" His eyes were glaring; he looked angry as could be.

"Robert, you—" She caught on to his anger. "You really don't want me to—"

"Not a word, Eddie." He brought his finger to his lips. "Not one word."

"Robert, she's my flesh and—"

"Please. I'm not saying anything one way or the other about your cousin, I'm not . . . I just don't want anything complicated. Things—things here are complicated enough." There was the concern, clear again in his voice. "Promise?"

Esmé could take this to heart. "O.K., I promise—I swear." But what was she swearing to? That she wouldn't tell her alter ego that Robert might have eyes for her? How could she do that? She gave her head a quick shake, then responded to the other thing he was saying. "What's wrong?"

Robert let out a long sigh. "Well, for starters, I found this guy—program director of WMAC—who was going to help me. Went to see him, and they said he'd just been fired. I think . . . think it might be for playing your record. But I don't know. And I can't find him."

"Robert!"

"What?"

"This strange thing happened. A few hours ago I heard my—I mean Essmay's; no, I mean *my*—record on the street. It was amazing, but then I was hearing it again when the radio station just went dead. When they came back on, I think they said it was . . . what were those call letters?"

"WMAC."

"The Good Guys—yeah, that was it. Then they played something by Little Evie Stone. She's on NRC, right?"

"You heard this?"

Esmé involuntarily touched an ear. "Yeah."

"I don't know, Eddie," Robert said. He was looking down at the ground, and his voice was burdened. "I—I just don't know."

＊ ＊ ＊ ＊ ＊

"PASS THE BREADSTICKS."

"Pass the—"

"The breadsticks." The Reverend Octavus Chapman pointed right at the big basket of bread at the center of the table. He was a big, round man: round moon face, round belly swelling up under his cardinal-red sweater, round rings of muscle fat on his arms and legs.

"Please?" his sister, Ramona, said. Ramona, in contrast, was bird thin, with a long nose and thinning faintly wavy hair and a nervous way of clicking her fingernails against hard surfaces. She was a high school social studies teacher in Detroit.

Octavus gave her a baleful look. "Yeah, yeah— *pleeeaaassssse*."

Ramona spun her eyes. "My brother. You'd think a preacher would have some manners, like the Lord would open him up and say, 'You're workin' for me, boy, so we gotta make you presentable.' You'd think that." She gave a short, taut laugh. "But sometimes I think the Lord just passed this big ol' boy by."

No, Octavus's first glance wasn't truly baleful, but this one was. "Ramona?"

"Least when you got food in front of him." Ramona turned to her left, where the Captain was sitting with a cool, poker-faced smile on his face. "Where you get your manners from, Captain?"

"Oh, I don't know," the man in the beautiful white suit said. "Here and there."

"Bones always had beautiful manners," Ramona said. She let out a sad sigh. God, did she miss her brother—especially right now. Never more than right this second!

"I'm sure he does," the Captain said.

"You ever meet him?"

"No, ma'am, can't say that I did." The Captain dabbed his mouth with his thick-cotton napkin. "I'm sure it's my loss."

Ramona lifted her chin a fraction, then simply let her head nod downward, as if to say: That's the simple truth. Amen.

"I miss him, too," Hermione Chapman said.

Ramona reached over and patted her hand. "Of course you do, dear. He's your husband."

That comment left everyone quiet. There were five people dining at the round, white-tableclothed table: the Captain; Rick Lapidus; Octavus Chapman; Ramona Chapman Bowden; and Mrs. Bones. The Captain was wearing his pure white silk-wool suit, and Ramona had to say, it was one gleaming example of the tailoring art. Yes, there were many things to behold in this New York City. But she had promised herself that no matter what they threw at her, she'd keep her wits.

Right now they were throwing lots of money. More money than she'd ever imagined. When Bones had started his first, jazz-oriented company, he barely had enough left-over change for gas for his Oldsmobile after he'd paid to have discs pressed. Now FDL was a real company, with records well into the Top 10 and evidently enough promise to make the venerable giant NRC come forward with hats brimming with dollars. Evidently they thought there was heaps of money to be made from the singers Bones had put together, though Ramona knew they were talking about pop music, where every release was a gamble, and the winds of taste could blow any ol' which way on any given day.

You ask her, NRC was wildly overpaying, but maybe they

had other reasons to make their offer. Ramona didn't really worry that. She was just trying to think what Bones would want.

She knew her brother liked his money, no lie. Knew that from Day One he'd thought FDL would make his fortune, and . . . here the fortune was. Would he go for it? If she took NRC's offer, she knew none of them would ever have to work again, and that Bones, when he was better—and there had been some encouragement out of the hospital in Florida—would have enough to do whatever he wanted: retire to the south of France, take a trip around the world, buy the biggest goldarn house in Detroit, even start another record company if he wanted.

But what would he do right here and now?

Bones loved Fleur-de-Lys, it was his baby, his passion, probably more a wife than the difficult woman sitting across from her. It was what he thought about first thing in the morning, and she was sure, the last thing he'd thought about before he was hit by that Ford station wagon.

She also knew that FDL was having its troubles. Their star Maisy Columbine had already gone over to NRC—Ramona could use the words *poached by*—and Mary Hardy had left, too. The resident dreamboat, Orlando, had left also, though from what she was hearing, he'd come back.

So there was still a company, still the Cravattes, the Shags, and the Daisies on the Soul Cavalcade, and others like Penny and the Thoughts and the Corvelles back in Detroit moving through the pipeline.

No, she didn't know what Bones would do. God, she wished she could talk to him, or put off this Captain till he was out of his coma, but the Captain was saying that this offer—this eye-raising, breath-stealing offer—was the only one. It was take it or leave it *now*.

Hermione was all for it, Octavus had told Ramona he wouldn't go for the offer unless she agreed, but Ramona knew he was already counting how much extra would be coming to his church. Still, the way it stood now, Ramona had to decide it all. Right there at the table her head spun, her fingernails clacked rhythmically against the empty bread plate in front of her. She was just a simple schoolteacher, with a husband with 18 years on the Ford line and two kids in high school. How could she decide something as huge as this?

But like the Lord said, You never know day in, day out how you'll be tested.

Ramona was being tested—right here and now.

"And I can assure you, Mrs. Bowden, that we will put the full force of our people behind all the artists." The Captain had evidently realized Ramona was the final sell, and he was speaking directly to her. "We have a proven track record over 40 years. We've taken acts from the days of 78s to the 45s and long players we're selling now. You know, NRC helped invent the LP, and we can put them out in a way that FDL hasn't utilized much so far. Tell me, wouldn't a group such as the Cravattes love to have an LP out on them?"

Ramona leaned back and gave the Captain the long eye. "No reason Bones couldn't do that."

"I'm not saying that. Just that we have the proven track record—the marketing, the distribution, all the modern advantages."

"Modern advantages," Ramona mused to herself. She could feel Hermione's sharp eyes on her, and her brother's softer but just as snaky gaze focused her way, too.

"All of them." What a bright shiny face the Captain had. He was a little like her brother, a honky preacher glad-handing all the way.

Which meant Ramona didn't wholly trust him. She was certainly no fool, and that only made sense.

"Well, anything we do, we'll need a good lawyer."

"Of course." The Captain nodded earnestly. "And we'll make sure you have the best money can buy."

"Well—"

"That sounds generous," Octavus said.

"The whole arrangement will take awhile," the Captain said, "of course. Everything will be done by the book. All you have to do now is join your sister-in-law in giving your assent."

"Welllll—"

"Just to get the ball rolling," Hermione said. Ramona looked over at her, in her fur even though it was a relatively warm May night out there. Oh, her sister-in-law was loving the taste of all that money; it was bubbling like the champagne she lived on just under her nose. It crossed Ramona's thoughts that Hermione might not mind it that much if Bones, well, didn't pull out of his—no, she couldn't think that about anybody. *Stop it!*

"Just one thing bothers me," Ramona said.

Everyone leaned forward.

"I'd like to talk to the artists. I don't—well, Bones never brought me around much, so I can't say I know them—but it just seems that since they're actually here with us in New York, and playing right down the street, that maybe we should all go talk to them." A rustling around the table. "Yes?"

"I'm not sure that would be proper," the Captain said.

"Proper?"

"Because we're at such a delicate place in our negotiations."

"Not proper?"

"There are rules to all of this. Lawyer rules—" he folded his pink hands before him "—but there you are."

"You mean I can't walk over a couple blocks and go talk to all the people most directly affected by this?"

"It might be awkward," Octavus said.

"It might be the only damn right thing to do!" Ramona erupted. " 'Sides, if what you say is true, Captain, they'd be like horses chompin' at the bit to go over to NRC, now isn't that so?"

"I'm sure they are, ma'am." The Captain spoke more softly. "Look at Maisy Columbine and—"

"Well, then, that's all I'm asking."

A silence at the table, glances caroming right then left, and finally Octavus said, "I think, Ramona, this is awfully. . . ." He winced, looked as if he couldn't quite get the word he wanted. " 'Sides, they got their show to do."

"Seems the perfect time. They're all in one place. What's the problem?"

There was no answer for a long minute, then the Captain said, "I think we'd better consult with the lawyers, make sure there really is no problem." He looked down at his Rolex watch. "That might take a couple days."

"All right, here's my offer." Ramona put both hands on the table, faced everybody directly. "I know that after tonight Bones's Soul Cavalcade has one more show at the Apollo Theater, and it's a matinee tomorrow. You do what you gotta do with your lawyers, Captain Bryant, but I'm going to go over there and talk to 'em all before I give my agreement to anything." Ramona stood up. "If that's all right with you, then I'm going to the Ladies', and then my brother is going to escort me back to that very fine hotel you've put us up in." A smile at the Captain. "And thank you for a most wonderful dinner."

* * * * *

THE SHAGS HAD a new number: *Like a Barracuda*. This was now their last song, and after *Men on Fire* the spot on them went dark, and when it came up, the four backup singers had masks on their face. Their central feature? Long, gray-sleek snouts with three-inch-high gleaming-white, spike-sharp teeth.

The song was a kind of rumba, and Collie Farquhar, the lead singer, moved into the spotlight, his arms making swimming motions, followed by the four other men in their shimmering sharkskin suits and their jutting masks doing the same. Blue and yellow lights splattered off the exaggerated teeth. The group sang up a furious storm, peaking with the song's chorus:

> *Think of all the ways we can do ya*
> *We're comin' at ya like a ... barracuda*
> *Yeah, comin' at ya like a ... barracuda*

The five Shags spiraled through the special new choreography, making like prime attractions at Sea World—singing, dancing killer fish—and the audience erupted in hoots and wild cheers.

In the wings Esmé grew more and more nervous. She wasn't sure what was getting to her. She'd been performing now for weeks with the Cavalcade, both as a Cravatte and a Daisy, and she'd never known more than the common flutter of feathers inside her. But this was different; she felt much as she did when she was waiting to be called on in kindergarten to stand up and do a fashion show with her dolls or show off the cupcakes she'd baked at home.

It must be because she was going out there as Essmay, who was so close to Esmé, who, as well as she could remember, was herself. There was nothing left to hide behind.

But these thoughts to her were vague, lost to the swimming lights and the fizz of anxiety gripping her. It felt all over again like the first time she'd ever performed.

The Shags, fish masks and all, dashed off the stage.

"Hey, hey," Rags Doheny said into the mike, "what about them wild Shags. You girls gonna be dreamin' about those teeth tonight? Those big ol' pearly whites?" He wiggled, half lascivious, half goofy, then wiped his brow with a handkerchief. "All righty, we got us something special now. Maybe some of you know we got a new FDL song out by a new artist, and it's been gettin' all kinds of play here in New York on WMAC, the *former* home of the Good Guys." A glance offstage toward Robert, who gave Rags a thumbs-up. "We call it *My Eyes Go Wide*, and it was written and produced by our very own Robert Warwick of the Cravattes."

Sweet applause from the audience.

"Right, and unless you been down at the bottom of a mine today—" and Rags ostentatiously leaned over and looked down past his shoes into the audience, eliciting squeals from girls right in front of him "—or you been up there on the moon—" and up shot Rags's motley-suited arm "—well, I bet you heard it. I think *Eyes Go Wide*'s one of them songs first time it enters your ears, it's like you already know it. You know what I mean?" Shouts, cries, even to Esmé's astonishment, a male voice from the far-away balcony crying out, "I love *My Eyes Go Wide*! I love Essmay!"

"Hey, hey, and that, my friend, is the little lady who sings it. Just in from the Detroit City, here she is, your newest FDL star, Esssssssmaaaaaaaaaaayyyyyy!"

She took careful steps out onto the Apollo stage, placing her tangerine-dyed shoes one in front of the other. The lights were brighter than usual, and seemed to be in far more colors, and as she moved to the microphone, it was as if she were swimming through a colored mist, almost blinded by the glare and the noise. The stage seemed far wider and more empty than when she performed with the Cravattes or the Daisies; and the lights far brighter, somehow, than when she'd gone out as Eddie pretending to be Essmay. Esmé reached up and touched her head, surprised to find that there was still a wig there, she felt so nakedly herself. Then the spotlight hit her, lit the very air around her, as if she were encased in fairy mist, and she walked slowly, not wanting to trip or lurch out of this magic moment. The applause rocked and swelled with each step. It was all just about too much.

But not. When she stood before the microphone mid-stage, out there all on her own, the band starting the count-off to her song, everything went very still and very quiet, and for a curious long moment she could have been alone—could have been twelve years old and back in front of the mirror at her house, her mother working at her beauty parlor and Esmé left by herself all afternoon with nothing but her dreams and her voice and the long mirror in her mother's bedroom. For a flickering second she beheld that long-ago vision of herself, and then the vision started floating slowly toward her—it became her.

There was no more time to hallucinate or even think. The band cranked up the intro to *My Eyes Go Wide*, and the whole performance was all on her. Her notes came out natural and easy, and she threw herself into the song as if it were all that existed in the world, her and Robert's song. She wasn't aware of singing it, not actually aware of anything, and yet when she was done, the applause was so raucous that Rags came up right next to her and gave her a big-smacking kiss.

"We love it!" someone called out.

"Sing it again!"

So even New York, even the Apollo Theater, wanted Essmay. The applause washing over her snapped her strange present-past hallucination; as the band fell into the song again, she was simply Essmay, the hot new girl singer from Detroit with the burgeoning hit. This time she knew just what she was doing. She sang the tune well, sang it fine, put it over. She was a little dismayed that the magic moment had burst, but relieved, too. This was her job, her business, and she could simply get it done. And she did.

She had a couple of other songs to sing, covers, and she pulled them off well, too, though the pizzazz wasn't there as it was with *Eyes Go Wide*. Still, she had to deliver a solid set, and she did it.

She left the stage to enthusiastic applause, everyone ready to see and hear her again. But by then Esmé's mind was elsewhere. It had hit her as she basked in the glowing audience pleasure that she was also one of the Cravattes; and that she had to run onstage with them—not just as a man but a whole other person—in less than five minutes.

"You were great," Priscilla came up and said. "Really super."

"Fabulous!" This was Robert, his eyes aglow. "You knocked 'em out."

"Thanks, thanks. That's great."

"Really good, Essmay." This was Orlando, standing back a few feet and looking down at Esmé with a benign, pleasant gleam. He drew her name out slowly, with a faint kiss on the final syllable.

"You really liked it?"

"Yes indeed."

All this was good to hear, but Esmé could see Mitch and Otis warming up a couple dance steps to her right, and they must be wondering where the hell Eddie was. Damn, she was wondering herself.

Priscilla swooped over and took her arm. "Hey, Essmay, let me show you around. You might—" a look at Robert and Orlando "—need a tour of the facilities. They're sort of hidden."

"Oh, thank you, thanks," Esmé said. She made a squinched-up little-girl-has-to-go-to-the-bathroom face. "You're a life saver," she whispered to Priscilla as she led her away.

"Don't I know it," Priscilla said with a laugh.

Priscilla led her down a corridor, up a couple of flights of stairs, then along another narrow hallway till they came to a small empty room. "I brought your suit up here. You only have a few minutes."

"What're we going to do about Essmay?" Esmé said as she pulled off her fine dress and slipped a leg into the trousers. "Aren't people going to wonder?"

"You know, when I was a girl I used to steal my older brother's *Superman* comics. That boy had the same problem." Priscilla gave a light laugh. "Had to pray there was a phone booth nearby and that nosy Lois Lane didn't catch on. But he pulled it off."

"Yeah, but—" In went Esmé's other leg.

"What, you don't got the wherewithal of Mr. Superman? You think you can actually *be* in two places at once?"

Esmé's eyebrows flew up in alarm.

"Come on, sweetie, I'm joking. I'll come up with a good story for you, don't you worry. And as soon as you're done with the Cravattes, we'll get you into your dress to sing with us Daisies."

"My head's already spinning."

"Yeah, spinning—spinning in the bed just the way you made it. But here's an idea. Why don't we get Essmay, since she's a 'real' girl, to sing with us Daisies. That way you'll only have to be two people, not three."

"I don't know if it'll make much difference." Esmé shook her head. "No, I think that might just be more confusing."

Priscilla shrugged, and Esmé sighed. "Pris, do you think they'll buy any of it?"

"Darlin', everybody's smitten with you. Haven't you noticed? You're the sweet new thing around here. I think all anybody's seein' is how pretty Essmay is, how sexy—"

"You think?"

"Hey, Orlando's eyeballin' you." Priscilla said this with a high-voiced kind of nonchalance. " 'Course, that ain't no terribly difficult accomplishment."

"I'm not wanting it, Pris. Not wanting it at all." Esmé gave her head a sharp shake. "And it's soooo damn confusing."

"Ain't confusing at all! Look at you. Behold: It's Eddie Days!" And that's who she now was: in her tight men's pants, the well-pressed linen shirt, the pencil-thin tie. "You just be the man or woman you gotta be in each moment as it comes at you, you'll do fine."

Esmé started to say she was still not sure when Priscilla held up her hand. She spoke quickly: "Listen, Essie, there's your cue—you better run. Run so fast you ain't got no time to think."

"Jesus, you're right," Esmé said, hearing the opening to *Doorbell*. Before she ran off, she leaned over and gave Priscilla a kiss on the cheek.

"Mercy!" Priscilla rolled her eyes, then winked. "Well, I got to say, Eddie, I always thought you made a good-lookin' man. A real good-lookin' man." She tsk-tsked. "And we women, we can always use us another one of them running around."

Esmé laughed in sisterly commiseration. "Don't I know it."

Priscilla flapped her hands before her: "Go. Go! Right now! Knock 'em dead, girl!"

✳ ✳ ✳ ✳ ✳

ROBERT WARWICK WAS hoping to talk more with Essmay after the show, but she didn't appear. He'd noticed that she and Priscilla had seemed to hit it off, and he went over to the Daisies' singer.

Priscilla shook her head, said, "Essmay just got really tired. She was up ungodly early this morning in Detroit, flew here, then aced the show. I told her I thought it'd be all right to head back to the hotel."

"O.K., fine," Robert went. "I guess I'll see her tomorrow."

"Oh, yes. Final show. She'll be there, I promise."

And what was that playful light in Priscilla's eyes?

Well, no time for that. Robert had more business to contend with. "Eddie," he called out to Esmé after the finale, even though she was dressed in her Daisies dress. "Can you come with me? I gotta go talk to this guy."

"Like this?" She fluffed out her skirt to make it more obvious.

"I don't care. But, yeah, if you can change back to your normal clothes quick, I can wait. Five minutes?"

Five minutes? She could become *anyone* in five minutes—why not? Maybe even Superman.

So five minutes later she was back, pants on again, men's shirt tucked in, light sweater. Hair quick conked down. Breasts still bound. Eddie Days ready to go.

Out on 125th Street, Robert tried to hail a cab—took a while for one to come by, and even up in Harlem the first cab didn't stop for the two black men. When one finally pulled up, Robert gave the name of the Bluebird on 138th Street.

On the short trip up Lenox Avenue, Robert filled Esmé in on Jimmy Devine and the tape he said he possessed that would bring NRC down—and how he'd said he'd bring it to the Fleur-de-Lys concert that night, then didn't show.

"And you think he's going to be at this bar?"

"It's all I got," Robert said. "But way it sounded, he's one stone regular."

The carved wooden bar, the sad-sack boozers, the dust-mottled yellow-gray light, the neon sign that fizzed BUD-WEISER in the window . . . this was a truly deadbeat joint, Esmé saw right off, the kind she'd stopped going into after Chicago. Robert, though, charged straight in, winked at the bartender, and got a nod to the end of the bar. There, just as Robert had found him the night before, was Jimmy Devine.

"So here I am," Robert said. "Though I thought you were coming to the show—"

Devine turned around slowly. "I got thirsty."

"Thirsty?"

"Hey, I got canned today, boy. What's it to you?"

Esmé could hear Robert inhale deeply. She laid a hand on his arm. Devine looked deep into his cups. His nose was so red it was almost blistered, his eyes were bloodshot, and his words came out slurred. She thought that this wasn't the time to get into an altercation with the guy.

"Have you been. . . ." Robert started to say. Esmé gave his arm a squeeze. "O.K., O.K.," Robert said after looking at her. "We're here about that tape you promised me?"

"Promised?"

Robert flashed a sharp look, then said quick to Esmé, "Let's go."

But she couldn't let these men do their animal thing. She stepped forward, saying, "Mr. Devine, Robert tells me you have people from NRC on tape shaking you down. We just came to hear it, and to work out some kind of deal."

"He knows the deal I want."

"Robert?"

"I don't see a contract in your hands," Devine muttered.

"What's the deal, Robert?"

"He wants a cut of *My Eyes Go Wide*."

"A cut?" Esmé said. "What percent?"

But Robert wheeled back on Devine. "I'd think you'd want to hurt NRC. Wasn't it them who got you fired today? For playing our song. Our 'hit'!"

Devine's head wobbled. He said slowly, "Man's gotta look out for himself."

"What's the percentage?" Esmé said again.

"He wants thirty percent of everything."

"Fifty," Devine said.

"Fifty—"

"Have you even heard the tape yet, Robert?" Esmé said.

Robert didn't answer her. "I'll go thirty, not fifty. That's all."

"I thought we was gonna be partners," Devine said, with a smirk.

Robert stood up, his eyes flashing. "It's my fuckin' song. I'll give you thirty percent. And only if your tape stops NRC cold."

"Fifty."

"Thirty!"

Esmé held Robert back again.

Devine let out a long cackle. "You putz, I always get fifty, and I've gotten it from better than you." He pushed himself up by his hands and faced Robert straight on. "And for just playing somebody's damn song, too."

Robert turned and started toward the door. Esmé said,

"Robert!" but he didn't stop. His head was high and he was walking with true purpose. She hurried after him, catching him in out on the street. He was so angry she saw heat rising off his flat black forehead. "I'm not going to be robbed," he hissed. " 'Specially by a fuckin' creep like that."

"You're right," she said. "And we haven't even heard the tape."

"Oh," Robert said, "I'm sure the tape's good, just what he says it is. Everything I hear about NRC ... they're just thugs, I'm sure of that."

"So what're we going to—"

Robert was glaring. "We got the music," he said after a moment. "We still got the goddamn music. Nobody's taken that from us yet."

Esmé stood there a second listening to Robert's boots clatter on the sidewalk, then quickly followed after him.

* * * * *

BACK AT THE HOTEL THERESA, Robert excused himself, telling Esmé that he had more things to check on and that he'd see her up in their room. And that's what she should have done, just gone to bed as Eddie and left it at that. But she was feeling that fizzy excitement, as if she had a brand-new toy and she couldn't wait to try it out. She dashed up to the room and changed into her getup as Essmay.

That is, she dressed as herself. That still felt odd to her, and she looked in the mirror and saw her thin eyebrows, her smooth skin, her short but cute-cut hair with a simple, profound delight.

She was headed down to the elevator when she felt someone behind her, then heard her name. "Essmay. Hey!"

She recognized Orlando's voice even before she turned around.

"Hey, darlin', where you headin'?"

"Oh, um, just out for a walk." She smiled at him. "I couldn't sleep. First day in New York City and all."

"I love this city," he said expansively. "It's a great place."

"Seems that way."

"So, hey, babe, let's go," Orlando said, taking her hand.

His hand surprised her. It was very soft, with fine nails buffed to a velvety edge. He didn't overpress or tug on her own hand; instead, having her hand in his felt like . . . well, as if his hand were black velvet in a box, there simply to support the jewel of her own flesh.

"Where?" she said softly.

"I'll go walkin' with you." His wide smile. "It's a lovely night, and you're a lovely girl—"

Did she blush? What else could that warmth be that instantly suffused her face?

"You say that to every girl?" she said flippantly, and even though her line felt corny to her, she really did want to hear his answer.

He gave his shoulders a rustle, like a bird about to show plumage, then fixed her with his wide, bright eyes. "Tonight, darlin', I'm sayin' it only to you."

Well, that wasn't too bad. Probably even . . . true. Now how would Essmay take it? Who was this Essmay right now? Was she a young, naive girl dazzled by her first time away from home, walking hand-in-hand with a dreamboat singer whose picture she'd had on her wall for years? Or was she a manifestation of Eddie Days, who had been around this Orlando Calabrese on and off for a month and seen his doggish ways? In this moment only one answer came to her: She squeezed his hand back.

"You were great tonight," he said as they strolled out of the hotel lobby. They turned left, up to 125th Street. The night was rose-petal soft, a light breeze gentle on their arms. "A little jewel."

"I thought it went all right."

"Hey, give yourself credit, darlin'. What you did? Hey, no audience ever asked me to sing a song twice in a row."

Esmé blushed again. "That's 'cause it's such a fine song. Your friend Robert Warwick did such a good—"

"Oh, yeah, Robert sure did," Orlando interrupted, speaking quickly. Esmé understood he didn't want to talk about Robert. At this moment with Orlando this close to her she didn't really want to either.

They strolled along 125th Street, hands tight, and the longer they were together, Esmé was noticing (with the part of her that was still noticing things) how Orlando had some mysterious way of making her feel wrapped up in him. He wasn't doing anything special she could note, but with every few steps there was just more of him there, a warm man-body closer to her, enveloping her more tightly, making her feel that the two of them were simply floating together in a world of just-them.

"Would you like a drink, sugar?"

"Um, I don't know if I'm old enough," Esmé said.

"How old are you, baby?"

Honest answer? Why not. "Nineteen."

"That's a sweet age. Not exactly sweet sixteen—" Orlando began to frown, then said, "But, yeah, hey, sweet nineteen." He laughed. "I don't know the drinking age in this town neither, but if you are or you ain't, don't matter. I got me a bottle back in my room."

She raised an eyebrow. "Orlando—"

"Just a nightcap, celebrate your success tonight. Besides, I'm missing Detroit. I'd like you to tell me 'bout everything been going on—"

How'd he do this? He'd steered them through their Harlem perambulation so that at this crucial moment they were standing again right in front of the Hotel Theresa.

"Just one?" Esmé said. How much trouble would one drink get her into?

Orlando held up his right hand, showing three fingers. "Scout's honor."

"Why, that's three fingers—"

"Why, was it two? Or just one?" He fumbled through different versions of the Scout salute, all the while with his eyes making it clear he wasn't talking about Scouts at all.

Esmé laughed. "Not much of a Boy Scout, were you?"

Orlando winked, and it was like the whole top half of his head crinkled. Ooh, that creamy skin. Then he threw one of his stage smiles at her, that huge one that lit up his whole face, made his features soften and melt together just enough to make you think warm cookies and milk. "Well, truth was, they didn't have Scouts for little black boys like me." A shrug. "Always thought I'd've made a good one."

They were in the lobby now, waiting for the elevator. Esmé cast a glance around to see if any of the Cavalcade was there to see the two of them. She didn't see anyone. "Why?" she said.

Orlando took his time answering, till they got in the elevator, and then off on their floor. "Well," he said, "I was always pretty good at rubbing two things together and starting a fire."

Esmé laughed. "Yeah, I bet you were."

"Here," Orlando said a moment later. "This is my room."

"Who're you roomin' with?"

"You wouldn't know him, one of the band, the bass player. Bunny?"

"Haven't met him yet," Esmé said, shaking her head, though of course she knew Bunny Alexander well. "And is he here?"

"He might be." Orlando opened the door, held it back. "Bunny? Bunny, you there?"

Esmé knew this was for show. Bunny and the rest of the band had been talking all day about a card game they'd found up on 142nd Street—the kind of game that went all night.

"Guess he's not here." Orlando lifted his arms wide in a what-can-I-do shrug. "Well, darlin', if you'd feel better, I could keep the door open—"

The door . . . open? Her room with Robert was another forty feet down the hall. And anyone walking by could easily look in and. . . .

"It's all right," Esmé said softly. "You can close it."

To Orlando's credit he pulled the wooden door shut without making anything much of it, then walked over to his bureau, where a bottle of gin and four glasses stood.

"Gin all right?"

"Looks like it's gotta be." Esmé smiled. She wasn't nervous or wary; wasn't much of anything but enveloped in Orlando's musk.

She took a proffered glass, they clinked, and the next second Orlando was right beside her, his hands on her shoulders. "You're pretty tense, baby," he said, cooing.

Now this was truly corny. Esmé started to pull away and laugh, but she couldn't. His hands were . . . just right. She knew he was trying to seduce her, and that she should right this minute get up and. . . . What she said was, "That feels good."

"I can feel it in you, baby. Slow and easy. Down deep." What was he doing with his voice? It was sing-songy, like his on-record voice—that voice she'd felt her whole spirit soar into when she first spun his 45s on her personal record player—but he'd dropped his tone, well, not a whole octave, but down there where each word came out as if it'd been run around the rim of a barrel before touching her ear. Doooowwwwnnnn Deeeeeeeeeeeeeeeep. Indeed.

His hands kept going, but now they were moving, feathering the bottom of her neck, those velvety fingernails just brushing her collarbone. She felt her skin stiffen. Orlando must've felt it, too, because he made his next move right away: He let his fingers drop so that they ran just inside the scallop-necked front of her dress, right above her flowery bra. Just at the beginning of the most tender skin on her breast.

Tingles burst through her body.

"Oh, you're comin' along nice, baby," he said in that echoey deep voice, right up now by her ear. And—good God, was that his tongue? Dabbing right behind her ear? Da-ha-haaammmmmnnnnnn!

She'd necked with guys in Detroit, of course, and some of them were pretty smooth, but nobody had gone behind her ear before. She remembered one fellow, name of Stick, who smushed his tongue flat in her ear, like that was supposed to do something, but nobody had found that secret indentation behind the lobe flap, that tiny bowl there that right now was getting flicked with Orlando's tongue and shooting more shivers all through her.

Even as her body went just where he took it, she wasn't losing all her senses. She knew this was the Orlando who seduced women just because he could. Figured that he was with her now because she was the new woman, the latest challenge. That he was the man who'd left the Soul Cavalcade for Maisy Columbine, then come back as if nothing had happened.

She also remembered that it was the poster of his face, so close and breathily warm to her now, that she'd put up on her bedroom wall at home. Looked at for years. Held in her gaze as her hands moved experimentally down her sides. That face, those eyes, those magical hands. . . .

She saw Orlando's eyes glowing at her. But even as he slipped his hand under the stiff cap of her bra, then took her own hand and moved it easefully down his muscle-thick leg, she felt a part of her just watching all this happen—as if she were still back in her girlish room. Was this how it was supposed to be on your first time? Was it normal to be a little distant, a little removed?

Right before he reached out and turned off the bedside light, then undid her blouse and skirt and lowered his bulk over her slender body, another curious thing happened: She had a glimpse in her mind's eye of Robert Warwick. What was he doing there? Even as her own eyes closed and she welcomed Orlando into her, it was Robert's eyes she saw. Robert's eyes reaching into her and touching her soul.

Chapter Fifteen

Sunday, May 10— New York City

SHE CAME BACK to her hotel room at dawn, blushing, and though the morning light was just beginning to streak pink and yellow light through the half-pulled-down shades, Robert was already up and waiting for her—or him. Esmé had slipped out of Orlando's room as soon as she awoke, before the singer stirred, then quickly decided she'd better become Eddie as quick as possible. She thought about sneaking into her room but worried about Robert's being up, then she remembered that she had a set of Eddie Day's clothes back at the Apollo. The theater was locked up tight, but by pounding on the stage door she was able to rouse a night-watchman, who was dubious about her until she pointed to a photo of Essmay, which was actually the photo of herself dressed for the Daisies, and said, "I'm with the Soul Cavalcade. I've left something important here, and I have to get it right this minute."

"You're in the Cavalcade?" the watchman said woozily. He looked a little drunk.

"Yes, that's me." She pointed again to the picture then threw out her legs and preened next to it. The guard was convinced.

On her way out, in her sleek sharkskin suit and trilby hat, she lowered her voice and said, "Thanks, that was a big help."

The watchman jumped up in a flurry of limbs and a sputter of words: "Hey, who are you?"

Then back to her normal woman's voice: "Oh, I'm with the Cavalcade. You just let me in. Don't you remember?"

"Hey, hey, wait, hold on," the watchman shouted, fumbling under his wool jacket and pulling out a gun-metal flashlight, which he bumbled and watched clatter to the floor. A silver-polished whistle and a long wooden billy club followed, both of which also flew from his butterfinger hands. The watchman stooped and picked up the whistle first, and after sticking it in his mouth backward turned it around and started blowing it wildly after Esmé, who by this point was halfway down 125th Street.

"Hey," Robert said as she let herself in with her key. "Where've you been?"

Esmé was startled to see him up and awake. "Oh, um, out." Out?

"Doing what?"

Esmé shuffled from side to side. "Well, I—"

"You hook up with somebody?"

"Well, yeah." Esmé blushed.

"Finally!" Robert gave Esmé a sly smile. "And?"

"I don't think I oughta talk about it."

Robert smiled. "After all this time on the road you get lucky, and you turn out to be a gentleman. Good for you, Eddie. And you know, I'm not gonna pry. Not like some of the guys around here."

Esmé pursed her brow.

"You know, like Orlando. You ever hear him get going on about some piece of ass he nailed?" Robert frowned. "That man, I think he likes to brag about it even more than do it."

"Really, I don't—" Esmé was blushing again, deeply this time.

"Oh, that Orlando's a terror. You know, I always say, one of the best things 'bout being a guy is you don't have people like Orlando coming after you." A short pause. "So can you tell me anything?"

"Well, it was . . . unexpected. I was sort of—I know this sounds weird—but I was kind of swept off my feet."

"Like that, eh? Some chickie in the audience?"

Esmé gave a half-nervous half shake of her head. "I really can't—"

"It wasn't some girl on the Cavalcade?" Robert frowned even as he leaned forward with vivid curiosity.

"Oh!" Damn, was she blushing again? "Robert, please, I really can't say another word." Esmé was feeling distinctly unsettled. "Please."

"Well, we know one thing—it wasn't Essmay." Robert laughed. "Hey, Eddie, I'm just trying to be friendly with you, not embarrass you. You gonna see the chickie again?"

Oh, God! Esmé hadn't given a moment's thought to the next step with Orlando. "Um, that's not clear. Aren't we heading back to Detroit right after the show today?" There, that should throw him off.

Robert fell silent at that.

"Robert?"

"Um, nothing," he said. "Just something I'm—" He looked down, then clearly changed the subject. "So, hey, tell me, how's your cousin doing?"

For a minute Esmé was at a loss. Her brain just fritzed, like an overloaded electrical circuit. She felt Robert's suddenly intent gaze on her. Her cous—? "Oh, Essmay." Yes, of course, her cousin! "I haven't talked to her today." Esmé yawned. "I'm sure she's still asleep. I always remember she was quite a sleeper." A faint smile. "I'm sure she'll pop up sooner or later."

"But far as you know she got tucked in safe in her room last night?"

Esmé heard true concern in Robert's voice. How sweet. "I'm sure she did, yes."

"That's good." Robert nodded.

Esmé had been moving around the room, taking off her shoes, eyeing the bed with longing. Just then she was struck by a furious need to be alone. "Robert, excuse me for a sec," she said, then went into the bathroom. She pulled the door tight behind her, dropped her trousers, sat on the toilet and quickly peed, then got up and looked at herself in the mirror.

eyes, which Esmé strongly wanted to see, were hidden in shadows. "Essmay, hey." A faint smile. It looked like he, too, wanted to pretend the whole scene with Orlando hadn't taken place. "Yeah, I was thinking we could add another song or two to your set. Maybe a couple new ones. What do you think? You did good last night, and we could keep that going longer."

"You're not pulling anything, are you?" Orlando said quickly.

Robert shook his head. "I just want to make sure we're giving the best show we can." Robert was speaking in a tight voice, clipping each word. "Orlando, this goes for you, too."

"What you want from me, boss?" Orlando parted his lips. The *boss* sounded sardonic to Esmé's ears. "Something other than my usual . . . great performance?" At the last two words, he gave Esmé a visible poke in the sides.

Robert sighed. "Just the best you got. We got a lot riding on it, man. A lot riding on it."

"I'll do whatever you want . . . Mr. Warwick," Esmé said, and waited a second, hoping that he'd tell her to call him Robert. "Another song, or—"

"Good," Robert said, simply business. "We'll work it out at rehearsal this morning." He looked past both Esmé and Orlando. "Where's your cousin?"

"Um, he's—" Esmé was going to make an allusion to Eddie's alleged adventures the night before, but that no longer seemed appropriate. "Um, he said he wanted to go get a paper. He should be back any minute."

"Well, if you see him, send him along." Still that tight, business-only voice. Esmé found it curiously depressing.

"Right, boss," Orlando said with his big smile. He put his arm around Esmé and led her out of the room. She tried discretely to shake his hand off her shoulders but wasn't able to till they were out in the hallway and Orlando had pulled the door shut behind them.

She gave a shimmy and was free.

"Hey, sugar, you want to get us some breakfast?" Orlando was flipping his orange again.

"No thanks."

"You sure?" Orlando's mouth opened and his tongue crept over the corner of his lips. "Something really tasty?"

"I don't think so." She heard herself take a deep breath. Then she leaned up and kissed his cheek. She knew he was the kind of man who needed at least that to get him to back off. "But thanks, though."

"Well, there's always lunch, sugar. Or dinner? Or another . . . nightcap. . . ."

Esmé shrugged noncommitally, then turned away far enough so that Orlando could only take the hint and leave. When he was gone she stood there. Should she go back and talk to Robert? But as Essmay she hardly knew him, and she didn't know what she could say. She couldn't deny what had happened. She tried never to lie (well, except for her whole existence on the Cavalcade being one big lie after another, but that—that was different). So she had nothing to say to him, and that fact unsettled her heart. She had a tremendous need to see Robert again right then, to try to begin to make things right. Another long sigh. O.K., she thought, I'll send Eddie in. Maybe *he* can make things better.

She ran back to Essmay's room, pulled off the yellow sun dress, left on her bra and panties, though, and quickly stepped into Eddie's pants and shoes. She was dressing so quickly she buttoned her shirt wrong. Damn! She grabbed a deep breath then rebuttoned the shirt, matching up the shirttails and climbing each silvery button one at a time. By the time she tucked in the shirt she was half out the door. Then she realized her breasts were rising noticeably against the cloth, and she grabbed a loose-cut jacket, slipping it on and buttoning it over her chest.

"Hey," Robert said as she slipped into their room. "Get your paper?"

"And a quick egg sandwich. You eaten yet?"

Robert shook his head. "I don't have time."

"My cousin come by?"

Robert looked away, then said, "Oh, yeah."

"And?"

"I told her I was thinking of having her sing another song or two."

"And?"

"She said she would." He said just that, nothing more.

"Robert, you seem sort of—" Esmé winced, then moved over to her bed, sat on its side. "Something happen between the two of you?"

"Why do you say that?"

Why do I say. . . ? She stood up. "Didn't you tell me yesterday you were interested in my cousin?"

"I never said that."

"You—? Hey, we talked it all over."

Robert was looking away, shaking his head. "I remember you tryin' to get me to say something." He popped up his forehead. "I never did."

"And that's all?"

Now Robert got off his bed. "Eddie, what're you gettin' at?"

"I just thought, Essmay came by, you were alone with her. . . . You know I don't want to pry."

"We weren't alone."

"What do you mean?"

"We weren't alone, that's all." He looked over tight-lipped. "Listen, brother, the sooner you get off your silly fantasy about me and your cousin the better." Robert was furious; Esmé could hear it. "You hear?"

✳ ✳ ✳ ✳ ✳

ON HER WAY DOWNSTAIRS Esmé bumped into Priscilla. "Hey, hey!" the fellow Daisy called. "Eddie. Eddie Days, my man! Wait up." Priscilla ran over, catching her breath. Close to Esmé, she smirked. "It is Eddie, isn't it?"

"Girl, I hardly know myself," Esmé said, then laughed.

"Yeah, you look a little—" Priscilla dipped her head toward Esmé's unbound chest.

"Oh, jeez," she said, looking down. "I thought the jacket covered them."

"Guess again, sweetie." Priscilla let out a laugh.

"So how're you?"

"Oh, I'mmmmm fine." Priscilla drawled out the middle word. "And how's Essmay today?"

There was a sharper look than Esmé was used to from Priscilla, her eyes partially hooded over. She recognized it as the exact look Priscilla used to give Maisy Columbine.

"I heard Essmay had herself a little adventure last night."

"You heard—" Esmé shook her head. "How'd you hear about that?" she said, though of course she knew. She uttered a silent curse.

"So, it's true?"

Esmé had a quick thought not to admit anything, though this was her good friend Priscilla. "Well, she was out late, yeah, if that's what you mean."

Priscilla took that with her shoulders tight. "Seems like everybody loves your Essmay."

"Just 'cause she's new."

"Yeah, right. And what did Robert say?"

That stung Esmé's heart. "Oh, Pris, he wasn't happy!"

"I'll bet he wasn't."

"What? Why do you say that?"

"You know as well as I do," Priscilla said. She had her hands planted on her hips, elbows cocked right at Esmé. "He's got a stone thing for your Essmay."

Esmé gave her friend a tight, half-simpering, half-smirking, all-uncomfortable smile, the look of a little girl caught. "So what else am I missing around here?"

To that Priscilla didn't say a thing, though her gaze bore down on Esmé. There was something Esmé wasn't getting, though she couldn't figure out what it was. Then Priscilla said, "One question: What'd you tell Robert last night that his roommate was up to?"

"Oh, that was good!" Esmé brightened. "I told Robert that Eddie finally scored—"

Priscilla leaned toward her. "What'd he say to that?"

"He said, 'About time.' " Esmé smiled, tried to get the friendliness going again. "What else could he say?"

"Who'd, um, Eddie say he was with?"

"Oh," Esmé laughed, "Eddie, he don't kiss and tell." Now her smile was genuine, if biting. "He's an honorable man."

Priscilla didn't say a word for a long minute, then whispered under her breath. Esmé wasn't certain what she'd said, but she heard something like, "I just can't help myself."

✶ ✶ ✶ ✶ ✶

ROBERT WAS OFF to midtown, to a studio on West 40th Street. The surprising call had come at a good time, right when he needed to get away from the Cavalcade and Orlando and Essmay—needed to clear his head. "Robert, you gotta get down here," Maisy Columbine had cried through the receiver. "They don't get it. They just don't get it at all."

"Maisy, you O.K.?"

"Nooooooo!" she cried. "I'm dyin' here. I'm at the NRC studio, and they just don't get it. Can't get the beat to fall in the right way, can't get the band to swing. And then they want to put violins on everything, drizzle 'em over my voice like hot fudge on a sundae!"

Hearing this was deeply gratifying to Robert, but he knew enough not to gloat. "So, what can I do?"

"Way I hear things are goin', you're practically part of NRC now," Maisy said in a matter-of-fact way. Robert winced. "Why don't you just come down and hang around. Maybe give 'em a nudge here and there."

"Who's going to listen to me?"

"I don't know." Maisy snorted. "They damn well ain't listenin' to me!"

"They aren't?"

"It's worse than with Bones, Robert. Worse than with Bones! Can you believe I just said that. One thing, these guys are white."

"One more reason they won't listen to me."

"Please, darlin', just come down to the studio, be with me. Might not do no good, but can't hurt. *Pleeeeaaaaase?*"

Well, Robert agreed to go, not only because the vision of Maisy on the other end of the phone begging him—him!—unnerved him, but also because he was seeing glimpses of a way that she might be helpful to the cause.

His first thought after being buzzed into the NRC studio was Wow!

What he'd known best was FDL's cramped basement, each instrument on top of the other, and the control room in a former closet with a small rectangle of scratched glass to see through. This room was . . . huge. It was wholly covered in acoustical tiles. The control room was about the size of the whole FDL studio, there was enough room on the main floor for a small orchestra, and here and there were true isolation booths: enclosed glass boxes with expensive mikes dangling head-high. The mikes! Robert knew a thing or two about gear, and he saw immediately that these studios had everything top of the line. The mikes and signal processors looked well used but just as well cared for. Those back in Detroit were bought secondhand to begin with, and though everyone was professional enough to respect the equipment, when you were recording in that small a space, well, somebody was always knocking a tube Neumann mike over or sending feedback through the large Celestion speakers.

As he walked in, Maisy was inside one of the isolation booths, and there was a combo behind her, the basic players they would've used at FDL but also, as she'd said, a double

"I like that," Lapidus said into his P.A. mike, and somehow his volume knob must've been spun up, because his words boomed through the studio: "I LIIIIKE THAAAAAAT." Robert's and the band's fingers flew to their ears; Maisy in her isolation booth wasn't affected at all. "Sorry," Lapidus said, his voice now at a normal level. "But I think that's a keeper. Maisy?"

"Whatever you say, boss."

Lapidus took that as full affirmation, nodding and saying, "All right, gentlemen, that's a wrap."

The mustached A&R man came out of his booth and approached Robert. "So, whaddya think?"

"Interesting."

"It's gonna be a hit for her, I feel it in my bones," Lapidus said fast. "Gonna take her right to Number 1." He looked down at Robert and added pointedly, "Finally."

Robert gave a nod, then noticed that Maisy had slipped out of her singing booth. He excused himself and went over to her.

"Well?" she said.

Robert laughed. "I don't know whether I want it, got it already, or would pay any price to keep it away from me." He hummed, *The knicky-knicky, knickety-knock.*

Maisy rolled her eyes. "They want that the A side. Funny thing, the B's actually not that bad, but, jeez, you think some program director's gonna turn the disc over after he hears *that*?"

"Anything you can do?"

Maisy lifted her eyes, shot them toward Lapidus, up in the booth with the door open, talking to his engineer. She called out, "Mr. Lapidus, I'm gonna go outside and catch a smoke with my old friend. O.K.?"

"We're doing playback in a moment, Maisy."

"Oh, I'm sure it's gonna be great. You guys give it a listen, let me know what you think."

And before anything further could be said, Maisy led Robert out of the studio, along the hallway, ignoring the elevator—"It takes forever"—and pushing open a door next to a red-painted sign that read EMERGENCY ONLY. A few flights down, and they were in a small concrete courtyard behind the studio building.

"So what do you really think?" Maisy said with a laugh. Under the guard light the white panels of her dress shone silver.

Robert just laughed back.

She shook her head. "I don't know, I thought it'd be a good idea, and I still think I'm better off out of FDL, but—"

"Maybe you just gotta work with them."

"I am." Maisy held out a pack of Lucky's. Robert declined. "That's what you saw in there, me working with 'em. 'Yes, Mr. Lapidus. Another take, Mr. Lapidus? Anything you all want.' Jeez! I want to have a talk with the Captain, but he's spending all his time trying to buy up you guys."

That's one reason Robert was here, to learn something he didn't know. "How's he doing?" he said quietly.

"Looks like it's a done deal, my friend." Maisy laughed. "Welcome to NRC."

"You want us all there with you?"

Maisy took a moment to answer. "Not really," she said softly. "Nothin' personal." She trilled out a laugh. "You know me, I like bein' the queen bee." A shrug. "But like I said, Robert, nobody listens to me about business." Then she tried to change the subject. "By the way, how's Orlando?"

Robert bristled inside, felt the tips of his ears redden. But he chose not to answer. "When's it going to happen?"

"Hmnnn? Oh, the deal? Any day now. The Captain, he's got Bones's whole family in town. They all just gotta sign you guys away—"

"And they're going to do it?"

"What I hear—though I don't hear everything."

"Maisy, what do you know?" Robert leaned in toward her. "Can you tell me anything else? This is important."

She puffed at her cigarette, blew out gray smoke, then made a lighthearted shrug. "Well, Ramona, Bones's sister, she's not sure yet—the only one not humming the NRC tune. But I'm sure she'll be coming around. Got Hermione going for it, and you know what that means." Maisy gave out a loud snort. "Hey, what do you hear about Bones?"

Robert shook his head. "No real change."

"Damn!" Maisy nodded slowly. "You know, he'd hate this, what NRC is doing. Even I know that." She took one last puff on her Lucky, then tossed it to the concrete and ground it out with the heel of one of her near knee-high boots.

"You're sure it's all over for us?" Robert was hoping for a new idea, some way in. "Nothing we can do?"

She shook her head. "I don't know what. What I hear, the final signing's planned for this afternoon, after Ramona goes to see you at the Apollo—"

That caught Robert up quick. "She's coming to the Apollo?"

Maisy nodded. "That's what I heard. Wants to see you guys one last time." Maisy paused, then said with apparently detached curiosity, "By the way, what're you doin' about me?"

"In the Daisies?"

Maisy gave a tight nod.

"Priscilla's taken over."

"Oh."

Robert loved that *Oh*. It was soft, delicate, as introspective as Maisy ever got. There was a deep, satisfied smile in him, but he tried hard not to let it out. He didn't hold any ill will toward Maisy Columbine; indeed, he thought the Daisies were better with Priscilla and was basically glad Maisy had decamped. He saw no reason to antagonize her. "This afternoon's our final show. You're sure Ramona will be there?"

"Unless something's changed."

Robert gave a quick nod. "Great." Then he started to back away. "Listen, I gotta go. But good luck."

"Good luck?"

"With *The Knicky-knock*." Now the smile was full on his face.

"Yeah, sure."

They left smiling at each other, a good thing, Robert was certain. Back in the cab uptown he had one thought: We gotta give the performance of our lives this afternoon. Gotta go out there and knicky, knicky, knicky-knock 'em dead.

✳ ✳ ✳ ✳ ✳

"WELCOME, HARLEM, U.S.A.!" Rags Doheny called into the mike. It was 3 p.m. and the house was full. Cheers and shouts greeted him. The energy was wildly high. "We're the FDL Soul Cavalcade, and this is our first matinee here in New York City—and our final show. And I want you to know, we're gonna simply knock the socks right off of your . . . heads!"

Laughter rang out.

"Now I hope all of you did the right thing and went to church this morning, had yourself a nice Sunday dinner—I'll tell you, I did, chicken and waffles and some mean green beans in fatback, mmmmnnn, mmmmmn, mnnnnnn." More laughs from the audience, and Rags leaned forward and pointed to a woman in the front row, saying, "Tell me, ma'am, what'd you have for Sunday dinner?"

The woman blushed but right off answered up, "We had us a ham!"

Laughter. "I bet it was a good 'un."

"Oh, mister, it was!" More laughs.

"Well, I hope you didn't get yourself too full of that ham, 'cuz, you know, we got us some ham, too." The crowd was in Rags's hands now, smiling, tittering. "Oh, yes we do. Got us some real wild hams, they jump all over the stage just like barnyard animals." He threw his arm out to the stage wings. "Ladies and gentleman, give a big New York City Harlem Apollo welcome to the fabulous Shags!"

The group ran onto the stage, Buzz doing a somersault, Collie grabbing the mike and starting to climb up it, Reggie the bass man, standing still and so storklike he got his own laughs just being there. They ran through their usual set, and maybe it was something about the Sunday afternoon, or maybe Rags had it right, everybody'd had some church in them, then some fine food, and they were feeling fat and sassy; but whatever, the audience was all over the five men, laughing as loud as they applauded, and calling out each man's name as they took their solos.

Robert, with Esmé as Eddie standing next to her, looked out from the curtain wings.

"That's them," he said.

"Which? Oh, the people around the old white guy, right?"

Robert nodded. "Can you—O.K., what do you think from looking at them? First impressions."

Esmé peered forward. "The white man, that's this Captain guy, head of NRC? Yeah, he looks pretty sharp, could talk a snake out of its skin, easy." She moved her gaze along. "Guy with the big stomach, that's Bones's brother?" She smiled. "He looks like he'll follow the next plate of food set in front of him. And that other woman, the one with the pinched chin and the high-piled hair—which one's that?"

"Hermione, Bones's wife."

Esmé shook her head. "Forget her. And that leaves Bones's sister . . . hey, she looks sort of nice. Didn't you say she was a high school teacher? I don't know, Robert, but maybe. . . ."

"Show of our lives," he said half under his breath.

Right then the Shags dashed off the stage. "O.K., Eddie," Robert said, "let's hit it!"

The Cravattes had a new first song, *Big Bouncing Boy*, and Robert was the lead. Otis, Mitch, and Esmé lined up as usual to his right, and after the band's horn intro, the three back-ups dipped and bobbed, and Robert stepped to the mike and launched powerfully into the first verse.

Things went wrong right from there. Esmé, after the embarrassment of her unbound breasts this morning, had before the show tied them down extra carefully, but she'd made the gauze too tight, and as she leaned in for her high harmonies, the wrapping bound up her chest so that she could hardly get a note out. Damn! She wriggled and shook, trying to stay at least close to the choreography of the act, but she couldn't get the gauze to loosen. She'd tucked in the end of the cloth behind her back, and she darted her hand there to free it, all the while bobbing her shoulders in time with Mitch and Otis. Her fingertips tugged at the tight-wrapped gauze, but she couldn't find the end. Damn again!

Finally, she couldn't take it any longer and simply stepped out of the lineup and glided to the side of the stage, where she saw Priscilla. Robert let his voice soar into the glissando of high notes of the chorus, *"Baby, I'm more than a bundle of joy / I'm your very own big bouncing boy,"* then looked over to see if everything was all right. She nodded to let him know it was nothing serious, then turned to find Priscilla right beside her. Esmé quick whispered, "My breasts, the wrapping's too tight. Pris, you gotta loosen it." She twirled, lifted her jacket. "Behind me."

Priscilla deftly lifted Esmé's suit coat, then untucked her shirt and found the gauze. She picked at its end, freed it, then said to Esmé, "Spin a few times."

That did it: The gauze was free. Esmé felt it slide down her torso. "Can you get it back up?" she said to her friend, but when Priscilla tried to tie it again, Esmé's clothes got in the way. As Priscilla moved her warm hands under Esmé's silk shirt, she just couldn't seem to get the gauze stuck enough to start wrapping it again. Finally, the filmy white stuff fluttered to the floor.

On the stage *Big Bouncing Boy* was soaring into its finale, when the four Cravattes would raise their hands, point to the heavens, then bow deeply. Esmé, not wanting to miss that, felt Priscilla fumble again and simply said, "It's O.K., let it go. I gotta get back out there."

"You sure?" Esmé never wore a bra with the gauze, and without the wrapping, her breasts were free.

"It'll be all right, Pris, let me go."

But it wasn't. As she joined Robert, Mitch, and Otis for the final bow, she leaned over and felt her breasts fall loose, her nipples clearly indented on the white silk shirt, barely covered by her open suit coat. The silk shirts they were wearing were low cut with wide, flaring collars, and it struck Esmé that somebody in the front row could look all the way down her chest.

Good God! As the applause clambered up to the stage, she looked carefully into the near rows of seats. Was anybody—look, there were two men, and one of them was pointing right at her. She flushed a fiery red, pulled the jacket tightly around her. Then the second man elbowed his neighbor on the other side.

Song Number Two. This one, *Moving On*, commenced with all four Cravattes with their backs to the audience, then spinning as one and stepping forth like a line of gunslingers to their mikes before starting the *"Oooh-ooooh-eeeee"* that led into the tune. Later Esmé tried to figure out just what happened. It was Mitch, just a scintilla off the beat, that threw them. He spun around before anyone else, and Otis tried to catch up with him. Esmé was diverted enough worrying about her chest that she was simply waiting for the proper cue. When it came and she started to slide toward the mike, Otis's foot was right in front of her. Her Italian boot caught on it, and she tripped and fell face forward to the wooden stage, breaking her tumble with her hands.

A loud "Ooohhhh!" came from the audience, and there Esmé was, on her stomach, facing right at them. She was less embarrassed about that, though, than knowing that those men in the front row were looking straight at her again. She tried to scrunch herself up so that her blouse didn't flap open, and basically succeeded, but in doing so she pulled back far enough that the shirt cloth pulled tight across her chest; and this time her breasts pressed tight against the very expressive silk fabric. Not only were her nipples vivid points, but the gentle curves of her full breasts were clearly outlined.

Now it wasn't just a couple men in the front row; there was a wide tittering across the front of the audience. Esmé blushed again, with even more heat than before.

Robert was looking at her, too, with a puzzled look. Esmé prayed that all he was thinking was *Why did Eddie fall?* but she had no way of knowing.

Her tumble had stopped the intro to *Moving On*, but now Candy kicked the band into it, and this time Mitch found the beat and they all glided forward at the same time. Otis leaped on the lyrics, and, thank God, they got through the song— and the rest of the set, culminating in rave applause for *Doorbell*—without any further trouble.

Now she had to be back onstage in minutes as Essmay. As soon as the Cravattes were off, Robert started over to her; but she didn't think she could talk with him then, even if he hadn't seen her full breasts so visible under the white silk. She ran right to Priscilla and whispered, "Come help me. Get me out of here."

Her friend led her off the stage, then up a flight of stairs into the same small changing room they'd used yesterday. There was her Essmay getup, her wig, dress, high-heel shoes.

"I need a bra," she said, pulling off Eddie's suit.

"It should be here," Priscilla said. She was pawing through a trunk of clothes. "Where the hell is it?"

"We didn't touch anything yesterday, did we?"

"I don't know." Priscilla pulled out scarves, blouses, long glistening silk stockings. She found a couple showgirl bras, but they were rhinestone festooned, and even when she held them up for Esmé, it was clear they were way too big.

"Oh, well, it doesn't matter. I'll just button this up far as I can." The dress she was holding, though, was a rayon ice-blue chiffon with an exaggerated low-cut opening down from her neck.

"But—you're showing."

"Oh, so what?" Esmé said, exasperation catching up with her. "At least it's a girl showing her tits. Did you see what happened to me out there just now?"

"You fell—"

"And gave these creepy guys in the front row a peep show. Damn."

Priscilla had her head up as if she were hearing the clock tick. "You're right, we can't worry about it. Gotta get you right back out there. Come on."

"My hair," Esmé said. It was the shmused-down process look she affected as Eddie Days. "Can we get it to look like Essmay?"

Priscilla shook her head. "Listen, let's just get a wig on you." She reached over and pulled one off a mannequin head, then held out the fountain of black curls. "Here, quick."

Rags was telling the audience all over again about Essmay, the newest star in the FDL firmament, with a record busting out all over New York and the rest of the country, and there it was, the slip-sliding intro to *My Eyes Go Wide*; and then Esmé was alone under a pale-blue spotlight the same color as her dress, moving herself right before the microphone, looking out into the blur of the audience, feeling the music more than hearing it, waiting for her cue—and hitting it right on.

Oh, *that* felt better. Esmé knew this song down to her bones, and loved it—Robert's wonderful gift to her—and a vision came to her from the day before out on 125th Street, the way the tune flowered from transistor radios and open-door storefronts. It was that magic moment she threw into the performance now, and it worked. The audience was with her from the first verse, and as she hit the chorus, *"You make my eyes go wide / With surprise and delight / Every time . . . you walk on by,"* she was thrilled to hear the audience singing along with her.

Thrilled. They know the song, they love the song—it's a hit. She could hardly believe it. Here was verse two, and this time as she hit the chorus, she reached out to the crowd and waved them along with her. She sang, *"Every time you . . ."* but dropped the final three words, letting the audience carry it on with a loud and hearty *"walk on by."*

Wow! That was amazing. She swung into the bridge, *"Early in the morning, only one thing that I hear / Just like that: Sweet words are in my ears / They're in my ears,"* and as she did, she twirled around the stage in such joy and delight that, well, her wig slipped.

Not off. Just akilter. She could feel it pulling down on one side, this tumble of black curls not made to fit her, and now it was weighted wrong, not sitting right at all, looking . . . God knew how it looked.

She reached up to adjust it, but right then the band blew into the instrumental section that followed the song's bridge, the horns all standing and blasting away, and when the sound hit her, it threw her off-balance a second. That was all it took. She inadvertently tugged the wig off her head and was standing there now with her short Eddie hair, all puffy and matted and spiking out in the most horrible way—like that crazy comedienne Phyllis Diller.

Her first impulse was to run, simply to flee the stage, but she was a trouper—a seasoned performer now—and so she fought down the hysterical impulse and just kept singing, right through the third verse, then out with repeats of *"Every time . . . you walk on by."*

They applauded, they still loved her, they didn't care that she was wearing a wig, and who knew if anyone connected her with Eddie of the Cravattes who had just been on the stage—well, how could anyone in the audience know? What Esmé dared not do was look to the wings of the stage to see what her fellow Cavalcaders were seeing and thinking.

She went to the mike and said in her sexiest voice, "I'll always be . . . hair for you," gave a breathy laugh, then took her time setting the wig back in place.

What else could go wrong? Well, nothing as Essmay, thank God; she got through the rest of her set, including the reprise of *Eyes Go Wide*, flawlessly. And this time the crowd sang along with the whole song.

"That was crazy," Priscilla said as soon as Esmé was off the stage. "I almost fell over laughing."

"Thanks!"

"No, it was great, though."

"Anybody catch on?"

Priscilla looked left, then right, and said, "I don't know. Don't think so."

"You sure?"

Priscilla made a ditzing move with her shoulders, fully noncommital. "I don't think we got time to worry it. You and me, we're back onstage in a couple more minutes."

"Yeah, I better go change." Esmé ran up the stairs, back to the dressing room she'd just been in, but when she got there, she found it padlocked. Padlocked? Who could've done that? Jeez, no time to worry, she had to get into one of the matching Daisy dresses, couldn't go back out there dressed like Essmay, could she?

She ran back down the flight of stairs. "Priscilla, the door's locked. Do you have any other outfits? One I could get into?"

Priscilla called over to her compatriot Linda Strong and said, "Tell Rags to get out there and stall for us, O.K.?" Then to Esmé, "Come on, I think so."

The Apollo was fancy enough that each act had its own room, and they ran to the Daisies', which was only one floor up from the stage. Both women were breathing loud and hard. Esmé was pretty much an average size, but the two other Daisies were a little smaller, and Priscilla was a size larger. "Which way do you want to go?" Priscilla said, holding out one of her own dresses.

One of the great things about the Daisies was how well they dressed—true for all the FDL acts—and Esmé had a vision of excess fabric flying around her midriff. "How about one of Linda's or Annie's dresses?"

"You're gonna have to really suck in your stomach."

A flash of being out there with the Cravattes and trying to sing while bound too tightly hit her, and she said, "Can you pin me up if I put on one of yours?"

"Sure."

In a minute it was done. The Daisies this night were wearing the pale organdy number that swept the floor, and when Priscilla had wielded half a dozen pins, Esmé saw herself looking svelte and grand in the peach-colored dress.

"And now, here they are, the hottest female group in America, welcome the Daisies!" Rags called through the theater, and to whoops and applause, the four ladies strolled heel and toe, heel and toe out to their mikes. The vision of them, all dressed the same, in the folds of peach organdy, and each with a bouffant hairdo coiffed just so—Priscilla, her own hair clean from the hotel, had given Esmé her wig—and their moves that were pure charm-school girls flaunting their wanton sides sent the audience to the rafters. Up to the mikes they sashayed; Priscilla took the lead one, and into *Man Alive* they went.

The act seemed to be going great, but Esmé kept hearing a little voice in the back of her head saying, What else can go wrong? This whole afternoon's been one wreck after another. What possibly could—

She cut a particularly tight but swooping move the girls did, heel down, pivot on it, hands out beckoningly, hip to rise and follow, when she felt one of the pins pull loose, then heard the dress rip. If it was too big for her, how could it tear? The organdy had ripped, though, and she was too caught up in performing to stop and figure out where. Nothing to do but keep her feet moving in line with the other girls.

Now one side of the dress was hanging low, too low—scraping the floor; Esmé noticed this as she cut left, following Linda Strong, and there a swath of glowing peach organdy was, almost under Annie Sylvester's feet.

Esmé pulled hard right, to yank the cloth away from Annie, but that threw off her own moves, and her elbow slipped over and bumped Linda. The singer gave Esmé a look, and Esmé did her best to shrug and tip her head toward her dress, but of course that gesture wouldn't make sense to anyone.

The Daisies were two thirds through *Man Alive*, and the choreography called for them to drop back six steps, then like victorious soldiers march up three in a line until they flanked Priscilla. Esmé made the retreat fine, but when she spun, the hem of the loose panel of her dress ended up under her own feet, and her shoes got tangled. First thing, she heard her heel crack off; then her stomach spun wildly and her hands reached out and flailed at the air to keep herself up. But it wasn't going to work. She was falling, but just then two arms caught her from behind and lifted her back up.

It was Robert. He said quickly, "Eddie, thank God I was watching. What happened?"

"The dress, it's—"

"I see. Come on, off the stage, let 'em finish the song. I'll get Bee to fix you right up."

On Robert's arm she made a quick exit, and to her surprise she heard a solid smattering of applause as she half-hobbled off. In the wings he said, "I can see it's been pinned, but it's torn there. Hmmnnn."

"Can it be pinned up again?"

"I don't know dresses—like some men." A quick flash of his eyes. "But I'm sure Bee can work her magic."

Bee turned up a moment later, with a long needle trailing thread. She stitched up the side panel of the dress, then felt around under Esmé's arms, checking for another tear. A second later Esmé felt Bee's fingers brush lightly against the sides of her breasts. Bee pulled her hand back. Esmé turned to say something—what, she didn't know—but Bee just gave Esmé a long, curious look, then glanced back on the stage where the Daisies were finishing up a song called *Won't You Remember Me?* In a low voice Bee said, "O.K., I can get you back out there 'cause it's an emergency. But we're gonna have to have a talk later, all right, *Mister* Days."

"Yes, ma'am," Esmé said in her best Eddie voice.

As she went back onstage, the audience cheered her far louder than before. Priscilla looked over at her and laughed out loud; the other two girls didn't quite get it but looked happy that Esmé was back. And the rest of the set, including Esmé's song as lead, *Here We Go*, went great.

As the Daisies left the stage, the band kept playing, a soft vamp, and Rags came out. He said, "Hey, hey, this is the final show of the Fleur-de-Lys Records Spring 1964 Number 1 with a Bullet Tour, and we thank all of you for coming out this afternoon. Yes we do. And to show our appreciation, we're gonna have all of our acts out here on the stage together to sing a song we all have always loved. Come on Shags, come on Cravattes, get yourself out here Miss Essmay, you, too, Orlando Calabrese, and you girls—you lovely, lovely Daisies—come on back out, too."

Though the principals often sang a final song together, whatever Rags was getting at came as a surprise not only to Esmé but to the rest of the troupe as well. Esmé glanced over at Priscilla, who couldn't help herself; she was shrugging widely with a What you gonna do, girl? look, then she doubled up with laughter. Esmé looked over at Robert, lined up with the other Cravattes, and begged him with her eyes for help.

He broke away and came to her. "I'm sorry, we should've talked about this before, but I left it to Rags to decide if the crowd would be into it enough."

"So what should I—"

"Well, there's no time for you to change back to your normal clothes, so go on out with the Daisies."

Esmé nodded. There's was only one question she dreaded hearing, and—

"Where's Essmay?" Robert said, glancing around as the groups took the stage.

"I don't know."

"Where could she be?" Robert looked rattled. "I have a special surprise for her."

"I really don't know, Robert. I haven't seen her since she did her own set."

"You haven't—"

"Have you?"

He shook his head. "I guess not. But that doesn't explain anything now."

"No, it doesn't." Esmé shook her head.

"This is bad." Poor baby, he sounded so dejected.

"Let's just start the song, get it done. Then I'm sure we can find her." Esmé took his hand and led him toward the stage. "What're we doing?"

"It's—"

But Rags beat Robert to saying it, telling the audience, "We're going to end with the classic *Somewhere over the Rainbow*. But I guarantee you, we ain't doin' it like Judy Garland. We're doing it FDL-style."

Priscilla started them off, easing gently into the timeless words about floating away, high above it all, to a place that could only exist in song, singing the tune clean, supper-club style; then in the second verse she started kicking it out, and the Daisies fell in around her, along with the Cravattes laying down a low *mmmmnn-mnnnnnn*, and the Shags bottoming even that. At the chorus, when it was wishes and stars and life in the clouds far, far away, Priscilla started jumping notes on top of notes, and Orlando soared in behind her; then it was the third verse, and when nobody stepped forward to take it, Esmé realized that that was the place Robert had planned for Essmay. She debated for only a second, then stepped up and took the verse herself. It was huge having the full band and the whole Soul Cavalcade troupe behind her, like standing in a jet stream. But she carried it easily, soaring just as high as the bluebirds in the song. Priscilla moved beside her then, and the two women traded melismas through the whole fade of the lyric: "*So-ho-homm-hommmm whe-wheee-wheeeeeere o-oooo-oooooo-verrrrrrrr the ra-haaaa-haaaaainnnn-bo-ooooow-oooooooooooooow. . . .*" It was glorious music, hitting churchlike heights but scraping down and dirty—doing just about everything singing could do. When the two of them had finally dueled the song to a close, the audience, already on its feet, was shouting and crying and jumping up and down.

Esmé turned to Priscilla just as Priscilla turned to her, and the two women flew into each other's arms. "That was fabulous," Esmé whispered to her. "You're the best."

"No, you—you were great."

"No, it was you, all you."

They both gave a laugh, then pulled back, keeping their

hands linked and beaming at each other. Finally Priscilla said, "So, girl, looks like we were missing somebody. Where was your cous, Essmay—" and they both cracked up again so hard they nearly tumbled onto the floor.

The applause swelled over all of them, and each group took turns bowing, Esmé curtsying with Priscilla and the Daisies. Then the curtain rang down and everyone headed off the stage.

Robert was right up next to her. "Where could she have been?" he said. Esmé looked closely at him and saw he looked a little frantic.

"I don't know, Robert. Maybe she thought that after her set she was done, went outside for some fresh air or something. I'm sure it's as innocent as that."

"We need her," Robert said. "Right away!"

"Yes, sir!"

"Eddie, come on, this is it!" Robert was all business. "Go find her. Then get yourself back here, too." When Esmé started to protest, he added, "Things we gotta do."

Esmé spun around. How the hell was she going to. . . ? But there Priscilla was.

"What's wrong?" Priscilla came up and took Esmé's hand. "You look like you just saw a ghost."

"Maybe I did."

"What is it?"

"Oh, Robert wants me to go get Essmay, then be Eddie again, just like that."

"Darlin'," Priscilla said with a shrug. "That ain't nothin' you haven't done a thousand times before. Come on, let's go."

Once she was moving, everything was better. They decided just to change Esmé's wig; as Priscilla said, "If Robert can't tell what's up now, he ain't going to lose it over the same dress." That only took a minute, and then the two girls ran back to the stage.

Robert started when he saw her, Esmé clearly saw. (She was looking.) More than surprise, too, as if he was jolted just by the sight of her. She ran over to him and gushed all girlishly, "I'm sorry, Mr. Warwick, I just got so ex-ci-ted after my singing that I couldn't stand it. I just had to get some air. Went out for a walk. I didn't know—my cousin, Eddie, just told me—well, that everybody got up and sang *Over the Rainbow* afterward. I hope it went all right?"

"It's all right," he said.

She bubbled on: "Well, I thought it was all just so amazing, I mean, the audience already knew my song. How terrific is that?"

"You were very good."

"You mean it?"

Robert considered this, or considered something, for a moment, then said, "I do, yes."

"Oh, Mr. Warwick!" And Esmé, perhaps tossing herself into her role with more gusto than was needed, threw herself at Robert, opening her arms and wrapping them around him, almost lifting the smaller man off the ground, then planting as wet a kiss as she could make right on his smooth-skin cheek. She pulled back, saw the startled look in his eyes, then hugged him so tight it was like she could make his bones pop. And surprised herself: She thought she was doing this just to divert him, but she found with her arms around him that part of her was holding on to him for dear life.

"Um, call me Robert, please," he finally said, though he wasn't letting go of her.

Esmé kept holding him close, unexpected feelings running through her. Maybe it was because she was Essmay, so close to herself, but pulling Robert to her made her swell with the warmth and ease of finally being back home.

She felt a tap on her shoulder.

"Hey, darlin', mind if I cut in?"

The voice was low and familiar. Esmé stepped back from Robert and turned around.

"Orlando," she said, startled. Robert had loosened his arms around her, too, but his fingers feathered slowly down her bare arms, then over the palms of her hand.

"Hey, sugar." The tall singer stood there stolidly, his feet planted well apart, his arms folded across his chest. One of his fine plucked eyebrows was crooked below his high forehead. "I thought you were savin' them dances for me?" His left eye cocked higher than his right.

"What do you want, Breeze?" Robert said, the final word out with a lightly veiled sneer. It sounded like *sneeze*. The tips of Robert's fingers had just kissed Esmé's fingertips, but now they weren't touching at all. Robert faced Orlando straight on.

"I thought it was clear, buddy boy." Orlando reached out to tickle Esmé under her chin with his long fingers, but she pulled back. He then said, "I thought we made it damn clear this morning."

"Orlando—" Esmé started to say, but Robert moved around behind her, and Orlando slid over to face him.

"I didn't ask what went on last night, that's not my business," Robert said through tight lips. "But it ain't your business now, right Essmay?"

"Robert, I—"

"It damn well is." Orlando stretched on the balls of his feet. Then his arms unclenched, and he pushed at Robert. "You poachin' on my woman. It damn well is [push] my [push] business—"

"Orlando, I'm not your—"

"Get your hands off me, you shit," Robert said quiet but steady. His eyes narrowed, his thin nose was fluted. He rode gracefully back at each of Orlando's jabs.

"You called me—"

"A big dumb shit." Robert had balled his fists. He reached

over and pushed Orlando, his open palms butting the much taller man's chest.

Orlando looked surprised. "You little creep. I shoulda—" He cocked back his right hand. "If you weren't wearing glasses—"

"Stop it!" Esmé cried. She spun from Robert to Orlando. This was all over her, and it was making her sick. "Both of you, stop it!"

But they weren't listening. Robert, glaring at Orlando, tugged off his thick black glasses. Up went Orlando's fists, but it was Robert who ducked to the side and threw the first punch. Orlando feinted aside, and Robert's fist grazed his sweater but nothing else. Then Orlando swung and clipped Robert right under his ear. Robert's head jolted back; he shook it for a second, then in a cat-quick move lunged forward. Orlando was half turned away, and when Robert's body hit his, the tall man went down. Robert threw himself on top of him, throwing punches at Orlando's upper body and head.

"My God!" Bee Williams bustled up, shouting. "What is this? Robert! Orlando! What're you doing?" She stood behind Robert, tried to grab his shoulders. "You two, stop this. Stop it right now!"

Orlando was twisting under the smaller man, trying to buck him off.

"Stop it!" Bee cried shrilly, loud as she could. This momentarily froze them.

The commotion had drawn a crowd, and other men stepped in. Though Robert was flailing, Otis Handler was able to pin his arms behind him; Buzz and Reggie reached down and tugged him up. When Robert was safely off Orlando, two other Shags, Collie and Jerry, pulled Orlando up, holding his arms tight behind him.

"Jesus, you two," Bee said now that everyone was under control. "What the heck's going on here?"

Robert looked at Orlando, and Orlando glared back at

him, but neither man said a word. "Essmay, you were standing there. What is this about?"

What could she say? "I'm not quite sure," Esmé slowly answered.

"I bet it's fraternization," Bee said. "I told you all the first day on the bus, no fraternization! That's the root of all trouble! Orlando? Robert? It's fraternization, ain't it?"

Both men, still in the grips of their handlers, chose not to say a word.

"You guys ain't talking?" Bee looked around. "Does anybody know?"

Silence. Even if anybody did have a clue, the code was: No ratting on anyone in the troupe.

"All right, O.K." Bee was pacing back and forth before the two men, her black helmet of hair bobbing between them. "I have the power to fine you, and I am going to do it. You, Orlando, and you, Robert, are both fined $200 to be taken from your paychecks. And I have to say, Robert especially, I am amazed by this."

Tempers had cooled, and the men who were holding the two combatants relaxed their grips. Nobody left, but it was clear that nothing more would happen, at least right then.

Esmé stood there flustered. Now this on top of trying to be Eddie and Essmay and everything else! As she stood between the two men, she felt a close, heavy pressure on her.

"Hey, Essmay, over here." This was Priscilla, about twenty feet away. Esmé turned her sharp eyes from Orlando to Robert, lifted a shoulder huffily, and went to her friend.

"What was that about?"

"They were fighting over Essmay."

Priscilla laughed. "Ain't you smooth, girl."

"No, Pris, it was horrible. I just stood there, feeling so helpless—"

"Oh, come on, you had to be digging some of it." Priscilla's face was all mischief.

"Well," Esmé admitted after a moment, "maybe a teentsy part."

"So who was winning?"

Esmé looked straight into her friend's eyes. There was a question there, but she couldn't see enough of what it was to know what the right answer was. She keep peering at Priscilla. Finally she said, "Neither of them."

Priscilla nodded. "That's good enough, sister." Then she said, "I think the smartest thing all around is to get you out of here—at least, get that troublemaker Essmay out of here." She laughed again. "Come on, lady!"

✳ ✳ ✳ ✳ ✳

WHEN PRISCILLA AND ESMÉ as her alter ego Eddie Days walked back to the stage, they found the curtain swung back again and on the stage the full FDL troupe surrounding the group from NRC: Bones's wife, Hermione; Bones's sister, Ramona Chapman Bowden; Bones's brother, Octavus Chapman; and the white-bowler-hatted Captain Bryant. Just turned up from their recording session were the A&R man, Rick Lapidus, and surprising everyone, Maisy Columbine.

Maisy had changed from her recording-session dress and was wearing a flamboyant black-and-red polka-dot number, with wide shoulders and big white buttons with three black spots on them. To Esmé, they looked like two eyes and a nose. It was as if Maisy had little baby faces up and down her front.

All eyes were on the former Daisy. The unasked question: What the hell you doin' here, girl? Maisy wasn't speaking, just taking in the long, curious glances, but she kept her chin high, and everything about her answered, Never you mind. But can't you see I'm doing great?

Apollo workers were still breaking down the bandstand, but there was plenty of room, so the six members of the NRC party stood there among all the FDL singers and players.

It was Hermione Chapman who spoke up first. "You all have gotten better." Her thick, crustily mascaraed eyebrows fluttered. "This was nothing like what I used to see in Detroit."

"Thank you, ma'am," Bee said. She was standing in front of the group, with Robert and the other Cravattes next to her, and Priscilla, Rags, and Cotton Candy on Bee's other side. Esmé dressed as Eddie was right next to Robert's shoulder. "We're really happy to see you," she added brightly. "Any word from . . . Bones?"

"I called down there this morning," Hermione said, shaking her head, "and there ain't any change."

A long, whiskery sigh rose up from the members of the Cavalcade.

"You know how sorry we all are about that," Robert said, taking a step forward. "It's been hard without him."

"Yes, it has," Hermione said. She brought the back of her hand to her forehead in a gesture that Esmé was certain came out of an old Theda Bara silent movie.

Captain Bryant, his eyes on Mrs. Bones, though his expression was undisclosing, stepped forward and said, "I want to tell everyone that I was very impressed tonight, too." He had a gruff, commanding voice that pulled attention to him. "You put on a very lively show."

There was notable silence to this statement.

"So, could *you* make it better?" a male voice came from farther back on the stage.

"Who was that?" the Captain said, chin tilted.

Nobody said anything at first, and the Captain stood there, a faint smile on his upturned face. The rim of his white bowler cut a sharp slice through the heavy air. Finally, he started to say, "Well, if. . . ." when Otis stepped forward.

"Sir," he said firmly, "I'm Otis Handler, of the Cravattes." The front row of the group parted enough to let Otis through. "And I think I'm askin' what everybody's thinkin'."

The Captain gave him a faint-smiling look, then said, "Well, Otis—" hands sweeping out to the full Cavalcade "—everybody. I think I could."

"How?" Cotton Candy said, not missing a beat.

The Captain simply smiled, then gave a nod to his assistant Rick Lapidus. Lapidus said, "We have oceans of experience in these things." A grin beneath his wide mustache. "Got deeper pockets, too."

"So you all know what's going on?" Ramona Chapman said. She had been off to the side, next to her brother and Maisy Columbine.

Silence. Then Robert spoke up. "We've heard rumors." His sharp tone made it clear he wasn't going to pussyfoot. "NRC wants to buy us, and—well, you all came up here thinking they should get one last good look at what they're getting."

Ramona caught the young man's eye. "Nothing's been decided yet."

Mrs. Bones walked over and put a hand on her sister-in-law's arm. "Now, Ramona."

"Mrs. Bowden here thinks we should all talk this over before we make it official." Captain Bryant lifted his nose. "I'm not so sure, but—"

"I just want to know what you all think." Ramona took firm steps forward till she faced the troupe straight on. She was speaking the way she did to her high school students, bringing them into the discussion, doing what made her a good teacher.

But nobody spoke. The silence was deep and it was cold.

"I guess this is a little awkward, but—" Ramona started to shrug.

"Are you going to do it?" Robert said to Bones's sister point-blank.

"And you are?" This was Captain Bryant, stepping in front of Ramona.

"Robert Warwick, also of the Cravattes. I've been—well,

since Bones's accident, I've been helping Bee make sure things went off all right."

"Ahh, yes. You're the young man behind that new tune *My Eyes Go Wide*?" The Captain had a thing where he wasn't looking straight at anyone, yet Robert could feel his gaze forcefully on him. "I was just telling my A&R man Rick here that that disc sounds like a hit."

"We know it is."

"Well, we at NRC like hits. Don't we, Rick? Maisy?" Captain Bryant lifted his thick white eyebrows, let them seem to laugh for him. "Tell me, is the singer here, what's her name?"

"Essmay." Robert made a production of looking around the whole stage, then said, "She's not." He shook his head. "I don't know where she is."

Ramona said, "That's one of the things that gives me some hesitation, if I can speak honestly. That this young man, Mr.—"

"Warwick," Robert said.

"That Mr. Warwick could write such a good song, then discover a new singer for it, and, well, if—if NRC takes over, you'll keep on working with talent like Robert, won't you?"

"Of course," the Captain said in his bland but potent way. "At NRC we do nothing but respect talent." He turned to Lapidus and said, "Rick?"

"He'll work within the NRC system, of course," Lapidus said. "But, yes, the Captain's right, we always fully utilize our talent. That's what makes NRC so potent in the marketplace."

Potent in the marketplace. Robert tightened. For a second he wished he had Devine's tape . . . but no, that had been too high a price to pay.

"That new song really is catchy," Bones's sister said. "You're certain you'll be able to do just as good work with a new singer like this Essmay?"

"I can assure you," the Captain said, "that anyone who

can make hits for us, well, we'd be crazy not to use them."

"How're you doing with Maisy?" This was Robert.

"She's doing great!" Rick Lapidus said.

"Maisy?" There was a barbed hook in Robert's tone; everyone heard it.

All eyes turned to the former FDL singer. "I don't have a complaint in the world," she said calmly, though with an overly bright inflection.

"I think without Bones here," Ramona said, sighing, "well, I don't know, but it seems that you'd all just be better off with NRC. It's a huge, professional company. The Captain assures me they don't waste time and that they know how to get records made and sold."

"But we do, too." A female voice called out.

"Who's that?"

"I'm Priscilla Bondrais," she said. "I took over from Maisy in the Daisies. It was—well, we got it together really quick, and really well."

"You looked smashing up there today," Ramona said.

"Damn right! And we'll keep on, too. We can do it all ourselves, ma'am." Priscilla's voice was sharp and sure. "I think, with all due respect, ma'am, we can be just as professional. And with Robert here we can do it better."

Now it was said. Breaths were being sucked in all around them, everyone could hear it.

"Is that how you all feel?" Ramona said.

Murmurs, half nods, feet shuffling.

"You all have to speak up. I really do want to hear what you're thinking." Ramona turned to Mrs. Bones. "I haven't decided anything yet."

"Yes," Robert said. "We *can* do it all. And that's what Bones would want, we all think that—"

"Bones, I don't have to remind you, is in a coma." This was Octavus. He spoke through his wide, round face, his double chins. "He's been like that for weeks now. And he may, God forbid, stay that way." His large Adam's apple bobbed. "We know that none of this would have come up if Bones were here, but he ain't." He turned straight on to his sister. "And we got to do the best for what is, Ramona. What is now."

Ramona sighed. "I know. This is—so hard for me. Bee, Mr. Warwick, all of you. I just got this gut feeling that we have this opportunity now. NRC loves your music, the Captain's assured me of that, and, you know, they are a big, serious company. Nobody's going to have to live from week to week anymore." She sounded frightfully resigned. "They're going to make everything just so—"

"White?" The one word popped up from the back. It startled everyone.

"Who said that?" Captain Bryant said sharply.

Nobody would admit it. The speaker was far in the back, probably one of the band.

"I resent that!" the Captain thundered. "How dare any of you say that!" He lifted his head back, his long thin chin pointing gun-straight at the FDL troupe. "Sure, we're no . . . fly-by-night organization." His patrician features scrunched up in distaste. "We've been around a long time, and we have a proud history. Certainly we have shareholders we're responsible to, but—but the bottom line has always been: We know how to make hits!"

"Do you?" The voice was sharp, and at first no one was certain who had spoken. Everyone's eyes swept the stage.

"Maisy?" Rick Lapidus finally said. He was still standing next to the singer.

Maisy in her grand black-and-red dress strode forward. The button baby faces glinted. "I want to say something."

The whole stage was startled silent.

All but Captain Bryant. "Maisy?" he said softly, his tone much lower than his outburst a moment before. His eyes were lifted again, curious, distant, cool.

"Yes, it's me." She gave the Captain a huge, bright smile, then turned around and faced the FDL Cavalcaders. "There's just a couple things I want to tell everyone—"

"*Maisy?*" Again the Captain, but with a vivid flash of darkness under his imperturbable tone. "I don't know if you want to—"

Maisy went on as if she hadn't heard. She spoke in her straightforward, breathy voice, not unlike her singing tones. "I'm just thinking about Bones, what he'd be saying if . . . well, if he was here." Everybody could see it: a thin, wet shine in her eyes. "I know—know that some of you would say I betrayed him—betrayed all of you." She sucked in a long breath. "Well, we'll see about that." And, *bang!* There was a sharp retort as one of her heels hit the wooden stage floor. "But what I'm getting at is that Bones wanted only one thing: a Number 1 record. You know it, we all knew it—hell, that's why the goddamn stinky bus was called the Number 1 Express."

The whole troupe was silent now, hanging on Maisy's words.

"And, damn—" Maisy's voice rose, as if whirling up a fluted glass "—he got us close, cracked the Top 5, but we ain't got there yet. None of us have. And me, I left 'cause I just got—got frustrated waiting around. NRC said they could do it, could kick me right up to the top." A glance at Rick Lapidus. "And I damn sure hope they can, because that's why I'm there."

"You'll get there." This was Captain Bryant, softly under his breath. "I promise—"

"But it hasn't happened yet," Maisy said, turning directly to face the older white man, "and I—I got to be honest here. Sometimes I have my doubts. I just don't know if . . . if they . . . get it."

It was quiet, mostly a flaring around his eyes, but the Captain looked furious. Everybody else's eyes were stuck on Maisy.

A sharp look from Maisy now back at the Captain. "I know I got a Number 1 in me," she said firmly. "I know Maisy Columbine's gonna hit the top no matter who or what helps me."

The Captain started to speak, but Maisy thrust up her hand palm outward and stopped him. "It may not take money, may not take a fancy studio. I don't know if even *I* know what it does take—if anybody does. What I do know is that Number 1s can pop up in strange, strange places. They can be tricks, goofs, funny things, unexpected, like, like—"

"Magic." This was Robert, finishing her thought. He smiled at Maisy, who gave him a bright nod back. Robert then turned directly to Ramona and kept going: "That's what we can say here to you, Mrs. Bowden. We might not have the money or the security, we sure as hell ain't white—" The Captain started to speak again, but Robert rushed right on past him. "And we don't got radio stations doin' just what we say." Another tight, sharp look at the Captain, who now clearly chose not to interrupt.

"But Bones," Robert went on, "he put us all together to capture the magic. Like you get lightning in a bottle—you gotta reach out and grab it, right when it's starting to glow in front of you.

"That's what I tried to do when Bones went into his—had his accident. I took this song I'd written, then got Ed—I mean, his cousin Essmay—into this deadbeat studio in Washington, D.C., and we scooped up all the lightning in the room, Ramona. We slammed it all on that record you love, *My Eyes Go Wide*.

"And look: Now that song might hit it, hit Number 1. Even though we had us some trouble getting it on the air, we got people out there singing it on the streets, we got 'em—the record's been out only a couple days—and we got 'em already singing along at the Apollo. Who could've planned that? Who could have—"

"God, son?" Octavus Chapman interrupted. "Could it have been God?"

Robert turned to Bones's brother. "Sir?"

"You talk about your magic—don't you understand talk like that takes the Lord's name in vain. To the Lord, son, there is no . . . magic. There is only the Lord's way—"

Robert, his eyes open wide, spoke slowly. "I don't mean no disrespect, sir. But I also don't know if the Lord up there in his majesty is lookin' down on us trying to make a Number 1 hit."

"Everything, son. From the lowliest leaf to the grandest sunrise—"

"I know, sir, I understand. But all I'm saying is, well, you can't always know what the Lord is willing for us. Can't always know that, sir. So you just do the best you can. Making these records for us, it's—it's like pushing a boulder up a hill, we all know that, but we're doin' it. Trying to catch something . . . something glorious—the FDL magic. It's Candy and the band, and it's everything we learned from Bones, and everything we know as the Cravattes and the Shags and the Daisies. It's all of us. And it's us also taking a chance on somebody new, just like Bones did when we needed somebody to fill out the Cravattes. Eddie here just walked in the door and wowed him. And his cousin Essmay, well, she wowed *me*—"

"I appreciate that, Mr. Warwick," Octavus Chapman started to say. "But I still think—"

Robert turned back to Ramona. "Mrs. Bowden, respectfully, all Maisy's saying—all any of us are saying is that nobody can guarantee a hit, and if they do it once, ain't no certainty they can do it again."

"Son, I think your vanity—"

"No, sir," Robert went on, speaking to both brother and sister now. "I'm not saying *I* can guarantee a hit. Neither can NRC. But, Mrs. Bowden, what all of us at FDL can promise

is that, you let us stay as we are, let us do things our way—
Bones's way—and we'll always, *always* put our blood and our
love and our guts and everything else we got into our songs."
Robert's speech was rising like a swift wind. "Every damn
song!"

"Well, I've never heard such Godless non—" Octavus
rumbled out of his deep chest, but then a curious thing happened: Maisy Columbine reached over and touched his ham-
thick shoulder. That was it, one touch on his black suit.
Octavus looked at her and, after a confused play of emotions
on his face, fell silent.

Ramona took a step in front of her brother and said simply, "I want to see her."

"Who?" Bee said.

"The girl—the new girl with that song."

"Essmay?" This was Esmé, alarmed.

"Ramona, I think we've heard more than enough,"
Octavus said gruffly. "Why do you want to—"

"I want to hear about it from her, how she found these
people, how Mr. Warwick worked with her—I want to hear
about this . . . this magic straight from her."

"What will that—"

"Octavus, you just be patient." Ramona spoke as she
would to one of her unruly students. Then she turned to
Bones's wife. "You too, Hermione. I said I got it all on my
shoulders, and I do—I got it *all* on my shoulders. And I'm
gonna do right by Bones. And to do that, I want to see . . .
that . . . girl."

Robert's gaze flashed around the stage. "Mrs. Bowden,
she's—I don't know exactly where she is." A sharp look at
Esmé. "Eddie, can you go find her?"

Esmé felt everyone's eyes on her, but none more than
Priscilla's. "I could try, I guess."

"She's probably just off like she was before, getting a walk
outside." Robert was almost pushing her. His words skittered

out like stones over water. "I just—it'd be really great if she was here."

"I'll help you look for her," Priscilla said, and she took Esmé—who, truth be told, was almost paralyzed standing there, caught in all the twists and bends of her deception—and dragged her back behind the stage into one of the dressing rooms.

"I can't do it again, Pris."

"You got to."

"I know, but I just—" There was a pair of well-stuffed, nubby-fabric-covered chairs, and Esmé sank into one of them. "Pris, I don't even know who . . . I . . . am."

Priscilla got down on her knees and looked her friend right in the eyes. "You're Esmé Hunter, that's all you ever been. You're just you. That's all."

"But who am I out there?" Her high, tight voice surprised even her, it was so shaken.

Priscilla sighed. "I guess you gotta be Essmay one more time."

"But who is Essmay?"

"Honey, only you know that." A quick, sharp look from Priscilla. "And maybe Orlando."

"Jeez, is there anybody who doesn't know about that?"

"Girl, there's only one secret around this place, and that's you—who you really are. And only because nobody's got the imagination to imaginate something so crazy."

Esmé shook her head, shook her shoulders, too. "I'm sorry—sorry I started the whole damn mess."

"No, you're not."

"I'm—"

"Listen, sister, you're the best thing that happened to us. You got the Cravattes going 'cause you loved them, you bucked up Robert when Bones had his accident, and now you've got the single that's gonna save FDL. Just get out there and tell Bones's sister that."

Esmé's head was wobbling on her shoulders. "I just—I'm afraid I'll—what if I screw it all up?"

"You won't."

"I—"

"Just the one more time, be Essmay. Come on, let me get you out of those pants and into a dress." Priscilla lifted Esmé's arms and pulled off her suit coat, then undid her shirt. "What, did you run out of brassieres?"

Esmé shook her head. "I don't remember."

"O.K., girl, just you let me take care of you. Come on, here, look at this dress—" Priscilla held out a pale lavendar number that immediately picked up Esmé's ebony skin tones "—this gonna work for you?"

Esmé was still lightheaded when Priscilla took her back onto the stage. "I got her." She beamed.

"Where's Eddie?"

"Oh, um, Eddie—guess he's still out looking for her. But . . . here she is!"

Ramona walked toward her and took her hands. "You're Essmay, then?"

"I am," Esmé got out.

Ramona gave her a warm, motherly smile. "That's a fine, fine record you made."

Esmé tried to smile, but not much showed.

Ramona brought a steadying hand to the young singer's elbow. "You look a little faint, dear. Are you all right?"

"It's a lot—it's all been a bit much for me."

"Do you want to sit down?"

Priscilla stepped up and gave Esmé support. "I think she'll be all right."

"That's good." Ramona patted down the front of her suit dress. "Now, child, Mr. Warwick here's been telling us how he discovered you, how he got that great performance out of you." Esmé saw her warmest smile, and smiled wanly back. She took a step back, away from the helping hands. "Now I have one question. Do you think anyone else could've worked that way with you? You know, with your background and all. Did it have to be Mr. Warwick and Fleur-de-Lys Records?"

Esmé turned her head just enough to see all the faces and all the eyes bearing down on her. No, she wasn't all right. A high, bright wind was whistling through her head. Faint, she felt faint. She breathed in deeply and felt so lightheaded, and so—

"I—I—" she started to say, then stopped as everything got wobbly and teetery. Oh, no! Her legs weakened, and she was reaching out, and there was somebody—oh, it was Orlando!—and he was trying to hold her up, but she . . . she squirmed away from him. She took a step back, but she was so dizzy, her head spinning, and . . . oh, I can't help myself. It's so complicated. Her brain fritzed, and she couldn't remember who she was supposed to be at this moment, herself, Esmé, or Eddie, or this girl they all wanted to talk to, Essmay . . . and just the thought of all those E's made her head whirl again, she wasn't getting enough air—not enough oxygen—and she was suddenly lighter than a leaf, her head floating up and tipping over. . . . She threw a hand out, and there was Robert coming to catch her, but everything was going black, her fingers waving, but she couldn't reach him, and. . . .

When she came to, she was lying on the stage of the Apollo. She could feel the well-heel-trod wood underneath her, and what was this over her—oh, a blanket. Somebody had turned up a scratchy wool Army blanket, and it was draped on her. There were people's heads, she couldn't make them out; they floated in shadows before the overhead lights . . . wait, there was Robert and there was Bee, and there was that nice woman, Bones's sister.

"Dear, are you all right?" she heard, sharp concern. It was Ramona. "You must have fainted. You're looking brighter—are you O.K. now?"

Esmé did her best to nod. It was funny lying there on her

back in her dress. Her bare legs stuck out from under the blanket. Somebody had taken off her shoes.

"We think you should rest," Bee said, above her, too. "Do you want a doctor?"

Esmé shook her head, then reached behind her and propped herself up on her elbows. "No, no, I'll be fine." She started to struggle up, but everything went light again, and she lay back down.

"Take your time, Essmay," Robert said.

That name! Essmay. She—it sounded—oh, yes, that's who they thought she was, somebody named Essmay. Not Esmé, but Esssss-maaaaay. She gave her head a cobweb-clearing wiggle.

"Just take your time. Here—that's good, here, drink this. It's a Coca-Cola."

Ramona handed her the cool, fluted green-glass bottle, and Esmé raised herself up again, then took a sip of the beverage. It was quick-reviving. "That's good," she said.

"Here," Robert said, "let me help you up." He offered a hand, and Esmé grasped it. It was solid and strong. Robert leaned over and put a hand behind her head, helping her sit up.

"Oh, my, this is . . . embarrassing."

"You're looking much better, dear." Ramona took the Coke bottle from her, but Esmé reached out, and she handed it back. "O.K., yes, drink as much as you want."

A minute or so later she felt almost normal. "I think I can stand now, thanks." Robert gave her a hand again, and she was upright.

"I'm sorry if I said anything that—" Ramona started to say.

"No, it's not—I don't know what happened. I just got . . . lightheaded."

"Mrs. Bowden." This was the Captain, stepping forward. "I really do think we should call an ambulance. This is nothing to trifle with." His cool smile. "And besides, I want everyone to know that NRC takes care of its own."

Oh, that was it! That's what was going on! It all flooded back to her. She was Essmay, and it was all on her to persuade these people not to give up on FDL. Her head flew light again, and everything started to spin, but she fought it—she held tight.

"No, no, please," she insisted. "I'm fine now."

"Well, I don't see we should bother this poor little girl anymore," Octavus said. "I'm thinking here of her health. Sister, I think we certainly do know enough."

Ramona looked from her brother to Esmé, and there was a deep concern in her eyes, but what she said was, "Maybe you're right. I guess maybe this whole . . . inquisition was just too much." Like that something clicked inside Ramona's head, Esmé could see it. Oh, no! she thought. I've ruined it.

"Please, Mrs. Bowden," Esmé said, reaching out to her. "I do want to answer your question, it's just that—that the answer is more complicated than you think—than any of you think—" From the corner of her eye, Esmé could see Priscilla move toward her. O.K., she knows what I'm going to do. But I have to do it. "There's something I have to tell all of you, and I really am glad you're all here—all of my friends on the Soul Cavalcade."

She could feel the curiosity pressing on her. But now that she was determined, she felt stronger, not lightheaded at all anymore.

"The answer to your question, Mrs. Bowden, really is yes—yes with all my heart. Nowhere else could this have happened, that I could come out of nowhere and find Robert and make such a good record. I—I truly believe that.

"And I did come out of nowhere. It's just that, well, I'm not this girl Essmay—"

Lifted eyebrows, shaken heads. What could she—

"Well, I am—I mean, my name is Esmé, E-S-M-and an

E with a funny mark above it that my mother, bless her heart, gave me to make me special. I'm Esmé Hunter."

The eyebrows stayed up, the heads stilled.

She went over and took Ramona's hands. "Mrs. Bowden, this is how much I love FDL Records. A month ago me and my girlfriends went to the FDL office to audition, and Mr. Chapman, well, he didn't take us." A swallow. "Then I heard they were looking for a fourth Cravatte, and it was really crazy, but I—I went and dressed as a man, and—"

"You what?" Bee said.

"Eddie?" This was Robert, loudly.

"I did it," she said to all of them. "I bought a suit, cut my hair, and went in and aced the audition. I became Eddie Days!"

Swirls of whispers, questions, outright disbelief spun around her. She went on.

"And it was the best thing that ever happened to me. Mrs. Bowden, it was my dream come true. There I was, on the bus as a Fleur-de-Lys singer." Esmé could feel questions bubbling up, but she ignored them.

"And then, well, things got complicated. Maisy left the Daisies, and one night we were playing around and I—I mean, Eddie—dressed up as a girl, and Mr. Bones, he thought it would be a good idea for me to sing with them— as a girl. As Esmé." The uproar was building all around her, but she held out a staying hand.

"And then—oh, God, then Robert had this great song, and he needed somebody to sing it, and even though he thought I was still Eddie, he liked my voice with the Daisies, so I did sing it, but he wanted a real girl to do it with the Cavalcade, and that's where—that's when I suddenly remembered I had a 'cousin' in Detroit." Esmé gave out a sheepish shrug. "We called her Essmay and Robert met her and . . . it seemed right."

Bee had a hand to her forehead, her eyes round. "I don't think I—" she started saying.

"How many people are you?" Robert interjected.

"Oh, Robert, I'm just one person—just myself. Esmé Hunter from Lombard Avenue in Detroit."

"But you're also Eddie?" This was Orlando, seeming quite alarmed.

"Yes."

Orlando made the face of a child just told that the Santa whose lap he'd sat in was actually a derelict in a stolen white beard. "Essmay, you're telling me that you're a *guy*?" He gave a visible shudder.

"Orlando, shut up," Priscilla said. "She's saying she's a girl who pretended to be a guy." Orlando's face stayed blank. "A girl pretending to be a guy," she repeated. "Get it?"

"So all the time that you were Eddie helping me," Robert said, "you've really been Esmé Hunter—and Essmay, too?" His face was nearly indescribable: still mystified, a touch horrified, yet also robustly amused.

"That's it."

"And why, dear?" Ramona said. "What were you saying about—"

Esmé took Ramona's hands again. She felt close to this warm woman. "Because, Mrs. Bowden, I'd do anything—I did do anything—to sing with Fleur-de-Lys Records." Her head was spinning again, and she took a deep breath to steady herself. "I wouldn't—I couldn't imagine doing that for NRC. Not after all I know about them. After what Maisy said. After what all of us think—"

"You all think—"

"Can we take a vote?" Esmé said.

The Captain stepped forward, but Ramona was in front of him. "You know, if I'd just thought of that before," she said, then shook her head in wonderment at Esmé's coming clean. "A vote. Can you all hear me? Will you raise your hands if you want me to keep FDL together. To not sell it to NRC."

It was surprising, Esmé and Robert decided later, that it

took so long for the hands to go up, but understandable, too; everybody was so certain that NRC was going to take over the company that they were cowed. But slowly one by one hands did go up, and when it was all over, every last soul, from Bee to the band to all the Cravattes, the Shags, the Daisies—even Orlando—had their hands in the air.

"I can't do it," Ramona said. She turned to her brother and her sister-in-law. "I'm sorry, but it's all their lives, and their wonderful music, and—and it's Bones's legacy."

A jubilant cheer went up. It started low and ran around the floor, but like a rush of warm air, it swelled upward and cascaded through the whole theater.

And that was that.

✳ ✳ ✳ ✳ ✳

ESMÉ COULDN'T BELIEVE the tour was over. The drums were packed in cases for the last time, guitars and horns stored away; word was out that they weren't staying another night in the Hotel Theresa but instead taking the bus back to Detroit tonight—Trip promised them he'd get them home by lunchtime. Lunch with her mother? The gossip from her church. Latest personnel problems at her hair salons. Her weight. . . . No, Esmé couldn't imagine it, or believe it.

But there was no question everything had changed, and not just because of her revelation and the successful fight for FDL. The energy of the Cavalcade had simply rushed off, like a tide shifting; everybody was distracted, a little air-headed, probably exhausted, and no doubt both relieved and dismayed to be discovering that what they'd so intensely given themselves over to for the last three weeks was evaporating like a puddle of water out on sunny Lenox Avenue.

The other thing that was different was that though her deception was of course over, in a weird way for her it wasn't. She still felt she was one of the Cravattes; and why not? She'd come along at the right time and kept them going. She also loved it that she had become a Daisy, even if just a backup singer to the stronger than ever Priscilla Bondrais. Did all that have to end?

She'd meant to ask Robert about that—about everything—but after the showdown with NRC, Robert had gone off with Bones's sister. The implication, as everybody understood it, was that by making her decision, she'd assumed power over FDL. Mrs. Bones had overplayed her hand, and Octavus would have to throw his lot in with his sister. So now nothing was going to happen without Ramona weighing in—at least till Bones was back. Esmé was surprised how optimism about the boss had flowered. The mandate now: Keep the company together, even move it ahead, till Bones returned and could take them all to the top. There was no longer doubt that that would all happen soon.

"Hey." Esmé looked around and saw Priscilla coming up to her.

"Hey, girl."

"And, 'Hey, girl' back to you." Priscilla gave a little laugh. "Guess I don't have to worry anymore about who I'm saying that to."

"Yeah."

"Essie, what's wrong?"

Esmé shook her head. "Nothing."

"You look sort of . . . distracted."

"I guess so. Aren't you?"

"You mean, 'cause the tour's over and all?"

"That, yeah."

"What is it?"

Esmé shrugged. It was 7:30 p.m., and she was just hanging around in the Hotel Theresa lobby. The plan was the bus would be leaving at nine, but nobody had said anything about dinner, so maybe she was just cranky because she was hungry.

"Maybe you're just hungry?" Priscilla said.

Esmé gave her head a shake. "Damn, I was just thinking that."

"Well, what I'm thinking is that the whole thing is falling apart, all the discipline, and it's making everybody a little nuts. Only thing I can think of is we go feed ourselves. We're back in the real world, lady, and that is the simple fact." Priscilla gave her head a nod. "Come on, there's a coffee shop next door."

Nothing on the menu looked that good to Esmé, but finally she ordered a grilled-cheese sandwich and a Coke. She'd loved a toasted-cheese when she was a girl but hadn't had one in years. Still, it was the only item that said anything to her.

"I think we're all feeling it," Priscilla said as the pink-uniformed waitress walked away. "Deep kinda letdown."

"I know I am."

Priscilla nodded. "Yeah, and you got it worse, I'm sure. It wasn't me who fainted this afternoon. You had a lot of stuff on you, girl."

"And now it's all . . . off." Esmé pursed her brow, trying to decide how much of a question for Priscilla that was.

"I guess."

Both women were silent a while, till their Cokes came.

"I don't really know what I'm going to be doing," Esmé finally said.

"Hey, you're gonna be a brilliant member of the FDL troupe, that's what," Priscilla said. "*Hits-a-Poppin*'s gonna be writing all about you—the real you."

"So that's the deal? Essmay is going to be me—Esmé Hunter?"

"Essmay is Esmé—just the way you say it. I say you stay Essmay. But we'll see what Robert thinks—and Bones, when he's back."

"I was just thinking about Robert—"

"Oh, is that it?"

"What?"

"Why you got the gloom bugs hoverin' round you?"

Esmé slowly shook her head.

"Oh, tell sister Pris about it!" She shook her waves of black hair. "I think Robert not being here has got you in this funk."

Esmé considered this a while, then said, "Maybe." A moment later she added, "But only because I don't know where I stand. Am I still gonna sing with you? And what about the Cravattes?"

"We'll have to wait and see, though I don't see those three boys really cottonin' to having a female Cravatte, if you know what I mean."

"But—"

"O.K., now, how should I put it?" Priscilla flashed a big smile. "Let's say, a commonly-known-to-be-a-girl female member." She laughed at her phrasing. "Come on, darlin', it'll all get sorted out. Like I said, everybody's chasin' the funk tonight. Ain't nothin' going to get worked out till we get home to Detroit."

Esmé sighed again.

"Girl, you don't know your own mind, do you?"

"What do you mean?"

Priscilla leaned back. Their food had just come, and Esmé picked up her cheese sandwich and gingerly nibbled at a brown-toasted corner. That was all it took, one bite. She was so famished, she started gobbling it all down.

"I mean just that," Priscilla said. "Look at you and that sandwich. When you want it, you just gotta have it."

"But—" Esmé took another big bite of the sandwich's other half. "But what do I want?"

"Oh, you know."

"No, Pris, I don't. If I still don't know who I'm going to be, how'm I gonna know what I want?"

Priscilla lifted her chin, shot an eyebrow-up look at her friend.

"Oh, you know it. And if you think you don't, you gonna find it out soon enough." She tipped her head at the last bit of Esmé's toasted cheese. "Once you finally take yourself one little ol' bite, you'll know just what you want."

"How about you?" What Priscilla was saying to Esmé had shaken her just a bit, and she wanted to turn things back on her friend.

"How about me what?"

"What do you want?"

"Oh, I don't have no problem knowing that, girl." Her eyes were bright. "No problem."

"And?"

"I got me some secrets, too." Priscilla's eyes were bright. "You just gonna have to wait and see."

✳ ✳ ✳ ✳ ✳

THE BUS WAS READY, pulled up in front of the Hotel Theresa on 125th Street, and it was already full except for Robert and Esmé. She hung back on the sidewalk waiting for him; well, she wasn't quite admitting that to herself, just that she did want to talk to him and still expected that they'd be seatmates, even though she was no longer Eddie Days, his fellow Cravatte. But where was that man? He hadn't shown up after he'd taken off with Ramona, and nobody else had said anything about his whereabouts. Indeed, it was like Priscilla had said: Nobody was saying much about anything. The bus held a lot of quiet, somber, generally down people. You take the fizz out of the champagne, it's just grape juice, eh? Even the band guys in the back were just sitting there, not a flickering ace or king in sight.

Finally she couldn't stand it any longer, and she called through the door to the bus, "Bee, you know anything about Robert?"

"We're expecting him." Bee was in the first seat, catty-corner to Trip at the wheel, puffing away at her Tareyton. "That's why we're waiting."

"He didn't say anything about heading back to Detroit with Bones's sister and brother?"

"Not so he told me, and if he didn't tell me, I'm gonna skin him."

Esmé smiled. "After he saved us?"

"Girl, I think *you* saved us."

Esmé didn't say anything to that, just paced up and back ten, fifteen feet around the bus's entrance. It was another warm but gentle spring night, and 125th Street was filled with people, all dressed fine and out having a time. She liked New York; hoped she could get back here soon. As Essmay or Esmé or . . . whoever.

A few minutes later she heard Trip say to Bee, "You sure Robert's coming? Maybe the girl is right. Hate to push our leavin' much later if he don't make it."

"He would've said something," Bee said, and Esmé heard her next words in her own head even as Bee was saying them. "We're talkin' about Robert Warwick here. He's the one man on this bus you know would tell us."

"Hell, I guess so," Trip said. "Just wish he'd get his smart little ass in here. It's gonna be a long drive no matter how we cut it."

It was now 9:25, and Esmé's intuition told her that Trip would want to be leaving at 9:30. That would be half an hour late. That, with Robert, would seem definitive. "I know he's coming," she said up into the stairwell of the bus. "I can feel it."

"I hope you're right, girl," Trip said.

Good, that would hold Trip off till 9:45. By ten, though, all bets were off.

She heard a shout from back in the bus, male voice she couldn't make out: "Hey, what's holdin' this crate up?"

"They're waiting for Robert."

"Oh, yeah, and you think they'd be waiting like this for me?" Esmé could tell now it was Mitch Williams speaking.

"Hey, fuzzball," Trip turned around and said, "we'd be in Pennsylvania now, it was you off losing your money. We can wait a little longer for him."

Dammit, Robert, get here. Esmé was a true bundle of nerves. Something very large inside her seemed to be riding on her friend's showing up, but all she knew was the pacing unease.

At two minutes to 10 Trip finally turned the bus engine over. That was probably just to warm it up, Esmé was hoping, but she couldn't think of any way to keep Trip from shifting it into gear, except that . . . oh, there he was. Finally! Robert came dashing down 125th Street, waving his hands and calling out, "Oh, thank God. Hey, here I am—here I am."

He came up breathless, and Esmé said, "Where were you?"

Between gasps of air Robert said, "Oh, Jesus, I had a lot to take care of. But I think I got it. Come on, you've all waited for me? Thank you." He clambered up the bus's steps. "Bee, that's great. Trip, thanks. Sorry everyone." He turned then, realizing he'd jumped ahead of Esmé. "Oh, Esss—" He shook his head. Didn't he know what to call her? "Hey, I'm sorry, get on up here. You were waiting for me?"

Esmé was feeling absurdly flustered. "Um, well, I was just getting some air, and—"

"Another one of those . . . walks?" Robert said with a smile.

"Um, a, I, um—" Esmé stuttered out.

"It's all right." Robert reached down and offered her a hand, then turned and faced the whole bus. "O.K., everyone, here I am, sorry. Trip, let's go. We gotta hell of a drive ahead of us."

There was a fully empty seat in the middle of the bus that Robert grabbed. Esmé was following him down the aisle, and though she saw the seat open next to Robert, she had a sudden anxious moment. Better just sit anywhere, let Trip get going.

So she was all set to drop down next to Linda Strong when Robert looked right at her, patted the seat next to him, and said, "Eddie, hey, come on, sit with me." A wink. "Like always."

There were laughs around her. Eddie? What did he mean by that?

"That's all right." She started to lower herself into Linda's seat, but Robert raised himself on the metal bar behind the seat in front of him and said, "Come on, I'm serious. I need to talk with you. You want to sit next to Linda so much, you can later. Come on."

There wasn't much traffic in upper New York City, and Trip had them crossing the George Washington Bridge in no time. Nobody had said much as they'd driven up to the bridge, and now that they were heading into New Jersey, the Cavalcade if anything grew quieter. It was the silence after a booming storm had blown by.

"So what is it?" Esmé finally said. She had been looking out the window and was surprised how quickly out of New York City they hit farm land.

"I think—" Robert started to say. His voice was soft and in-turned, though not at all hesitant. "I think it's going to be all right."

This cheered Esmé startlingly. "What were you doing?"

"Trying to hammer everything down." Robert raised his thin eyebrows, made a gesture of whapping a hammer against a nail head. "All the different corners just popping up like in a *Mickey Mouse*."

"Like what? I thought with Ramona we had it all settled."

"She's only a minority holder of FDL. They don't even need her to make a majority to sell the company. In truth, she doesn't have enough to control anything—"

"She seemed to be doing a pretty good job to me."

"Yeah." Robert's eyes lightened. "I was impressed. But truth is, anything that happens, we gotta get it around Mrs. Bones and that fat preacher brother of Ramona's."

"And?"

"I think that's what I got hammered down. Ramona seems to have persuaded them; hell, *you* seem to have persuaded them. They loved what you did—how you made them see how much FDL means to you." Esmé nodded. "So it looks like FDL's going to just keep on going. We're all going to make our records, and nothing's gonna change—at least for now." Robert was silent a moment, then added, "We all still gotta pray that Bones gets better."

"Who's going to run things?"

Robert made a strange sound, halfway between a hiss and a sigh. "That's the tricky part. It's gotta be Mrs. Bones."

"But she wants to sell, right?"

"That's what's tricky. She's gotta be the head, but we can't let her actually do anything."

Esmé raised an eyebrow. "It's you and Ramona, yes?"

"For now. Ramona's going to take a leave from her school and be the family member most involved. We've had to promise Mrs. Bones that she'll be consulted on every move we make, and as long as we make her think we're doing just what she wants done, well, we can do what we got to." A small but deep smile. "I think Mrs. Bones is a little excited about being in the loop. Maybe she's been someone who just spends Bones's money long enough."

"Robert, I'm really proud of you!"

"Yeah?"

"Yeah, damn straight I am."

He gave a small, pleased nod, then said, "That means a lot to me."

Now it was Esmé's turn to go, "Yeah?"

"Because I'm proud of you. Way you saved—"

"Proud?"

Robert leaned back, considered the word for a moment, then said, "Yep." A wink. "Damn straight."

"Why, 'cause I fooled everybody? That impresses you?"

He moved his head side to side, meaning, well, meaning anything Esmé wanted to read into it. What he said was, "No, that really pissed me off."

Robert's sharp words hit her hard, and she pulled into herself, fast, like a turtle diving into its shell. A minute later she got out, "Really?"

Robert nodded. "Yeah, how would you like to be—be around somebody who was tricking you all the time? Just playin' a goof on you—"

"But I wasn't—"

Robert sighed, then held up a hand. "I know. That's what I've been thinking. You weren't really ever just, well, trying to bamboozle us, were you?"

"Bamboozle!" Esmé guffawed at the word, then saw Robert was serious and fought her giddiness down. She shook her head. "Of course not."

"No, you—"

"Robert, I just wanted to sing!" Esmé cried, her heart in every word. "That's all I ever wanted to do. Everything else, it just—"

"Just followed." Robert shrugged. "So, O.K., yeah, I don't think *I'm* mad anymore."

Esmé heard the emphasis and thought of the rest of the Cavalcade. She didn't have a clear fix on how they were taking the revelation of her masquerade. "What about—"

"Everyone else?"

"Well, yeah." Esmé nodded. "Like Bee and Trip and . . . Orlando—"

Robert exhaled so fast it was a loud sputter. "Who cares about him?"

Ah, this was a turn. "Oh, Robert!" Esmé cried, air rushing out of her, too. "You're not—"

"What?"

She caught herself then, not wanting to say the word *jealous*—worried it might be too inflammatory. But she couldn't help but think back to that time with Robert and Orlando. She felt a warm feeling sweep through her. She started to say, "Robert, you know, a couple days ago, you were so. . . ." A pause. She reached for a flock of words: *cute, darling, wonderful,* but thought better about actually uttering any of them, too.

"I was so . . . what?"

Esmé sighed. Could she get herself out of this? Did she want to? "I just thought it was . . . funny."

"Me and that bozo fighting over you?"

"It wasn't over me," she said quickly.

"Uh-huh." Robert furrowed his brow. "And instead it was. . . ?"

"Essmay."

"Ahhh!" His brow furrowed even deeper. "And Essmay is. . . ?"

There it was, that undercurrent of anger Esmé had hoped they'd moved past. "Oh, Robert," she said in a quiet explosion. "I don't want to go back to all of that, I just don't!"

Time passed. The bus rolled along the four-lane road through darkened New Jersey. As always stockings fluttered down from the overhead bins, gray smoke swirled around everyone's heads, that close-in tightness like a fever not yet broken.

"So what about me?" Esmé finally let out the question that had been building all through the drive into the near midnight blackness.

"You?" Robert seemed surprised by her voice. "What do you mean?"

"About what I'm going to be doing?"

He took a long time to answer, then said, "I haven't really thought about that."

"Oh."

"Don't take it like that."

"Like how?"

Robert considered a second. "What do you want to be doing?"

"Singing. With FDL. Singing as much as possible."

"I understand."

"And?"

"Well, you're definitely Essmay now, right? You got yourself a hit record, lady. Nothing wrong with that."

"So I'm out of the Cravattes?"

"I—I think so. Yeah. I mean, we can't be a freak show."

"Robert!" Esmé flew around in her seat.

"You know what I mean. All the attention being on the guy who's really a girl." Robert winced, as if he saw that curious public story trailing them endlessly into the future.

"What about the Daisies?"

Robert took a moment to answer, then said, "I think you're going to be awfully busy as Essmay. Won't that be enough?"

Esmé settled back. She hadn't thought it out fully, either. But if she did have a hit record, that could be . . . enough. "I can cut some more sides?"

"You're a star, darlin'. You're gonna be able to do whatever you want."

Esmé settled back again, contemplating this. The word *star* seemed enormous, a whole galaxy of mystery and magic. She was suddenly a little scared.

"You got yourself awful quiet all of a sudden," Robert said softly.

"Yeah," Esmé said. It was all hitting her at once. A star! Who knew what that would mean. "What about you?" she finally said.

"What about me?"

"If I'm this . . . star."

"Well, darlin', I'm just Robert Warwick. Hope I can write a few more songs good as *My Eyes Go Wide*."

"That's it?"

That full-shouldered Robert Warwick shrug again: "That's who I am, babe."

That *babe*—no, she didn't want to hear that word like that, whatever it meant. It confused her even more. It was so . . . distant.

"Robert—" She started to speak to him but, again, wasn't sure what she meant to say or even how to begin to say it. She let his name just hang there, and curiously, he didn't respond. This was not good. There was something cool and, yes, distant here. This was not at all good.

But she couldn't find a way out of the box of silence around them now on this late-night drive. What had been decided? O.K., she'd be Essmay and ride her first song as far as it could go. Good. She'd also record more songs, and they might be Robert's, and he might be there in the control booth coaxing just that perfect vocal out of her. All right. But all of a sudden on this rumbly old bus that she'd been on so long now she knew it better than any home she'd ever had, at this moment the bus felt as icy and remote as a rocket ship blasting toward Mars.

The first noise came from the back. It was 12:30 on her watch, and it was dark all around her, but she wasn't asleep and she didn't think anyone else was either. Just so quiet. But then it started: One of the musicians tapping a tambourine. It's skin-brushing, rattly *thwomp* in perfect swing, not loud, but in the silence vivid.

A minute or so later, in came a couple of the Shags, laying down a *Vooooom-voooooooom* bass line, a breathy cushion floating around the tambourine beat, and they carried it for half-a-dozen measures until it was clear what song they were moving toward: the gospel number they often closed the show with, *Peace in the Garden*.

It was a slow, doleful tune, perfect for this enervated bus. A couple go-rounds, then Otis Handler lifted gently into the verse, *"When the lamb lies down with the lion / When the living find ease with the dying / There'll be Peace in the Garden, By and By."* His mellifluous tenor floated over the bass bottom, then Priscilla Bondrais joined in, topping him in alto harmony. Soon the whole bus had joined in, not loudly, but in hushed, night-rich tones, each voice coddling the words, letting them out delicately but firmly, carrying the mournful gospel through the ever-darkening night.

They sang all the written verses, then started making them up; Robert coming up with *"When the longer we search, the less we find / When the blessed sighted learn they are truly blind / There'll be Peace in the Garden, By and By,"* and then Esmé trying her hand, *"When all our disguises have fallen far away / We can only pray it's the start of a new day / There'll be Peace in the Garden, By and By."*

Robert looked over at her as she sung this, and his gaze was so warm and sweet and proud—yes, proud of her—that it took everything she had to not lean toward him and kiss him.

How long had they been singing *Peace in the Garden*? Were they in Pennsylvania yet? Ohio? Well, James Motion in the back with his tambourine must've gotten finally too lulled by the endlessly bluesy gospel because he right then started whapping his tambourine in a double-jump-time beat, and like that the gloomy must of the rumbling bus was dissipated; that was all it took, just stepping up the sharp tambourine snap, letting the jingles crackle like bursts of silver light through the darkening, and Esmé felt people shift in their seats, heard their feet start tapping against the floor, was sure she felt the air displaced as their shoulders and torsos began to wiggle away.

John Smith had uncased his guitar and sent a snappy strum over the double-time rhythm, and the chords were clear. It was the Cravattes hit *When the Doorbell Rings*, so it was perfectly natural for Mitch to take lead and Otis and Robert to fill in the harmonies. Esmé heard the verse turning and felt—no, she could actually see her part, her rising alto, right in front of her—but she was too self-conscious, she wasn't Eddie Days any longer, to sing it; but moments later a couple Shags and the Daisies joined in, and she knew she could too.

The bus rocked through *Doorbell*, then kicked into *Man Alive*, Priscilla taking the lead, of course, and everybody else working backup; and then Orlando followed up with *Our Hideaway*, the girls especially enjoying crooning along behind him; and when he finished up, Linda Strong, then Priscilla, were standing and moving into the aisle. James and John cracked their rhythm tighter, and the two women started to dance. In their slinky dress/nightgowns they slipped their hips and waggled their butts and dipped their shoulders, shimmying up and down the open aisle to claps and shouts of delighted encouragement.

"Hey!" Robert said, then held out a hand to Esmé. "Come on."

He led her into the aisle, now filling with bodies, with not much room at all to move, yet everybody shaking it, bouncing against each other, elbows knocking, butts clacking, shoulders nudging; and then more people joined in, and it was as tight as a rush-hour subway car, everybody locked in the groove . . . and every last soul moving together.

It was an astonishing feeling. Esmé, coming in uncertain and self-conscious, now just part of this bouncing mass of bodies; all her friends, her sometime enemies, her whole life this last month . . . no, the only life she ever wanted.

It was more than heady, it was delirious; more than joyful, it was . . . unsettling, and the sensation swept through her legs and her middle and up to her burning forehead. Robert danced his suave cuts in front of her, and she followed as well as she could, and everyone was so tight that they were pressed together; she could feel Robert's leg up her leg, his arms around her, and hers around him. They dipped and lifted and dipped again, and the way they moved, it was funny, but she didn't feel at all taller than he was, as she had all along; felt just the right size.

The beat kept snapping and popping, and Robert was on her front, and Priscilla—she thought it was her friend; caught a glimpse in the muted light—was behind her, but on her too, they were so tight she was hardly feeling where her body stopped and the next began; everything around her an undulant blur, this rocking, rolling bus of dancing fools.

The whole Soul Cavalcade was in it, that's what was amazing: The band playing hot as they could, Trip Jackson tooting the horn on the downbeat, and Bee—ol' Bee, who hadn't boogied once since Jackson, Bee was up and moving in the stairwell. But most of all it was Robert, movin' and groovin', all over her.

How long did they play and dance? Pennsylvania? Ohio? Michigan? On to the North Pole? The rockin' rhythm bus hurtled through the blind night.

Of course it had to stop, everybody lathered up, panting—it was, after all, nearly 2 a.m. now—and exhaustion crashed down on them.

Everything had changed. As the dancers found their way back to seats, people weren't sitting next to those they'd been with before. It was Linda Strong now there with Collie Farquhar of the Shags; Annie Sylvester settling in with Norris Rowland, the band's baritone sax; and to Esmé's surprise, Priscilla in the same seat as Orlando, right behind her.

Esmé stayed in the same seat as before; just got there first, so she was against the window. Robert came up and eased in next to her, lowering himself slowly then dropping the last few inches with a swoop, as if something still tight inside him had finally let go. The loose vinyl seat cover made a whooshing settling sound as the air bled out of it.

"Tired?" Esmé said gently into the quiet night.

Robert took a moment to answer, then said, "I can't even tell anymore."

"I know what you mean."

The bus kept hurtling through the darkness, and soon Esmé heard whispering behind her, too low at first to make out. Against her judgment she listened more closely. Priscilla was saying, "No, no, for a long time, really."

"I never knew," Orlando said.

"And I didn't want you to."

Esmé's thoughts were sparking. Did this mean. . . ? She listened with ferocious attention, all the while a curious emptiness opening up within her.

More incoherent words passed, and then she heard, "And that Essmay or whatever her name is, who was a guy. *Eccch*." She could feel Orlando's shiver.

"She's my friend," Priscilla said.

"But she's—"

There was silence then, followed by the faintest of liquid sounds.

Esmé suddenly felt so alone. Priscilla and Orlando? Well, you never knew, but what hit her was just that: On the bus right now, up and down all the rows around her, this soft, unleashed canoodling in the gentle night; and unaccountably she felt so damn alone.

"You got an awful lot to learn," Esmé heard Priscilla say after a long minute. Her voice was so soft she could tell it was mere inches from Orlando's ear.

"What do you mean?" Alarm from Orlando.

"About women—true women."

Orlando was silent a long moment, then Esmé heard his brassy, sort of fake bravado voice. "And you're going to teach me?"

"If you're lucky," Priscilla said with a low, throaty laugh. "If you're goddamn lucky."

Esmé couldn't help it, she looked over at Robert. Had he been listening to any of this? His eyes were shut, his breathing regular; his face was cool, impassive. She thought it would be pretty quick for him to have fallen asleep, but she couldn't really tell.

She kept looking at him. She could always see the intelligence in his face, the cut of his cheekbones, the clarity around his eyes. She liked that about him, of course, but she wondered now if he was somehow too smart—meaning, too wrapped up in his own designs; seeing too many details till he got blinded by them; too divorced from what ultimately mattered. Wasn't this night about something more than silently worrying about the next song, the next record date, the fate of FDL Records?

"Robert," she said in a whisper. "What're you thinking?"

No answer. Maybe he *was* asleep. She took her hands, one of which had been very close to his thigh, and folded them together right in front of her. Tell her that that was the posture of prayer and she'd deny it. She would.

"Robert?" Just a little louder, still no response. O.K., he must be asleep. Oh. She could hear Priscilla and Orlando behind her, whispering and canoodling, and she found words in her head that wanted to come out. "You know," she said, "you were like the best friend I ever had, when I was Eddie, that is." She smiled to herself. She didn't know what she was going to say, not really, the words surprising her even as she said them. Of course, she was just speaking to herself. "The way we got that record together, you letting me help you go up against NRC. It was—you know, girls usually don't get to do that. It was special."

Nothing from Robert.

"If you were awake now, I think I'd ask you about Essmay—you did have a crush on her, right?" Not a stir. "It was so obvious. Then you got in that fight with Orlando over her, that was just crazy." She said it that way, *over her*. It was over Essmay, who was, she understood, not really herself. Essmay was . . . a creation of both their imaginations. "Yeah, I love the way we cooked up Essmay. It was like we were both—" She caught her breath. "We were both so . . . so right there. You know what I mean?"

Nothing.

She dropped her voice so low that it couldn't have been any louder than air blowing from a heater. "And can you believe what's going on behind us now? Orlando and Priscilla? Jeez! I knew he'd go after anything in a dress, but I thought she'd be smarter." A long pause. "Still, if anyone can show him what's what, it's her. Right?"

Not a motion. He had to be asleep. Esmé smiled. She was really getting into this.

"So what're we gonna do now?" She waited a couple beats, then said, "Yeah, you and me. Whatta you think?"

There was of course no answer to this either. Robert's breathing if anything had grown more regular, more like the breathing of a man fast and deeply asleep. The regularity of his breathing emboldened her.

"Really, what do you think? I'm not Eddie anymore, and I'm Essmay only on the stage or a record. No, you got a whole other animal here: the real Esmé Hunter. You know anything about her? You dig her?" A long pause in the whistling night. "Does she dig you?"

Her hands remained folded before her as before.

"Yeah, I don't know either. I'm not sure what she feels . . . about you." A pause. "I think I'd feel better if—if I knew whether you even wanted to know, but you're dead asleep. Can't blame you. I'm exhausted, too. It's been an incredibly long, crazy day. I should probably let it all go, right? Is that what you'd say to me? You always have the right thing to say, you know? Robert?"

Her voice had risen a little, and she hoped that nobody around her had heard. Probably not. They were either all asleep or doing their secret stuff in the dark.

"O.K., well, that's enough." She gave a shrug, then felt silly, realizing that she was having such an involved conversation with nobody but herself. "Yeah, enough for one night. Tomorrow—I wonder what will happen tomorrow?"

Esmé settled back in the bus seat, closed her eyes, and listened. It was only the soft whoosh of the bus down the road, the faint sighs and occasional titters around her. It was so very peaceful. She was sure she'd be asleep in—

What was that? She turned and . . . Robert leaned over and placed a kiss on her cheek.

She jumped.

"Hey, sleepy," he said. "I have something for you." Then he half-whispered, half-sang, " *'Tomorrow, I wonder what will happen tomorrow?'* . . . Think that might make a good song?"

Esmé nearly shrieked. She flinched away, her heart suddenly pounding ridiculously.

"Robert! Were you—"

He reached over and put his finger across her mouth, "Shhhhh." A moment later he took her arm, lifting her against him and lowering her head on his shoulder.

"Go to sleep now, darling Esmé." A faint smile that she could feel like a warm breath on her cheek. "Esmé Hunter, whoever that is."

Her thoughts were still spinning wildly, and she was beyond embarrassment, but she was so tired, and there was something lulling and infinitely comforting here, too. She reached out and took his hand. It too was warm, and tougher-skinned than she'd have thought.

"*Tomorrow*," he whisper-sang again. "*Will love be ours . . . tomorrow?*"

It was funny; he was mocking her, or mocking himself, or . . . just making her smile. Smile she did, but close and to herself. She laughed also, but tried not to let him know. The laugh rattled deep inside her, a fuller, more overwhelming laugh for its being kept so secret.

Turned out, it didn't stay secret long at all.

Epilogue

Sunday, February 19, 1989—Los Angeles

FDL RECORDS: TWENTY-FIVE YEARS OF HITS. Not bad, eh? Scooter McGafferty, who was producing the TV show, knew they had to give it a nice, comfortable number, and since FDL Records had started as a jazz label in the '50s, there was some thought that it was more like the 32nd anniversary, but that number wouldn't fly, so Scooter pegged it to the first FDL record to hit No. 1, in the summer of 1964: Essmay's *My Eyes Go Wide.* Ergo: *Twenty-five Years of Hits,* though in truth the Top 10 records pretty much peaked about 1966, which made it Two Years of Hits, though that hadn't stopped the company from already becoming a fondly remembered legend. Hell, that it was only a short but intense burst of winners from the Cravattes, the Daisies, Penny and the Thoughts, and one more from Essmay probably helped.

It had been more work than Scooter had expected to put it all together. I mean, who wouldn't jump right away to be on TV? And sure, it was easy to get members of the Shags, those still alive, and the backup girls of the Daisies to sign on. Hell, one Shag, Buzz Stone, was working at a car wash in Crenshaw; another, Collie Farquhar, who'd picked up writing royalties, actually had a ranch in New Mexico; and a third, the master bassman, Reggie Calhoun, was working as a prison guard in Atascadero. Linda Strong of the Daisies? Ran a franchised temp employment agency in El Segundo. Annie Sylvester? She'd married a shipping magnate and lived in Luxembourg—cost a penny to fly her in, but at least she was game.

Which was more than Scooter could say about Priscilla Bondrais. She was still singing, small clubs mostly in the Midwest, and she billed herself as Lead Singer of the Daisies, which of course was true, though the biggest hits had been under Maisy Columbine, who also was still singing—and also billed herself as Lead Singer of the Daisies. Just that Maisy played concerts throughout the world and traveled with a 20-piece orchestra.

So the show was shaping up as:

DUELING SOUL DIVAS
THE BATTLE OF THE DAISIES

Which made for great publicity and a show that was quickly shoehorned into sweeps month, but which also meant that neither Priscilla nor Maisy had actually committed.

Scooter tried to get Bones Chapman to referee, but since Bones had sold the company in the late '60s to Music America, which in '74 merged with High Plains Steel, which in the mid-'80s was sucked up into the maw of IG Düssell, the huge German corporation (which ran FDL simply by repackaging its catalog in ever more inventive ways), Bones kept saying he had no power over anyone. Bones had promised to show up and take a bow, and Scooter knew that would be an emotional high point. People still remembered his accident and his recovery, and the way he'd helped push six more FDL songs to No. 1. Bones would move the heart, but it was Maisy and Priscilla who were making for drama.

The producer still had hopes that Robert Warwick could intervene, or his wife, Esmé, who had both committed. Indeed, they hadn't ruled out a re-creation of the legendary story of how Esmé had portrayed herself as a man and sung with the Cravattes. Scooter for one didn't quite buy that it had ever happened, or at least not for the months or so the story had it that she'd faked everyone out, but it was a good tale, and he'd already storyboarded a scene in which Esmé, after singing *My Eyes Go Wide*, goes offstage and returns in sexy top hat, tails, and fishnet stockings to sing *When the Doorbell Rings* with the old group . . . or at least what was left of them. Robert would be there, of course, but Mitch Williams was dead, shot in an alleyway in Detroit in 1968, and Otis Handler was nearly gone from cancer of the esophagus, which meant he couldn't sing or even talk. Scooter hadn't decided yet whether to wheel him onstage or not. He thought that he should, but there were also the four guys who were still touring through the Midwest in the current version of the Cravattes, and he could fill out Robert and Esmé with two of them—might be safest. Sponsors wouldn't want too much of the true stink of passing time around the show, would they?

Which was also a problem with one of the two single acts. Mary Hardy, who'd left FDL around the time Maisy Columbine did, was, God rest her soul, dead by her own hand, but Orlando Calabrese was very much alive—and a bit of a worry. You couldn't say that many people knew his story, or even knew he had AIDS; but when Scooter tracked him down in a halfway house in Cleveland, he read the look in his assistant Marcy's face: This man does not look good.

The tall, regal beauty still haunted his face, and the voice that had had half-a-dozen chart placers all through the '60s was solid—Orlando, with a desperate look in his eyes, launched into *Smoke and Mirrors* and *Crybaby* right there in the linoleum-floored reception room of the establishment he was living in, and he still sounded good—but there was something about his forlorn, haggard face that might, if they didn't package him just right, spin the gala evening in a morbid direction.

Well, Scooter would have to decide about Calabrese later. No, the real problem was the Soul Diva situation. Robert Warwick, who pretty much had run FDL until Bones sold it, simply said they were dealing with tough women and he couldn't promise anything.

And his wife, Esmé—Scooter called her Essmay once, with the long, drawn-out *s*'s, and she gave him a wilting look—didn't offer much hope either. She said she was still good friends with Priscilla, and that she respected Maisy, especially what she'd done to help save the company back in 1964, but rumors said that the two Daisies hated each other beyond passion.

So that was the show: some dead, others lost, and one great, big cat-fight controversy at the center that might or might not happen.

Par for the course in the TV biz.

At least there'd be a lot of great music. Those FDL hits, they were still all over oldies radio, and more and more turning up in commercials; even for Scooter, who was all of 12 when the Cravattes and the Daisies were first coming out, the songs called up a wonderful time of freedom and possibility: music that had the wonder and ebullience of the whole mid-century nation in it. Yes, he couldn't wait to hear the songs live. That—plus his usual fee—was why he'd signed on to the network proposal.

The intercom barked; it was Marcy: "Call on Line 2."

"Who is it?"

"Esmé Warwick."

"Good, put her on." A crackle over the line, then he heard her voice, still carrying the soulful richness of her old hits. "Esmé, hey, it's great to hear from you."

"Hey, Edwin." For some reason Mrs. Warwick had problems calling him by his nickname; instead she'd found out his Christian name and used it exclusively.

"That's me, ma'am."

Esmé laughed. "O.K., just this once: Scooter."

"That's me, too."

"Well, glad we cleared that up. Reason I'm calling is, I just talked to Priscilla, and she said you've already signed Maisy Columbine. That true?"

How to play this? "Um, not technically."

"Meaning, it's . . . not true."

"Well, Maisy hasn't said no."

"And Priscilla?"

"She hasn't said no either."

Scooter could hear Esmé sigh. "That's what I thought. So it's a stalemate." A moment of silence, then, "Robert was wondering how the network feels about that, neither of 'em hooked on yet."

"Tell him not to worry."

"Meaning?"

"They're committed any way it shakes out."

"That's good," Esmé said.

"It's going to be a killer show. *Killer*."

"And that's good, too, right?"

Scooter laughed. "These days, yeah, *killer*'s good."

"Haven't heard Lateesha or Nick use it, that's all."

"Your kids, right?"

Scooter could see her nod into the phone.

"You know, Robert was also thinking, maybe Nick could fill in with the Cravattes—I know you're needing people for Mitch and Otis."

"Your son?"

"He's got Robert's talent, that's for sure."

"And some of yours?"

"Well, he sings great—and he doesn't hate the old-school songs like some kids these days. Course he likes hip-hop, too."

"Don't we all."

Esmé laughed. "It's a different world, that's for sure. God, when I think of that first bus tour—"

"Was it true, the stories—" Scooter started to say, then had second thoughts. He didn't want to say the wrong thing to Esmé, but she was clearly in a good mood and answered him anyway.

"About me dressing up as a man?"

"I've heard that, yes."

Esmé laughed, loudly this time. "I've heard it, too, and all I gotta say is, they're good stories."

"But I've seen pictures—"

"Of four handsome men? Of a cute young 19-year-old girl with her first hit on her hands? We've all seen those pictures, Edwin."

"Sure." Yeah, no percentage in antagonizing her. "So you think your friend's going to do it?"

"Priscilla?

Scooter nodded into the phone, and Esmé seemed to hear it.

"I think she will, yeah. As long as you promise to present her right."

"How's that?"

"At least equal with Maisy."

Scooter rolled his eyes. He was remembering talking to Maisy Columbine's people on the phone. Their simple demand: The whole show be billed as *The Maisy Columbine Homecoming Special.*

"What, Maisy wants the whole damn thing, right?"

Scooter gulped at her prescience. "She says she is the Daisies. The one who gave them the hits—"

"Not all the hits—not even the biggest."

"True enough," Scooter said. "But you know Maisy."

"Oh, I do—or did. I doubt she's changed much."

"Me, too." Scooter got out a laugh. "I doubt it, too."

Esmé was silent on the other end, then said, "You know, though, she came through at the end for us."

"The end?"

"When NRC was trying to buy FDL—you know about that, right?" She must've seen his nod again. "She was at the big blowout, didn't have to be, she'd already left the group. She stuck up for us—for me and Robert and Bones—"

"You know what they were saying, that she had an affair with Bones—"

"Oh," Esmé said, "I've heard that."

"Is it true?"

"That could be—it would've been before I got there. But—"

"You've got something else to tell me, right?"

"It's all coming back, us talking like this, but what I remember is that Maisy had another little secret. One that definitely helped us out."

"I'm all ears, girlfriend!"

Esmé laughed. "Girlfriend?"

Scooter blushed. He wasn't a bad sort, really, and had just gotten caught up in the moment. "Sorry."

"Think nothin' of it. Anyway, Maisy, yes, she had herself a secret that day. I didn't know it for years; actually, it was Bones who told me later. Maisy, well, she messed around a lot, but there was one nobody knew about: Bones's brother, Octavus."

"I don't—"

"He was a preacher. Big fat stomach, way I remember. Maisy, she had her reasons, I guess, and she climbed up that ol' stomach, and—pardon me."

"And that saved FDL?"

Esmé took a long moment to answer. "That she was there, yes, it quieted Octavus down, made him go along with his sister, Ramona." A pause while she probably shrugged. "Guess it didn't hurt."

"Any hope that—" Scooter was thinking fast "—do you think I can use that somehow to get Maisy in the show?"

Another pause, then Esmé said, "I'm not sure how. It's not that big a thing, and Octavus has retired from his church."

"Damn!"

"Oh, I have faith in you, Edwin, you'll sweet-talk her into it, I'm sure."

"I just want the show to be great."

"I'm sure it will. I gotta go, though. We'll talk later? And you'll think about using Nick?"

"I think it sounds great. Bring him along to the rehearsals."

"Done."

"And best to Robert."

"Done, too."

When they'd hung up, Scooter sank back in his chair and sighed. This was his reward for doing this show, the true reward: to get a glimpse of that life, the tiny, reverb-rich studio, the musicians and singers crowded on top of each other; the rush-rush bus tour; all those timeless groups crowding the same stage; the magic of trying to hear those songs when they were new. In this age of mega–stadium tours and three years between records, it seemed so distant and amazing. He reached back and hit his CD player, cued up these days to one of the two discs on *Soul Cavalcade: the FDL Collection*. He hit PLAY, sank back in his chair, and let those great songs swell around him: *Man Alive, Our Hideaway, Sugar and Spice, Men on Fire, When the Doorbell Rings, My Eyes Go Wide*. . . .

He listened to them all, his eyes closed, feet tapping, half singing along, and they made him happy.

Coral Press publishes fiction about music.
If you enjoyed *Soul Cavalcade*,
We're sure you'll like our other novels.

Pink Cadillac

Real rock 'n' roll literature—a book with all the wily grace of a Chuck Berry song.
> —David Hajdu, author of
> *Positively Fourth Street*

Isbn: 0-9708293-0-2
391 pages $14.95

Lone Star Ice
And Fire

First-novelist Brady writes with energy and authenticity.
> —*Kirkus Reviews*

Isbn: 0-9708293-3-7
412 pages
$14.95

Cutting Time

A heady mix of blues myth and blues nitty-gritty.
> —Michael Lydon, author of
> *Ray Charles: Man and Music*

Isbn: 0-9708293-2-9
302 pages $12.95

Please visit our website: www.coralpress.com
We Love Rock 'n' Roll ✤ We Love a Good Story

Robert Dunn is the author of *Pink Cadillac—a Musical Fiction*, which was chosen for the prestigious Book Sense 76 list, and *Cutting Time: A Novel of the Blues*. *Soul Cavalcade* is the third in a series of novels tracing the history of rock 'n' roll, blues, and R&B. Look for *The Annas*, a novel about the fabled early-'60s girl group, to be published soon. More info: www.coralpress.com.

Dunn has published poems and short fiction in *The New Yorker*, *The Atlantic*, and the *O. Henry Prize Story* collection. He teaches fiction writing at the New School in New York City, where he lives. His band, Thin Wild Mercury, plays often in Manhattan. More info: www.thinwildmercury.com.